Forgotten Fallacy

The Chronicles of Xannia, Part Four

M.J. Moores

Forgotten Fallacy: The Chronicles of Xannia

Copyright © M.J. Moores, 2018

Published by Infinite Pathways Press 2018
P.O. Box 4, Caledon Village, ON Canada L7K 3L3

ISBN 978-1-988044-10-1 Paperback Edition

10 9 8 7 6 5 4 3 2 1

The Chronicles of Xannia

The Lost Chapters

Times's Tempest

Cadence of Consequences

Rebels Rein

Forgotten Fallacy

To my characters.
Thank you for taking me on this journey and
opening your lives to me and the world.

Acknowledgements

It's hard to believe that over five years the stories of Xannia have found a home within these pages for all to read. It is a dream come true. A dream that wouldn't have happened at all had it not been for the wonderful people I've met along the way who helped me learn about the craft, the business, and the comradery between like-minded and inspired individuals.

First and foremost, I would like to thank Mark Koning for his detailed insights into brain injuries and their repercussion to both the individual and those around them. His memoir series covering this topic painted a vivid picture of the challenges and barriers someone can face.

I'd also like to thank my writing buddy and fellow author Nanci M. Pattenden. She has been with me working on this project since I brought book one out of the shadows and started getting serious writers to critique my work. She, Melissa Barker-Simpson, and Linda Francis took time to beta read this, and other, books in the series. Without their professional input as both writers and readers, I might still be scrambling to get this series done.

A big shout out goes to my new editor, Val Tobin. It took me four books and as many lost chapters to finally find a kindred spirit who not only "got me" and my work but scrutinized my writing down to every last detail just as I would for one of my editing clients. Her awareness of craft is phenomenal and I can't thank her enough for helping birth the last baby in this series.

Behind it all, though, lay my writing and critique groups – my alpha readers and support system: WCYR, BWG, and Caledon Writers' Ink. Without their poignant insights, Godzilla-like critiques, and love this journey would have been lonely and frustrating.

Last, but certainly not least, I'd like to thank you – my readers. A writer can breathe live into a book but it's a reader who teaches it to live. You've taken this journey with me and for that I will always keep you in my heart.

MJ

Forgotten
Fallacy

Chapter 1
Split Decision

Dezmind

I blinked. Everyone else gaped at the guide as if expecting a punch line. Heat radiated from behind me. Taya must have moved closer at the guide's pronouncement, but she hadn't made a sound – she rarely did at these meetings.

Twenty-five council members sat around the conference table in the small council chambers, their faces ranging from pale Talian to multi-hued Commoner, but none looked to me – *the Kronik*. No. They all stared at the light-blue face of the young Balanis man temporarily assigned as Desert Guide, Kronik Council Liaison.

Benrek, the Talian representative for the illustrious Shoris-Mar, swallowed. He opened his soft mouth, set in an equally soft face, squinted, and then shut his trap.

Unusual.

Guide Aelix looked up, hands clenched, and met my gaze. I tried to give him what felt like a reassuring smile, but my lips had also frozen at the news.

"A *spacecraft*. You're sure?" Taya asked, a faint note of uncertainty creeping into her tone. Her breath curled hot against my ear. "He did say spacecraft, right?"

"Did you see it yourself, or is this just hearsay?" I asked what everyone was thinking.

Each magistrate's gaze slid from the guide to me and back again. The tension in the room all but pleaded for him to say "no" and waited for the release that comes with the certainty of scepticism.

"I saw it. The General and the two men who discovered it rowed me out and showed me." An accusation of disbelief laced his words, and I could almost hear General Kipling command them to take the guide out as a witness to silence the questions from Council – from *me*.

"The sea is surprisingly clear. There was no mistaking what lay below the surface. It looked identical to the buildings in the city. Same fabricated metal. It was huge. Bigger than six heilos but without rotor blades."

Magistrate Benrek finally choked out, "How do you know it's a *spaceship*?"

Every person at the table betrayed their curiosity.

"It looked like a cross between Tresdian and Hittition airplanes."

And there it was: an audible sigh as the bomb turned into a fizzling firework instead of a mushroom cloud. The species on those planets didn't have to deal with the magnetic field we had within our Deserts, making air travel a normal occurrence. *Normal for aliens.*

Several Talian magistrates spoke at the same time, all versions of a dismissal of the information, completely ignoring the brass ring protocol. Thousands of years ago, when the aliens came to our world, the Deserts hadn't existed. The comparison to simple aircraft reassured the councillors. But Aelix frowned. His gaze, both piercing and confused, shot up at me before he glared at those gathered.

"No, you don't get it. Bazdin and Raylan swam down. Saw it firsthand. It matches the artwork in several of the preserved journals found in the library." His eyes flashed with barely managed restraint. "It's a lot smaller than the descriptions, but it's definitely a spaceship." His cheeks purpled.

I had to do something, quickly, to defuse his anger. I stood and held my hands high, making eye contact with each magistrate-turned-councillor sitting at the oval table before me, but I spoke to the guide. "We don't doubt you believe the truth of your words and those of the divers. Regardless, whether it's a spaceship or an aircraft or something else, it's Dakturian tech, newly discovered." I leaned onto the table. "Are you able to postpone your return trip for another thirty hours so we can deliberate the news?"

"Sir, no, sir. If I wait another day, the receiver we're building risks damage from exposure to the elements. We're striving to keep the nodes and connector ports protected but—"

"You have to get back with the remaining pieces. Yes. From day one, our goal has been to set up stable satellite communications between us and the colony." I looked around the table at the council, more than double its traditional size, then turned to Taya. She now stood in her usual place by the inner door to my office, arms crossed,

4

grim face surveying the room.

"Jutaya." I used her formal name. "Would you join the table?"

A succession of needle-like pains stabbed at my chest. I immediately regretted the impromptu invitation when her tan face blanched. A wild terror I hadn't seen since the Pit of Chance dissolved the steel-nerved woman before me.

* * *

Taya

What! I must have sent the thought to Dez telepathically because he repeated his inane request.

Join us... The hesitation shifted it from command to question, but I couldn't say no without making a scene. Well, not out loud anyway.

I gave him and the council a stiff nod before taking the empty seat next to Dezmind, the new leader of the known world.

I didn't like speaking telepathically with him anymore. Too much effort. Clearing my mind while fighting to take everything in made me lose too much during the transition. He knew about my condition. We'd made a deal...

Why are you doing this?

He answered me by addressing those assembled. "Jutaya has first-hand knowledge of the alien language and culture. Her input in these matters will be invaluable."

We don't do this, Dez – I don't do this. You promi—

"The Kronik is right. Regardless of what the object is or is not, it's alien tech. The more we know, the better prepared we'll be," Magistrate Plithis said, slipping his hand from the brass ring inlay of the council table. Rarely did the Commoners willingly work with the Talians. An unexpected peace offering, but not surprising it came from the Prime's representative. Five other hands shot to the ring, and Dez nodded to each in turn. I squinted in concentration, trying to follow the thread of conversation.

"I agree. The advancement potential alone is enough to warrant raising it." The Talian magistrate, Olekk, – I think – stared at Guide Aelix as if he were *meeka* scraped off the bottom of his shoe. "Do any of those journals you saw have schematics or operational procedures?" The list of things he rhymed off went by so fast I couldn't take it all in.

I barely noted Aelix saying "no" before the next magistrate spoke. "We must have Internals on this—"

"You won't push us aside again," Common-Sector 7's – or was it 12's? – magistrate cut off the Talian. "Anything you learn needs to be—"

"Anything we learn goes straight to the Kronik," another official said.

The brass ring forgotten, Dez spoke over the competing voices to rally for order. I let my head fall, chin to chest, desperately trying to focus on just one voice…

"What do you think, Jutaya?" Dez asked.

My skin crawled as he tried to get into my head, tried to soothe the fire inside me. Rather than wrap my sizzling mind around the potential balm, I shoved it away. I was tired of being placated.

"About what?"

Silence.

The weight of it suffocated me as I desperately grasped

at the snatches of phrases I'd caught. Dez pushed against my scattered thoughts again, but I couldn't piece anything together with him poking around inside my head. It was just too much.

"Yes, I can help with managing translations. I agree the craft should be raised." I scanned the faces crowded around the council table. The Talians smiled and nodded, and the Commoners either sat stunned or looked at me with a mixture of horror and disgust.

Oh, meeka. What did I just agree to?

Chapter 2
Violation

Taya

I stood and backed away from the table, making eye contact with the two security officers on the other side of the room. My hands shook. I turned and held them in front of me as Dez shifted the conversation to the final item on the agenda: the measures being taken to deal with the Faction.

Normally, I'd resume my position by the door to the adjoining office, but today was not a normal day. Today, I walked straight through and let Ynell close the door behind me as she assumed my post. A question had lurked behind her eyes, mingled with pride. I'd never trusted her alone with Dezmind before.

Fire crackled through my veins as I forced one foot in front of the other toward the door to the hall instead of staying and readying Dez's office for our after-council debrief. The thought of Dez made my teeth ache and my temples pound. I marched into the hall not bothering to shut the door. This was not where I needed to be.

My fingernails, short as they were, bit into my palms as I walked with measured steps past each councillor's office down the east wing of the Capitol Building. None of those rooms would do. None except...

I turned into the only space with an open door and closed it behind me. No papers littered the expansive desk, untouched by the two rogue liaisons assigned here: the guides and the Underground. No surveillance cameras webbed the upper corners of council offices, and no one bothered to bug a room never used.

Grabbing one of two guest chairs, I leaned the weight of my entire body onto its skeletal back, forcing all the air from my lungs. Wildfire ignited across my neural pathways, constricting my breath. *What in Zola's name happened in there?* I staggered back, bringing the chair with me. Swinging it over my head, I smashed it against the perfectly polished surface of the desk. The ache in my chest constricted more.

"Why?" The wood reverberated in my hands as it splintered. "Why did you do that?"

I attacked the innocent desk, cracking and flinging broken pieces of chair around the room, losing myself to the rage. Turning with the carved leg in my hand, I smashed the standing lamp with a full swing, knocking myself off balance and into the wall of books. Dozens of old volumes pummelled me from above. I swung my arms up and let loose another guttural cry to the vaulted ceiling before punting the trash can across the room.

"You promised! You promised!" I rasped, but still the fire coursed through my veins. A hysterical sob escaped. Channelling all the anger and frustration of the past months, the past weeks, of *today*, I spun around and kicked the innocent desk, assaulting it like the android trainers at the Contractor Training Facility. My knuckles throbbed and my hands ached from scratches and gouges until only the husk of the desk remained.

Panting, I raised the battered chair leg and set my sights on the bar across the room and all that sparkling glassware reflecting the façade of this lie, of my life. As I shifted my weight to attack, two solid arms pinned me from behind, lifting me from the floor.

* * *

Jezetek

A muffled crash penetrated my mask of concentration as I sat waiting in the lounge for the final notifications to clear. I looked down the hall behind me and then over at the security desk. No one moved. No one even showed the slightest interest. *Maybe it's a test.* I slipped from my chair, straightened my suit, and hurried down the corridor. Another crash reverberated from behind the second door on the right. I depressed the handle and peered into the office.

"Sweet Zerameteth," I cursed under my breath and slid into the room, locking the door behind me. Before Taya had a chance to hurtle herself or the chair leg at the pristine bar on the other side of the room, I grabbed her from behind, held her tight and tilted my head to avoid getting cracked in the nose by the back of her skull.

"Taya!"

She raised her knees. I knew what was coming, and I also knew I wanted to keep my kneecaps right where they were.

"Augh!" she bellowed, seconds before I slammed her to the floor and let the full weight of my body plaster her to the woodwork. She shifted her head to the side.

"Get off me!"

"No," I whispered in her ear.

Her every muscle tensed, readying to toss me aside – and she might have done just that if she hadn't been trapped in my arms.

"Get. Off. Me. *Now.*"

"Taya, you need to calm down."

A slight tremor quaked her muscular frame.

"Tek?" The second she said my name her body slumped.

I rolled off her, but she didn't get up. So, I lay there with her, nose-to-nose, resting my chin on my hands in the middle of a war zone of splintered wood and battered books.

"You do realise you're not at the Facility, right?"

She refused to meet my eyes, burying her head in her arms instead. She didn't shudder or make a sound, so I doubted she was crying – just blocking out reality. I didn't rush her.

When she gave a sigh that melted the remaining tension from her body, I knew it was over. Whatever "it" was. She popped her head up and laid it on her arms. Her lashes glistened but the absence of wet tracts meant she was still fighting.

"Hey. Come on. Tell me what's going on. This isn't like you. I mean, look at this place. I'm surprised no one else came running."

"They knew who was in here," she mumbled, shifting her gaze around me, taking in the absolute destruction.

"Who knew?"

"My security team. They would have seen me on the hall's surveillance system. They're not stupid."

"And I am?"

"Well…"

"Now, that's not fair. Is this something you do on a regular basis?" I motioned with my head and we both sat up. I didn't like the curved line of her back or her hunched head and shoulders. This wasn't the woman I knew.

She stared at me, straight in the eye, as if she'd heard my thoughts, and gave a wan smile. "Vent? Yes. Destroy stuff? No. So, did they hire you? I told them to, you know."

I laughed. "Yeah, they hired me. I was waiting down the hall for confirmation of the transfer when I heard you venting. I'd be a pretty poor Special Ops commander if I hadn't checked it out."

Her gaze flickered to the door and back to me, the smile gone. Taya shifted to stand, but I caught her arm and pulled her back to the floor.

"Hey. We've known each other for ages. Spill it already."

She rubbed her face with her hands, then ran her fingers through her shoulder-length black hair. The dye job on it and on her skin had faded these past months to reveal the woman I'd fallen in love with all those years ago – and yet not. The look in her eyes had changed since she'd woken from her coma.

"You can see it, can't you?" she asked.

"See what?"

"I'm not the same person I used to be."

"None of us are."

"That's not what I mean. Something happened to me in that cavern three months ago."

"Yeah, you died. Or nearly. I know. I was there."

She punched me in the arm.

"Hey! I'm just stating the facts."

"I have brain damage, you idiot." The defiant spark returned to her eyes and shone past the unshed tears.

"What?"

"Yeah. At least that's what the doctor told me. But I felt fine... I mean, I thought I did. When I was *taking it easy,* as Dezmind called it, I didn't notice anything different. Sure, things were a little foggy sometimes, but what else could I expect after being blasted at short range with a plasma gun? You can't use yourself as a grounding rod for indoor rain without some consequences. Meeka, that was stupid."

"No. It wasn't. You saved a lot of lives that day." I nudged her chin with my thumb. "But I don't understand. You say you felt fine. You certainly look all right."

"Well, that's the problem with a brain injury – it's all internal." She knocked her fist on her head a couple of times. "I didn't believe it until a month ago when The Faction nearly assassinated Dez at that rally." She got a far-away look in her eyes reliving those terrifying moments.

"But everything worked out. The security team—"

"Exactly. The security team, not me, saved him."

"Come on, Taya. You can't be at the top of your game all the time." She hit me again. Both fists, numerous times. I held my hands up in defense.

"Shut up, Tek! I'm trying to tell you something important. You're not helping."

"Okay, okay." She let her hands drop to her lap.

"I couldn't think straight. At first, I thought it might be PTSD but the more Dez integrated me into his security detail, the harder it was for me to concentrate." She stood and paced the room. "I wasn't afraid. I wasn't reliving what happened in the cavern. I was happy. Dez was in power, we were together, my mom was released, and we'd found a cure for the alien bacteriophage. Tek"—she stopped amidst the rubble of the desk and shelves and turned to look at me— "the more information coming at me at once, the harder it is for me to sort through it. I used to be able to do this stuff in nanoseconds. Now, after a minute, two minutes, I still struggle. My brain doesn't work right anymore."

I let the silence fill the room far longer than I should have, but I didn't know what to say. "Does Dezmind know?"

She quirked an eyebrow at me. "Yes, he knows. But clearly, he doesn't believe me. Hence"—she opened her arms to the room—"my frustrations." She sighed and dropped onto the only chair untouched by her earlier fit. "I told him after the assassination attempt. He assigned me a core security detail for back-up and promised not to make any council decisions until after we had a debriefing and worked through everything on the table together." She rested her arms on her knees and looked at the floor. "Today he broke that promise."

I shifted over and knelt before her, one knee up, one down. I didn't hold her hands, touch an arm, or caress her face – all things I wanted to do – but waited. My job at this moment was to wait until she was ready.

"Oh, Tek." She buried her face in her hands and leaned back against the chair, letting her arms fall. "I don't know what I've agreed to. One minute we're talking about a new discovery in South City, and the next, the people I'm trying to help are staring at me as if I've turned on them. I couldn't follow the conversation. I couldn't ask for clarification without revealing my disability. I couldn't say no, so I said yes. And then I lost it."

My brain jumped from one idea to the next, turning and twisting and flipping it over as I searched for the answer she so desperately needed. It didn't escape me that she struggled to do this very thing – what kept her from being at the top of her game. But, she said she could make connections and analyse things at a slower pace. Maybe—

"Oh, gods," she breathed and stood, fear highlighting her features. Voices filled the hall. "Council's adjourned." Taya stared at the door as though it might eat her alive. I rose, linked my arm through hers, and led her toward it.

"I've got an idea. Go to the meeting, figure this out, and then meet me at the CTF an hour after dinner when general training's over. I'll take care of the mess here." I unlocked and opened the door wide enough to send her through to the hall. "Now, go."

I closed the door and leaned against it as the image of her desperately hopeful face shattered my heart.

Chapter 3
The Details

Taya

Down the hall from his office, Dez waved for me to join him. For the first time ever, I didn't want to. I wanted to grab Tek, race over to the Training Facility, shut out rest of the world, and get my head on straight. But two things stopped me: one, I hadn't been back to the CTF since the governing council threatened my freedom; and two, I was head of security and the Kronik's sounding board. Right now, I had to walk back into gods-know-what and try to clean up my mess.

When I entered the room, I hesitated. We weren't alone. The second breach in protocol today. *I'll have to talk with Ynell about this.* I stood by the open door in the ready position, feet shoulder-width apart, hands clasped behind my back. Dez spoke one-on-one with Guide Aelix.

"Once your Com-Base is operational, we'll synch up and finalise the details. Have the General send any intel and a list of supplies needed to finish the project. I don't want to lose time on this. Safe travels."

Aelix gave a sharp nod to the leader of our planet and turned to leave.

"And get Gerrund to pick a permanent Liaison already."

The blue-skinned young man kept his eyes averted and bowed as he faltered mid-step. Both he and I knew that wouldn't happen any time soon.

When he left, I shut the door and turned to stare at the empty seat across the desk from Dez. He dropped onto his leather chair. Part of me wanted to rail at him for pulling that meeka on me in the council chamber, but another part just wanted to curl up and cry. I couldn't do either, so I sat and crossed my arms, waiting for him to apologise. When Dez finally made eye-contact with me, he frowned.

"What? What is it?" he asked.

"You promised."

He sighed. "There was no avoiding it, Taya. Aelix is on his way back tonight. We had to have tomorrow's discussion, today. The communication's array—"

"—is more important than a promise to your Soul Mate."

He balked, clearly not ready for that reminder.

"Do you have any idea what happened to me in there?"

"Apparently not." He leaned forward and rested his elbows on the desk. "I know you put your mental walls up and refused to talk to me telepathically. Twice. Something *you* promised wouldn't happen again."

I almost smashed my hands down on the desk. Almost yelled at him. I almost did something I knew I'd regret.

Almost. But I had to bottle the rage fuelled by my frustrations, my confusion. I clenched my jaw and swallowed all of it, opening my mind to him for just a moment:

I had to shut you out. I couldn't concentrate on the debate as it was. If I'd have let you in, I would've lost even the basic thread of the conversation. "I told you things were different now. I explained what happened to me and why we need these post-meeting sessions *before* decisions are made. Why we must—"

"But you looked fine. I watched you. Your eyes tracked the speakers, you were alert, and you agreed—"

"To what, exactly? Huh, Dez? Because whatever it was, it sure ticked off half the magistrates in that room. And not the half I'm used to ticking off either."

"What are you talking about?"

"Looks can be deceiving." I stood and paced, hugging my arms tighter to my chest, trying my darndest to keep from lashing out again. As I swept the length of the room and turned at the apex, I nearly walked right into him. I stiffened as he held my arms and searched my face. His thoughts entered my mind.

Stop talking in riddles, Taya. Tell me what happened.

But I had already told him so many times, in so many different ways. Instead, I said, "What did I agree to?"

I stared into his eyes. In a flash, he went from nearly pulling me into a hug to just giving up. He let his hands fall and then returned to his chair, nodding at my seat. So, I sat.

"You gave your support to raise the spacecraft and to learn what we can from the Dakturian tech."

"And…?"

"I don't understand."

"How will all this happen?"

"You'll co-head a team to analyse the ship."

"*Co*-head?"

"Yes. The Talian magistrates suggested that Professor Elix work with you in South City, reporting back to me every few days."

"Professor *Elix*? The Talian engineer who convinced the old Kronik to keep modern tech from the masses?"

"That was a long time ago."

"The hell it was! You saw what was in the warehouse where they tortured me. All the POWs keep telling us—"

"Stop it Taya."

"—that the secret agents tried out new tech on them—"

"I said, stop it."

"No! I won't stop it, Dez." I jumped up and finally slammed my hands down on the desk. "He can't be a part of this! I'm not working with him and I'm certainly not going to the alien city."

"But you are. You said you would. The council is counting on you. *I'm* counting on you. Elix swore the Oath. He's loyal to me now. He was acting under the old Kronik's direct commands before. He listened then – he'll listen now."

My ribs ached. A desperate shriek threatened to claw from my lungs. My heartbeat hammered faster and white spots flashed before my eyes. I tried to blink them away but only more came. I staggered back toward the door. The scrape of chair legs across the floor told me he'd sprung to his feet. I gulped in a breath, turned, and stumbled out, disappearing around the corner long before my name echoed down the corridor.

* * *

Taya

As the chill from the concrete knee-wall spread from my ass into my thighs and up the small of my back, I glanced at my watch-com for the tenth time. I'd wandered Klax Square for more than an hour before walking over to the Contractor Training Facility and plunking myself down at the base of the stairs that led to the main entrance. That was three hours ago. Tek had said to meet him an hour after dinner. Cadets usually broke for an evening meal around five o'clock and then had study time for two hours.

It was three minutes past six.

In my mind's eye, I saw past the hedge on my right and followed the stairs up to the employee entrance. I blinked and looked over at the main doors. *Am I a guest or an employee?* I had signed an Infinity contract with Dez. Yet another first accomplished by the youngest graduate ever – although, this time, it wasn't necessarily something I was proud of. Until today, I hadn't planned on ever stepping foot inside that building again. Not after everything that had happened.

I looked from the guest entrance to where the hidden door would be. The cold crept farther into the core of my body. I pushed myself off the half-wall and walked around the bottom of the long hedge and up the stairs to the employee entrance.

21

At the top, I stared at the scanner. My arm felt heavy, my hand like an anvil. Still, I managed to raise my thumb to the ID pad. The light flared up and then down. When the door unlocked and swung into the double-mirrored hall, I swallowed a sob. The CTF still saw me as one of them.

One shaky step after the next, I forced myself back into the place I'd called home for nearly four years — a place that built me up to be the best and then conspired to have me killed because of what I became.

Through the process of elimination, I found Tek warming up on Level 6. The gym there was utilised specifically for personal training. Halfway through the level, it was up to cadets to devise a physical regimen while the faculty focused on guiding our minds. That didn't mean the final exam was any less stringent. It just meant we had to figure out how to pass by ourselves.

I walked out barefoot under the glassed-in observation deck and joined Tek on the mats. He frowned at me and cocked his head to one side. I hadn't brought a change of clothes. I challenged him with my eyes to go ahead and make a big deal out of it. I wanted to hit something again. But he didn't take my challenge.

Instead, I ground my teeth and spent fifteen minutes brooding while loosening up.

"So, what's the plan?" I finally asked.

He popped to his feet from a handstand and shook his arms out, flexing his biceps. I used to say, *just go ahead and kiss them already*. To which he'd respond, *I'll leave that to you in the ring*. Then I'd smack the side of my thigh in a *kiss my ass* move. Tonight, I just stared at him and he stared back.

"You said you still know how to do stuff, right? That it just takes longer to find the information?"

"Yeah. Pretty much."

"This afternoon, I did some research on your condition."

"My *condition*, eh?" He didn't get it; brain damage was brain damage.

His frown deepened. "You need to re-train your brain. Build new neural pathways to help you connect the dots faster."

"Great gods, I can't learn everything all over again. That's insane."

Then his eyes took on that old familiar spark. My heart jolted a nanosecond before he lunged at me. I grabbed his arms, kneeled, and flipped him over me. But he didn't land on his back – he never did. I twisted around, expecting he'd come at me again.

But he didn't. He just stood there, smiling.

"What!"

"You." He crossed his arms. "You did exactly what you were supposed to do. I didn't have to re-teach you anything."

"Oh, for the love of the gods, Tek. I wasn't using my brain."

He laughed. I was offended at first, then broke into a smile.

"Then what were you using?" He stepped forward, leaving only a foot between us.

I missed this: Us working together to be the best. Having a friend to rely on. I didn't let my thoughts go any further.

"Muscle memory."

"Right. Your brain identified the initial situation and then your body took care of the rest."

My smile dropped away. "But that didn't happen at the Rally. That's not what happened at the meeting today."

"You're right. Here, we're one-on-one. No distractions. No other incoming data to process. You're not watching a crowd, checking sightlines, listening to coms, or trying to track five conversations at once."

"Exactly. And that's what I need help with." I heaved my arms up and turned away, fighting back tears. I was useless as a bodyguard. I couldn't fulfil my contract. I couldn't protect the man I loved.

The smooth whoosh of pistoned limbs drew my gaze to the wrestling ring. Two training androids stood at the ready beyond the raised mat. Tek came and stood beside me, shoulder-to-shoulder.

"So, we practice with multiple distractions. You'll find a way, Taya. You always do. Now, come on. It's time to take a beating."

I gave him a grin as he nudged my shoulder and sprinted to the ring. Tek had a plan.

Chapter 4

Co-heading a Team

Taya

I slipped into the hidden passageway between the insides of the walls and crept to the side entrance of the apartments in a central courtyard of the Capitol Building. The double-thick walls provided extra protection and sound-dampening. No direct public access to the interior was permitted. The office of the Kronik, like any other ruling institution, was paranoid. However, as head of security, I was privy to all their secrets. I despised being monitored. This, at least, gave me some modicum of personal mobility and privacy. Besides, only a handful of key people knew Dez and I lived together – or were in a relationship.

I exited the tight space into the shadows ten paces down the hall from our rooms and quietly entered the main foyer, nudging the door shut behind me.

No lights shone and the opulent entryway looked

abandoned but for a dark mass pretending to be a rug. I tucked my work boots into the hall closet, and then I knelt down and buried my face into my lynx Jadis' fur. She nuzzled me back and put her large paws on my shoulders, trying to knock me down.

"We'll play tomorrow. I'll take you to the park." I kissed her soft forehead and rubbed the fur around the sides of her neck. A deep, throaty purr rose and followed me as I moved through the house in my sock feet.

Dez wasn't in the den or even having a late-night snack in the kitchen. *He must be exhausted.* I bypassed the formal living room and the office to the master bedroom, my fingers drifting over the panelled walls. The raised ceiling in our bedroom made my heart jump, as always. It reminded me of the sand ceiling in the Pit of Chance, the ancient covered-over amphitheatre buried under thousands of years of static-electrified sand particles out in the Deserts.

The sheets on the large four-poster bed mounded to one side. *Maybe he's not asleep yet.* I removed my weapons and placed them on the bedside table before tucking the Clinex into the drawer and the Whipstaff under my pillow. It didn't take long to kick my clothes to the side and crawl under the covers. I leaned over to put my arms around Dez only to have the blankets collapse. Neither of us had bothered to make the bed that morning.

I sighed, rolled onto my back, and stared up and up and up at a ceiling carved into a whipped cream dome, lined with ribbons of gold-leaf. I couldn't close my eyes. Sleep only ever came when Dez lay beside me – at least in this room – but I didn't want to move. After the beating I took, my muscles threatened a night filled with pain if I so much as thought about shifting to the couch in the den. Maybe Dez would be done soon. Maybe—

My watch-com buzzed, vibrating on my wrist. I never took it off. Flipping up the casing to reveal a tiny screen, I read the text message:

> *Working late tonight, sorry. Meeting with Elix set for 8.*
> *Escort in MF. See you tomorrow.*
> *~Dez*

"Sweet Zerameteth." I let my arms fall to each side and stared back up at the peak of the vaulted ceiling. I hit Dez's pillow, biting back a scream – or a sob.

* * *

Taya

Zola's rays pierced the cloudless morning sky. I held a hand to my brow and noticed a tall Talian man wearing a black suit, black shirt, and black tie walk to the left of the first pillar outside the Main Foyer of the Capital Building. He stood at the ready. The brim of a black driver's cap shaded his eyes. He didn't call out to me, wave, nod, but he did raise his nose and left it in the air pointing in my general direction. Few people came and went as the offices weren't officially open for another hour – all Talian.

I didn't move.

These games, I knew how to play. Even though I was half-Talian, I looked all Commoner from a distance. I watched as the transport left the new Tourist Depot across the quad. The fountain tunnel lay just beneath it. I shuddered at the memory of what had happened there. Crossing my arms, I leaned against the half-column to one side of the main double doors.

I didn't acknowledge the man in black.

The fountain sat silent. Since the explosion and the underground infiltration into the Compound, no one had bothered to fix the plumbing. I let my gaze drift around and tested myself. Tek said I needed to incorporate multi-level cognitive functions into my daily exercise regimen, just like any other task I worked to perfect. *Not that I'm anywhere near perfecting it if the beat-down my good friend and his android buddies gave me had anything to say about it.*

Glancing right, I caught sight of a dark figure flanking the inside door as it swung open to admit a new visitor. Farther along, another shadowy figure blended into the side of the building. I tracked three businessmen walking up the grand steps and then relaxed back into my peripheral vision to—

"Ahrum," the man in black cleared his throat.

I startled a little and turned to look at him. *Dammit. I shouldn't have missed that.*

"Miss Doir."

"Yes? Oh! You must be my escort. Hello." I managed to sound mostly genuine and gave him my sweet smile.

"This way." He inclined his head toward a sleek, black hover-rider parked in the drop-off zone around the circular drive. As we approached the vehicle, I breezed past him along the sidewalk toward the north-east section of the complex.

"Ah… um… Miss Doir." He twisted around and hurried

to match my strides. "The rider—"

"Won't be needed this morning. I prefer to walk."

"But you don't know where you're going."

"That's why I'll need you to escort me. The professor's lab is on government property within the Capitol's complex. Since your rider is facing north, you intended to at least drive in that direction. Therefore, I know I'm going the right way and that it will take no more than ten minutes to get there." I looked him up and down as he panted trying to keep pace. "Maybe fifteen."

It actually took us twenty minutes. Between my escort's lagging and the lab sitting on the far side of the complex, we lost more time than I thought we would. In fact, when he left me by the receptionist's desk, it was five after eight.

Elix greeted me with a snide "You're late." He sat dwarfed behind a large desk in a relatively small office and didn't bother to look up. I smiled my polite new smile and nodded my head to the stocky, pale Talian with matching white hair when he finally deigned to acknowledge me.

"I apologise, Professor. It was unfortunate that my escort didn't recognise me right away, nor I him."

He narrowed his eyes at me and scrunched his nose as if inhaling a bad smell. I plastered *polite* across my own features. The day after his inauguration, when suddenly I was the only person of colour living inside the Compound, Dez warned me about Talians with powerful positions. He also warned me that flying off the handle and spouting ethical conduct was not going to win them over. So, I was working on playing nice.

"Is this where we'll be operating from?" I scrutinised

the simple layout.

"This should be sufficient until we're called on to travel." Elix reclined in his seat. The only other chair in the room stood across from him, stiff and formal looking. He did not invite me to join him. "Where are your things?"

I cocked my head slightly and pursed my lips before walking over to the desk. I was going to sit on the small stack of papers resting on the corner but chose the chair instead. I crossed my legs and tapped my head with a finger.

"Everything we need is right here."

He quirked an eyebrow. "Is that so? I would've thought with your *brain damage* that the Kronik would demand more checks and balances from you."

I froze. Only three people in the world knew about my condition: Dez, Tek, and my doctor. Yet this conniving excuse for a man had found a way to breach doctor/patient confidentiality.

"If you've read my private file, you'll also know that my memory is just fine, thank you. Now, pass me a tablet and stylus, and I'll write out the Dakturian alphabet for you. It's time you learned your ABCs, Professor."

When he didn't move fast enough for me, I nabbed what I needed from the supplies, pushed several files on the table aside, and started writing.

"Here." I shoved the device at him and grabbed another. "Start memorising." I leaned over the new tablet.

"The council will hear about your insolence, Ms. Doir. This—"

"—is exactly how everyone else has learned the Dakturian language. I don't have any of their books here.

The only one brought back was the Journal, and that's in Dez—the Kronik's possession. If you want to understand the tech we'll be working on, you first need to learn the language." I refrained from telling him to shut up, but only just. Dez had said I'd agreed to help, that he and the council were counting on me. That meant biting my tongue a lot more than usual.

As I returned to copying out simple sentences in Dakturian, Elix gave a silent scowl, then sat back with the alien cipher and did as he was told.

Chapter 5
Return of the Lost

Satie

In the wee hours of the night just before Zerameteth slept, the slap of sails, rattle of rigging, and smack of salty waves reminded me we were on a new adventure. That leaving Darius' Island wasn't just our only decision, but the right one. Daria leaned over the ship's rail beside me and nudged my hip with hers as she looked out into the night for something we hesitated to name. We were ghosts on a ship with no designation come to haunt our past.

"Can you see it yet?" she asked.

"Maybe. Is Teena sure?"

"Something dark on the horizon she said. You can see everything from up there."

"I know." I shuddered, recalling the one and only time I'd ever climbed the rigging up to the crows' nest. "I remember."

"Look, Satie. Look!" Daria grabbed my arm with one

hand and pointed out to sea with the other. "We did it!"

In the half-light, the outline of new land grew in the starlight, giving form and purpose to the speed of the old museum-ship. We turned to each other at the same time and fell into a bouncing, jostling hug of squeals and laughter.

We'd survived. Again.

* * *

Satie

Marxx crossed his arms tighter as several more lights flared to life on shore. He scowled. "It's the Kronik's lands. Turn about and—"

"We can't," I said. Daria's daughter, Teena, and Tony, our Quartermaster, stepped to either side of me, our shoulders touching in a united front. Daria hung back. I glanced over my shoulder and watched her frown deepen.

"And why's that, All Mother?" he growled. I turned back.

"Ya know perfectly well why, Marxx," Tony said.

"We can re-supply once we're past the lights," he said, tone clipped.

"I don't think that'd be wise." Tony signalled to Daria to join us.

"It's been twenty-two years"—Daria stepped forward, standing closer to Marxx than her daughter—"but that doesn't mean anyone has forgotten what happened." She stared at each of us, especially Teena.

"Well, now, that may be true. But likely, the Kronik has expanded housin' and whatnot all the way to the edge o' the Expanse by now. If we keep goin', we'll find no supplies in the Deserts. I say we risk landfall. If this is Kronik land, it's probably part of the far sectors across the continent from Darzeth and the Compound. We've always had sympathisers out this way—"

"Again, that was over twenty years ago." Daria crossed her arms and frowned at Tony. For the first time ever, my best friend and ally aligned herself against me – against *us*.

"What's going on, Daria? You of all people know we can't survive without verrin and fresh fruit. Teena and I have eighteen people under our care in Med-Bay. Nearly half the ship's complement. The next thirty hours are critical." I tensed for a battle I wasn't sure I'd win.

"Mom, we could have one team watch the ship and another sneak ashore during twilight and gather the basics." Teena placed her hands on her hips in a very "Daria" pose. Under different circumstances, I might have smiled.

Tony gave his support. "In and out and on our way."

"What does Delenon say?" I asked and looked toward the stairs leading to the lower decks.

"Doesn't matter what he says. I'm the captain." Marxx straightened to his full height, but Tony still towered over all of us.

Teena, though adopted, suddenly took on Daria's strongest traits. She stepped up and poked Marxx in the middle of his chest. "Don't be an idiot. Listen to us. We can still make this work without sacrificing our friends' lives."

But Marxx didn't look to Daria to call off her daughter – he looked at me. The last mutineer on board this ship. Our peace remained tentative at best, even after all this time. I had to be careful.

He pushed home his point, "We have no idea how deep the shoreline is or how hostile the natives are. This is still Kronik land and if word gets out that we're back, that we survived the Massacre, he'll send his contractors until every last one of us is dead – not just the eighteen in Med-Bay. Besides, we can't safely make landfall at night." He held his arms out as if we ought to know better.

"What if you sent a scouting party first?" Teena asked.

Everyone looked at her.

"What?" she asked, shifting around to rejoin the circle.

"Now, that might just work," Marxx muttered. "Who will go?"

Teena gave a wicked smile but Daria frowned. She'd once struggled with the death of her family and the loss of her baby; and now her daughter, who'd never known the depth of the Kronik's hatred for us, was willing to risk her life. Noble, but to Daria, deadly.

* * *

Satie

The rope eased through my hands, sending the heavy metal toolbox filled with whatever we could find headed toward the sea floor as our sounding-weight. A hush fell now that we were in the cove halfway to land. The water lapped against the rowboat with gentle slaps. Salt permeated the night air along with a crisp, fishy-seaweed odour mingling with excited fear. My fingers touched the fabric tie I used to mark the current depth of the water near the hull of our rowboat.

"Same," I whispered, knowing full-well how voices

could travel over water. The small crew dipped their oars as I hauled the length of rope back up into the boat and tied it off, the weight just below the surface. The boat listed.

"Shift," Tony prompted and we moved more to the opposite side.

As we drew closer to a series of piers lining the rocky shore, I checked the depth again. It was shallower, but not by much. I tied a new marker and nodded to the team. Raised eyebrows and loose jaws punctuated their surprise. Our plan might work after all. Tony and Jip dipped their oars into the calm waters of the inlet as the others rested.

We needed too many supplies to be able to row in and row out multiple times over the course of twilight when the suns slept. The only way to get what we needed, and fast, was to bring the ship in to dock, grab what we came for, and leave before dawn.

The closer we rowed to the end of the middle pier, the more aware I became that no boats moored along the five long docks. Strange. We didn't see anyone fishing the waters on our way in either. *Why would there be so many docks and no boats? Why would there be docks at all if we can't go in the water? Unless…* I gasped. *They aren't above but below the waterline.*

"Go slow and test ahead of you the closer you get to the pier."

"Why?" Jip asked.

"A hunch. Be careful." But nothing untoward banged into the rowboat or the oars as Tony tied the vessel to a mooring ring at head-height on the end of the pier. I conducted the final depth test – just a few hands lower than before – and gave everyone a thumbs up. Our ship could safely dock in this inlet, making resupplying faster. With three hours left until dawn, time was no longer on our side.

A rung-ladder hung from the end of the pier down into the dark waters. As the ladies and I made our way up to the deck, the rowboat drifted to starboard with the weight of the sounding anchor. The hull bumped something invisible under the water. I clung to the ladder as the rowboat shifted under my feet. My insides clenched. I held my breath but nothing happened.

"What is it?" I asked as Tony leaned over the edge of the boat. Jip counter-balanced as Reena lay flat on the dock and peered down from above. She and Tony locked gazes.

"What?" Teena echoed.

"What did you think we'd find, All Mother?" Reena asked as I climbed the rest of the way up and knelt beside her. I glanced down into the water just as the star shine caught something metallic. My hunch had been right.

"Underwater boats," I said, and shook my head in awe. A lot had happened in twenty-two years. I leaned over the edge of the deck toward Tony below. "Seems they're not in use right now. Lucky for us. But, we'll have to move a few for the ship to dock without incident." I shifted and glanced over my shoulder. "Get Marxx to bring it to the last one, over there."

"Will do," Tony said, then released the mooring and pushed against the dock with his paddle. The gentle dip and trickle of water from even strokes took the men back to our ship to inform Marxx and the crew. Still crouched low, I signalled for the other women to follow suit. This was enemy territory. *One wrong move could mean we lose everything.*

"So, what's the plan?" Teena asked.

"Ree was a high-ranking Resistance fighter. She's got more experience than either of us." I turned to Reena, her short-cropped hair had lost its dyed strawberry hue and curls shortly after we'd made land all those years ago, but I still saw it when I looked at her. "You scout the shore. Be ready with a report once Marxx and the crew arrive. Teena, we'll shift the underwater boats away from the far pier. We'll have maybe twenty minutes. Ready?"

"Let's do this." Ree clapped us each on the shoulder and moved off down the sturdy dock, hunched over to scout the area. All too soon her steps vanished amidst the lapping water. She became the night. I drew in a shaky breath.

"Hey, it'll be all right." Teena bumped shoulders with me. I shook my head and motioned for her to follow. I had to keep an eye on her. She only knew stories, and few at that, about the evil of the Kronik. We'd lived it. Daria kept her sheltered though. Probably never imagined we'd come back.

By the time Teena and I reached the shed at the bottom of the pier, Reena had completely disappeared. Teena moved to skirt the far side of the hut.

"Wait," I whispered, and checked the door. It wasn't locked. I waved for her to join me. The small shed had no windows. I motioned for Teena to keep the door open and let the starlight in. Diagrams, safety procedures, mooring instructions and all things nautical lined the walls. *Perfect. Everything we need to shift the submerged boats around.*

"Okay, come on." I tapped Teena on the arm as I walked out. She made sure the door whispered shut and followed close. At the base of the far pier, I waved her to me and explained what we needed to do.

We released the lines from the mooring loops. The steady slap of the water against the legs of the pier made me tighten my shoulders every time. I glanced out to sea to check on the ship and then back to shore, searching for shadows. We couldn't afford to get caught, not after what we'd all been through.

In the weeks before the Resistance, black-clad contractors, cloaked in night, monitored the streets. One could slip up behind us at any moment. It still might happen.

I tugged up on the rope, away from the side of the deck, and a smallish oblong glass casing nosed above the waterline. It wasn't heavy or cumbersome. It clunked against the first unit, but the two underwater diving crafts politely jostled for space in the water. I tied the line closer to shore. A plank groaned. My heart leapt into my throat as I flattened myself to the pier.

"Sorry," Teena whispered, coming up beside me with her lines.

I sent a silent prayer of thanks to the Sun Guardians and moved on to shift the other devices down. Teena and I made quick work of the task.

As the museum ship eased toward us on the momentum of its oars, the rigging remained mostly silent as the sails clung tight to the yardarms. Teena and I stood with our backs against the small shed at the base of the last pier until the vessel nosed toward the end of the dock.

We moved into position.

Tony tossed a line over the rail to Teena. I looked back over my shoulder and around at the other piers and sheds. No shadows moved out of place and only the snap of water broke the silence of the night.

I gave Teena's arm a squeeze. She glanced at me, waiting for another line to drop. I inclined my head back toward shore. She bit her lip and nodded, mouthing "be careful" before turning her attention back to the ship.

Reena was late.

Chapter 6
Missing in Action

Satie

Drax's warm breath played against the back of my neck as I stood watch near the hut by the shore. I leaned back into his warmth. His arms encircled me and he kissed the side of my forehead before I turned to face him.

"Where's Reena?" he asked.

"I don't know."

"What do you mean?"

"She should have been back ten minutes ago. We gave each other twenty minutes. But we don't have time to wait for her intel. I only hope the gods are watching over her."

"She'll be fine." He rubbed my back as he turned toward the ship.

A few minutes later, all those healthy enough to work gathered on shore in the shadows before the little hut. Jippon ran point.

"Okay, you know your groups. Stay together and watch

each other's back. Daria, take your team up the north street. Teena, you follow, then break off when you spot an opening. Drax, you head south. Tony, follow up the rear with your team. I'll go through the middle of town. Magistrate, you stay here and relay messages and supplies to Marxx on board. Whatever you do, *don't* engage with any of the locals. Don't break anything or break *into* anything. Take only what's accessible. Get in and get out. We have one hour before we have to leave. Let's do this."

The five teams of three hunkered down and branched out. I followed Drax and Neeka through the deserted streets. I'd never visited any of the farther sectors in my youth, but I heard they were more rural than most, a lot like those creeping closer to the Expanse, only less nerve-wracking to live in. In the city, no matter the time of night, something was always happening – not always legal – but there were some businesses and factories that worked on fifteen-hour shifts to cover the whole day. Mind you, there could be a curfew in effect we didn't know about. It wouldn't be the first time.

Drax navigated the streets as if he knew the place. Maybe he did. We never really talked much about our lives before the Massacre. Still, Talians rarely set foot outside the Compound, so it was more likely confidence and not familiarity.

After raiding a nearby orchard, we wove our way toward the docks when his back stiffened. He stopped short and held up a hand. My heart rate jumped. Neeka and I flattened ourselves against the side of a house, a sack each filled with fruit on the ground between our legs. I crouched down and peered around Drax's legs, holding my breath.

Two uniformed men walked the streets. Their footsteps echoed steady and slow. Drax signalled for us to move farther into the shadows away from the spilled light of the street lamps. Justices on patrol or maybe security guards for a nearby business. I couldn't tell this far away, but they certainly didn't look like Kronik mercenaries, contractors, or government soldiers – too relaxed. We waited them out.

Back at the ship, I checked in with Magistrate Delenon after unloading my supplies.

"Nothing yet," he said. Meaning no one had found Reena nor had she checked in.

"Not good. If she's not back before daybreak, we risk exposure…" I let my words trail off. Knowing Marxx, he'd sacrifice her before allowing the ship to be exposed. I couldn't fault him for that but I also couldn't let it happen.

Daria's team swept in carrying two bags of flour among the three of them. I stepped in to help Daria as her mates focused on the other bag. After unloading, using the well-oiled winch system for the rowboat to send our finds up to the main deck, I pulled Daria toward the end of the pier out of the way.

"Reena's not back yet."

"Meeka," she swore and looked at me with narrowed eyes. "What are you planning, Satie?"

I raised my eyebrows. "Nothing… yet. But you know what'll happen if she's not back in the next fifteen minutes. We can't abandon her here. What if she's hurt? What if she's lost? What if—"

"—one of those patrols found her. I know. I know. But

she's a fighter. She understands the risks."

I shook my head. It didn't matter that she was a fighter – she was family. "Come on. Let's see where the others got to and check out a few of the missed streets. I'll never forgive myself if we don't even try to find her."

Daria's gaze followed Teena's progress up the pier. She looked to the main deck, high above, where several teams now helped unload. Then she locked eyes with me again.

"Okay. But we do this my way."

I nodded and Daria headed back down the dock toward shore. Delenon was on his way up and gave us a questioning look. "Where are you ladies going? All the teams are back now."

"But Reena's not," I said.

"I know."

"We have to do something," I pleaded.

"I know, but…"

"It's dangerous," Daria finished for him.

"She's family, now. We can't leave without her. It's not right."

He nodded. "Wait here." We watched as he spoke briefly to Jip before coming back. "All right, let's go."

"Wait. What?" I asked. "No. We can't put you at risk, Magistrate." I grasped his elbow. Daria agreed with me.

"And yet we can risk our All Mother?" he asked.

I opened my mouth but nothing came out, so I shut it again. He had me there. He was the heart of our family, I was the spirit, and he knew there was no way our "brawn" would leave us both behind.

"Right. We're out of time." I turned to Daria. "Where

should we start?"

"This way." She led us into the middle of the city where we'd only sent one scouting team. Daria took point, pausing when necessary to allow for the occasional patrol to pass. She wove around businesses and along alleys. Delenon and I took turns as lookout at the back and in the middle.

We crouched, waiting for some early risers, likely on their way to work, to pass on the main road. A muffled knocking and banging drifted across the narrow street. I was acting searcher, so I visually scouted it out. An old shed door rattled before a hand waved at me on the other side of a grimy pane. My heart leapt. I reached for Daria and the magistrate.

"There," I said.

They both risked a glance at the rattling shed and nodded. Delenon gave me a tight smile but Daria's frown deepened. When the sound of the walking workers' conversations drifted to nothing, Daria led us across to the small building. A forehead and nose pressed against the tiny window.

Reena!

I reached to lift the slide-latch but Daria grabbed my wrist and shook her head. She twirled a raised finger twice by her ear and disappeared around the back. Delenon looked up. I followed his gaze. The stars faded as Zola's rays breached the black of night. I hugged myself and bounced on the balls of my feet. *Hurry up, Daria.*

"All clear."

Delenon slid the metal bar up and Reena came tumbling out of the shed.

"Thank the gods! Come on." She grabbed me and Daria by the elbow and inclined her head for all of us to follow her.

In one quiet moment, as we waited for yet another patrol to pass, I whispered, "Who locked you up?"

"I did." She looked over her shoulder meeting three confused stares. "A patrol caught me by surprise. I hid in the shed but didn't force the lock open far enough. It fell back into place when I went to leave. I'm just glad you found me."

As we slid alongside one of the faded merchant buildings across from the docks, the faint silhouette of our ship broke the horizon as the first sun rose.

"We have to make a break for it. Now!" Reena pushed us all from the shadows as we dashed across the worn street to the far pier. Before my feet touched the dock, a voice cried out from behind us.

"Hey, look! A ship!"

Then the door of the hut swung open to block our way and out stepped a rubber man with large fish eyes.

Chapter 7
A Changed World

Satie

Daria and Reena flung their arms wide as they used their bodies to shield Delenon. I shifted behind him and did the same as the gathering crowd blossomed. The divers, covered head-to-toe in rubber suits, had removed their head-gear to reveal ordinary Commoners beneath, not strange aliens.

"No, it can't be," someone off to my left said.

"It is! It is! Magistrate Delenon and the Resistance fighters. It's them, I tell you."

Daria smacked someone's outstretched hand, reaching past her shoulder. "Back off!"

Up the pier, those of the crew who were still mobile swarmed over the side of the ship and amassed behind us on shore, forcing the curious on-lookers toward the street. I prayed Drax would stay on board. He knew the dangers of showing his face around here, but people did stupid things when they thought lives they cared about were at risk. I'd risked myself when I jumped into the sea to rescue him. He'd do the same for me, only this time it would be a sea of Commoners.

I shifted around to join Daria. Jip came forward to flank Reena, and together the four of us formed a wall between the town's folk and the magistrate. I felt every one of us stiffen at the sight of the four uniformed justices piercing the crowd equidistant from one another. Their simple formation twisted my guts. The three Resistance soldiers I called family growled. Our suspicions were confirmed the closer the officers got – bright red lettering embroidered "CTF" under their local justice badges.

Contractors.

In my peripheral vision, Tony and Marxx fell into line beside Jip and Daria. I stepped forward, pulling Daria and Reena together behind me. The four contractors' hands hovered over their Whipstaffs. We knew what those weapons could do as well as they did. Everyone ran scenarios through their minds, analysing the potential body-count.

"Stop!" I held up both my hands. Surprisingly, they listened and the crowd shrank back a step from the officers. My arms trembled but my voice held, "We don't want any trouble. We'll just be on our way." Before I could wave everyone back to the ship, a short barrel of a man trundled through the masses and burst past the line of justices.

"Magistrate Delenon, you old rabble-rouser, you!"

"Gedrix? Is that you?"

Delenon burst through his protectors, as Gedrix had the

justices, and the two men grasped each other's arms in a vigorous shake before pulling one another into a hug. Then Gedrix turned to the crowd and opened his arms wide.

"It's true! The lost Resistance fighters have come home!"

A deafening cheer rose, and the contractors fell into ready-position, no longer on high-alert.

I looked at Delenon, confused, then spoke to Gedrix, "Sir, I don't understand. Why is everyone cheering?"

His smile widened. "Why, my dear, the Resistance won."

"What?" Delenon and I gasped.

"It's true. Three months ago, the children of the Resistance, the Cause, overthrew the Kronik with a coup."

I watched as every single surviving member of the Resistance shifted their gaze to the four contractor-justices standing behind Gedrix.

"Um," I cleared my throat. "Then why are you still using contractors as justices? Isn't that a little counterintuitive?"

Gedrix laughed. "It's a long story. Come, join us in the Town Hall. I'll explain everything."

"We thank you for your hospitality, Gedrix—"

"Keeper Gedrix," a few voices from the crowd cut Delenon off.

"*Keeper* Gedrix. I guess you've had twenty-two years to climb from being my assistant to sector keeper."

"More than a few ups and downs, but yes, I finally made it."

Delenon smiled. "Old friend, we've been travelling the seas for weeks. My crew is tired and hungry and half of them require medical attention – specifically verrin – the whole reason we risked coming to shore. My executive team and I will gladly meet with you later this afternoon, but right now, we need to feed our people and rehydrate them."

Delenon read Gedrix's disappointment just well as I did. At least no one asked where we got our supplies from.

"However, if you'd like, I could personally give you a tour of our ship and we can talk freely of days past and this recent political turn of events."

Keeper Gedrix glanced over at the ship looming tall in his harbour, and his eyes widened with pleasure. "I would like that indeed. Farez." The justice in front of me stepped forward beside Gedrix. "You will accompany me."

But the moment that contractor moved, the front-line behind Delenon crowded closer, encircling the four of us.

"Keeper Gedrix." I signed thanks to the Sun gods and his eyebrows shot up. "The crew of this vessel has not yet come to terms with the idea that contractors are on our side, so to speak. Would you mind being accompanied by a Guardian?"

The man's happy eyes sharpened in thought. "How about two career justices instead?"

I looked at Delenon. One contractor easily equalled two or more standard officers. A public figure, such as this sector's keeper, would prefer his own protection as he ventured into foreign territory.

Delenon nodded in agreement.

Gedrix inclined his head at Farez, who slipped away through the crowd.

We didn't have to wait long. Word travelled of our arrival, and likely every person in town stood shoulder-to-shoulder on the dock-side street. It was so full, movement was almost impossible.

Our front-line team remained where they were as Delenon waved for the remaining crew members to re-board the ship. He and Gedrix walked the pier slow and steady, the two officers following behind, and me bringing up the rear.

It didn't take long for our guests to climb the ladder embedded into the hull at mid-point. An eerie sensation settled over me as I watched them willingly board the vessel. Twenty-two years ago, on the opposite side of the continent, a moment like this had heralded the war lost – but now the *drezek* had flipped. Yet, I couldn't shake that odd feeling.

"Glorious Trinity," Keeper Gedrix breathed as he stood in the middle of the main deck by the central mast. He gazed up to the observation nest. Most of the crew had either climbed the rigging to get out of the way or had gone down to the quarters below. Still no sign of Drax. Marxx stood at the wheel as Tony, Jippon and Reena waited around the edges, watching the justices watch Gedrix. I hovered in the space between the two men and their bodyguards – a physical reminder of peace to all sides.

"And you learned how to sail her all on your own?" Gedrix asked.

"Yes. The museum curators described the basics, but it was up to us to remember their teachings and put them into practice. No mean feat," Delenon said.

The sector keeper turned full circle, then placed his hands on the base of the mainmast just over the sail ties.

"You do realise your group became legends, right?"

"Oh? How so?" Conflicting emotions played across Delenon's features.

Daria had told me of her frustrations during the end of the battle when the Resistance could have maintained their ground if only the average citizen had bothered to care and help. How was it those same reluctant participants now held the fighters in such high esteem?

"The old Kronik knew how to spin a disaster. The city of Darzeth is now called Darzeth Prime, you know. He claimed you willingly set out to find Darius's Island as a way of solving the problems you fought for. That your journey toward Neto Darzeth was a more valiant way to end suffering than war. So, those remaining saw you as intrepid explorers trying to find another solution with the aid of the Kronik."

"Is that so? Well, I guess it's better than being remembered as *rabble-rousers* as you so congenially put it." Delenon smiled at his friend, but something in his eyes spoke to diplomacy. "Come, let's take the tour to the lower decks. You'll want to be truthful when you tell the world that you were the first citizen to step aboard this legendary vessel."

Gedrix's eyes sparkled. He practically danced over to the landing. Delenon winked at me over his shoulder and signalled to the watchers. Reena and Jip caught the double-blink signal and flanked the group as we descended.

"Oh my, you can really feel the boat sway once you get below." The keeper kept a hand on the wall as he made his way down.

"This is our Medical Bay. I advise you to just pop your head in. We're dealing with a number of health-related issues right now."

Teena nodded to the group as she bustled about Med-Bay while we passed.

"There are crew quarters to either side of this wall." Delenon banged his fist on the panel in the middle of the ship. "On our way back up, I'll show you the other side. Below is our galley, the mess, extra sleeping quarters and the rowing deck."

As the group traipsed down another level, I spotted Daria overseeing the serving of cut fruit to several crew members. She glowered at Gedrix, or rather, his escorts. She'd lost so much twenty-two years ago, I couldn't blame her. Besides, we still didn't know what happened three months ago or who exactly was in charge now.

Chapter 8
Wild Fire

Daria

Satie's gaze flicked to the darkened stage, past where Sector Keeper Gedrix sat on the edge, swinging his feet like a small, round child. The rest of the town hall was well-lit. *Come on, Daria, she's the All Mother. You disrespect her every time you call her Satie.* The bad habit had started over twenty years ago, but All Mother never called me on it. In fact, I think she preferred Sister Satie. *All Mother* just landed in her lap due to circumstance. *Either way, I guess her prayers were finally answered.*

"So, the old Kronik, the one who massacred the Resistance fighters, is now in prison? A Talian prison?" Delenon asked.

"Yes."

"But another Talian helped organise the coup? I don't understand. Why would he do that?"

It made no sense to me either. In fact, it sounded like

another trap. Lull the Commoners into thinking he's on our side and do an about-face once he's in power.

"No one fully knows his tale, except that he became disillusioned with the system at a young age, left the Compound willingly, and joined the Cause – the new arm of the Resistance. He believed the government kept secrets from everyone, not just the Commoners. And that they weren't doing everything they could to solve the problem of the growing quakes. So, he took a group into the Deserts to find the lost Chronicles in order to learn how to deal with the planet's problems."

"And did he find them? Did he actually figure it out?" Delenon asked, speaking for all of us.

"Yes. At least, I think so. The super quakes stopped shortly after he came to power, but he has some strange claims about why the quakes were happening in the first place."

"Oh?"

Gedrix cleared his throat and steadied his feet. "Aliens."

"Excuse me?"

A collective gasp came from the room full of able-bodied crew.

"Says that they came to our planet over three thousand years ago and tried to terraform it to suit their needs."

"How?"

"By putting a fake sun in orbit. Gamma."

"Who?"

"Zerameteth. We tend to refer to the suns by their rotational sequence now: Zola is Alpha, Zita is Beta, and Zerameteth is Gamma. When the old Kronik brought about the New Renaissance and encouraged more learning about science and technology beyond the Compound walls, the names were adopted. Of course, the Sun Guardians and orthodox FOL, Followers of the Light, still only refer to them by their religious names, but most of the new generation has adopted the change. After the Massacre, the government did its best to wipe everyone's memory of what had happened. Trust that General Kipling made sure there was a way to remember."

I leaned forward. "Who now? Kipling? Gerrund Kipling?" Everyone in the room stared at me. My blood ran hot, then cold. A shiver rattled my bones.

"Why, yes. He took up the mantle of the failed Resistance and created the Cause. Enlisted the Talian dissident who now stands as Kronik and the head of a new governing council. Everything's changed." Gedrix went on to explain how the new council was made up of twenty-six councillors, each former magistrates for the corresponding sectors in both the Compound and Greater Xannia. The council included a place for a representative of the Underground and the alien city as well.

Pins and needles pricked my skin from the inside out. Teena squeezed my elbow but I didn't look at her. She didn't know. I should have told her more but...

"So, it's true then? There really were aliens and Zera – I mean Gamma is fake?" Delenon asked.

"I can't speak to whether or not our smallest sun is real, but yes, the aliens existed. They lived in the southern hemisphere." Gedrix spoke of many crazy and amazing things, but I couldn't get over the fact that my baby brother had helped bring about the change that our parents, that our older brother and I, couldn't. *General Kipling*.

A deeper shadow at the back of the stage moved again, seeming to draw near. None of the crew took notice though; we'd been warned not to. I had a hard time sitting still, so I could imagine how difficult it was for the shadow.

Our reintroduction to life on the main continent swirled around my head for another hour before Delenon finally clapped Gedrix on the shoulder and thanked him for the extensive update on what we'd missed these past twenty-odd years – especially what had developed over the past three months. As the sector keeper slipped through the door to a bustling crowd outside the Town Hall, Drax emerged from the shadows. He and Satie looked back and forth at each other, but never spoke or reached out to one another as they had grown accustomed to.

For the All Mother, news that Zerameteth might not be real had her blinking and shaking her head. And Drax, who'd made a new life with us, with *her*, might be able to return to his family. We all might – at least, those who were left.

My ribs contracted, gripping my lungs. I gasped. Kaynee, my baby sister… Gelden, my baby boy…

The hall door burst open amidst our silent reorganisation of the folding chairs into a circle. Lights flashed from reporters outside. The door swung shut but left a sputtering Gedrix staring at Drax, our resident Talian.

Delenon stepped forward as those of us closest to Drax formed a barricade around him, two and three bodies deep.

"Yes, Keeper Gedrix?" Delenon placed an arm around

his old friend and turned him back toward the door. But the portly politician glanced back over his shoulder and rolled out of the magistrate's grasp. Unfortunately, Tony was the only other person present as tall as Drax and unless he decided to sit or crouch down, Drax's pale silvery-white skin acted as a beacon in a room full of Commoners.

"Wh-huh? Who?" Gedrix cleared his throat. "You never mentioned having a dissenter join the Resistance."

"That's because he didn't join us, Gedrix. The old Kronik caught him sympathising, trying to burn down the ship before it could be used as anything other than a museum. The Kronik made sure he was on board when we set sail. Truly cleaning house as it were. Now, why have you returned unannounced?" The hint in his words echoed Delenon's displeasure at the man's abrupt appearance.

Good. He needs to know how serious a breach this is.

"Oh, uh, right. The council has extended an invitation to all the surviving Resistance fighters to return to Darzeth Prime to meet with and exchange ideas with the new Kronik."

"That was fast." Delenon looked at the crew surrounding Drax and then back to Gedrix. "We haven't even discussed if staying more than one night is an option."

"What? Why – what do you mean not stay?"

"I mean, the plan was always to restock and keep heading south, especially now that we know most of our surviving loved ones have chosen to migrate to the alien city."

"Oh! I thought now that the Resistance had won—"

"We have yet to discuss anything we've learned here this

afternoon, old friend. While I am still recognised as their magistrate, we operate very differently now than we used to. No one makes unilateral decisions."

Marxx coughed and stared straight at Delenon. Because of his decision to help Satie and I look for Reena, we ruined the plan everyone had agreed to: get in, get out. Still, he couldn't fault us for that. We're also soldiers, and as such, we don't leave anyone behind.

"Please, give us some time to talk about this and I'll let you know what we decide." Delenon guided Gedrix back toward the door, using the bulk of his body to block prying eyes as he ushered the keeper out a second time.

A blast of voices shouting questions crashed into the quiet room before Delenon shut and bolted the door. He waved at us to take our seats. Satie gave Drax's hand a squeeze before selecting a chair next to him. I couldn't read him – body language or expression. He'd become blank, a wall. A lot like the creature I'd first encountered in the bowels of the ship's hold over two decades ago.

Delenon sat down last, as was his custom. "I'd like to open the floor to comments. Now that we're here, and we've been brought up to speed on the changing landscape of the government and Kronik lands, what are our options?"

"Do what we agreed to, regardless. This still isn't the rebellion we wanted." I leaned forward and placed my elbows on my knees. "I say we stick to the plan and go south where we'll find our brethren."

"We should at least consider their offer ta meet the new government," Tony said, and Satie nodded in agreement.

"Now that we're not considered hostiles or rebels anymore, we have a rare opportunity ta learn more 'bout this new world than the average citizen. We could get a read on the modified council and take a measure of the Talian who claims ta speak for all Xannians. Besides, Gedrix also said that the Underground was still runnin'. That some chose ta stay, some ta go, and some ta return topside."

"Personally, I'm tired of being on the water." Jippon ran his hands over his face and through the spiky hair at his forehead, then looked around the circle. "I don't want to risk getting that alien virus, and I don't care if they've found a vaccine. It's not a cure, which means any one of us, or those who've already gone south, might end up dead for no reason. We didn't struggle to live on that blasted island for twenty-two years just to let some long-dead aliens kill us off."

We talked through our options until Zola set. Eighteen crew deciding the future of thirty rebels, all that remained of the more than one hundred fighters launched aboard the death-barge after the Massacre. The only thing we readily agreed on was that any Talian in power wasn't to be trusted.

Chapter 9

Movement

Satie

I stared at the male reporter wearing a strange headband with the smallest View-X ever strapped to the side above his grey ear. I shifted on my chair before the town hall stage and frowned, absently gripping and releasing the journal in my lap.

"What does it matter? I am Guardian to these people and have been since the Kron—old Kronik yanked my sisters and me from the temple for aiding the Resistance."

"Other sisters made the journey as well?" He leaned forward.

Drax's hand twitched where it rested on his knee. He either wanted to hold my hand or slap some sense into the man. Probably both. I took a slow breath and released it. Magistrate Delenon and Captain Marxx completed the semi-circle of the honoured crew to be interviewed. Thank the gods only Gedrix and his assistant sat watching. It was bad enough we'd agreed to have the interview, but the reporter wanted to record it as well.

"My sisters gave their lives in order for the gods to hear our prayers. I became All Mother once we reached Darius's Island. You see, there was nothing special about me. I was simply the only one left who knew all the practices. Necessity is the mother of invention. The ancient term was renewed due to our circumstances and nothing more. So, please, don't put words in my mouth." I ran my fingertips over the soft leather binding around the old journal, willing my heart rate to calm.

He turned his attention to Drax, the final interviewee requested – for posterity, they said. "And you, sir, how did you find yourself on the ship?"

Now my arm twitched. These were old, deep wounds we did not pick at.

"The Kr—old Kronik found out I didn't like the idea of him using my ship to send people to their death."

"Your ship?"

"I was lead engineer on the build for the museum."

"Why do you suppose the old Kronik didn't arrest you?"

"Oh, he did. But the attempt to burn down the ship was seen as an act of treason, and he'd decreed that all rebels should be purged from his lands."

"You were a Resistance supporter, then?"

"No, I wasn't."

"But you said—"

"I said I didn't agree with how he wanted to use my ship. I might even have implied that I was morally against treating any Xannian in that way. I was not a dissident. I was merely a man with a conscience."

"And yet, you helped navigate the ship and have been living with ex-Resistance fighters for over twenty years. That couldn't have been easy."

I glanced at Drax, my eyebrows raised. He gave a half-smile.

"The first few months were, shall we say, challenging. But after we made landfall, we realised we all wanted the same thing – to live peacefully."

The reporter slowly tracked his head-cam back over to Delenon. "And were you successful?"

"Yes."

"Then why return home?"

"Ah, the Big Question. We always assumed we'd try to come home one day, maybe not so soon. But practicality drove us from our peaceful lives – the gradual disappearance of the only source of verrin on the island. We had to leave or die. As you well know, we don't prefer the second option."

Glimmers of smiles and smirks tweaked our lips. It was true. We'd come close to death numerous times before reaching Darius's Island and we refused to give up now.

"Have they told you the same problem exists here?" The reporter said it so off-hand that it took a moment to resonate.

"What?" Marxx leaned forward as if to stand but remained seated. "What did you say?"

"Our verrin is disappearing too."

I blinked and blinked again. A haze wavered across my vision. I tried to take a breath but my lungs refused to obey.

Arm extended, I turned to Drax. Everything went black.

* * *

Satie

My head bumped against a familiar arm as dozens of voices filtered through the haze of my brain.

"—are you doing here?"

"What happened?"

"Is the All Mother hurt?"

"Why is a Talian carrying the All Mother?"

"Why is a Talian with the Resistance fighters?"

"Where are you taking her?"

Why are so many people worried about me? How to do they know I'm the All Mother? I cracked an eye and realised Drax cradled me tight in his arms as Delenon led the way to the waiting lidez. The journal, tied to my waist by a length of cord, swung below me. Marxx shoved off searching hands and too-close bodies as Gedrix and his assistant parted the crowd next to the large transport vehicle. I sat and bumped my head into Drax's jaw but wrapped my arms around his neck to help pull me taller and bring the journal closer. *The lidez is hovering! What in the world?*

Gedrix had mentioned a New Renaissance encouraged by the old Kronik – no doubt another way of diverting attention away from the truth of the Massacre. But vehicles without wheels? How was that even possible?

The steps up into the transport were narrow, so Drax set me down on them, holding my shoulders as we walked up in tandem past a driver with wide-eyes and a slack jaw. It looked almost comical, except that I knew he was staring at

Drax. Past the sliding divider, the vehicle opened up to plush seating for thirty with swivel recliners and an extra-wide aisle. Drax directed me to one of the chairs. I perched on the edge, the journal in my hands again, looking out the large windows at the giant crowd. Metallic things hovered in the air around the lidez as Zita rose, rich in her deep-orange gown, to greet the day. I whispered a prayer in honour of this momentous occasion.

We were going to meet the Kronik.

"Are you all right, Satie?" Drax crouched beside me. I could hear Delenon's "speech" voice muffled by the vehicle's walls as he and Gedrix finalised our voyage across the nation.

"I'm fine. What happened?"

"You fainted."

"I did? I guess I must have." I sighed and clasped his face with my hands. "I'm sorry. This isn't how I wanted them to remember us here."

He smiled, kissed my palm, and then shifted to the vacant chair beside me. "It shocked us all, but you've been putting on a brave face for longer. Are you sure you're feeling all right? You don't normally get light-headed."

"I've been taking advantage of the abundant fruit and verrin... though, perhaps not as abundant as we first thought."

Delenon walked through the divider and made sure it shut tight behind him. "I'm glad that's over."

"Are you sure we're doing the right thing?" Daria asked, seated farther back. Delenon moved to the empty chair near the middle of the aisle, and we all swivelled to see him better.

"Yes. We agreed that a reconnaissance mission was vital to understanding our next move. It sounds like even though your brother is running things in the south, he still reports back to the new Kronik. And if this is the only other landmass across the Nine Seas, we need to know just what this new Kronik's policies are and exactly how far their reach is."

"Too many people know we're back." Tony rested one ankle on the opposite knee and leaned back into the luxurious chair. "Even if the new Kronik isn't all he's cracked up ta be, he'll not be makin' us disappear any time soon."

"Speaking of disappearing," Reena said, looking out the back windows, "not everybody from town is doing just that. Look."

Those of us closer to the front of the lidez shifted toward the back windows. A variety of vehicles ranging from network cube-riders to family and single riders hovered like a long train behind us.

Chapter 10
Pressure Cooker

Dezmind

"I will carefully consider everything you've brought to the table today, Councillors. As prior magistrates for each sector, you are the voice of the people and those voices need to be heard." I stood and surveyed all those present in the council chamber. This time, the chair for the desert guide liaison sat empty and a new face for the Underground stared wide-eyed back at me. The petite girl couldn't have been much younger than Taya, yet she was still so naïve to the topside world. *Why on Xannia does Kaynee insist on sending her friends? I need to visit her – get this straightened out once and for all.*

"Now, let's move onto matters affecting all sectors and lands." I nodded to Ynell, the guard by the main door. She opened it wide for Professor Denali. Ynell directed him to the vacant chair and closed the door. The professor remained standing.

"You have the floor." I inclined my head to the man.

"Thank you, Kronik. Councillors. My research regarding climate change is now fully complete." He had no papers, no charts or handouts. The man just stood there, his dark-grey skin sallow around faded navy-blue coliths. Even the markings around his eyes drooped, distorting his usual clown-like appearance.

"And?" I prompted.

"And we've hit critical mass."

Those magistrates who'd heard his last two updates understood the gravity of this simple statement and shifted forward.

"How bad is it?"

"If we don't stop the warming of our planet *today*, all sources of verrin will evaporate within the next twenty to twenty-five years."

A collective gasp broke their raw silence.

"That's impossible." Sir Hetrick, Sector 4's magistrate, pushed his chair back and folded his arms. "The verrin isn't just going to disappear—"

"Yes, it is, Magistrate." Denali cocked his head slightly toward me as if to ask for support. Then his gaze slipped past my shoulder to the guard standing by the door to my office. The professor squinted and wrinkled his nose. I shifted to block his sightline to Taya. She'd warned me she'd been contracted to help with the early phases of his research the second time around.

"Go on," I said.

"My research is flawless. If we don't stop global warming, the remaining pockets of verrin will evaporate and we will die."

"What are the figures, Professor?" I leaned forward, hands on the table. "What is the exact point of no return? Next week? Next month? Next year?"

"Next year will be too late. Far too late. I told the council, *today*."

Madam Quellen's fingers reached for the brass inlay of the table. "We cannot achieve miracles in one day, Professor. Give us a time frame and we will work toward a realistic deadline. Do you have these numbers?"

Denali bristled and some of the old piss and vinegar Taya had told me about resurfaced. "Yes, I can calculate the numbers. But I'm telling you, this has to be resolved *now*. It cannot be put off. It cannot be ignored a second time. There was nothing wrong with my research the first time around and there damn well isn't anything wrong with it this time, either." His gaze flickered past me to Taya again. I couldn't figure out if he was mad at her for being the one entity he couldn't account for during his time in the field, or if he was angry she wouldn't step forward to back him up.

"Thank you, Professor Denali. We look forward to receiving those numbers from you so we have an accurate time frame within which to work toward a solution." I nodded to Ynell. She opened the door wide, and the room waited for the obstinate professor to take his leave. When he finally stepped out of Chambers, Ynell motioned for the next speaker to enter. A trim, well-dressed Talian man walked in and stood by the empty chair.

"Specialist Reegan, an update please."

"Certainly, Kronik." He turned and addressed the entire

council, familiar with his place and the men and women in this room. "The communication satellite link-up with South City is now fully operational. We've been able to bypass the volatile electrical residue across the Deserts by bouncing a signal from a tower in the city to the newly launched array in geostationary orbit above Xannia. For the past thirty hours, the General has been sending detailed images of the sunken ship's site and the exterior of the craft itself. A community line has also been established and com-calls can be placed using the prefix dialling sequence of 999. We are now looking to expand the network band across the northern lands and the General is seeking to do the same throughout the city."

He paused, looked around the room to open the table to questions and nodded to me when no one spoke.

"Excellent, Specialist. Carry on."

Reegan gave a slight bow and left. Ynell waved in the next speaker. Behind me, Taya released a nearly imperceptible sigh and moved to stand next to Professor Elix across the table from me. A slight limp highlighted her stiff bearing, but the puffiness under her left eye told me her make-up hid a lot more than usual. Work kept me at the office late, and we'd barely had time to talk let alone look at one another these days. *What are you up to now?*

"Professor Elix, report," I said.

"Yes, Kronik. Preliminary images and discussions with the General and the two divers who discovered the spacecraft have helped us determine that the vessel appears *not* to have been breached by the seawater and likely was submersed relatively recently. Perhaps even as recently as the first super quake six months ago – the one that levelled the historic Solar Plex."

I noticed Taya's eyes unfocused as if looking inside herself. She'd told me what had happened that day, how she and Zaith had tried to help. It was hard to tell if she hurt more about not being able to save everyone or if she battled something deeper. To this day she refused to talk about what happened with her best friend once the three of us got to the City.

"How do you know?" I asked.

"There appears to have been a naturally occurring pedestal of rock rising from the water. The angle of the craft, drag-marks along the slope of the column, and the lack of significant sea growth on both the ship and the surrounding boulders under water imply the Dakturians likely parked the craft on the pedestal and used it as a launch platform."

"I see. When does the General think they will have the devices ready to raise the ship?"

"Approximately two to three weeks. He will update us regularly, but the supply chain is slow."

Taya's expression sharpened at those words. She'd helped institute that network. A brief battle waged inside her. When her facial muscles returned to neutral, I knew it was safe.

"I'd like another update next week. Dismissed." He nodded and left.

Taya remained where she was as the new leader of the Special Security Division walked in. One of two men I'd found sleeping outside Taya's hospital room after the coup.

Now that Zaith had passed, Taya spent a lot more time with this old friend. Her entire frame eased as they stood nearly shoulder to shoulder, he a head taller, both more confident in the other's presence.

"Special Operations Commander Jezetek, update."

"While we thwarted yesterday's attack on the tour transport heading from the gates to the Capitol, none of the civilians wanted to follow through with the trip into the Compound. However, our on-site team was alerted to this attempt in record time and we've gained new intel. The Faction is led by ex-military and possibly even someone affiliated with the special agent operations previously run by the old Kronik's double agent. Not everyone who participated in the trap underground on Talian soil was captured."

"And why can't we find them? The Compound is only so big, at best the size of one of the larger sectors. We should have found them by now." I studied the contractor, the man Taya said could stop the Faction and help restore peace. He'd made headway in only four days, but this might be a fluke.

"Sir, due to the ease with which the members of the Faction are able to disperse and disappear after an attack tells me two things: one, their training equals or exceeds my own, and two, they have help."

"Help? What do you mean, help?" The Talian magistrate, Sir Olekk asked.

"They're either using Talian hideouts and hidden tunnels, or the locals are supporting them and helping them hide. It's my bet both options are in play."

Olekk smacked his hand on the brass inlay and stared hard at Tek across the table. "So, as a Commoner, you're saying that Talians are disobeying their Kronik and harbouring fugitives? And you're telling me this on a hunch!"

"No sir, as an Elite Contractor who has studied both warfare and criminal tendencies, my expertise in these matters shows that Talian terrorists are being aided by the general population."

I held a hand up to keep anyone else from responding. "If what you say is true, how do we even begin to find them?"

A sharp rap on the main door caused every head in the room to turn. I nodded to Ynell. She placed her body between the room and the crack in the door. Tek angled himself between her, me and the door, and Taya slipped from my peripheral vision only to show up beside me, resonating heat along the left side of my body, though she never actually touched me. Every security agent in the room tensed.

Ynell spoke in soft but formal tones to whoever stood on the other side. When she turned back, shutting the door behind her, an audible sigh from those in the room floated toward the ceiling.

"Sir, if I may?" She waved her hand toward the council table.

"Indeed."

She stepped forward and placed her hands behind her back in ready-stance. "It is my duty to inform the room that the Lost Resistance Members are due to arrive just prior to second sundown."

News of their arrival two days ago, reported by Magistrate Kelum and Keeper Gedrix, had catapulted the Chamber into chaos. Today, while actions and expressions remained neutral, the fire that burned in every single councillor's eyes either screamed elation or fear. The return of the Lost broke open not only twenty-two-year-old scars but also twenty-odd weeks' worth of fresh ones, too.

"Ynell."

"Yes, sir."

"Initiate Alpha protocol."

"Yes, sir."

She stepped from the room and another security officer took her place by the door. SOC Jezetek turned to face me.

"But sir, the last time you initialized Alpha protocol—" He glanced at Taya who stepped into my line of sight. I placed both of my hands on her shoulders and spoke to the room.

"The Faction tried to assassinate me. Well, Special Operations Commander, let's make sure that doesn't happen on your watch."

Chapter 11
Between Life and Limbo

Taya

My feet flew out from under me as the cap-gun discharged. I smashed my elbow against the raised mat as I scrambled upright. The android holding the toy gun stood over the android wearing the tie – *Dez* – while a third waited patiently behind me for instructions.

"Reset!" I shouted. We recreated the mock scene. Dez-bot stood next to me as the other two droids hid in the gymnasium. Dez-bot played the recording of the Kronik's speech from the day of the assassination – the only recording of his voice I had access to and a clear reminder of my failures.

I looked at the gym equipment stacked or hung on the far wall as if each piece might be a person in a crowd. Then, I eased into the awareness my special abilities afforded me and listened to the room breathe: ropes swayed, fans whirred, chains clanked, all while Dez-bot spoke to the people.

A shift of shadow depth caught my left eye. I focused on tracking it as I touched base with the fake crowd and the ambient noise in a discernible pattern, one after the other. Shadow Android slipped from the gloom but didn't make any telltale aggressive movements. *The decoy scenario.*

I shifted to Dez-bot's right side and angled my body back in anticipation of the hidden bot's strike. But Dez-bot stuttered as shadow-bot walked around to the join the crowd of equipment. With the blast of the cap-gun, Dez-bot hiccupped and collapsed at my feet. Shadow-bot had concealed the weapon and taken advantage of my distraction.

"Argh!" I heaved my arms in the air. "You changed it! Of course, you changed it." I spun away from the androids and kicked a free-standing boxing bag. "I. Can't. Do. This." I punched and kneed the bag with each word.

"Taya!"

I whipped around in fighting stance and snarled, "What?"

Tek stood in full combat gear, from the com device in his ear all the way down to his… "Socks?" He couldn't wear his boots in the gym.

I dropped my fists and let their weight pull my shoulders down. "What are you doing here?"

"I've been calling you for over a minute, now. What's going on?" He crossed his arms. "Why didn't you wait until later when we could—"

"What's the point?" I shoved stray strands of hair off my face. "I programmed the droids to alternate the attacks each time. The muscle memory isn't working."

He shook his head. "Come on. It's nearly second sundown."

"Already?" I grabbed the tie from Dez-bot and waved the droids back to their resting positions. Tek turned and walked toward the change rooms.

"We can talk about this later."

"Why bother." I wiped sweat from my forehead with my bare arm. He turned back and I walked right into him. Frowning, he held me at arm's length.

"You're doing too much all at once and not following the plan." His gaze searched my face. "Maybe you need help with more than muscle memory."

"What do you mean?"

"You need to talk to someone."

"I'm talking to you."

"Taya—"

"No. I already know what's wrong with me and I'm fixing it."

Tek frowned. "Maybe that's the problem."

"What is?"

"Forget it. Go get changed. I'll meet you at the rally point. They should arrive in twenty."

I watched my last friend pad away to do the job I'd trained so hard for and shook my head. Under normal circumstances, twenty minutes would have been a lifetime to change and head out the door, but I couldn't muster the energy required to be efficient. Besides, what did it matter? I had only been kidding myself. How could I be head of security and not be integral in setting up the rally stage? My team was out there but I wasn't.

I shoved my workout clothes into my locker, armed myself, and stood in the foyer waiting for the elevator. When the door dinged open, I glanced up into the face of my past.

Niless.

I couldn't wave the elevator off and take the stairs: that access was for emergencies only. And if I waited for the elevator to come back, I'd be late getting to the Rally. What was probably only a nanosecond of hesitation felt like forever. Averting my gaze, I stepped into the metal box beside the contracts coordinator and pseudo-mother to every trainee who came through this place. I stared at the floor indicator, but my peripheral vision saw anyway. My chest tightened as I struggled to take a calm, even breath.

Her golden coliths radiated under the simple lighting as the elevator dinged its way to the main floor. I glanced at the black space below the upper floor listings and shuddered at the memory of being hauled to the sub-basements the last time I saw Niless. In fact, the last time I spoke to her was six months ago when I sealed the deal with Dezmind to act as his bodyguard and guide into the Deserts. My Infinity contract had been signed by the old Kronik himself and the master keeper of the Facility, who personally came out to the Capitol to watch the deal sealed.

The petite Metek woman beside me had always placed my best interests at heart. Or so I believed. But she'd been the one to encourage me to take on the Max-View technician contract *and* supported my friendship with Zaith – reporter and double agent for the old Kronik. Zaith, the woman who'd been sent to assassinate both me and Dezmind out in the Deserts. The only person who—

I blinked the thought and the ache of betrayal away.

The elevator dinged for the last time and I walked out never having made eye contact with the woman I'd always thought held the best of intentions toward me. While a part of me doubted she ever knew the endgame of the master keeper, the ethics committee governors, or even the secret agent pretending to be a renowned reporter, she'd still had a hand in shaping my destiny.

Chapter 12
Homecoming

Satie

"And what do you think about this new Kronik? What do you know about him?" Delenon asked the driver through the open passage between the cab and the back of the transport.

Beside me, Drax leaned forward, keen to hear more about the Talian who'd done the unthinkable. In fact, I think we all turned a head or cocked an ear to hear what the man might say. I was likely to be the most receptive, given my connection with Drax. I reached for his hand and gave it a slight squeeze. He squeezed back but kept his eyes riveted to the man talking.

"Well, sir, I don't think anyone but the Underground knew much of him until five or six months ago. You see, he was a follower of the Spoken Truth and believed in what the Cause was trying to do."

"And that was...?"

"Huh? Oh, right. You've only just returned. The Cause built up the Underground into a fully functioning city where those the previous Kronik targeted unjustly could seek asylum. My boy happened to have a habit of speaking his mind and got on the former Kronik's radar. Three times bizarre accidents nearly took his life, and we realised the powers that be were trying to silence him for good. Anyway, once you go below ground, the only contact with the rest of the world is through the tabloids."

"The tabloids, really? Ingenious," Delenon muttered.

"Yep. The General managed to keep everything under wraps as he amassed an army of volunteers to help with the coup. I hear the new Kronik had been working with them for nearly five years. But I don't think his trip into the Deserts was smoke and mirrors. Nope. I listened to him speak before he became Kronik, and he truly believed he'd find the answers to our weather problems and the quakes by finding the Chronicles."

"The Chronicles? But that's just a legend, a bedtime story."

"Nope. They're real. Been brought to the Museum of Darius to be kept with the Tablets and other artifacts from the time of the Great Migration."

"And they helped solve the problem? Then why were we told there's something wrong with the verrin?"

"Yes and no. You see, it was the aliens who lived in the south what caused all the problems. Things are better since the new Kronik and his followers restarted an ancient device. Now, I know what you're gonna say, but I've only seen pictures and all this talk about the verrin comes from a scientist who the old Kronik tried to have silenced. It's just speculation if you ask me. All the Kronik has said is that they're looking into it. Sounds a lot like the old Kronik sometimes."

"And why is he any better than the old Kronik?"

"Well, you see, he – oh. Here we are."

I looked out the tinted window as a rainbow sea of people parted in the street and our driver broke off the conversation to focus on not running anyone over. A large stage spanned the entire gateway into the Talian Compound. On the stage, twelve Talians stood side-by-side with twelve Commoners. *Which one is the new Kronik?*

The lidez glided to a stop and a dozen or more justices created a double-sided barricade with their bodies leading from the transport door all the way to the stage.

"Come on, Satie." Drax tugged on my hand.

I closed my eyes and shook my head trying to make sense of the pageantry of it all.

"Hey." He pulled me close and kissed my forehead as we joined the queue of our fellow Resistance fighters to meet the one Talian who managed to remember there was an entire world outside the Compound.

As I stepped down from the hovering transport that had brought us across land from sea to sea, horns honked and people cheered – even a brass band blasted enthusiastic music. The caravan of vehicles that had followed us from Nova Leau had grown exponentially as we passed from one town to the next. People knelt and stood on the roofs and hoods of their riders waving and laughing and even crying.

My hand slipped from Drax's as a flare of deep orange

light from Zita winked over the promenade, and I stepped away from the transport. I signed a blessing to the setting Sister and then one to sleeping Zola and bright Zerameteth as I followed Tony, Marxx and Delenon past justice after justice. Some wore the contractor emblem under their sector badges, some not. All *smiling*. I honestly never thought I'd live to see the day.

I glanced over my shoulder past Drax who refused to acknowledge the glint of surprise in the gazes of those surrounding us. Behind him, tension radiated off Daria as she used her body to shield Teena. Jippon and Reena stood stiff and tall, avoiding eye contact with anyone, especially those who bordered our path.

As I approached the edge of the large make-shift stage, a silvery-white hand with outlined black coliths stretched toward me. Without a second thought, I reached for the proffered hand just as I'd reached for Drax's over the past twenty-two years. My gaze barely had time to register the Talian face of a young man who might have rivalled my feelings for Drax had their places and ages been reversed. As I shifted past the helpful gentleman, a gasp rose from the crowd. I grasped my journal, glanced over my shoulder and stumbled. Tony shifted back to steady me.

Before a crowd of hundreds, on both sides of the wall, Xannians learned that their new Kronik wasn't the first Talian to work and live amongst Commoners – amongst rebels. And then the dramatic moment passed almost as fast as it happened. Cameras flashed and View-Xs recorded the eighteen of us who'd been healthy enough to travel across the lands to return to the beginning. No smoky pyre, no soldiers with strange hi-tech weapons shooting at us, and no death march down to the distant docks, of which there were now several. But, like the docks in Nova Leau, no ships cluttered the landscape.

A female security officer shifted for a better view of the young man who'd helped us onto the stage and who now moved to stand behind the microphone at centre stage – the dividing line between us and them. *Dear gods, is he the new Kronik?* I reached for Drax's arm and squeezed just above his elbow, then let go when I realised I was making a scene. Several people in the crowd pointed our way.

The young man, amidst muted cheers and general crowd chatter, turned his back on the twenty-four officials standing opposite us and spoke to both the Talian crowd and the Commoner crowd as one.

"Fellow Xannians, it is time for us to properly welcome home these intrepid souls." He opened his arms wide and the volume from the Commoners' side erupted with the band and streamers and balloons.

I covered my ears. Turning from side-to-side I made eye contact with each member of my flock, most of whom stood dumbfounded with tears threatening to spill. We'd had no idea what to expect when we agreed to meet with the new Kronik, but it certainly wasn't this. My heart ached with the clash of joy and sorrow. This show of support was truly bittersweet. I drew in great gulping breaths to keep my own tears in check even as a tremble shot through me from head to toe.

As the new Kronik waved the excited voices down to a dull roar, a few more security officers shifted away from the shadows, some on stage, some surrounding it. The intense woman who'd shadowed him earlier now stood with the officials. Her body fairly vibrated with tension as a mix of emotions animated her eyes, fear and confusion dominating.

"I pledge before everyone here today to honour those souls who fought for a cause far greater than themselves." The new Kronik extended one arm toward us and swept it around to the Commoner crowd. He swung his other arm toward the Compound, drawing a marked hush from jubilant onlookers.

"On both sides of the conflict. Those of my race and the elite Commoners who worked for the old Kronik are just realising the lies and half-truths that came from a man they trusted to watch over all of us. This civil war has touched every person present whether from twenty-two years ago or twenty-two weeks ago."

The female guard shifted to the space between the officials and us, turning in marked degrees toward the Talian crowd. A sheen coated her bronzed Matin skin. The trace of a red colith flashed along one side of her neck as she strained to look over and through the crowd, searching for something — as if she knew his words did not speak to everyone. My heart jumped at the thought.

"The only person to blame is the man who's been stripped of his ranking and power and who no longer whispers distorted truths to the representatives and people of Xannia. We will build a monument to *all* the souls lost in this conflict because regardless of race, we were all equally lied to. This monument will serve as a reminder that we need to hold ourselves accountable to the truth and to the sanctity of life. We are no longer a divided people, and that is what we are here today to celebrate."

A volley of streamer blasts exploded into the air as the cheers renewed – more from the Talians and less so from the Commoners. Still, I could see now why this young Kronik stood before us today. His ability to see past the veil and unite all people might just heal a long-fractured land. But the presence of the female officer who'd separated herself from the shadows and now clearly stood by the young Kronik spoke volumes about his idealism versus the reality of his vision. Still, as a Commoner, she was willing to sacrifice herself to keep him alive. To keep the hope for a new beginning alive.

The young Kronik then motioned for each group on the stage to meet in the middle. Within seconds, two lines formed and the mix of old and new government officials extended their hands toward us, the old Resistance whose ideals now echoed in the new Cause, and we too bridged the last of the gap and accepted their offering.

As the new Commoner-councillors did their best to welcome us, Delenon and the Kronik, along with his personal guard, walked toward the microphone stand. Another wave of excitement burst from the crowd as the young Talian introduced the famed and much-loved magistrate of old.

While the last of Zita's rays slipped below the horizon, everyone on stage – Commoner, Talian, official and rebel – moved onto the street to meet the media up close. All of the shadow officers emerged as the rows of justices who'd parted the crowd for us earlier did so again. Only, this time, they stood shoulder to shoulder between the bulk of the excited masses and us. A small microphone hovered in front of my face.

"Is it true that you're the first All Mother in nearly five hundred years?"

"What? Really? Has it been that—"

"Were you a Sun Guardian before the failed Resistance—" another mic shoved the first aside.

"Uh, yes. Zera—"

"—or were you a fighter who's self-anointed?"

"No! I studied with temple Guardians for years." I glanced around and noticed the networks had effectively separated us from each other.

"Are you in a relationship with the Talian dissenter?"

"Excuse me? Drax isn't – what?"

"How is it possible to be a Sun Guardian, let alone an All Mother, and yet break one of the four fundamental oaths to the gods?"

I recoiled. *How do they know any of this?* Three more microphones joined the other two vying for a position to get the best soundbite.

"What do you think about the claims that Gamma is a fake sun?"

I held my hands in front of my face to ward them off. The officer shadowing me did nothing to help. I tried to back away from the media mob, but more caught wind of the questions and repeated them over and over.

Then, out of nowhere, a pair of strong hands turned me away from the onslaught as the Matin security officer placed herself between me and the reporters. I glanced at the fierce features of the woman who'd been guarding the young Kronik. She glowered at the justice behind me. I glanced back and watched him flinch from the non-verbal reprimand. Before I knew it, I found myself at the edge of the stage next to the Compound wall where a vine bushed out and helped block sightlines.

"Are you all right?" The female guard straightened my blouse and signalled for a different justice from the wall of guards to join us.

"The Kronik will extend an invitation for your group to stay with us at the Capital Building."

I blanched. As she nodded, I caught sight of the ribbon-like colith creeping beyond her neckline and noticed the fine black tracing around the deep red wave.

"That's what I thought. So, I've arranged it with the current leader of the Underground for you to stay there as long as you're in the city. Would you like me to take you there now?"

"Thank you, but I need some space. I'd like to go for a walk. Away from here."

She stared at me for a long moment. An inner argument waged as her eyes flickered in response to her question.

"Certainly. Officer Nylin will accompany you. I will inform the others of your wishes once we leave the area." And just like that, she was gone and Nylin was using his body to shield me from the crowd as we left its crush and mass ignorance.

The back streets were surprisingly quiet, and by the time we'd travelled a block away, life appeared normal. My breathing slowed and soon my steps followed. At first, I just took in the wonder of the modern buildings, but when I could see hints of the older architecture consumed by larger structures, I got a better sense of where I was.

I hadn't realised it, but after an hour of seemingly aimless wandering, my feet brought me to the steps of the only original untouched building in the area. Its modest columns and faded brickwork contrasted with the metal and tinted glass surrounding it. My guard and I stood out front staring at the structure as the occasional acolyte or believer walked through its doors.

"You can go in, All Mother. I'll keep you in sight, but I can stay by the inner arches. I doubt you're at risk here."

I glanced up at him. Kindness radiated from sincere eyes.

"It'll give me time to check in with base again, anyway." He smiled. I returned the smile, nodded, and then walked back through the very doors men like him had dragged me from on the day of my Devout ceremony – the day of the Massacre.

Chapter 13

Hunting the Past

Taya

I didn't want to endure yet another tour of the Capitol Building, so I put Ynell in charge of Dez. Tek's team had the LRM, Lost Resistance Members, well-protected, so instead of being in the way, I caught a lidez to the Klax Square Transpoint to follow-up on accommodations for our visitors in the Underground. At least, that's what I said I was doing.

The bistro café sat two streets over from where Dez and I had hidden under a lidez back when the old Kronik tried to blow up the Spoken Truth Rally. I caught sight of new signage to the left of the door, UNDERGROUND *Transpoint* Access 8. Kaynee convinced Dezmind not all the known transpoints needed to be revealed, but a total of twenty-five from Darzeth-Prime to Vrazeth were now open. She'd agreed that free access to the Underground was essential – but still wanted to monitor who came and went.

It had been particularly helpful in keeping Faction supporters and fanatics out.

I followed another sign at the back of the crowded café through a door that now stood permanently open. A security camera was mounted on the other side of the doorframe. The dark orb appeared harmless enough but recorded a picture of everyone who entered and exited and stored digital footage in thirty-hour batches. Gerrund had ensured the orbs were installed before shipping out.

He'd taken my advice: Go where you can make the most difference. He chose to leave and watch over those UGC, Underground Citizens, who wanted to live above ground but not within the immediate reach of the Kronik – even if the new one did seem to be a nice guy. It was the right move. Gerrund's disposition only grew surlier the longer he stayed in the Prime.

Bright lights set into the smoothed rock walls guided me down the winding staircase to the what-not shop in the tunnels below. The clatter of cutlery and animated chatter faded the farther I got from the café. Below, the door at the bottom opened after an old, re-purposed palm-reader registered my identity. Government agents signed in and out. I wanted it that way so I could track my people at a moment's notice.

Malik, the exuberant shop owner, raised his hands as if he could hug me from across the room. "Taya! I haven't seen you in ages."

"How's the system behaving?" I asked.

"Ah, much better now. I haven't called for service for over a month."

"Good to hear." I stopped to chat even though I wasn't in the mood. "How's business?"

He knew what I meant. "Busy at first, but things have levelled out as the novelty of the Underground wears off. Even though there are fewer UGC, those who've decided to stay have topside family that visit regularly, which tends to even things out."

"I'm glad. Dez – I mean – the Kronik and I were a little concerned when so many people jumped at the chance to go south." I reached out and clasped his arm over the counter. "I'll see you on my way out then."

I slowed my pace the closer I got to Major/Minor Street, passing familiar shops lining the edge of the grand tunnel, lights ablaze overhead to mimic the daylight topside. The wall frescos looked brighter, touched up recently with the influx of trade and support from the new government. A flash of memory from the first time Gerrund took me on a tour of the Underground invaded my thoughts. Gods. I had so many questions and was so certain of what I had to do. But it was easy then: save Dezmind. He didn't need saving anymore.

I hesitated at the entrance to the side tunnel, remembering my first Daily meeting with Gerrund, arguing with Thenticia about training and how to make a formidable soldier. An ache surged from my gut up into my chest and throat. I inhaled a shaky breath and forced one foot in front of the other. *Maybe this is a bad idea.*

The old Desert Vehicle Shop stood dark, relegated to a storage bay once again. Gelden took everything and set up shop topside after the coup, near Vrazeth's border. Less of a hassle moving supplies and vehicles around, and I'd heard he'd expanded the design, too.

The large chamber that once housed Gerrund's stage of operations, a set of barracks, and the Cause's training grounds, sat almost empty. Picnic tables with bright umbrellas surrounded a platform now used for entertainment instead of battle plans. I didn't know how I felt about that.

I skirted the leisure grounds and headed for the old shop that connected to another chamber where we'd housed the additional barracks months ago. Kaynee, Gerrund's sister, had bought out the shopkeeper so he could move to one of the recently vacated locations on the other side of the commons. I nodded to the two Underground guards leaning against one side of the newly refined opening and then slipped down the short tunnel to the small cavern beyond.

With a cursory glance, I knew at once Kaynee had everything under control. She always did. Just like her brother, yet different.

Several small tents in various stages of construction circled a common area with tables and chairs. Trunks upon trunks of old supplies lined the rough-hewn walls, pushed aside for the temporary accommodations. Magistrate Delenon asked that his people not be separated. This was the only place nearby we could think of that might accommodate them. Dez wanted them to stay in one of the apartment buildings with proper plumbing and furniture, but it would have placed them on the outskirts in the abandoned construction zone where I had once helped

Gelden, my mentee, on one of his volunteering jobs. At the time, I hadn't liked that the Underground needed to expand, but now I felt a strange loss at the number of homes that never got to keep a family.

I completed a circuit of the action, looking for Kaynee. A sharp surge hit my chest at the thought of having to enter the commotion. I couldn't find her. The mix of shouted directions, conversation, and laughter formed a living cloud as I forced myself into the action. But I messed up an intuitive choreography, barely avoiding an elbow to the head. My pulse quickened. I helped steady a long pole, then got bumped in the shoulder. Someone else hurried by. I tried to focus on my breathing but nearly tripped when a length of tent cloth yanked out from under my foot.

I have to get out of here.

A flash of straight, pale blonde hair disappeared into a mobile tent. The four volunteers carrying it set it down and then went to help elsewhere. I ducked inside.

"Kaynee," I said. She looked at me from atop her portable stool, hands still poised to straighten the elbow of a roof support.

"Taya!" She jumped down and enveloped me in a hug, lifting me off the ground even though her head only came to my chin. "What brings you here?" She let me go and knocked her palm against the side of her head. "Of course, Kronik business."

"No. You don't need me watching over your shoulder. But you do know he'd like a permanent liaison for the council, right? Not just whoever you can spare when you remember to send someone?" Talking shop helped even out my heartbeat, doing what the breathing exercises couldn't. She rolled her eyes and shifted her stool over to the next support elbow. I helped straighten the one closest to me. "Okay. I've kept my promise to Dezmind, and you can verify that I asked."

She made a face and stuck her tongue out. I laughed, something I hadn't done in so long. In the early days, after Gerrund had left with the exodus south, Kaynee would steal me away from whatever light-duty task Dez had assigned me to help her grapple with leadership. Everyone treated her like their younger sister, just like Gerrund had, but she was the High Ruler of Underground now and a tiny one at that. She still had no formal title, but at least I'd managed to get people calling her Kaynee instead of "Gerrund's little sister." Bringing Dias Betauni in as an advisor had also helped.

"So, what brings you to my neighbourhood then?" She grabbed her stool and headed for the tent opening.

I snagged her elbow and guided her in an arc back inside, heaving a sigh.

"That bad?" she asked.

"No. I don't know. A friend said—" I waved the air around my head. "I need you to contact Bijak."

"Jak? Someone in need of his particular services?"

"Yeah, you could say so." I crossed my arms.

"For you! Oh. Okay. Well, we don't do the clandestine thing anymore." She searched her multi-pocketed pants and came up with a pen and a small notebook. "Here." She shifted the tent flap into the brighter light to jot something down. As she ripped the sheet from her booklet, a helper breezed in with a rechargeable light-tube to hang from the ceiling.

"What's this?" I shifted the piece of paper in my hand.

"His office. Well, his new office." When I looked up from the note, three more helpers stood around us. "I wish I could walk over with you but…"

"I know. The LRM will be here in less than an hour. A tour of the Capital building doesn't take that long. Go." I waved her, and her accumulated helpers, away.

As she weaved through the chaos, each person received a new task, and Kaynee disappeared once again… as did the bubble of joy that floated with her.

I stared at the scribbled directions on the page. A familiar chill settled over me, but I had to admit Tek was right. He could only do so much, and now he had a new job to focus on, with a whole new set of people placed in the Faction's crosshairs. I had to stop relying on him so much. I shook my head. Nothing had happened at the Welcome Home Rally, but that was all thanks to him and my security team. I crumpled the page in my fist and headed for the exit.

I'd taken the easy-out: followed the All Mother when the press descended, left Tek and Ynell on Dez's watch. I was nothing more than window dressing these days. It was time to change that.

As I followed Kaynee's directions, the eerie stillness of the streets weighed on my mind. Malik, the transpoint shop owner, hadn't told me everything. No bicycles whizzed by with impending messages for Gerrund and his people, fewer patrons sat at the cafés, and nearly as many shops stood closed as remained opened. The hustle to get the LRM's tents ready belied a coma-like silence to a once thriving city.

The quiet seeped into my bones and rattled around in my chest as I walked down a tunnel I'd never visited when the Underground became my sentence for exposing myself to save Dez. A business vibe came from multi-tiered buildings that resembled small apartments but displayed a number of different signs – still just pictures on metal or wood posted on a single pole sticking out from the tunnel's rock face. Under a third-floor window hung a plaque with stylised grey matter and what appeared to be a swirl of stars or glitter coiling up like smoke. *Brain Magic? No. Brain Science? Maybe.*

I opened one side of a double-glass entry and climbed the sweeping twin staircase at the back of the foyer. I chose the one on the right. A separate smaller stairwell climbed to the third floor which opened onto a large reception area nearly the size of my old apartment. Clearly, Jak wasn't the only specialist who worked here.

"May I help you, Miss?"

I glanced at the blue-skinned man sporting a shock of dark purple and blue hair shaped like a flame. His small, thin, silver coliths clustered so tight he looked more like a mirror than a man. I could see why he worked here.

"I'd like to see Jak."

"Do you have an appointment?" He glanced at the ledger resting under his forearms.

"No."

"Do you have a referral?"

"I'm an ex-patient."

He scanned down the page and flipped to the next, and the next. "I can fit you in for a half-session in about a week."

A week.

"Can you just let him know I'm here? Taya Doire."

"I'm afraid I can't interrupt a session."

"When will it be over? I have to get back to work soon."

"Hmm… I honestly can't say. Why don't you leave me your com number and I'll—"

I closed my eyes a moment and waved him quiet. "Never mind. I just wanted to talk to him for a minute. I had no idea all this"—I motioned to him and the grand office—"would be… I don't know. Convoluted. Forget I was even here." I turned and walked out the way I came.

The last thing I needed was someone telling me what was wrong or how to fix it. Tek and I were doing just fine. We had a plan. It was just going to take longer to work through the muscle memory patterns than I thought. I had to adjust for more time. I always had to adjust for more time. Why would this be any different?

Chapter 14
Unfixable

Jak

I opened my office door and leaned my shoulder against the frame as I loosened my tie. Virtual therapy sessions always put me on edge.

"How long until the next one?" I asked my assistant.

"You've got a dinner break and then two more this evening before lights out. Oh, a young woman by the name of Taya Doire was here a moment ago."

"Taya? Really? What did she want?"

"To talk to you. She was going to make an appointment but changed her mind."

"What? Why?"

"You're booked solid this week and—"

"When did she leave?" I took a few steps toward the landing.

"Maybe five minutes ago. But she said not to bother."

"Wipp, I told you, they all say that. Hold my calls." I

jogged down the two flights of stairs and crashed through the doors, stumbling out into the tunnel. *Dammit. Which way did she go?* I scanned the road to my left and then right. *Think, think, think.* I ran to the right. Left only went to a suburb. Right connected with Main Street and all the major locales.

Several UGC were on their way home for the night. One stiff-backed, combat-booted woman turned the corner at the T-intersection. As I rounded that same corner a minute later, something told me to back off. I studied her gait, following at a distance. Her straight spine and militaristic pacing verified it was Taya, but the dipped head and absence of haughty ambivalence spoke volumes.

I tracked her to the tunnel that once led to Gerrund's base of operations, but she hesitated mid-step before passing the old shop. I curled my body into a pocket of rock and waited. A commotion of voices and movement told me she'd been headed toward something – something she clearly didn't want to be part of right now. She turned back to the shop door. From the pocket of her cargo pants, she tugged a key free. Her hand shook as it hovered before the lock, and then she plunged it home and wrenched the door open. An emergency light at foot-level glowed to life, but she didn't turn on any other fixtures.

I moved down the tunnel and fit myself into another nook, watching her through the large-windowed door. My stomach grumbled, and I debated jogging to the concourse at the end of the tunnel and picking up something to go, but I couldn't leave her. She'd come all this way to find me and left without making an appointment. Something very much in character with the woman I'd met four months ago, but not the woman who'd sacrificed herself for something so much bigger than herself; the one who'd made it possible for Gerrund to continue to lead even though he was never destined to be Kronik; who helped keep the Underground alive for those who'd come to see it as home.

"Why has she regressed?" I whispered to myself. With that in mind, I walked across the width of the tunnel and opened the door.

* * *

Taya

I stared up at the rough-hewn ceiling, willing the tears back into my eyes, turned, and stood to face the interloper. After blinking the last of my failings away, I squinted at the dishevelled businessman, tie loosened and hanging at an odd angle, top button of his good shirt undone, and sleeves rolled back over his forearms. But it was the rainbow coliths and ambiguous features that fired the right synapses in my brain.

"Jak?"

He tried to finger-comb his hair but gave up. I'd never seen him so... normal looking.

"Where's your cloak?"

He laughed. "I told you once there was another side of me."

"More than one, actually. Masculine, feminine, *and* businessman." I hugged myself. "But I don't understand. Your assistant said you were with a client. Couldn't see me for a week. What are you doing here?"

"The session ended early. Wipp mentioned you'd just left. You've never visited my office, so I thought I'd catch up to you. May I?" He held his hand toward one of the stools by the work counter.

I nodded but sat in the chair by the old drafting board collapsed by the wall. I tried to picture him in his non-gender-specific disguise but had a hard time seeing the man who'd so easily broken my resolve to remain silent all those months ago.

"You know, you could have made that appointment, right?"

"Why? I shouldn't have bothered."

"Bothered what? Finding me? What's going on? Are the nightmares back?"

"No."

"Then what?"

I shrugged one shoulder.

"Come on, Taya. Talk to me. I know I look different and things don't work the same as they did before the coup, but there's a reason you wanted to see me. Cough it up." Now he sounded like Gerrund, but a little of his old self squeaked through.

"A friend advised me to talk to someone. I've talked to all of three people in my life: Dezmind, Jezetek, and Zaith. The only other exception I've made is you. Right now, I'm lucky if I see Dezmind outside of work hours, Zaith is… gone, and Tek's the one I go to for field advice and training. But our new regimen isn't working."

Jak frowned. By the tilt of his head, I could tell he struggled to understand.

I sighed. "Do you know what happened to me three months ago?"

"The night of the coup? No. I just know you were hospitalised." He leaned his elbows on his knees and clasped his hands together. "What happened, Taya?"

"I got beat up pretty bad. Used my body as a lightning rod and got shot with a Clinex plasma gun, short-range. All this after having survived sodium shock only weeks before." I met his gaze. "I died. At least, that's what the doctor's said. Tek saved me. When I woke up ten days later, my doctor told me I had brain damage. I didn't believe him because I felt fine. Problem is, fine never got any better. If anything, it's gotten worse."

I told him about my slowed reflexes, the overwhelming confusion, and how all of this almost cost me Dez's life.

"Tek's been trying to help me re-train my brain but…"

"It's not working."

"Not really. But I haven't given it enough time. It's just…"

"You're noticing a pattern? A block? Something you just can't get beyond?"

"Yes. I'm broken and I need to be fixed. I can't live like this."

Jak shifted and took a deep breath. He sat up tall, pushing his palms into his knees. I recognised that look in his eyes, the unspoken words… *you can't be fixed.*

Chapter 15
Rumblings

Satie

The temple stood exactly as I remembered it, from the worn stone floor to the traditional benches facing a sun god each, to the central altar where the Devout performed rituals. My calloused hands brushed over smooth carvings and columns as my gaze darted around the dim interior. A fluttering in my chest and stomach made my breath hitch.

I knelt before the wall of white candles surrounding a painting of Zerameteth in spirit form. Over my shoulder, the red candle wall honoured Zola, and the orange one, Zita. Now were the hours of the Child of the Light, and the clear glass high above cast a pale round glow on the floor between the pews and the shrine. I tilted my face up and raised my arms in prayer.

Snatches of whispers floated closer as a pair of women, likely FOL making their Worship rounds, sat a few rows back.

"They have everyone else represented on that new council except a Guardian. That's a slight in and of itself, but to blatantly claim that Zerameteth isn't real?" The gruff voice halted.

"I know. And that scientist talking about aliens and terraforming Xannia – ridiculous. Just ridiculous. But what will we do if the Kronik decides to take drastic measures?"

"We must be prepared to do the same. He will not destroy our gods."

A chill settled over me at their words, but the women moved on after singing the Solemn Prayer. As I made my way around the room, similar whispers overrode the usual quiet surrounding prayer – and not just the Followers of Light talking, but Initiates and Faithful too. The Devouts observed quiet contemplation.

A male Guardian watched me from the shadows of the outer corridor as I prayed at each station, arms and face raised to open myself to the gods during prayer. The FOL bowed their heads. With a tingle, I realised I'd paid the highest respect to all three gods and not just the Child god who'd seen fit to guide me through my travels and to whom I'd formally devoted my prayers all those years ago.

An older matron Guardian joined the man. They spoke in hushed whispers before she scurried away. Unease crept over me as pairs of eyes in the corridors beyond the walls flashed around pillars and through paneless windows. Something was wrong.

I glanced at the main entryway and caught sight of my security guard standing perfectly still. The outline of his shoulder and arm was a reminder of the new world we'd returned to. The physical architecture of this building may not have changed, but the people within its walls had.

The male Guardian spying on me slipped into the shadows before rounding the wide column. I stood and faced him. His measured steps slowed noticeably. I met him at the foot of the round altar in the middle of this sacred place and bowed. He nodded, clearly of the Devout and uncertain what to make of me.

"Greetings Brother. I wish to speak with the Guardian overseer. I am the once Sister Venra now All Mother to the Lost."

He blinked several times, obviously not expecting me to speak first. Whatever his intention had been, my request now superseded it. He nodded a second time.

"This way." He did not address me with an honorific as he should have.

In the corridor leading to the sanctuaries and kitchen, no eyes followed me as they had during my prayers, but all sanctuary doors remained open. I sensed small groups gathered here and there.

"Wait here, please, while I relay your request." He knocked twice and entered the office of the overseer. A heated conversation cut short when he entered. The second the door shut, I slid over to the wall beside it. The thick decorative glass muted the shape of the people inside the room, but I caught snatches of the muffled discussion beyond. I hadn't intended to speak to the overseer when I stood outside the temple weighing my soul, but I also couldn't ignore the obvious. A dark shape beyond the door grew. I shifted back across the hall.

"The overseer will meet with you now."

I nodded and walked past the Brother who'd never given me his name and into the office I'd spent many a session in. Discussions of what it meant to become a Devout and how to find the right name of honour popped to mind. Again, the people were the only thing different in the room. I stood before the large antique desk as the Brother and the Sister I'd spied earlier stepped into opposite corners behind me. This overseer had her own security.

I bowed in traditional greeting and glanced at the name plaque on her desk, nearly hidden by a mix of files and thin electronic note-takers. *Tablets.* "Guardian Megrhan," the name caught in my throat. "Apologies, one of my Lost Sisters shared your honorific."

"Shared?" The matronly woman asked with a soft yet commanding voice.

"She and Sister Ellanir did not survive the crossing of the Nine Seas. Which leads to my request to see you."

"Oh?"

She'd been expecting me to say something else. "Yes. During the crossing, we lost many lives to a vicious storm on the White Sea." The weight of that account nestled against my thigh in the journal dangling from my belt. "I asked Zerameteth to bind their souls to me so that they would not be lost to the death waters. I have yet to learn how to release them to Zola for the journey home. I came today with renewed hope, seeking your guidance."

"My guidance? Interesting. I would have thought that the All Mother would know the answer to this fundamental question." I didn't like the sharp edge to her gentle tone.

"I am not *the* All Mother, Guardian. I am *their* All Mother. Surely, you understand my position as the last living Guardian who'd sailed with the Resistance survivors. This is not a title I bequeathed upon myself, but one my flock has taken to using because I came to speak for all the gods. My overseer taught me much as I prepared my heart and my mind to become a Devout. Perhaps she might have included this lesson had we foreseen the consequences of our actions in helping the Cause. And so, I now seek this guidance from my brothers and sisters at the temple of my induction."

She drew up to her full height and narrowed her eyes at me. "Is it true what the media are saying?" she asked, her voice barely a whisper.

Startled, I glanced toward the door as if they stood right on the other side.

"What are they saying?"

She clicked a remote on her desk and a modern-looking screen came to life near the ceiling between the other two Guardians. She flipped from one network to the next, each one showing a different image of Drax and me: me placing a hand on his knee during the interview dockside; him carrying me out to the lidez, our hands unclasping a nanosecond after we disembarked from the transport; me holding his elbow up on stage… As all these perfectly harmless moments flashed by in a slideshow, I recalled those reporters questioning me as All Mother and then asking about a relationship with Drax. I paled.

"So, it's true then," the overseer said.

I faced her, my gaze steady, but remained silent.

"You have desecrated the ancient honorific by becoming

romantically involved, and with a Talian no less." She snapped the images off the screen and tossed the remote to her desk. "If you truly do carry the souls of the lost inside you, the only way to release them is with your death."

The two Guardians behind me shifted forward. *She can't mean now?* My chest tightened as my pulse raced. I glanced toward the door, wishing Officer Nylin had followed me all the way in. Two sets of firm hands gripped my arms and led me to the door.

"Satie Hithkrest, you are hereby disavowed."

Had this happened before the turmoil of the Nine Seas, I would've bent my head and allowed them to drag me from the temple. But if the gods had taught me anything these past twenty-two years, it was that I had a destiny to fulfil regardless of title or perception. The overseer assumed I'd returned to beg back my position and repent my decisions. Instead, I'd address her as an equal.

Yanking my arms across my body, I caught my captors off guard and grabbed their thumbs and wrists just as Daria had taught me. I squeezed the pressure points. They released me, snatching their arms tight to their chest. I turned all five feet two inches of myself around and stared down the overseer. Her grey skin paled and her eyelids fluttered.

"I do not answer to you, only the gods." I stalked out of the office, head held high. Back in the main chamber, I called for Nylin as I made my escape. He followed me down to the cellar. A stack of trunks hid the old transpoint, but together we shifted them aside and travelled down the darkened rock-cut stairs to the Underground.

At the bottom, another door waited. Nylin held up his hand for me to wait as he listened with one ear to the wood. Cautiously, he turned the knob. The door didn't budge but it also didn't appear to be locked. He stepped back and kicked the wood. A loud crack echoed as we stumbled through to an Underground temple and a mass of followers saying evening prayers to Zerameteth.

"Dear gods, It's the All Mother!" someone cried, and the congregation surged forward.

Chapter 16

Ally

Satie

Nylin gave a slight nod and raised his eyebrows. Our escort had arrived. I looped my arm through the crook of FOL Wentae's arm and headed for the door.

"Will you visit us again, All Mother?" she asked, a wistful quality to her voice.

"I mean to. I think it's time your little enclave had a proper leader."

"You're going to stay!" Excitement lit her eyes and lingered in her smile.

"No, my dear."

"Wha—oh. I don't understand."

I smiled at her. "My place is with my people, my extended family. No, I plan to train you as an Initiate. What do you think?"

"Me? Really?" She bounced up onto her toes and hugged my arm.

"Yes! You're nearly there. The UGC is an extension of my family now as this is where many of them lived before the Massacre. But I warn you." We paused at the open archway to the tunnel street, and I turned to face her. "I am not recognised by my old order. Your standing as a Guardian will only hold down here... and maybe in the south."

"I understand, All Mother. It isn't easy for others to adjust to change." A shadow crossed over her eyes, likely a memory of the time before the coup or maybe something more recent. Even a positive change could be challenging.

A deep, genuine laugh drew my gaze out onto the street. A group of FOL stood around the female security officer who'd rescued me from the media. She stood tall, hands behind her back; her ease in speaking with the group showed me she was no stranger to these Believers. They trusted her even though she helped protect the Kronik. The new Kronik.

Nylin's towering presence behind us reiterated it was time to go. I thanked Wentae again for her hospitality and slipped my arm from hers. Nylin and I stepped forward, but I wasn't ready to disrupt the young woman who'd come for us. I touched his arm.

"Wait."

He glanced between me and the girl.

"Who is she?" I asked.

"What do you mean?" As formal as this young man was, the hint of a tease played in his question. I looked up at him and smiled.

"She's special." I looked at her again. "She has a foot in

both worlds – above and below, Common and Elite."

"You've seen her maybe all of ten minutes this evening, and you know this about her already? How?"

"I can't explain it. There's something about her."

"She's a walking contradiction," he said, a slight frown on his face. "I heard she was the top contractor at the CTF, but after helping the new Kronik find the lost Chronicles, she ended up sacrificing herself for the Cause."

"Sacrificing herself? My goodness, what did she do?"

"I wasn't there, but I've heard soldiers talk about the battle for the Underground the night of the coup. Made it rain in the cavern under the Compound. Some people say her connection with Gamma – uh, Zerameteth – and the Alien City changed her. I don't know. She's kind of a recluse. Does her job and then disappears. But one thing is certain: without her, the new Kronik would never have survived the Deserts and stopped the super quakes… would never have made it into power."

"Is having him in power better than having the old Kronik?"

He didn't answer right away. The girl looked up and nodded toward us. Excusing herself from the group she strolled over.

Nylin took a half-step back, but I heard him whisper "Yes."

"All Mother, welcome to the Underground. The others are waiting for you." We walked side-by-side with Nylin just behind us. The young woman had reverted back to security officer posture. Her smile disappeared and with it the ease she'd allowed herself moments before. She was back on duty, hands still clasped behind her.

I didn't quite know what to say to this girl who seemed so unassuming and yet clearly carried a great weight upon her soul.

"Have you visited the Underground before?" she asked.

"No. My fellow Guardians and I allowed the Resistance fighters access to the streets through the cellar in the temple. We had no reason to venture below."

"I was wondering how a Guardian got mixed up in all this." She tried to keep her comment light, but something in her tone echoed the weight of her experience, of her choices. She pointed out a few specialty shops along the way and provided a pleasant tour-guide-view of the tunnels: a little bit of history, points of interest about the lighting and wall frescoes. But our pace slowed once we left Main Street and turned onto Major/Minor. She wiped her hands along the side of her hips and her whole body stiffened as if bracing for yet another battle.

As we entered a side tunnel, Nylin said, "Ladies," and double-timed it toward the distant ruckus at the end of the street.

"What's your name?" I asked, turning and clasping her hand in both of mine. She snatched it back. A flash of fear and apology painted her features. But I felt the scars there.

"Jutaya Doir."

We stopped adjacent to an old shop about halfway along the tunnel.

"May I?" I indicated her hand with a nod.

"Why? I mean, the others are waiting for you. We should—"

"They're not going anywhere. Besides, there's something I think you should know, and I don't know who else to trust with this information."

"Surely Magistrate Delenon…"

"Yes, but then he'd be in the same position I am – wondering who to trust with it. Wondering if it really meant something or if I'm reading too much into a world I haven't been a part of in over two decades. Something tells me you're a person with one foot on both sides, so to speak."

A war waged inside this young soldier. The battle played out in muted fierceness with the twitch of her brows.

"How can I help you, All Mother?"

I took a cursory glance around. No one walked near. I stepped forward and took her hands in mine, looking her straight in the eyes. "Trouble may be brewing."

Instead of snatching her fingers away again, she gripped mine tighter.

The girl lowered her voice, "What kind of trouble?"

"The sun you call Gamma."

She stiffened but leaned closer.

"The new Kronik's scientific beliefs may be true; I don't know. My gut tells me he's an honest man. But rumour has it that Gamma is the source of our climate change and the reason verrin is disappearing from our world. If… if anything negative were to happen to it, to the religious community's Child god, the new Kronik might just have another uprising on his hands."

"What are you talking about? You can't be serious? How do you know? You've only been back—"

"—for three days. I know. But with fresh eyes and a

deep connection with the FOL. A connection I can see in you, too."

"You're certain?"

"No. I'm not. That's the worst part. This is no longer my world. But in the past hour, I have heard things from all levels: Guardians and Followers, above and below. And I remember how the Resistance started all those years ago. The whispers, the concerns, the sense of injustice."

The poor girl deflated before me. Her hands now limp in mine, I turned them over and looked at the twin mass of scars riddling her palms. Sunbursts. My heart jumped in my chest. *No wonder the FOL have taken to her.* She curled her hands into fists, and I looked into her eyes.

"It's not what you think," she said, her jaw tight.

"And what do I think?"

"That the gods have marked me."

"What is the truth?"

Her eyes flickered. One question. One word and every mental wall this child had erected imploded at the same time. She staggered. I gripped her forearms to steady her.

"There's more than one truth, isn't there?" I asked softly. She nodded.

"Satie!" Daria's voice echoed the length of the tunnel.

I shifted to one side of Ms. Doire and waved.

"Come on, already. I'm hungry."

I glanced at the young soldier beside me.

"Go," she said. "I won't forget what you've said." She straightened her back and masked her features before turning and following me down the remainder of the tunnel, her steps slow and steady.

Chapter 17
Unspoken Truths

Taya

Dez and I followed the nurse down the hospital corridor. Three Special Ops officers trailed behind us. Leaving the Compound thirty hours after a Faction strike never went over well.

"Two of you can enter at a time." The nurse gazed up at us as we stood inside the trauma ward at the hospital in Darzeth Prime. Less than a week after the Welcome Home Rally, the Faction returned to targeting the innocent.

I turned to the Special Ops group and forced a confidence I didn't feel into my voice. "I'll take him in. One at the door, one at the window, and one by the elevators." I nodded in the direction of each location. They saluted and dispersed.

Dez smiled at the nurse who led us in. "The others have already been signed out, but these four were hit hardest." She led Dez to the closest bed.

I slipped past them to the window and shut the blinds.

"Rikk, the Kronik is here to see how you're doing." The nurse raised the upper portion of the patient's bed and slipped an extra pillow behind his head and shoulders. His pale pink skin held a yellowish hue. He winced when he tried to sit straighter, collapsing over on his right side.

Dez chatted with the man about how he was feeling, his family, and his job. His attentiveness became a balm. Rikk relaxed, speaking easily with the new head of the government – the very person he'd been hoping to meet when the Faction had blown a hole into the side of his lidez. Dez had decided to continue to run the tour of the Capitol at least once a week, but the escalation of attacks impacted everyone's safety. He compensated every tourist for lost time from work but refused to admit to an error in judgement.

The window muffled raised voices from below. I glanced at the door; Tek's man held his position. I twitched one edge of the blind aside and peered down three stories to the media frenzy at the entrance to the hospital. Two guards kept the reporters out. For now.

A low voice resonated from my ear-piece, "Situation at front entrance. Sending unit to check alternate exits."

I glanced back inside the room. Dez stood over by the bed opposite Rikk's, the nurse hovering nearby as he spoke to a woman with a bandage over her head and one eye. We'd been assured that everyone would recover fully, but some might take longer than others.

Something tickled my fingertips. I snatched my hand up and stared at the source. The tragic expression on the face of the boy in the bed broke my heart. I caught his gauze-covered hand lightly in mine before he let his arm drop back to the bed. His eyes lit up.

"You're like me," he said as he carefully turned my hand over to expose my scarred palm. This wasn't like those times with the FOL, with All Mother. This ten-year-old saw them for what they were. Battle scars. I gave him my other hand as well. The blast had burned his hands and arms. He'd likely tried to shield himself from the fireball that accompanies most explosions. The four citizens in this room had sat closest to ground zero.

"Sort of. I have a bad habit of doing things I shouldn't when I'm supposed to be healing." I gave him a small smile.

"What happened?"

I glanced at Dez, the guard at the door, the nurse, and then back to the kid. "The first time, I helped people out of a building damaged by the super quake."

"The Solar Plex."

"That's right."

"Mom and Dad were watching the news when it happened."

I nodded. "Yes. A lot of people were."

"Then what?"

"Well, I brought the new Kronik, before he became the new Kronik, into the Deserts to find the lost Chronicles. On the way, I climbed a cliff with sharp rocks, and I broke open the scabs before my skin could heal properly."

"Wow. It sounds like you were on a real adventure."

"Yes, I suppose we were."

His small, individually gauze-wrapped digits traced the

star pattern of the scars.

"Then, when the old Kronik tried to blow up the Spoken Truth Rally at Darius's Square, I broke the skin open again."

"What happened?"

I glanced over at Dez but spoke to the boy. "The new Kronik was trapped on the statue of the ship as it sank into the ground. I climbed down the statue to help him, but my hands still hadn't healed."

"We, my mom and dad and big sister, used to sit by the ship and have picnics on weekends when Jolly Green sang in the park."

I nodded. Jolly Green had been singing in the park for kids even when I was young and living on the streets.

He went quiet and chewed his bottom lip. This young boy's seriousness drew me in. I sat down in the chair beside his bed; Dez now spoke with the patient across from us.

"Why are they stars?" the boy asked.

My chest tightened. I took a breath to calm my nerves. He wasn't FOL. He wasn't asking about the gods. He was just a curious kid.

"I don't know. I think it has a lot to do with how I hurt them. You see, the first time and the third time I was holding onto thin metal that broke my skin."

"And the second time?"

"Well, the sharp rocks poked into the middle of my palm before the skin could heal properly, and the jagged rocks broke my skin in new places near where it had already knit together. Because—"

"Scar tissue is tougher."

"That's right."

"The doctor told me that." He looked at his arms, me now holding his hands. "They said the skin on my arms would be different. Stronger. It would show how brave I was."

Dez's hands squeezed my shoulders. I looked up at him and he smiled at the boy. "That's what I keep telling Taya, here. Maybe she'll believe it now that you've said it, too."

I opened my mouth to retort when a report came through my ear-com. I set the boy's hands on his lap and stood to face Dez.

"We must get back. The media's presence is growing and the General's communique has come through. It's time."

Dez looked into my eyes and then sat down. He wasn't going anywhere until he'd finished this afternoon's mission.

* * *

Taya

In the past, once we made it back onto the Compound, we could relax: no media stalking us, no crowds to manoeuvre around and through. But the Faction had changed all that. Each and every agent assigned to Dez's detail remained on high-alert until we whisked him back into the main building.

Usually, our pace reduced and our hearts had time to expunge the adrenaline surging through them before arriving. Today, we ran through the Capitol Building all the way back to Dez's office, where Coms Specialist Reegan stood waiting for us just outside the door. He ushered us into the room and over to Dez's desk where a vis-u-fax sat screen up. Dez plunked down, and I leaned to the side, resting my hands on the arm of his chair.

"It's about time," Gerrund grumbled. The lush green canopy of the southern forest framed his miffed expression.

Dez ignored the remark. "Are you ready, then?"

The green world swirled as Gerrund repositioned the device to face out. "The dive team is getting ready to inflate the canvas balloons."

I squinted. "I can't see anything."

"That's because nothing's happening yet," Gerrund griped.

"I know that. Can you zoom in to where it'll break surface?"

The camera lurched forward.

"Geeze, Gerrund. A little warning." I blinked back a wave of nausea.

"Better?" he asked.

"Yes," Dez said.

The dive team broke the surface of the blue water and waited along the shoreline. Nothing happened at first. The surface hardly rippled. But then, a few minutes later, small pools of bubbling water made the ocean boil. The frothing pools grew larger until they interconnected, forming a mass of lather twice as large as a long-haul transporter and three times as wide.

Something white and rounded broke the surface.

"A balloon," Gerrund said. "Jantice and Tamaine constructed a water-tight weave and lined the inside of each one with resin from one of the trees around here."

An enormous cloth balloon rose from the churning ocean as water cascaded from it. The roar echoed even through the simple speakers of Gerrund's old vis-u-fax. The balloon rose higher and higher until a metallic black dome breached the surface. I gasped.

"Dez, it's like Guide Aelix said: it looks like the alien houses. Do you think they dismantled their fleet in order to build their homes? Their shops?"

"It would explain why this is the first ship we've found. They must've kept one intact for a reason."

Two divers swam out with giant hooks that dangled from a tower crane on shore. Two large balloons hovered above the craft while three others supported it from below. Once the hooks were in place, the crane operator reduced the slack in the lines until they pulled taut.

"This is it." Half of Gerrund's face came into view on the monitor. "We've done all we can to see what the best lifting locations are, but there's no guarantee the weight of the ship won't rip sections of the hull off and send it crashing back into the sea."

Dez nodded. I pursed my lips and frowned. With proper Engineers down there instead of only those UGC interested in immigrating, the margin of error would be smaller. I gripped the top of Dez's chair until the leather complained.

Gerrund gave the signal. Dez stiffened and leaned forward. The cables connected to the crane groaned. A week wasn't long enough to build a machine like that from scratch. All of the materials had to cross the deserts on haulers with teams of guides, and inexperienced workers had built it: farmers, shopkeepers, artists. Dez and Gerrund had asked me, months ago, to go south to coordinate the general rebuilding efforts, but I'd declined. I'd told them my place was by Dez's side, ensuring his safety. In truth, I hadn't wanted to go back. I still didn't.

The heavy grind of metal-on-metal made me shudder, but I didn't look away. Balloons bobbed and wavered, raising the alien craft higher and higher, as waterfalls crashed around the ship back to the sea. I caught my breath when the boom arched toward land and the ship listed in the air. The grinding and creaking grated through my bones as they hauled the spaceship, mostly hidden by balloons, over the water and onto dry land. When the ground crew shifted the lower balloons away and the ship touched down, a wild cheer reverberated over the speakers into an office hundreds of miles away.

I dropped to my knees and pushed my face into Dez's arm. He turned and hugged me. I held him. Tears of happiness mixed with tears of fright washed over my cheeks.

Now, I had to return. I'd given my word.

Chapter 18
Dynamic Duo

Taya

I glanced up as Professor Elix crashed through our workroom door three days after Gerrund raised the ship. He slammed large roles of drafting paper and what looked like an old toolbox onto the table, scattering the latest pile of printed images.

"Hey!" I snatched the thick stack of photos off the desk and chased down the few I hadn't caught in time. "What are you doing?"

"I don't understand why we can't work at my lab. Everything I need is there, and I don't have a security problem," Elix grumbled. I kept my smile hidden. At least when he worked with me in the Capitol Building he didn't treat me like his errand girl. I'd gotten Dez to agree that any information regarding the spaceship should remain on the premises. Now we were in my house, so to speak.

"I repeat, what is all this?" I set the image back down

and waved my arm over the rolls of paper.

He inclined his head ever so slightly toward our mobile whiteboard plastered with squares of photos displaying every inch of the spaceship's outer hull. "That's not good enough. We need a scale drawing if we're going to collect any accurate data about this technology before we head south. Why haven't we left yet?"

"I'm surprised you're so eager to breach the Compound wall. You don't strike me as open-minded."

"You're the one with a closed mind, girl. The Talians have always had the brightest engineers, and the old Kronik knew how to take advantage of that. If anyone will figure that ship out, it'll be us."

"What, you and me? You've—"

"No. Not us. *Talians*, girl. Do you need me to speak slowly so you can understand?"

gods, I wanted to haul off and deck the guy. Instead, I separated any new external images from the pile and retreated to one of two stuffed chairs by a low table.

"Gerrund got some clearer shots of the control panels," I said, refocusing him to the task.

"Are you able to read anything this time?"

"Yeah, but it's all in short form. About half are pretty clear, but I'm not sure how easily the others translate. Like"—I stood again and walked over to him, shifting one photo to the top of the pile—"this one. It says CONT. SPHERE. 'Cont' could be short for anything, and we've yet to see something sphere-like in or around the ship."

Elix ignored the proffered image and kept plotting his base grid to transpose the ship's measurements. I still didn't see the purpose of it. *So, we make some blueprints. How does that help any more than looking at real pictures?* I dropped onto the stool by the table and immersed myself in the images as Elix kept blessedly quiet while he worked.

During a light dinner last night, Dez had mused about whether or not we could get the ship running again. If we could figure out how to turn the thing on, that's when the tech would become valuable. Right now, it was just more proof that someone else had been here before us and messed up our world.

My thoughts drifted to the All Mother's warning. I hadn't said anything to Dez, yet – wanted to do a bit of digging on my own first. But, really, I had no reason not to trust her. And it made sense. Xannia was founded on the belief in the gods. If we had to destroy one, especially the Child, to keep our verrin from disappearing, could we reason with the zealots? What would it mean if Dez's government destroyed Gamma? Would he be proving the gods don't exist? Or would he become the mortal who killed a beloved god? The latter seemed more plausible.

I shook my head, attempting to clear it, and focused on Elix's drawing. Squinting, I flipped through the new, untouched images I'd left on the table for him.

"That's not right," I said.

"What are you talking about, girl? It's exactly what we agreed to—"

"—yesterday. Yesterday, Elix." He glared at me for dropping his title. I didn't care. "If you'd bothered to look at today's images, you'd see the person standing here." I shoved the picture under his nose.

He frowned, glancing from the new image to the old one on the board and over at his notebook of stats. "Meeka," he swore and snatched the image from my hand for a closer comparison.

I left him erasing and re-plotting to sit on the floor by the chairs. After spreading out the images, I followed Gerrund's path as he entered the ship's side hatch and passed a large bulkhead before entering a corridor. He'd sent a video file too, but the signal corrupted and only the images arrived intact.

I counted three main chambers. The hallway separated the flight deck at the nose from an anti-chamber set slightly higher than an empty egg-shaped room.

"Oh, my," Elix muttered to himself. I knew he'd never willingly share whatever it was with me, so I got up to look. He checked and re-checked a set of measurements and then expanded the overall size of the craft based on the dimensions of that empty room.

"That's a big difference. It doesn't look that big in the pictures." I leaned over the drawing. "What are those?" I pointed to two large openings.

"The vents Gerrund mentioned. They flow into and out of that empty room." Elix continued to sketch in all of the corresponding dimensions.

"This anti-chamber is sealed off completely?" I asked.

"So far as I can tell."

I shifted back to the images scattered across the floor and brought three of them over. "The control panel here operates the access door to the empty room. Do you recognise this symbol at all?"

"You're the one who taught me how to read Dakturian. Why are you asking me?"

"Because Dez— the Kronik mentioned once that the writings on the Ancient Tablets he used to find the Chronicles shared some attributes with the alien language on the Orb. You've been trying to verify who set up the Museum of Darius and how such important items were kept beyond the Compound wall. The old Kronik had you track resources. You knew what was going on in that warehouse, didn't you?" My blood sizzled with the heat of the accusation.

He looked up at me, moving only his eyes. "Whatever do you mean?"

"I looked into it. Your lab was the hub of the intelligence network. You were supposed to track everything, including the whereabouts of Lady Lynnia's illegitimate daughter." *You were feeding them information about me, giving them new tech to torture me.* But I didn't say it out loud. I clenched my teeth and waited for him to admit it.

He refocused on the symbol in the image. "Hmm... It resembles the Ancients' graphic for *explosion.* It's a rare marking."

Explosion? That's not what I expected. Distracted, I looked closer at the instrument panel both in the anti-chamber and on the flight deck. One section near the quadrant I figured directed the propulsion of the ship matched perfectly. But there were no engines. Only those vents and that empty room. Then it hit me.

"Elix." I pushed the two images of the separate control panels under his nose and sent his laser-etching pen skittering across the desk. "What if it doesn't mean explosion, like a bomb, but a burst of controlled energy or a volatile propulsion core of some kind? I think these large blank areas are screens. If the ship's computers aren't damaged, we might be able to figure out how this thing runs!"

"Look here." He pointed to a series of small panels set about the chamber. "These likely open and link into something. An energy source of exponential power."

"But where did the old one go?" I asked.

"It was submerged. Maybe it was washed through one of the vents into the sea? Or maybe it had a finite lifespan. We won't know until we get down there. We'll have to bring a few devices along to see if we can power up the system."

"What do you use to launch the satellites? Can it be adapted?"

"Not likely. We use fuel in a rocket. It's nothing like this."

Gods! We were so close. I shoved away from the table and smacked my hands against my thighs. The fingers on my right hand brushed the top of my Whipstaff. I looked down and slowly removed the weapon from its holster.

Elix startled and shifted away from the table. I wasn't going to blast him. I wanted to, but I wasn't an idiot. Instead, I held it over the blueprints and said, "Now imagine it a thousand times bigger."

* * *

Taya

Half an hour later, when Elix finally left, I rushed down the corridors of the expansive Capitol Building, by-passing the apartments even though Dez should have been there, and into the Operations Wing. His office door stood closed. My heart hammered. I sucked in a great lungful of air and held it, releasing the breath slowly. It took five tries before the pounding of my heart left my ears.

I knocked softly, two sets of three in our unique pattern, and opened the door just enough to stick my head in. Dezmind sat at his desk, the vis-u-fax propped open, in the midst of a conference call with one of the Talian magistrates. I couldn't see the screen, but he didn't frown like that when it was a Commoner. They trusted him more.

I sighed. This was why he never came to bed at a reasonable hour. *Should I wait? Leave it for the council meeting in the morning?*

He remained intent on the conversation and not on who might be spying on him from the door, but he knew it was me. Still, it would have been nice if... I shook the thought away.

I slipped into the room and closed the door. I wouldn't be able to sleep, so I might as well get comfortable. The couch by the wall of old books called to me, so I skirted around the large book pedestal by his desk and sat down. After curling my feet up under me, I leaned into the plush arm of the furniture and flipped open my watch-com. Scrolling through the images I'd scanned when Elix wasn't looking, I re-visited everything we'd discovered that evening.

Sometime later, my eyes drooped and I couldn't focus on the images any longer. I closed my com and rested my head on my arm, listening to Dez talk politics.

I don't know how much later it was, but his strong arms

wrapped around me and lifted me up. I nuzzled my face into his shirt and breathed in his scent. I don't remember him carrying me down the hall, but the feel of his body lying alongside mine lingered long after his day started the next morning.

Chapter 19
Updates

Dezmind

"Well, in that case, the roads through Applex-Mar could use resurfacing," Sir Karok snapped.

I rubbed my face with my hand and leaned forward onto the edge of the oval council table. "This is the first you've mentioned it," I said.

"That's because he doesn't want the money to go to subsidizing the Sea-Markets out of Vrazeth," Sir Enay countered.

Magistrate Delenon sat still in the chair beside mine, as he'd done all meeting, quietly taking everything in. He knew what the old sessions were like, having been the one and only magistrate to represent the people beyond the Compound. I wanted his impression – and to maybe make him an offer.

Sir Olekk straightened and slapped his hand over the inlaid brass banding of the table. "The Compound's budget has been halved since the formation of this new council. The allotment of funds—"

"Is fair." I stood up, drawing all eyes to me, even the two security officers in front of me. Taya's gaze still burned holes in my back, as did Daria's, but for different reasons. Taya had twice tried to talk with me before the council session, but it hadn't worked out.

"You can't ignore that each sector in the Compound equates to the size of a small town beyond the wall. The Common sectors simply cover more land with more people and more opportunities for things to go wrong. The *budget* is no longer divided. One land. One people. Those that need it the most, get the money, and *I* have the final say. End of discussion." I took a breath. I wanted to stretch out my neck and shoulders, but that would be construed as a sign of weakness.

Today I drew my strength from Delenon. Just knowing his familiarity with the situation at hand, even from days past, reassured me. "For our next order of business, I'd like to thank Magistrate Delenon and his aid, Daria Myyup, for joining us today. The LRM were curious about how the new council works, and I hope it's been insightful."

Delenon nodded, stood and shook my hand. We gave each other guarded smiles, but I had a feeling he might yet be receptive to an idea of mine that had been growing since their Welcome Rally eight days ago.

"It looks as though we're on schedule and the Monument to the Fallen will be ready for unveiling in two days," I said. Polite applause filled the room.

"We can't thank you enough for your generosity and

recognition. We look forward to working with the new government toward a better tomorrow." Delenon met my gaze and those of the council one by one around the table before sitting down again.

I nodded to my security officer. Ynell opened the door and motioned for our first guest to enter: my new Special Ops commander. As always, Jezetek's gaze flickered to Taya, posted by the door leading to my office, but then he noticed Delenon and Daria before settling on me. I'm sure he'd taken in the atmosphere of the entire room, charged as it was. He and Taya were working on some kind of project lately. She was no longer around if I happened to get a break for dinner. That left me to explore the nuances of my predecessor's office where I'd made several discoveries of late.

"Report," I said.

"We have stopped all registered tours coming into or going out of the Compound. Lone individuals are still welcome to come and go, but even that has petered out since the increase in the attacks."

"Understandable."

"The bomb signature from the escalated attack on the tour transport leads back to an agent of the old Kronik, as we suspected. But now, we have a name and a dossier."

"Excellent."

"We're looking into previous patterns and known behaviours, but unless a Talian officer questions the Talian people, we'll get nowhere."

"I suspected that might be the case. It'll take time. Consider having a Talian and a Common officer work together on the canvassing. The more opportunities we have to acclimate my people to the rest of the world, the better. Anything else?"

"No, sir."

"You are dismissed. Ynell?" She escorted Tek out and brought Professor Denali in. "Welcome, Professor. You have an update for us?"

"I do. As you requested, I ran the numbers to get an exact range of time for when we could still work toward cooling the planet and saving our dwindling verrin supplies."

"And?" I prompted when he hesitated a little too long.

"The window closes within the month."

Gasps buffeted the air as several sector magistrates sat up or leaned forward.

"There's room for error, but I guarantee if global warming is left unchecked for another two months, no matter what measures we take after that point, our verrin will disappear within a generation."

The weight of the news left the air in the room heavy. Delenon and Daria stiffened but remained silent.

"What are our options?" I asked.

"Remove the source of the problem," Denali whispered.

"You mean, blow up the sun." Taya stepped forward, her blunt assessment ricocheting off every cranium in the room, their staccato blinks a visual recoil. "That's insane. We can't blow up the sun. What about fallback debris on Xannia? What about the Followers of the Light? If we blow up Zerameteth we—"

"Kill their god." Magistrate Delenon's deep voice

resonated low.

"What else can we do? That can't be the only way." I couldn't condone the destruction of something we knew so little about.

"Sir, you've said yourself that it's a fake sun. You said you fixed it when you journeyed south to the alien city," Madame Wekker spoke up.

"We stabilized it. It needed regeneration." I glanced at the empty chair for the guide liaison. If Gerrund would just pick a Rep, we could have first-hand knowledge of their efforts. "The General's team is still searching for any kind of documentation to help us understand the technology."

"They've been looking for months. Have they found anything yet?" Madam Saritt of Compound Sector 11 asked.

I didn't respond. Everyone in the room already knew the answer.

"Ynell, ask SOC Jezetek to join us again."

She nodded and slipped out past the door. Beside me, Taya's body vibrated. I risked a glance at her. She glowered at Denali, anger or frustration sparking in her eyes. I wanted to bridge the two-inch gap between us, grasp her hand and give it a squeeze, but no one in this room knew the truth. Not all of it. She was, for all intents and purposes, my personal bodyguard and the head of security. That's it.

Tek and Ynell re-entered the room. "SOC Jezetek, are you aware of all of Xannia's space and weapons-based programs?"

"I've been briefed, sir."

"Do you know if we have the capability to launch a weaponised rocket into space?"

Tek frowned. Taya grabbed hold of the sides of her pants and scrunched the material in her fists.

"Yes, sir. I believe so. We haven't had need of that particular combination before, but from what I've seen, it can be done."

"How long would it take to build such a device?" I asked.

"I'm not an engineer—"

"Your best guess, then."

Tek inhaled and the whole room balanced on that one breath. "Maybe a month? Three to five weeks depending on the size of the rocket, the weight of the payload, and any number of other calculations that would need to be made."

"You can't!" Taya burst out. Not at Tek, but at me. The magistrates in the room murmured their surprise. She was just a security officer after all, not a member of council, and this wasn't the first time she'd broken protocol. Even Daria narrowed her eyes from her spot in the corner.

"Sir, the aliens had to turn Gamma on at one point. We might be able to turn it off. The theory of nuclear fusion dictates that without a fuel source to supplement the reaction, it'll lose potency and fizzle out – just like what happened before we re-initialised the photon beam down south. We got the quakes to stop by recharging it. We need to find a way—"

"Officer Doire," I used her formal title. "We have one month. The numbers don't lie. There's no evidence that the General's team will find a manual for the fake sun in time for us to do anything about it."

"What about the spaceship?" she asked.

I frowned and turned my head. "I don't follow you." But something niggled at the back of my mind. Her falling asleep in my office last night, waiting for me. The two missed opportunities to talk this morning.

"Professor Elix and I think we can get the spaceship operational. We worked on the theory last night while going over the new images the General sent. All we need is a powerful enough energy source to activate the internal computer. If we can get the ship into space, we might be able to locate the source of Gamma's power and disable it."

This was huge, but... "You said theory and ended with a big *if*. And you have no power source in mind, which means the tech is still mostly a mystery."

Delenon cleared his throat. I turned my attention to him but Daria had pulled the magistrate's gaze with a sharp shake of her head. A silent argument played out between them in less than thirty seconds.

"Sir." He stood to address me. "I believe I may have a solution to the lady's power problem."

* * *

Dezmind

When the last magistrate had exited the room, Ynell shut the door behind her on the way out. Taya opened the way to my office and stood just inside. Delenon shifted to walk through but Daria caught his arm.

"No. I won't let you go in there with *her* around." She narrowed her eyes at Taya.

"What?" Delenon asked.

"I don't understand," I said and looked from Taya to

Daria and back again.

"She's a *contractor*." Daria spat the word.

I frowned, almost crossing my arms but caught myself, remembering it was a defensive stance. "I still don't understand. She's not a contractor anymore. She works for me now."

Delenon stepped between Taya and Daria, breaking their sightline. "It's difficult for the LRM to be around anyone associated with the CTF. The old Kronik used them to fight his war – our own people, Commoners, shedding the blood of Commoners."

"But Jutaya hadn't even been born yet. In fact, her parents were the first Talian/Commoner partners." I looked around Delenon's shoulder at Daria. "It was your brother who welcomed her into the Underground. Without Taya, we'd never have won." I whispered the last line, knowing just how much she'd sacrificed for a better world.

"Give us a minute, please?" Delenon asked.

I nodded and joined Taya in my office, leaving the door open. Their hushed voices parried back and forth for several minutes as Taya and I stood by my desk. Then it went quiet. The only way I knew they were still in the next room was the other door hadn't shifted.

I looked at Taya to mouth an apology, but she stared at the open doorway, her eyes livid. I didn't think she was mad at Daria. In fact, I was ninety-nine percent sure she was pissed at me. I'd broken the same promise twice in one week.

Daria stormed through the door, her distrust of both Taya and me, a Talian Kronik, etched into every line of her features. Delenon, however, continued to exude the stately qualities he'd long been known for and paced himself behind her. Daria searched and examined every inch of my office – even my drawers. We all knew what she was doing even if she was the only one who felt it warranted. We waited until she was satisfied and stood behind Delenon. Taya mirrored Daria's precautionary stance. The magistrate and I shared a silent chuckle in the span of a glance.

"Now, you said you might know of an energy source powerful enough to run a spaceship?" I asked, leaning forward and clasping my hands on the desk before me.

"Yes. There's a reason the tales of the great Captain Darius always had him *sight* land at a distance and then turn around and sail home through the seas."

"It always struck me as odd that he wouldn't have tried to restock, or at the very least look, at the land he'd discovered. But you know why. You've lived it now, haven't you?"

"We have. But unlike Darius, we had a Talian engineer on board."

"Now that is something," I said.

"There's a towering ring of oval-shaped boulders circling the entire island. At first, we couldn't pass them. Not because they were too close. We had plenty of room to manoeuvre the ship."

"Why, then?" He seemed to want the prompt for effect.

"Because an invisible magnetic field surrounded them."

"Lodestones?" Taya asked. I gave her a quick glance, then remembered her love of science and the extensive studying she'd undergone as a contractor. Likely the very thing that had tipped Daria off to her training.

"Sort of. You see, the lodestones we have around here are small and their magnetism comes from the compound of metal and stone that make up each one. These super lodestones, if you will, work more like planets."

"Geomagnetism on that small a scale? But how?" Taya asked.

"I don't know. We didn't have any scientific tools with us, but Drax said it made the most sense. Especially after what he, Tony, and Marxx found after cracking open a smaller one."

"How do you know one of these rocks will be strong enough to power a spaceship?"

"I don't. But one of the smaller ones generated enough energy to keep our town lit for twenty years. Once we figured out how to harness it." He looked over at Taya. "If you're looking for a miracle, this might be it."

She hesitated, licking her lips. "Would we have enough time for you to train a new crew? Would they be able to find Darius's Island?" Taya glanced from Delenon to Daria and back. She knew half of the LRM still recuperated in Nova Leau.

"I'll talk to my team. We needed to cross only four seas coming home in the opposite direction, not including the Crystal Sea protected by the super lodestones. Word came through last night that the crew we left in Nova Leau in Keeper Gedrix's care is doing well. I'll let you know by this evening."

"And, how long did it take you to cross the four seas?" I asked.

"Nearly two weeks." Delenon met my gaze. Professor Denali had given us a month. That Tek thought four to six weeks was all they'd need to weaponise a rocket...

I turned to Taya. "We shouldn't risk it. It'll take four weeks just to get a stone to you down south. You'd have to learn how to pilot it within a matter of days... it's unrealistic." Her whole body stiffened.

"Magistrate," Taya said. Delenon looked up as she approached the desk, her movements mirrored by Daria. "Do you trust All Mother?"

Delenon looked confused and answered carefully, "Without a doubt."

"If she gave you a piece of advice based on less than a day's observations of a new situation, would you weigh it with equal consideration to actual proof?"

"I don't know about equal, but she's never steered us wrong. In fact, if it wasn't for All Mother, we might never have made it to Darius's Island. She and Daria relied on their intuition to help us. The only absolute fact we knew for sure was that we would die if we didn't do something." He gave a wan smile and raised his eyebrows.

She turned to me. "Then we have to try. All Mother senses a deep unrest with the FOL and the Guardians. If we simply launch a rocket to blow up their Child god, we'll have another revolution on our hands. Besides, Elix and I have a theory that might help us activate isolated systems on the spaceship to learn how to control it. We just need some time."

I sighed and leaned back in my chair, drumming my fingertips over the end of the arm. If we waited a month and Denali's calculations were off, we might just be lighting our own funeral pyre. On the other hand, what good would saving the world do if the only hope at peace we finally found plunged us into another civil war? Could I kill a god? Could I destroy the last of our sacred beliefs and be satisfied that I'd done everything within my power to stop it because it was the only way to save ourselves?

"All right. Taya, you and Elix have three days to prep. Head south with the next guide. Magistrate, I hope your people rally to the cause, otherwise, we're going to war."

Chapter 20
Déjà Vu

Taya

What struck me most while I completed my survey of the Compound's access point wasn't the shift in the size and location of the rally stage, now a thin rectangle with walking room all around it; it also wasn't the huge drapes of material flanking either side of the Compound wall. No, the biggest surprise was the complete removal of the double-winged gate that once divided the Commoners from the Talians.

Tek's team secured the perimeter on both sides as the crowds continued to swell. Alpha protocol revised. We'd gotten lucky at the Welcome Rally when the Faction didn't show. This time, they'd be looking to make a statement. I only hoped I was ready for it.

My nerves jangled. I shook my hands out at my sides. The massive crowd filling the street both in front of and behind the Compound wall outshone any that had gathered there before. Dez would make history again, and no one wanted to miss it. I gave the signal.

Magistrate Delenon exited a long-distance lidez parked on Capitol Street near the stage. A wave of cheers started at the front of the crowd and rippled back as the local media networks live-cast the events on large screens attached to their cube riders. Daria followed close behind, as did the sixteen other LRM who'd travelled across the nation to be here.

Then, on the opposite side of the wall, exiting from a different lidez, came the more renowned Talian families who'd lost loved ones in the fighting. Dez had said they'd found a mix of families from both the Nine Seas Massacre and the coup willing to be recognised for their losses. Each line of citizens flanked two edges of the stage looking out at the people gathered. No one showed fear or shame.

I slipped past the front line of justices on the Commoner side of the stage and over to the lidez. Once in position, I gazed up into the face of the man I loved. Nervous excitement flickered in his eyes. I wish I could say I felt it, too, but I wasn't excited, just nervous. He smiled at me as he stepped down and walked over to the small stage with the single microphone. I followed him and knelt at one corner of the stage out of sightlines but still within reach. Tek and two Talian Special Ops agents follow suit with the other three corners. Dez had stressed the importance of equality and balance for everyone gathered here today, including his staff.

As he waved to both sides of the divide, the roar of the crowd deafened. Someone chattered over my ear-com but I couldn't make out what they were saying. Instead, I focused on my quarter of the immediate crowd, just as Tek and I had practiced: *narrow my focus, concentrate on one or two tasks, and trust the team.*

Dez motioned for the crowd to quiet, and soon only a hum of excitement remained. "My fellow Xannians, we rally on the precipice of the future. I stand before you today, not only as your Kronik but also as a man who's lived on both sides of this wall. Today is a day for looking forward. Yes, we're here to remember the fallen, but we're also here to celebrate a joining of forces, a world no longer defined by us versus them. Here"—Dez motioned to the war victims and soldiers surrounding the stage—"we stand together for a better tomorrow."

The large sheets covering either side of the Compound wall collapsed to the ground. Navy blue polished slabs of granite framed a city-scape surrounding each end of the wall where the gates used to hang.

"Behold, a nation united. Each window etched into this rare granite, excavated from the Underground caverns, holds the details of those brave souls who fought on *both* sides of the conflict for a better future. No ranks are listed. Instead, we've honoured the fallen with a reminder of their true spirit." Dez extended his arm and directed the crowds to follow Magistrate Delenon as he accepted a smaller microphone near the memorial. An undulation of movement at the back of the Commoner crowd caught my eye, then settled.

"Hytrin Neemer, age thirty-two; mischief maker and true friend. Talian," he read.

Then Dez motioned to the opposite edge of the stage. My mother accepted a mic and approached the other side of the memorial. My heart leapt. She had lost her brother during the takedown of the Capitol Building, and she herself had been imprisoned for wanting to live beyond the Compound wall. I hadn't seen her in over a month. She'd taken to touring museums, libraries, and art centres across the Commonlands – partly to show other Talian's there was nothing to worry about and partly to be as far away from the site of her imprisonment as possible. Either way, it worked to Dez's advantage if not mine.

"Marnee Utik, age seventy-seven; Mother to all Children. Danieth," she read.

Then Mom and Delenon took turns reading a few more names before returning to stand before the stage with the other families. Dez went on to explain that the majority of Talian names were listed on the Commoner side of the wall and Commoners on the Talian side. Delenon and Lynnia had stood where the hinges of the gates used to be – the one place where the names intermingled.

"Now, let us have a moment of silence to mark the sacrifices made to come this far." Dez lowered his head and closed his eyes. The crowd to either side followed suit. I couldn't identify anyone not participating in this sacred moment, but even I could only see so much.

"Thank you," Dez addressed a quiet crowd. "It is my pleasure to introduce you to some important game-changers."

I sighed and exchanged my position with another security officer before joining Professors Denali and Elix,

Magistrate Delenon, Daria, Captain Marxx, and All Mother up on the stage. An all too familiar tingling sensation crawled up my spine.

I no longer had my quadrant to focus on. Between the noise of the crowd, our clunky steps on the wooden platform, and the voices on coms echoing in one ear, my anxiety rose.

Too much happening.

Too many distractions.

I blinked and shook my head to clear it, then focused on the real estate beneath my feet, branching my awareness out only to the crowd near the line of justices.

"As you know, I have never hidden what I discovered with my Kahn-Lea when we travelled through the Deserts all those months ago. You've seen the Chronicles, the alien journal, and images of the abandoned Dakturian City. You also know that we discovered the alarming news that our smallest sun, Gamma, was set in orbit by these aliens to terraform our world. Because of that, our climate has changed steadily over thousands of years. Recently, rumours have alighted about a shortage of verrin. Our scientists have now confirmed the truth of this."

Gasps and worried chatter erupted amongst the gathered. Bodies shifted and swayed causing the crowd to move like boiling water as they turned around to talk to the people in front, beside, and behind them.

"But fear not! We have united to save our world as I said we must all those months ago. The people before you are working together – Talian, Commoner, Guardian, Patriot, and Resistance fighter alike – to combine both our natural resources and alien technology to stop these threats to our world. We have a plan, and only by utilising the unique strengths and expertise of those you see before you will we be able to set to right our beloved planet. I'd like to introduce our team"—he nodded for Elix and me to step forward—"who will be working on a way to stop the terraformi—"

Plasma scorched the air. The familiar sizzle discharged a nanosecond before the blast fired. My mind blanked and my body took over. I spun away from Elix and crashed into Dez, encasing him in my arms and twisting our bodies so that mine became a shield. We stumbled and collapsed onto the stage. Another security officer covered Dez's head as we landed.

Frantic cries tornadoed through the air. Another blast shot across the stage. A shriek pierced the din of panic. It sounded familiar. *You can't think about that right now.* I triggered a remote in my back pocket, and a square panel popped up from the floor nearby. I rolled Dez toward it and shielded him as he slid through the trapdoor head first. The other officer launched himself in the opposite direction, toward the fading scream.

I shifted around and angled my feet to follow Dez, but my heart stuck in my throat as I looked out over the rally stage. The wall of justices now surrounded the upper perimeter of the stage. Tek's team got the reps back onto the transports before spreading through the crowd, searching for the Faction extremists. Tek gathered a limp body over his shoulder and staggered to a nearby ambulance.

I ducked down and triggered the hatch to close, cracking a light-tube. Dez crouched under the low ceiling by a slight gap in the boards, muttering to himself.

"Dez! Get away from there."

He muttered something again.

"Where is it… where is it?" I scuttled around looking for the pry bar. The holder clamped to the underside of the stage sat empty. "Meeka! Not now!" I sunk two of my fingers into the breather hole of the storm drain cover and heaved. I groaned. It barely shifted. "Dez! Get over here! We're in trouble."

That got his attention.

"What do you mean?"

"We've been sabotaged. No pry bar." I grunted again. "Help me. Whoever's out there knows we're under here."

He straddled the heavy cover beside me and hooked two of his fingers into another hole. "Ready."

"One. Two. Three. NOW." We heaved together. The heavy iron shifted and we dropped it. A crack opened to the tunnel below. The faint click of a much bigger weapon registered in the back of my mind.

"Down!"

I yanked Dez to the asphalt, smacking my shoulder against the ground. An explosion rocked the earth as splinters of wood sliced at our exposed flesh. I scrambled up and shoved my fingers into the crack, scraping the skin on my knuckles. "Arugh!" The lid shifted. "Get in!"

Dez grabbed onto the metal ladder and slid down. I followed. Just as my head disappeared below ground, three sets of black-clad boots kicked at the jagged blast hole.

Chapter 21
Multiple Battle Fronts

Taya

Dezmind headed down the left passage, following protocol, but I grabbed his arm.

"No. This way!" I half-whispered, pushing my way through the buzz of contradictions in my head. Fighting off the muscle memory from running the drill a dozen or more times that morning, I clawed my way past the voices in my head telling me what I should and shouldn't be doing and listened only to my own advice.

"What? No, Taya. Tek told us—" He pulled me back the other way. A volley of fireworks exploded in my head, and the voices above grew silent even as I heard the shuffle of boots in the small space under the stage above us. The barrel of a laser pistol hovered by the edge of the metal casement lid—black on black.

I hauled on Dez's arm. He stumbled toward me as a red shot blasted concrete at us from the floor of the storm-water pipe. We bolted down the damp tunnel, our footsteps splashing and echoing throughout the dark. Muscle memory took over as I linked an arm with Dez and tried to push my shoulder into his, forcing us to counterbalance each other and run on a slight angle, above the shallow water instead of in it. But he wasn't Tek. He didn't know CTF field training, and we crashed into the curved wall of the cistern instead.

"What are you doing?" he whispered as we scrambled to stand.

I glanced into the dark behind us while my mind whirled to catch up to what my body knew. My heart smashed into my chest as fear and adrenaline pushed me to run; my thoughts flashed to the body Tek carried, the familiar scream, the voices from my ear-piece, and the dense clang of boots on metal rungs as Faction members followed us down into the tunnel. I couldn't find the words. My gaze scrambled across his face, into the dark, and back again. I wanted to scream. To hit something. To make my mind work the way it used to. I grabbed his arm again, held tight so our shoulders touched and managed, "Lean. Run above water. Lean. Now."

He finally listened to me.

"Move forward."

After three steps his feet climbed out of the water as the two of us angled into one another. We managed a jog into the heart of the Prime through a darkness only I could discern.

* * *

Taya

After twenty minutes and three interchanges, a new voice ricocheted in my head. I stopped when he said my call sign. Dez splashed into the puddle between us.

"Respond. Supernova, do you have the Package? Please respond!"

I tapped my earbud. "Supernova here."

"I repeat. Do you have the Package?"

"The Package is secure."

"Is your location compromised?"

I took a moment to concentrate on our surroundings: dripping water, a breathy echo. No footsteps, no immediate danger. "Negative."

"Then stay where you are. Activate your beacon. I'm coming for you."

I recoiled a bit at the informality over the com. They must have been trying to reach me for some time. Only Tek's voice had broken through the buzz of constant communication after the attack. I had to focus on two things at a time; he knew that. Dezmind and safety.

"Affirmative."

I turned to Dez. A thin ray of light from an access point wavered in the black depths. I didn't know how much of me he could see, but he looked more like the Kronik than the man I fell in love with.

"Report," he said, his voice low and husky.

"No one is following us. We've been ordered to remain here. Tek's team is on its way to intercept and retrieve us."

"Where are we?"

I frowned. "In the storm-water basin."

"Under the Compound?"

I didn't like the implication. "No. Under the Prime."

"And why is that, Jutaya?"

"Excuse me?" I crossed my arms, suddenly not knowing what to do with them.

"Why are we here and not where we're supposed to be?"

"We are where we're supposed to be, *sir*. We're safe."

He took a deep breath in. My body shuddered at the strip-down I was about to get. But I refused to stay silent. I waved my arms back the way we'd come.

"I had to alter the plan. They knew the plan. I don't know how. Maybe their Leader knew about the basin connecting to the underground caverns, maybe we have a mole. I guarantee you, they had back-up waiting to take us out farther up the tunnel. The Compound is their territory. I didn't think they'd risk following us this way. I was hoping they'd assume we went the way we were supposed to – and they did."

"I– I didn't– Taya…" He sighed and ran a hand over his face and hair. He deflated in front of me. "I thought I'd lost you."

"Lost me?"

"Your eyes couldn't focus. You went against protocol. You couldn't talk to me, tell me the plan. For the last twenty minutes, you've been in your own world, focused on… I don't know what. Then all of a sudden we just stop. What's going on?"

All I could do was shake my head. No words would come and the only ones that did had been said before.

"What do you want me to say, Dez? Huh? I did what I

had to do in order to keep you safe. In order to do my job."

"But you looked overwhelmed... scared. I've never seen you look like that. And your breakdown in the Pit of Chance doesn't count. You'd never been in that situation before. Even I was terrified of what I was about to do. But back there..."

"Back there, I had to find my way through the chaos of the moment, prioritise, and then follow through. My mind wouldn't allow me to do more than that. My damaged brain has been in training, every evening, recalibrating itself so I won't freeze in a moment like this. So I don't risk losing you again. Honestly"—my voice broke—"how many times do I have to explain this to you?"

I turned my back to him and stared up at the curved ceiling of the basin, blinking back tears. I hated being emotional. I hated not being able to think properly. And I hated that Dez—

A pair of arms encircled me from behind. Dezmind pulled me close and hugged me. I stiffened at first. It had been too long – since before Tek and I started training together again. The heat radiated from his chest into my tense muscles. His smooth, warm cheek pressed into mine. I closed my eyes and wrapped my arms over his for a moment before turning around and collapsing into his embrace.

I breathed in the crisp scent of his shampoo and breathed out the mildew that surrounded us.

"I had no idea... I know you told me it was affecting you, making things difficult, hazy. I'm sorry."

"I'm sorry, too."

Jak's look at the end of our last conversation flashed to mind, emphasising exactly how much I didn't belong here anymore.

"Dez… I don't think I can—"

A blast of chatter came over my ear-com. I pulled away just enough to yank the affronting tech out of my head when five simple words pierced my heart.

"Dear gods," I breathed.

"What?" Dez released my waist and held my face in his hands, tilting my gaze up to his. "What is it?"

"They've captured All Mother."

Chapter 22
Behind Enemy Lines

Satie

The blast hit Professor Elix in the chest and he collapsed. Two security guards lay over the young Kronik. Drax grabbed my hand and pulled me off the side of the stage. We crouched low, behind Magistrate Delenon, Daria, and Marxx as SOC Jezetek made a path to the lidez. A violent explosion knocked us to the ground, separating me from Drax. When I scrambled to get up, too many people blocked my way.

"This way," a Talian security officer said while holding my elbow and guiding me toward a bank of shrubs just on the other side of the Compound wall. My path to the lidez had been cut off. I ran with the guard past the inky-blue granite memorial, trailing my fingers over the blend of Commoner and Talian names as we ducked around the corner.

Two sets of rough hands grabbed me as a black bag

dropped over my head. A garbled choke cut off as it tightened around my neck and my arms wrenched behind me. I tried to scream past the bubble of fear blocking my throat, but they forced a cloth strap into my mouth, wrapping it around my covered head. Kicking and thrashing, I tried to get away.

"Satie!"

Drax! But my scream burned my throat, only coming out as a muffled whimper.

"Satie!"

His voice echoed from far away. Muffled calls told me he still searched for me. My captors dragged me farther into the bushes before tossing me into the back of an escape vehicle. I landed on my back. A heavy boot threatened to crush my chest as foreign hands patted me down. A slide-click announced my satchel opening. I squirmed, trying to free a hand trapped behind my back. The weight of the boot pressed harder and stole my breath until I stilled.

"Well, what do we have here?" A snide remark from the man crushing my ribs.

"Looks like a journal, sir."

The boot lifted. I gasped and curled in on myself. Someone yanked my hands forward and zip-tied my wrists.

"Let me see that." A presence leaned over me, then shifted back. "Hmm… interesting. Might be worth something."

It was worth everything. A one-of-a-kind account of what had happened once we'd reached Darius's Island. It was our history. Now it lay in the hands of ignorance.

* * *

Satie

A hoarse groan escaped my dry throat. It hurt to swallow. An ache splintered from the back of my neck out to my shoulder blades. I tried to hug myself, but my arms wouldn't move. I opened my eyes to a barren basement room cast in shadow. Zerameteth's faint rays broke the gloom and bathed me in hazy light. I lifted my face to the Child god.

Let wisdom rule my heart
Patience guide my soul
And truth breathe life into deed
Give me the strength to see when blind
And act as You doth heed…

The words of the Prayer for Guidance soothed my racing heart. I looked around my prison, slowly stretching the length of my spine as much as possible with my hands tied behind my back and my feet latched to the chair legs. My stomach growled but hunger was the least of my worries. Layers of dust-covered age-old chairs and desks stacked in the far corner of the room. A cracked board and chipped paint clung to the far wall. I sat with my back to the door.

An old classroom?

I struggled to remember anything about where I was or how I got there, but the only thing I knew for certain was that they brought me somewhere deep inside the Compound.

Chapter 23
The Blame Game

Dezmind

Councillor Olekk scrambled to match my pace up the front steps of the Capitol Building.

"I must insist that at least one Talian council member be present at the—"

"There's been a breach. No council. This is a Special Ops meeting, and only those individuals directly involved will participate."

"But, sir, surely you can see how—"

I turned to stare at the rotund Talian. "The other councillors who made it back to the Capitol are waiting in the lounge. I will update everyone when I can with the information I deem appropriate. Understood? This may be a new council, but I'm still the Kronik. Stop interfering." I waved to my bodyguards, and we rushed through the building into the soundproof Ops room.

Ynell followed me in, but the other three guards

remained outside. SOC Jezetek calibrated the wall screen. Magistrate Delenon sat at the head of the table, Daria and Drax pacing behind him. Four other SOs, two Talian and two Common, sat at the rectangular table. Ynell disappeared into the opposite corner from Taya.

The last time I'd stepped foot in this room was the day of my Reading. My father thought a tour of the Capitol Building might help cheer me up after the Oracle's pronouncement. At the time, the room had been empty, but the building and the halls were full of Talians. Now, the Commoners out-represented us nearly 3:2 in this room alone. Part of my heart warmed to the change, the other part dreaded needing to be here in the first place.

"SO Commander Jezetek, report." I sat down beside Delenon and waved for the others to join us.

Drax and Daria sat across the table from the other four SOs. I knew better than to ask Taya to join us. She'd already gone through her debrief about the change in plans. The rescue team had separated us. They brought her straight here but took me the winding back route to throw off anyone unsavoury who might still be in the area.

"All Mother has been missing for the past forty minutes. Here"—he brought the screen to life showing six camera angles of the rally stage at the memorial—"we see her with Drax seconds before the explosion tears a hole in the platform. The blast knocks her away from Drax, and a security officer arrives to help her away."

"Then where is she?" Drax barked.

I held up a hand.

"When I interviewed my team after the incident, not

one of them said they helped All Mother. This man"—he enlarged the back of the Talian to fit the screen—"is not one of ours."

"Then who is he?" Magistrate Delenon asked.

I sighed and turned to face him, Daria, and Drax. "He's part of the Faction."

"The Faction?" Drax echoed, grimacing.

"Yes. They're a small group of Talian extremists working to discredit the new joint council. They've opposed all attempts we've made to unite the people."

"Who are they that they could outsmart your best security operatives?" Daria shifted and crossed her arms, glaring at me. "Why weren't we warned about them ahead of time?"

I diverted around her second question and focused on the first. "Special Ops Commander Jezetek has discovered that four of the old Kronik's Elite Guard survived the underground attack and escaped, wounded, when General Kipling's soldiers took the Capitol Building above. These four soldiers have been targeting public events and tour transports into the Compound since they first tried to assassinate me a month after my inauguration."

"And why exactly did you think parading around at the gates would be safe?" Drax leaned over the table as if he might start a brawl with me then and there. But I didn't back down. I leaned forward to meet him eye-to-eye.

"No one in my position is ever safe. The added security measures at the Welcome Rally worked. Tek gains intel on this group every day, and we're closer than we've ever been to catching these extremists. Today shouldn't have been any different." I sat back and pointed at the screen. "That man is wearing one of our new uniforms. It fits him. We never get a clear shot of his face. He knows where the cameras are." I caught Taya nodding in the shadows. "That means we have a mole. If I'd known this prior to the Memorial Rally, I'd have postponed it. Nothing in our data or models indicated we'd been compromised. Tek?"

"Affirmative, sir. But I believe they've handled that problem for us." He called up six views of a shot one minute before All Mother's disappearance. A man lay sprawled on the stage, unmoving.

"The Faction's first shot was meant for the Kronik, but their second shot killed Professor Elix."

Taya sunk farther back into the shadows, the wall supporting her. No doubt she struggled between wanting to say *I told you so* and being surprised. They'd finally started making progress on the spacecraft and were supposed to leave for the alien city tomorrow.

"Are you sure he's the only one?" Daria asked.

"No," Tek said. "That's why this is a closed room. Anything we say here can be tracked according to who's in the room. We need to formulate a plan for locating All Mother. Fast." He cleared the screen and pulled up an audio file.

"This came in to dispatch fifteen minutes ago."

A voice modulator jumped across the monitor as a woman spoke. "We have the All Mother. Submit to our demands or we will make an example of her."

Drax clenched his fists and pinched his lips. His arms shuddered with barely restrained rage. Daria's bearing nearly mirrored the man beside her.

"We commit to releasing both the Guardian and her journal so long as the following demands are met within the next thirty-hour day: confine the Resistance survivors to the south colony, including the Kronik's personal bodyguard; collapse the new council; close the Compound with a stronger gate; no more tours; no more Commoners on Talian soil; no citizens moving beyond the wall in either direction – abandon your plans for integration. The Talian race cannot survive if its people are drawn away from the path of the Oracle. Our people cannot survive absorption into the masses without the threat of extinction. The last strains of Dakturian blood must be preserved and any trace of interracial relations abolished. We have no patience. Test us on this point and suffer the consequences."

Drax slammed his fists into the table and knocked his chair back as he stood. "What does she mean 'make an example of her'? What'll they do to Satie? How will we find her? You got us into this mess, by the gods, you'd better get us out of it."

Delenon stood as well, careful not to jostle the table or tip his chair. He straightened the jacket of his suit and addressed the room. "Now is not the time to bicker about how we got here or why." He looked from me to Tek and back again. "How can we make the best use of the thirty hours we've been given? What is the plan?"

I liked the magistrate. His forward thinking kept both of our peoples focused on the important issues. I nodded to Jezetek. "What do we know?"

Tek stood straighter and killed the signal to the screen.

"The Ops Team tracked the com signature used to leave the message. It originated within the Capitol Complex, confirming our most recent intelligence that the extremists have been operating right under our noses this entire time. We are in the process of checking the old underground tunnels in the area and are fairly certain that, while they may be using them to get around, they do not have a base within them."

Delenon nodded, glanced at Drax and then sat down. Drax picked up his chair and sat away from the table, his leg bouncing in agitation. Tek called up a map of the Central Complex on the screen.

"By focusing on abandoned or little-used buildings in the area, we can send out security teams to sweep and scout for evidence of the Faction and All Mother."

"Just because the call originated inside the Complex, doesn't mean that's where they're keeping her," Daria said, reminding me of Taya who remained in the shadows.

"Agreed. That assumption on its own is practically useless, but with the information we've gathered on when and where they strike the tour transports, their operational schedules during a strike, and the fact that there are still hidden sites nearby once used by the old Kronik's secret agents, we can narrow our focus with confidence. However, that still leaves a lot of ground to cover." He clicked a button and dozens of red spots showed up on the map. "These are our target locales. We send out teams of four and cycle through each location until we find them."

"And if we don't find them?" Daria asked.

"Then I speak to the people of Xannia and tell them

exactly what must be done to stop these attacks." I still held out hope that we'd find them before it came to that... but time was running out.

Chapter 24
Mobilization

Jezetek

I didn't like the idea that Professor Elix had been a spy for the Faction. He made a ready scapegoat at a time when they knew we'd be looking for a mole. If he was working for the extremists, I didn't think he was the only one. The Kronik agreed with me.

Taya followed him from the room after our other guests had left. My four Special Ops sergeants stepped forward once the door shut. Ynell stood guard on the inside.

"You have your orders." I tapped each of their watch-coms with the tech fob and uploaded the map file and their search quadrants. "Teams of four. Pick soldiers you trust and keep them need-to-know. Check in when you're within range of each mark and touch-base before moving onto the next one. Ynell will coordinate from here. Taya will shadow the Kronik. Dismissed."

I nodded to Ynell. She let my Sergeants out of the

room. Familiar voices filtered in from the corridor. I caught the edge of the door before it shut as Ynell activated the control centre consul at the vacated table.

I couldn't see through the tiny crack, but it didn't matter. The voices were unmistakable: Taya and Dezmind.

"It *was* my fault. I was so focused on protecting you that I left him vulnerable. Tek's SO got to you the exact same moment I did. I should have known they'd have you covered and refocused on the others standing there. Now, Elix is dead and All Mother is missing."

"You can't drag this burden onto yourself, Taya. I hired you as my personal bodyguard and head of security. You were doing your job."

"And how am I supposed to that job when you're sending me away? I can't do this alone, Dez. As much as I hated Elix, he knew his stuff and was committed to the project. That's why the Faction sacrificed him. He must've shown signs of regret. If he was their sleeper agent, he certainly didn't see his own death coming. Does that mean I'm a target now, too? Gods, my brain hurts. I'm trying so hard to get back to where I was." Her voice wavered.

It broke my heart. She'd taken my advice and gone to see her old therapist, but it hadn't helped. She'd only come back more confused than ever.

"Are you backing out? Quitting?"

I didn't like the Kronik's tone, but I knew he was goading her. I would have.

"If I can't do my job, then I don't belong here."

"You do belong here. Maybe not as my bodyguard but your experience makes you the best head of security I could ask for. If you hadn't pushed for Tek's hire, we'd still be in

169

the dark about the Faction and without a starting place to search for All Mother. Taya…" His voice softened.

My guts twisted, but I'd lost the chance to call her my own. I was too stupid to recognise what we'd had back when we trained together. How it might have been more.

"Focus on the mission south."

"But I no longer have help. I can't do this alone. I understand that now." Her voice broke. I knew she thought about the alternative – about destroying Gamma and inciting unrest again.

"Then find another scientist and do it fast. If we can't find the All Mother, it might be moot anyway. We have no other way of powering the spaceship, and if the LRM feel they've been duped or slighted, no super lodestone, no power source."

I couldn't wait any longer. I had to pull my own team together. I could only hope this moment had been enough for them as I shifted the door open and walked into the corridor.

"Taya, you're still here. Good. On your way back to the main floor, could you find Drax and send him to my office?" I asked.

"Of course." She stood taller and tugged her uniform straight. "What should I tell him it's about?"

"Joining the mission."

* * *

Jezetek

The cube-rider pulled to a stop a block away from our target. Drax double-checked his gear, lingering a moment over the top of the Whipstaff strapped to the side of his leg. In the dark-grey-on-black fatigues, he looked like he could have been a military man his whole life. Even the set determination on his face echoed that of my other two highly trained team members.

"Call it in, Ellis." I knocked twice on the divider between the back and the cab.

"On your mark, sir," came his muted voice between the steel layers. Then, clear and sharp over the coms, he said, "Ready here."

I locked gazes with the Talian, once ship-builder now LRM on a new mission. It was the same look I'd seen in Taya's eyes whenever Dezmind was at risk.

"Move out."

My second in command opened the back of the vehicle and we slipped out into the night, hidden by a large industrial sign. We slid down the alleyway, Drax in the middle, me at the rear. I watched as Drax imitated the soldiers before him: low posture, hands at the ready to grapple with someone or reach for his Whipstaff.

I'd gotten more than a few questioning stares when I'd handed the man CTF and military-issue weaponry. He'd practiced with it enough that I knew he could handle the electrified particle stream without endangering himself or my team. I also knew he shouldn't be here but would've found a way to follow us or make an even bigger nuisance of himself if I hadn't invited him along. He needed to be doing something tangible to get the woman he loved back, something I understood on a fundamental level.

We travelled on foot from one side-street or adjacent

parking lot to another until we reached the break-zone. With a nod, my team split up. Drax shadowed me. At the building, he checked any main-level windows and vents as I monitored the lower ones. The building sat still and dark, but that didn't mean this wasn't a viable option. The Faction might be using inner rooms to conduct their business. They might even have left All Mother in the dark.

If Taya was here, she'd know for sure. Being half-Talian, she'd adopted her mother's heightened sensory abilities. We'd just have to do this the old-fashioned way.

As we flanked the side door, I glanced at Drax, our backs plastered to the wall. I hadn't thought to ask if he had any special abilities – not all of them did.

I signalled my intent to Drax. He nodded. Holding a palm-size reader-redirector over the palm display, I disengaged the lock and Drax opened the door. We slipped into the building and headed straight for the stairs. No self-respecting extremist would operate a secret hideout on the main floor.

My other two team members remained quiet. We'd stay on com silence until we cleared the building. The basement of the warehouse spanned a lot more ground than the building specs implied. My internal warning system armed. Room after concrete room stood empty as we paced ourselves and eliminated them one by one. Odd stains marred pitted concrete that often held craters the size of fists equidistant from one another on either the wall or floor.

Drax and I prepped to enter the last room in the corridor's square footprint. We flanked either side of the door. I gave him the nod. He unlatched the handle, and I swung in, Whipstaff drawn.

"Holy Trinity," I breathed.

Drax followed me into the room.

"What? Did you find her?" He stood beside me and took in the wall of old monitors and dust-covered instrument panel. "What is this place?"

I walked over and flipped a familiar-looking switch. The tech was last-generation, but it practically mirrored the Ops planning room in the basement of the Capitol Building. A low hum accompanied the panel and screens as they flickered to life. Three smaller feeds bordered both the top and bottom of the space with a larger central camera feeding video to the centre rectangle. I recognised the interior of the rooms skirting the square hall of the basement, but the one in the middle was new.

"Are those chains set into the wall?" Drax asked, leaning forward.

I shuddered. "Sweet Zerameteth."

"What?"

"It's exactly as Taya described it."

"Described what? You're not making any sense."

"Jutaya, the Kronik's head of security."

"Yeah, what about her?"

"The old Kronik had her tortured in a warehouse just like this one."

"Tortured? Why?"

"She's a hybrid. Half Matin, half Talian. I'm sure you've heard the stories of Little Lynnia and the Lost Lady?"

"They ring a bell, yeah."

"Lynnia is the Lost Lady and also happens to be Taya's mother. You saw her at the Memorial Rally. She read aloud the name of a Cause fighter."

"Taya's a half-breed? I didn't think it possible."

"No one did, and the Kronik wanted to keep it that way. But they didn't kill her right away. They wanted to learn who knew about her and figure out what Dezmind's – the new Kronik's – plans were."

"So, the craters in the walls in these rooms"—he pointed to the six smaller feeds—"are all that's left of wall-mounted shackles?" He rubbed his wrists as he looked at the middle room. Something told me Taya hadn't been the only one wronged by the old Kronik. "Why didn't we find this room? Why is it still intact and the others dismantled?"

I frowned. "Maybe we did. Remember that darker patch of wall… about the size of a door?"

"You think they cleared up what they could then sealed off their main torture room? Why?"

"Maybe they ran out of time. The coup happened fast and we've been nosing around places like this since the Faction started making a nuisance of themselves. Guess someone forgot to dismantle the video feeds."

The other half of our team gave the all-clear above.

"Here too. Fall back to the safe zone." I turned to Drax. He stood with his arms crossed, glaring at the video feed. I shut it down. "Come on. All Mother's not here." I clapped him on the shoulder. "One down, five to go."

174

Chapter 25
Destiny's Betrayal

Taya

Dezmind and I watched from the shadows of the very bush All Mother was last seen walking toward as Tek and his Special Ops team oversaw the temporary border barricade. Tek's teams had failed to find the Faction's base and the All Mother last night. As the thirty-hour window to save her or submit to the unthinkable demands was now halved, Dezmind didn't want to give the extremists a reason to harm the innocent Guardian.

Dez shifted out of the shadows. I grabbed his arm and pulled him back again.

"Oh, come on, Taya. I can be seen in public. I should be seen in public, especially now."

"No. You wanted to check on their progress. We're checking. Your press conference isn't for another five hours. When the work is done." I sighed. "I still don't believe you're going through with it."

"What's not to believe? It's only temporary."

"I wonder if that's what the first Kronik said when the lands were divided. They won't hurt her—"

"How do you know that?"

"Fine. They won't *kill* her. You're setting a precedent here – and starting down a *very* slippery slope – by giving in to their demands."

"Yes. One that shows I won't let anyone take an innocent life and I'll do everything within my power to keep Xannians safe. We must be transparent about what's happening. That's the—"

"— the key. I know." Another cube-rider arrived from the Talian side with more supplies. Ynell stepped out from the passenger side of the cab and looked around. Dez stepped forward and waved to her. She waved back.

"What's going on? Why's Ynell here?"

Dez stepped back into the shadows and faced me, drawing me out of hiding, too. "You were supposed to be headed south by now. The next guide leaves for the City tomorrow evening. Are you ready?"

"Yes."

"You're lying."

"Maybe."

His hand twitched closer to mine before he shoved it into his pocket. He wasn't ready to announce our relationship to the world. The press harassed poor Drax and All Mother about their relationship, not that it was anyone else's business; in the absence of first-hand knowledge, the Networks speculated about their involvement and dragged All Mother's name through the dirt because of her choice to break with tradition. Even the Faction was using it against them: Talians don't mate with Commoners. It all reinforced how screwed up society had become, how having a drop of Dakturian blood suddenly meant you were better than everyone else.

Dez had never thought that way. Neither did my mother. I looked at him. He stared back at me, so many questions clouding his eyes.

"Why can't we just assign this to Gerrund? He's running things down there. For the love of Trinity, he's the *General*."

"He doesn't have your background, your training. You know that. It would take time to bring him up to speed on what you and Professor Elix have discovered just from photographs. It has to be you." He coughed to hide the hitch in his voice. We'd had this conversation before.

"I don't believe in fate, Dez..." My voice trailed off. The Oracle had revealed his destiny when he was twelve and he'd made it come true – even the part about not being with his Soul Mate. His intended was never born because of an accident. He challenged Fate, believing any daughter of Lady Lynnia could be *The One*. But right from the beginning, the choices we made only served to keep us apart even as we worked together. I could see it, but could he?

"I won't let the Universe tell me what to do. I want to be with you. I also want to do the job I signed up for, get married, and make sure no one kills you."

But can you even do that anymore? I squeezed my eyes shut. The voice of doubt taunted me. The look on Jak's face echoed my fears, and Ynell walking over to us did nothing but confirm it.

"Taya." Dez gripped my shoulders and guided us into the leafy shrub again, away from prying eyes. Ynell turned to help out one of the workers. "I love you. You know that. Neither of us knew what to expect that day under the lidez when we finally kissed. When we gave ourselves over to each other. All I know is that you promised to always keep me safe. You're the only one who stands a chance at getting that spaceship running in under a month. You'll not only be keeping me safe but everyone else, too. The innocent." He pushed every last button available.

"We'll use the rocket. We'll—"

"Blow up the sun? Destroy a god? If we must, yes. And then the cycle will continue. You may be by my side, in my arms... or Fate might find another way to keep us apart. Maybe even place you on the front lines of a new war. Don't second-guess yourself." He pushed a stray strand of hair away from my eyes, drawing his fingers across my forehead and along my cheek. I leaned into his hand, cupping it to my face.

"Gods, Dez. If we're meant to be together, *why* is the world constantly finding ways to keep us apart?"

He kissed my forehead, his lips lingering against my frown.

"I don't know." He pulled away and stepped out from our leafy confines back into the shadows. I followed.

"Have you found someone to replace Elix or are you going by yourself?" he asked.

"I can't go alone."

"Then I think you need to let Ynell take over your post for the afternoon so you can figure this out and get ready.

The council—"

"The council's suggestions for a replacement suck."

He raised both eyebrows.

I continued, "And you need to talk to Magistrate Delenon. There's no sense in me fixing a spaceship without a power source. And have you asked him about—"

"No. Not yet." His gaze shot past Ynell, the team working on the barricade, and beyond the Prime's buildings. It was that look where he saw both beyond and inside himself at the same time – the look that told me I'd lost him to thought. I could only hope I'd never lose him completely.

I exchanged glances with Ynell and left. There was only one person I trusted to go on this journey with me. And I could only hope I was wrong about his allegiance to the CTF and the master keeper.

* * *

Taya

The bank of elevators opened and a wave of young contractors surrounded me. They chatted and laughed, walking in pairs down the employee corridor and out into the world. Tek and I had been the only two graduates in our year. Everyone else had taken an extra year before passing the Level 7 Trials.

I stepped into the middle elevator just before the doors shut and stared at the floor numbers as they transitioned higher and higher. Sweat moistened my palms. I wiped them on my pants. Not having an appointment meant going through Niless to get the professor's schedule. I tried to calm my rapid breathing, but each moment before I exhaled, the force of my heartbeat bruised my chest... or maybe that was my memories.

The elevator stopped moving. I held my breath, wishing I'd arrived ten minutes earlier so we'd have the buffer of all those new graduates between and around us. As I suspected, Contracts Assignment held only one person. I hesitated so long the door started to close before I stepped out. They jostled in protest and reopened. Niless looked up from her workstation in the centre of the iris. Her smile froze.

I tried to swallow past the lump in my throat, but a dry mouth made me cough instead. Niless turned away from her screen and folded her hands on the empty portion of the band of table separating her space from mine. Her smile faded. She looked at me with her piercing stare, analysing me: my shorter, layered hair, the set of my shoulders, the line of my jaw, and the lack of sparkle in my eyes. That had been gone far longer than I cared to think about.

"Hello again, Jutaya."

And that said it all. I'd hurt her. But she'd hurt me, too.

"Niless."

"What can I do for you?"

I couldn't read her. That formal tone and restrained words could mean she was hiding something. If I'd been Taya from six months ago, I'd have said she was upset. But Taya of six months ago hadn't known about the sub-basement chambers, about Niless's hand in guiding me toward Zaith's job because of a government conspiracy to hide the truth. *Did you know?* I wanted to ask, but that's not what came out.

"I'm here to see Professor Gellik. Could you advise me of his schedule?" He taught science at every level, so I knew he was a busy man.

She paused a moment. The weight of truth slid the scales from one side to the other without finding balance. She turned and looked up his schedule on the view monitor. I looked away as she typed. The bank of monitors around the other half of the iris sat empty. I imagined the graduating class in here, moments before, finalising their first probationary contracts, laughing and joking with each other and asking Niless what she thought. Imagining her advice, words of encouragement—

"He'll be leaving Level 4 in ten minutes for a lunch break."

I should have said thank you.

I should have said a lot of things.

Instead, I activated the elevator and turned my back on the only woman in my life who deserved to be called Mom.

On Level 4 I walked through the change room to the smaller elevator that travelled between the classes and dorms. A long time had passed since I'd last ridden this elevator – at least, that's how it felt. My jitters, as I shifted between the levels, had nothing to do with excitement and facing a new challenge. The wary, hardened woman standing here sought only to protect... *my heart*.

I waited in the small transition foyer between three classrooms and a set of washrooms. It was similar to the foyer that led to the change rooms or observation deck overlooking the gyms but held an air of informality, smelled of learning instead of sweat. Ten minutes later a crowd of teens overflowed into the small space. None were as old as me but a couple looked close. I certainly didn't feel like a teenager. Never had.

I slipped past the remaining throng that didn't fit on the elevator and went into the classroom. The bank of lab tables at the back and personal tables scattered across the front transported me in time. My breath caught as I blinked past seven levels of images each filled with different trainees. I was the only constant every time.

"Taya! What a surprise. Welcome."

Well, me and Professor Gellik. He shut the clasps on his briefcase, then wove his way through the desks to the door and held out his arm. I linked mine with his. A smile twitched my lips for the first time in a long time. My growth spurt between Levels 5 and 6 had brought us eye to eye, but now I could easily see the top of his thick white hair. He tapped off his virtual reading glasses; the thin, clear transmitter coiled around his right ear.

"I'm on break – walk with me, please."

"Yes, Niless let me know. I don't mean to intrude."

"It's always lovely to see you, my dear."

We stepped onto the elevator and rode to the Main Floor. I opened my mouth to let him know why I'd come but was left gaping when the doors slid apart. I'd never seen the instructors' offices before. Everyone knew they were located at the back of the main floor, but only approved personnel could pass behind the central bank of elevators. Beige hall carpeting separated dozens of glass-walled offices of clear blue. The two-storey bank of rooms looked like a brightly lit patio carved out of the base of the dark inverted pyramid that was the CTF building.

As Professor Gellik walked me past a central lounge and down the far corridor, I peered into the offices we passed. Or I tried to. The glass had some kind of gas between double-thick panes. If an office was occupied, the glass became translucent so you couldn't see inside. At a large corner office, Gellik turned to face the transparent door. A retina scanner initiated and the door unlocked.

"Please, come in. Have a seat." He bustled over to his desk, set his briefcase aside and opened a mini-fridge behind him. "Do you mind if I eat while we talk? I have class again in an hour."

"Of course not. I don't want to keep you from your lunch." I stood in front of a cream-coloured leather couch but did not sit as instructed.

He brought his lunch box over and placed it on the glass table before perching on the edge of a cushion. I stared at the dark blue rug under my feet.

He chuckled. "Yes, I'm quite fond of it. Everyone else went with a solid colour or simple design, but that would have bored me."

"It's the celestial sphere…" I breathed in awe. "It's beautiful."

"Come, Taya. Sit down and tell me what's brought you to my door. I suspect this isn't a social visit. Did the Kronik send you?"

I blushed. "Sort of."

He took a bite of his sandwich. The jade-green coliths around his eyes scrunched with a wink, but nothing else marred his smooth, dark-grey skin. The white hair was an aberration. He'd been born with it.

I took a deep breath and let it out. "What I'm about to say cannot leave this room."

"Oh, my. This *is* serious."

I smiled and felt a small spark of giddiness – something I'd smothered since Guide Aelix first spoke to the council.

"Yes, but it's also exciting. Professor." I took a breath, but not for dramatic effect. I had to stomp down those pesky butterflies in my gut. "We've discovered a spaceship."

He froze mid-bite.

"I'm here to ask if you'll come with me to South City to get it working again."

A line of concern creased his forehead. Invisible hands grabbed hold of that spark inside my chest and squeezed. I should've known better than to come here. He'd been an instructor with the Facility for longer than I'd been alive.

"I'm sorry. I shouldn't have come." I stood up as he worked to chew his mouthful. "You've got trainees to teach, a contract to uphold." What had I been thinking? I hurried to the door. "It was nice to see you again—"

"Taya, wait…"

I glanced over my shoulder and shook my head. "No. I'm being selfish. I – I can do this myself." My voice wavered, betraying the lie.

"Taya, come back and sit down. Talk to me."

Had it been anyone else, I would've left, but I respected this man. I sat back down.

"Now, what's really going on?"

I clasped and unclasped my hands, avoiding eye contact. "What do you mean?" I stalled.

"You've been through a lot since you took that Deserts job. Even before that, I know the ethics committee brought you to chambers. You've been caught up in this government mess – Niless mentioned seeing you a week ago, training again."

I stiffened at her name. Had she been spying on me? No, we rode the elevator together.

"I also heard about an Infinity contract. And now, here you are before me talking about a trip south to work on resurrecting alien technology. So, I ask again, what is going on?"

"I don't know. Everything?" I sighed. Gellik was an instructor, not a therapist, and yet I felt more at ease talking with him than I ever had with Jak. "I've been the new Kronik's bodyguard since our time in the Deserts. The Infinity contract just made it official."

"But...? Look at me. What's brought you back *here*?"

I squeezed my lips together, started to speak and then stopped again and looked him in the eyes. "Do you remember my first time in Level 7 science class? You asked what we knew about Gamma. The two theories? Jezetek and I verbally squaring off?"

He smiled. "How could I forget? The two of you were at the top of your class. You both fed off each other's determination."

I nodded. "Turns out we were both wrong. Are you teaching about the third theory now? Do you believe it?"

"That Gamma is a fake sun, set in orbit by an advanced alien race to terraform Xannia?"

I held my breath and tilted my head to the side trying to

read him. But it was too hard to hold all those factors in my head. It was hard to see past anyone's façade anymore.

"Yes. I'm teaching it… as fact."

"Do you believe it?"

"I don't know."

"We stabilised it – the sun – when we went looking for the Chronicles. Turned the generator back on. The super quakes stopped and we anticipate the average quakes disappearing over time, but Professor Denali's temperature findings didn't change. We're in danger of running out of verrin. The planet is too hot. Gamma…" I couldn't say it for some reason. Now, in front of the man who'd taught me everything I knew about science and astronomy, I couldn't speak the truth. The council meant to destroy the alien sun.

"Fixing the spaceship might be our only hope of saving Gamma. We need to change it from a sun into a moon, and we have a month to figure out how to do that or we'll run out of verrin over the next thirty years."

"So why come to me? I'm just a teacher."

"You're more than that. You just chose to teach."

He smiled again. "Very true."

"All cards on the table? I got hurt during the coup. You might have heard I was in the hospital for a while."

He nodded.

I gulped. My stomach clenched tighter than my fists, and I tried to breathe past the ache. "I have brain damage. The Talian scientist assassinated by the Faction yesterday – he was working on this project with me. As much as I didn't like the man, I couldn't have analysed the images of the spaceship without him. He helped put things into perspective. He kept me on track and focused. The Kronik expects me to be on the next transport south. I need help. I'd like it to be you. I can trust you, and with your background in astronomy and physics, we can crack this puzzle together. I know I can't do this on my own. So, what do say? Are you willing to set aside your career to help save the world?"

"No."

My insides froze and shattered.

"But, for you, I'll think about it."

Chapter 26

Divine Intervention

Satie

My stomach grumbled. Every fibre of my being knew weakness wasn't an option – every fibre except my gut. I hadn't been this hungry since the launch twenty-two years ago. Not even our last days on Darius's Island led to these stabbing pains. It brought back too many memories. Remembrances of choices and actions I still couldn't bring myself to confront.

Zerameteth's glow illuminated the small window again. I hadn't seen much of his fortifying radiance last night with that hood over my face. I licked my dry lips, avoiding the corners of my mouth, still tender from the gag. If not for one kind guard, it might still be there. I leaned as far forward as my restraints would allow and whispered the Prayer for Guidance:

Let wisdom rule my heart
Patience guide my soul

And truth breathe life into deed

Give me the strength to see when blind
And act as You doth heed

Let passion be tempered,
Tempers run cool…

The click of the door unlocking echoed in the desolate space. I tilted my face up a little more to reach Zerameteth's pale fingers shining through the window.

And a level head reason the day

Bring me the peace to wrap clarity in mind
And strive for the light through the grey.

"Sorry to disturb you, All Mother." My guard approached, his boot steps firm, but his voice hesitant.

"Have they followed your demands?"

"Partially."

I nodded. "So, I'm to be released then?"

"No." He didn't whisper, but the quality of his voice resonated low and apologetic.

I nodded again. Not because I had any expectation about his answer one way or another, but because the answer itself confirmed the profile I'd built of the man. Daria had taught me to use such information.

He brought a glass to my lips and I drank. Verrin this time. I swallowed and he took it away.

I dropped my head and closed my eyes.

He hesitated.

I let a sigh quake my body.

When he shifted forward, I opened my eyes and lifted

my gaze to meet his. "If I'm to be detained, would it be possible—" my voice cracked. I shook my head as if to wave off the unfinished idea.

"What is it, All Mother? Food? I've tried—"

I shook my head. "No. I understand you're under orders. It's just— well, it's difficult to pray." I raised my shoulders and let them slump.

He glanced behind. His hand hovered to the Whipstaff strapped to his leg. The door remained open, but no voices travelled down the hall beyond.

"Maybe…" He looked at me and then back over his shoulder before shifting closer to the chair. A few deft movements on his behalf and my arms released, swinging beside me. I grimaced and inhaled sharply.

He muttered something. A line from the Prayer for Forgiveness?

I hugged myself, massaging my shoulders and rotating them in place.

"Hurry," he whispered.

I dropped to my knees in the small pool of light streaming in through the window and opened my arms, wincing but forcing them up and out to embrace the Child god. I raised my face to the pale sun above in the darkening eve and echoed his prayer with a chosen line of my own.

"My heart seeks Truth even in the midst of deceit."

In the blink of an eye, I lifted my knee and spun around tackling the kind guard. His surprise didn't last long. Daria's training echoed through my mind even as I spoke the prayer. I trapped his arms by his side, using my weight to my advantage. Gripping the line where his neck met his shoulder, I used the Perggle Hold, leaned in and whispered the last lines, *please forgive me,* before he fell unconscious. I released him. If I held on too long, I'd kill him.

I laid him down on the concrete with care, then grabbed the old school chair I'd been tied to and set it against the wall under the window. I hesitated, one foot up on the seat, and looked over my shoulder through the open door. I couldn't leave my journal behind. If I did, they would destroy it – destroy the last shred of proof about the actual voyage across the Nine Seas and the record of our time on Darius's Island. It was the only record of our lives and a truth that couldn't be erased.

I glanced back up at the window and a plan formed. I grabbed the unconscious guard's weapon, hopped up on the chair, and smashed the small pane – quickly clearing the remaining shards from the frame. I jumped down, dropped the Whipstaff, and ran to the door. Voices and footfalls chased me back into the room. *Maybe I didn't think this through.* I dropped to my hands and knees and scuttled under the stacks of old chairs three and four rows deep, fifteen to twenty high. At the back, I stood on the bottom of the lower chairs, suspending myself between them and the wall.

My wrists ached as I tried to hold myself still. Two other guards burst into the room.

"Innek is down!"

"She's escaped through the window!"

"It's too small for us. We'll have to track her from the side entrance," the first one said.

"I'll tell Vittina," the second one said, pulling Innek from the room.

I waited another two minutes; all my arms could do after being bound for a day. I slipped down, scraping my arm from the elbow to the wrist. I tried to shake off the pain, but it didn't help. I waited behind the chairs. Two sets of footfalls slammed past the open door. With Innek down and guard number two already looking for me outside, that meant the four guards who'd taken me hostage had left the immediate area.

I slipped out from behind the mass of chairs and crouched along the wall toward the door. The rapid beat of my heart reminded me how little time I had. I listened at the door and heard a far-away commotion, likely by the other entrance. When guard Number Two didn't find a trail to follow, he'd know I'd duped them and return.

The lights above flickered. If they were smart, the guard would shut them off the second they realised I hadn't left the building. Taking a chance, I raced down the narrow hall to the room at the end with its door open. A large desk with papers and blueprints drew my attention. The room had no accessible windows. Boards covered the two alternate exits.

I shuffled through the pages on the desk and even caught my breath twice mistaking two covered tablets as my journal. Each drawer contained a myriad of supplies, but no book.

I spun around. Three large metal filing cabinets crowded the far corner. I dragged open the top-most section. It grated metal-on-metal worse than an alarm. Fear crawled along my arms and up the back of my neck.

Time had run out.

I looked into the drawer – only more pages suspended

in folders. I pushed batches of them aside to feel along the bottom. *Nothing!*

My gut twisted. I had to leave. If I got caught again, Innek would not be so forgiving a second time, and the gods knew what the other Faction guards were capable of. I bolted from the room and headed back to my holding cell. Something moved on the floors above. Had I not been listening for it, I might have missed it.

They were back.

I launched myself off the chair under the window and scrambled through the tight rectangle. My hands landed on the broken shards on the other side, slicing part of my palm and fingers. I balanced on my stomach with my hands in the air, looking for a way to crawl out without slicing up the rest of my body.

"There she is!"

The hum of a Whipstaff charging ignited a fresh blast of adrenaline. I scraped my knees against the ancient masonry and leaped from the window. My kneecaps dripped blood down the length of my legs as the tears in my pants aggravated the brick-burn with every step. *Don't run in a straight line!*

I darted right.

A blast of electrified ions zapped the air beside me.

Chapter 27

Breadcrumbs

Jezetek

I signalled the team to split. Drax followed me along the outer wall of the dark daycare. The side entrance to the old school was boarded over, along with several windows both on the main floor and the lower level. A sense of futility floated around my heart. After four more failed raids, we were still no closer to finding All Mother. If we didn't rescue her tonight, we might not ever. The window of time for an abductee to be located decreased exponentially after the first day. The fact that the Faction had reneged on their promise to release her wasn't unexpected, but it did mean time was running out.

I whistled. Drax pulled up short and flattened himself against the side of the old building. Located on the edge of the perimeter we'd established as the most likely area the Faction would have a base of operations, this place represented the last of the potential locations. Drax nodded as I passed him, flattened myself against the wall beside him and peered around the corner. Two whistles came from the other half of our team. I signalled to Drax, and we rushed around the back to a door left swinging open. SOs Ginnee and Kellum had breached it.

Ahead, they signalled a search of the ground floor. The back half of the building wasn't used by the daycare. Records showed the school had reduced its operating footprint by a room or two every year due to reduced attendance. Seems the Talian's had due cause to be concerned about dwindling numbers even before we implemented Dezmind's vision of a united nation. I motioned to Drax to lower his night goggles and take the stairs.

He pointed down. Boot-prints disturbed the layers of dust. I caught Drax's gaze and raised my eyebrows in warning. A fierce glint in his eyes and hard set to his jaw made me wary. I shook my head. His lip flattened but he obeyed. I moved in front of him, searching the stairwell for signs of cameras.

On the lower level, we passed several locked or boarded-up rooms. No boot-prints disturbed the dust in front of them. Two doors at the end of the corridor stood wide open. A vice clamped over my chest. I struggled to pull air as I signalled to Drax to take the room at the end. I slipped into the closer one on the left and froze.

A length of rope splayed out in the middle of the room. An old chair lay on its side near a smashed window. I whistled. So did Drax. I went to him.

"What did you find?" I looked around the sparse office

littered with blueprints and schematics.

"This is it. What's in the other room?" he said, riffling through the abandoned documents. He looked up and squinted at me when I didn't answer right away.

"She's gone."

He blanched and clutched at the desk. "What's in that room?" He bolted for the door.

I called in the location and then followed. He righted the chair before climbing up onto it and reaching out through the window to touch something.

"She was here." He glanced over his shoulder at me and then lifted a bloodied shard of glass as Ginnee and Kellum burst through the door.

"Get the Sniffers," I said.

* * *

Satie

I didn't hear them, but I felt them. They were close.

I stumbled onto the front porch of yet another house and knocked on the door. My breath came in gasps. The curtains at the window flickered, but no one appeared. No one wanted to help a Commoner. Either that or they were afraid of what chased me. I couldn't blame them. I still remembered the faces of the Commoners peeking out their apartment windows as the Resistance battled agents of the old Kronik in the streets. Hadn't these people just gone through a coup? Hadn't they dealt with the very Faction chasing me, blowing up community transports all in the name of what they believed in?

I rolled to the left, pushed off the door, and hopped

over the railing. Pain spiked through my knees where the window sill had cut me. I changed direction and headed for the back door of the next house across the side lawn. Scrambling up the narrow back steps, I tripped over my own feet and fell against the door. Blood from my punctured palm smeared against its surface.

I used the knob for leverage and pulled myself up. I knocked, holding back my frantic nerves. I also might be the problem. The reflection staring back at me in the starlight looked wild, threatening. I tried to smooth my hair down without leaving trails of blood behind.

The door cracked open, an old chain-latch preventing the door from opening farther.

"Who's there? Whatcha doin' out back?"

"Sir, please help me. The Faction is chasing me. I need to hide. I need to get back to the Capitol Building." Desperation clung to each word. I might have doomed myself again.

But the slide and click of the lock made my heart leap.

"What's that now? Come in and let me look at you."

I slipped through the door before he'd opened it all the way and leaned to shut it. My knees quaked, but I managed to stay standing.

His eyes widened. "You're that Guardian what's gone missing. You escaped?"

"Yes. Please, can you call the justices? The Capitol Building? Someone?" My gaze couldn't settle. Whisking past the older Talian man, I greedily took in the simplicity of his kitchen. The remnants of a feminine touch were overshadowed by utilitarianism.

"Come and sit down. I'll call the authorities." He motioned me toward a much-loved wooden chair. My over-taxed legs gave way. I grabbed the edge of the table to keep from falling into it.

"Thank you," I whispered and lowered my forehead to the table, trying to catch my breath.

He moved across the room and over to a com-box affixed to the wall. The old tech surprised me, but then, not everyone embraced modern life equally. He picked up the cordless receiver and disappeared into the front of the house. He kept his voice low, but it still filtered back into the kitchen.

"Yes, I'm calling to report the missing Guardian. Yes. Rejje Critt. She's at my house, on the edge of the north complex just past the old school. That's right. Yes. I'll be sure she stays." He gave his address before shuffling back into the kitchen and hanging up.

"Thank you," I said again, stronger this time.

He nodded. "Tea?"

"I don't suppose I could beg a glass of verrin and a slice of bread? I will repay you."

He waved me off and set about shuffling around the kitchen to gather his supplies. My heart refused to listen to logic – *I'm safe. I did it. I'm safe.* As I watched Mr. Critt move about the space at ease and relaxed with a small smile on his face, I couldn't help but wonder about his situation. I took in the smiling face of a younger couple on a digital frame, which then flashed to him and a laughing lady about the same age. Likely a gift from the younger generation.

"Is your wife out this evening, Mr. Critt?"

"No, dearie. She's passed."

"I'm sorry."

"Don't be. Weren't yer fault."

But somehow I got the impression it was. The way his tone changed ever so slightly at the end there made the skin on the back of my neck chill. I watched him again. For all his bustling about, no food or drink materialised.

A dark shadow passed across the back window toward the door. My entire body vibrated and my breath hitched. I stood, scraping the chair over the floor as I moved to press my back against the wall.

A knock came at the back door.

I shifted over as the doorknob turned. Mr. Critt turned away to open the fridge.

The door burst open. Two Faction guards leapt through. I grabbed the door handle and sandwiched myself between it and the wall. A female guard ran in from the room beyond. Critt hadn't called the authorities; he'd called the enemy. Taya had been right – the locals were helping the Faction, or at least some of them were.

The fridge shut. Critt disappeared past the woman in black combat gear, never acknowledging the guards' presence. The fourth guard, Innek, likely hadn't recovered yet.

"Where is she?" Vittina asked. The woman scanned the room, then inclined her head toward the open door.

I held my breath and prayed to the Trinity.

The door jerked forward. I stumbled after it. The man latched onto my arms. I struggled and let loose a shriek straight from my toes. They hauled me out the back door as the Vittina aimed her Whipstaff at me.

"I've got it on stun. Just give me a clear shot—" As she passed into the yard, she crumpled to the ground.

"Hold her," the main guard said. He pulled out his Whipstaff just as two broad shadows broke free of the night. A pair of familiar grey eyes locked onto mine and then shifted to the man holding me. I became dead-weight, dropping and pulling the guard forward. In two steps, Drax moved in and punched him in the face. I curled into a ball and rolled out of the way into a clump of flowers.

Deep grunts resonated, and the air sizzled with electric current. I curled my body tighter as I tried to chase away flashes of a nightmare I thought we'd left behind twenty-two years ago.

A pair of hands gripped my shoulders, dragging me up. I opened my mouth, but the scream died as Drax pulled me to his chest and held me tight.

"I've got you. I've got you, Satie, and I'll never let go."

Chapter 28
Risky Business

Dezmind

I slumped forward onto my desk and rubbed my hands over my face. The morning sun shone through the window, warming my back. I hadn't slept more than three hours last night. Taya walked in through the door adjoining my office to the council chambers.

"They're here. All of them. Even Magistrate Delenon and Daria."

I didn't respond. I wanted to speak with Delenon one-on-one, but that wasn't possible now. I hated winging things. But after the abduction, no one was taking any chances.

A pair of hands massaged my shoulders. I sat up. Taya usually kept her distance when we were working. Lately, that's all I seemed to be doing. I closed my eyes and allowed myself one minute under her ministrations. Neither of us could afford longer. Our future hinged on what happened in chambers today.

A knock at the inner door startled her hands away. She walked over, every move efficient, belying any underlying change. Taya reached for the handle.

"Wait." I stood up, went over and grasped both her hands in mine.

She gave me a confused look. I wanted to say everything within the space of our thoughts, but that might throw off her focus. I couldn't risk upsetting her. Not now.

"I think it's time."

Her eyes widened. "Are you sure?"

I knew I wouldn't need to explain. We'd spoken of this often enough.

"Yes. For many reasons, which you'll hear me explain in chambers, but the most important is that I love you." I gathered her into my arms and kissed her. Her body stiffened. We'd agreed not to bring our private relationship into the office – it was hard to ignore habit. She relaxed and leaned into me.

The knock came again. She pulled back and straightened her black uniform, taking a deep breath.

"Ready?" I asked.

She nodded, opened the door and scanned the room before stepping aside. I walked in and those congregated stood. I approached the head of the oval table, Delenon to my right, Daria in the corresponding corner, and sat. Everyone followed. It wasn't as elaborate a ritual as Gerrund had constructed for the Underground Cause meetings, but the simplicity of it spoke volumes. The door clicked shut. I visualised Taya in ready stance, scanning the room. Her gaze had always been intense, but lately, it stripped me bare. I could only imagine how the others felt.

"Thank you for joining me at this early hour. There's much to discuss that can't wait for regular council hours." The mix of Common and Talian councillors nodded and shifted, a mostly positive response.

I motioned for Ynell to collect our first guest. In walked our new Special Ops commander.

"Tek, an update, please." He stood across the oval table from me and gave a nod of respect.

"We have located and rescued All Mother."

Everyone in the room expressed their relief.

"She is safe. Her minor abrasions are being tended to at the clinic in the Capitol Building."

"And her captors?" I asked, though I already knew. Still, certain appearances needed to be upheld.

"Two captured. Two tagged."

"Tagged?" Darzeth Prime's councillor, Sir Plithis, slid his fingers to the brass inlay. "What do you mean? Did they escape?"

"No, sir. We captured one at the remote holding location and their leader at a citizen's home. We knew we'd have a hard time getting information from them, so we devised a plan to track the others back to their main base. During the scuffle, my team placed trackers on the other two hostiles."

"Did you find the base?" Madam Quellen asked.

"What do you mean at a citizen's home?" Sir Olekk added.

Tek shifted his weight from one foot to the other and looked at me before answering any questions. I nodded.

"We have not yet found the base. It will take days, maybe even weeks, of surveillance and tracking before we can identify behavioural patterns. That being said, we're able to keep a close eye on their comings and goings, so no more surprises. We must wait for them to lead us to the jackpot. As for what I meant about capturing their leader at a citizen's home, it's true. We found the secondary holding location, but All Mother had escaped the Faction's custody." His eyes flickered over to Daria as if to acknowledge her hand in training All Mother during their time together. "All Mother sought refuge at a local citizen's home, but instead of calling the hotline to inform us she was safe, he called the Faction. This confirms our suspicions that some Talian citizens are helping the Faction and protecting their identity."

"Have you arrested the citizen?" Sir Hetrick asked.

"Not at this time. We have him under surveillance, too, though it's doubtful the Faction will maintain contact with him now that his cover is blown."

"Will charges be pressed? If they'd recaptured All Mother – well, the outcome might've been quite different. Harbouring vigilantes should fall under at least one of our laws. The fact that he's a Talian citizen shouldn't matter," Hetrick blustered.

"Agreed." I straightened my tie and placed my hands on the table. "We don't want to spook any other conspirators at this time. The plan is to lull them into a false sense of security, track their movements, and then strike when the time is right. Once the members of the Faction are in custody, we will revisit this, and other sympathisers', actions and mete out charges at that time. Tek, what news is there of All Mother's journal?"

"None at this time. My teams have scoured the building the Faction used to restrain her and only found documents pertaining to the assassination attempt at the Memorial Rally and All Mother's abduction."

"Any concrete intel about why they killed Professor Elix?" I asked.

"None at this time. Only conjecture."

"Thank you, Tek." I nodded his dismissal, disappointed it might take weeks before we found All Mother's journal. I'd hoped to use any hint of a lead to help sway my next case. Ynell escorted Tek from the room as I turned to face Magistrate Delenon. Daria and Taya stiffened simultaneously.

"Magistrate Delenon, I hate to broach this after our recent scare, but time waits for no one, I'm afraid. We are still planning to send our representative down to South City to examine the alien tech the General discovered. I'd like to know if this will be a salvage mission or the follow-through of Plan B for dealing with Gamma – Zerameteth. Namely, are you still on board with sending a crew back to Darius's Island for the super lodestone?"

Daria stiffened further at my request and a flicker of a shadow crossed Delenon's gaze. Maybe I'd read him wrong over the past few days and pressing for a commitment this soon after the abduction was just suicide. I searched for any sign he might still be on board and tried to keep the sincerity in my sad smile.

"We stand by our offer, but fewer than half the crew are

willing to return. We need at least a day to train your recruits in the basics, and it'll take three days to return to our ship on the west port. Do you have twenty citizens willing to sail? If not, it's a moot point. I won't force anyone to make that crossing – even if the west seas are more manageable."

I looked to the empty seat where the Underground Liaison should have sat. Kaynee rarely sent someone to the regular meetings; I don't know why I expected her to send someone to an emergency one. I couldn't afford to lose this opportunity though. If anyone was willing to help sail the ship, it would be Underground Citizens.

"I'll verify numbers immediately after this meeting. Both Tek and Kaynee have been collecting the names of willing recruits. Last count was fifteen between them. Will you be captaining the vessel back?"

"No, but our captain, Marxx, and his quartermaster are more than capable of making the journey without me." Daria visibly relaxed at these words, and I wondered what kind of tension there might be between the magistrate and his captain. Still, I considered this a win. That we managed to rescue the All Mother in just over a day might influence his current decision-making. I had to take a chance. I felt for Taya through our mental link, but her walls were up. I knew they would be, but if I could prepare her for the change… No. Nothing.

"Then, if I may be so bold." I stood up.

All gazes followed me. I bowed to Delenon. The councillors around the table shuffled in their seats.

"For every original Talian councilman's position in this government, a respected Commoner, many of whom are previous sector keepers, now has a transitional position as magistrate for their sector and an equal place on this council. However, we do not currently have a Kronik who adequately represents *all* the people."

Rumblings and mutters of displeasure and curiosity rose. I held my hands up to quiet those present.

"It's true, I have lived among the Commoners, but I am not one of them by birth, and as much as I'd like to think I represent every citizen of Xannia, I do not. So it is, Magistrate Delenon, that I humbly extend to you, on behalf of the entire population of Common citizens, the opportunity to be my equal on this council as we move toward refining how our government works here, to the south, and underground. Will you, Svelik Delenon, beloved Magistrate of the masses, accept the co-position of Kronik and rule for the good of all people by my side?" This was not the proposal I was supposed to make today, but it was the necessary one.

The room fell silent. I held my breath and extended my hand toward him. I had no idea what this great man would do, would say. I had wanted to speak with him about the possibility countless times since his return, but between the situation surrounding Gamma and then All Mother's abduction, everything fell into chaos. Still, I wasn't blind. The people loved him and he loved them. Gerrund knew his prejudices would only make him a target, so he agreed not to be the face of the new government. But this revered statesman had not only worked closely with the old Kronik but had also supported the rights of the Commoners and had lived as a rebel for the past twenty-two years. I could think of no one better – if he would only reply.

Delenon cleared his throat, then stood. He did not take my hand.

Fear stabbed at my heart. *Did I just make a complete fool of myself? Maybe he wants to retire and fade into obscurity. Maybe— I* lowered my arm, empty-handed.

He reached out and grabbed my shoulders. Taya, Daria, and Ynell took a half-step forward.

"I accept."

Smiles lit both our faces.

"Excellent, sir." I turned out of his embrace to those assembled. "During the course of our regular council meeting, Magistrate Delenon and his security officer, Daria Myyup, will sit in. At that time, we can discuss his inauguration and look at drafting a new government legislature that includes South City and the Underground with more than just liaison positions. This is the start of our new world."

The Common councillors cheered as the Talian ones looked on in disbelief. This world was larger than their backyard, and it was time equality became more than just an ideal. The Faction would be no match for the two of us. The Oracle had been right all those years ago. I was *destined to be King*. It was time to claim my destiny. I looked back over my shoulder at Taya. Her gaze locked onto mine. Was it also possible the Oracle was right about my Soul Mate, too? Was I destined to rule alone?

I tried to breach Taya's mental barrier one last time and failed.

Chapter 29
Tempting Fate

Taya

I crossed my arms and tapped my foot as the lidez driver struggled to lift my hiking pack out of the cargo hold. The glint of Beta disappearing below the horizon made me squint, but I still watched him. He slid it to the edge and heaved up. The top portion followed him but the bottom dropped off the edge and slammed into the newly paved road. I stormed over.

"I told you to let me get it. If anything's broken, you're paying for it," I snapped, hauling the elongated pack over one shoulder and stepping clear of the lidez. On the sidewalk, I checked for damage.

"You were told the weight limit. It's not my fault."

"And you were told—"

"Dalla!"

Only one person on this gods-forsaken planet called me that. I straightened up and looked over my shoulder at the front of the Desert Depot at the edge of the Expanse.

"Gelden!"

I waved the driver off and jogged over to meet my old friend. It was hard to believe I thought of him that way when we'd only met in the Underground four months ago. It might as well have been a lifetime.

His windblown dirty-blond hair bounced in the fading sunlight. I stopped short of running into him, but he plowed on through and lifted me up in a vice-hug. I let my pack settle on the lush grass and hugged him back… maybe a little too long.

He set me down and looked me over. "What is it?"

"What's what?" I asked.

The lidez hovered off to reveal a transformed Vrazeth. I gawked at the new infrastructure: a hotel, eateries, fresh siding on houses that used to peel with layers of paint, and a grand entryway to the Deserts Transpoint and Guide Headquarters – all smack dab on the edge of the Expanse and the gateway south. A fleet of D.V.s of various sizes sat parked in a large garage beside the Transpoint. I drifted away from Gelden, who grabbed my pack and followed behind me, laughing.

"Yep, here they are." He shouldered my bag with a modicum of effort and took me on the tour. "Here's model 1.0 – the one we developed for partner travel. It's still the fastest way to cross, but now that we're also doing caravan and cargo runs, I've remodelled your original hauler and made it solar powered."

I floated through the expansive garage, touching every machine parked or being worked on. Space for four mini-

D.V.s, two cargos, and two caravans sat vacant. One Caravan waited parked out front with all the supplies.

"So, where's the scientist?" Gelden asked.

My shoulders tensed. "Assassinated."

"The Talian from the Memorial Rally?"

I nodded.

"Tough break. Still, I hear he was mixed up with the secret agents. Helping them with interrogation tactics."

I sighed. "Yeah. But I get the feeling Dez was right."

"Oh? About what?"

"That he was acting under the old Kronik's orders. Being patriotic and all that meeka. He was annoying, but a big help. He didn't deserve to die." We stood silent for several minutes, looking at the array of D.V.s in the garage. I tried to take in what modifications I could see, follow the new team's design choices. I got so lost in my head, trying to work it all out, I didn't hear Gel at first.

"Sorry, what's that?"

"I said, did you get to meet them?"

"Who?"

"The survivors. The Lost Resistance Members."

And then it dawned on me: he, Gerrund, and Kaynee had lost most of their family to the Nine Seas Massacre and the failed Resistance when they were kids.

"Why didn't you go? You could have seen them." Something triggered at the back of my mind – something Daria had said about Gerrund – but the memory slipped away.

"I couldn't."

"You're not married to this job. You could've g—"

"No." He leaned against the nearest Caravan and rubbed his arms. "What if she was there? What if she wasn't? Only half made the trip from Nova Leau's port, right? I've built her up in my mind over the years… there's no way she'd ever measure up to the woman, the warrior, Gerrund used to tell me about."

And then it clicked. Warrior. Gerrund's older sister was Gelden's mother. Daria had called Gerrund her *brother*.

"What?" he asked.

I looked at Gelden and released a breath I didn't know I held.

"Your eyes are huge. What? She's there, isn't she? You met her? I know that face. You met her, didn't you?"

"I— I think so? I don't want to say for sure."

Now he was the one holding his breath. He looked so vulnerable in that moment: scared and excited all smashed together with a longing I'd never noticed before. Of course, I hadn't noticed. He grew up believing she'd died. Had accepted that as a fact. Now…

"A group of the LRM are returning to Darius's Island to get something we need to help us with our project in the south. They're looking for recruits. I don't know if she's going or not, but it might be a way to connect with her… see what she's seen. Think about it. Don't hide out here. Find her. When I found my mother it— well, let's just say it didn't go as planned. But since Dezmind came to power, I've gotten to know her better. I put a lot of ghosts to rest when she answered all my questions. You must have as many as I did."

He looked away. "Yeah, maybe."

I stepped into his personal space and held his face between my hands. We hadn't been this close, other than a friendly hug, since he'd kissed me all those months ago in the Underground. It could have been a lifetime. It certainly felt like someone else's life.

"Hey. Think about it."

"I will. I *will*."

I stepped back before I did something I might regret. Dezmind and I might not have a perfect relationship, but he did have my heart. Gelden ran a shaky hand through his hair and let out a breath to match.

"One of Dezmind's missives said you were bringing someone. We have enough supplies for three—"

"I tried. I—" I shrugged and gave a half-hearted wave. "It's just me." I breathed in but uncertainty stabbed my chest. "Wait. What? Three?" I turned to face Gelden just as a Network News Now cube rider halted on the street out front. I groaned. "Ugh… what are they doing here? Come on, reunion's over. Let's get me launched. Zita's almost set. I've got, what? About a night to reach the Ancient City? Maybe more?" I snagged my pack from the floor next to Gelden and trudged over to the Caravan.

"Hey, wait up!" A young, male voice called. I wasn't in the mood for an interview, and if that reporter came anywhere near me—

"Hey, hi. I'm Ky—"

I turned as he stumbled forward, and I gave him a palm-drive straight to his forehead for the trouble.

"Dalla!" Gelden rushed forward and caught the guy before he hit the ground.

"I don't do reporters."

"The Kronik sent him."

"What? Why would Dezmind— Oh," I groaned and looked up to the sky. "He promised the council full disclosure, so he'll pacify them with this guy. *Politics*."

Gelden had the reporter on his feet again when I turned back around. I squinted as I assessed him. He looked younger than me. I almost said as much but choked back my words. How many of my employers had discredited me about the same thing when I graduated from the CTF? It didn't matter how old he was. I still didn't want him around. But I'd promised Dez, *and* All Mother, for that matter, that I would try to fix this. Stop the rocket launch. The weight of responsibility pulled at my body and my senses.

My gaze wavered as I looked through the reporter back to this morning's emergency meeting and the afterward. Dez was supposed to announce our engagement. The wedding celebration was supposed to act as a balm for the masses as Tek cleaned up the last remnants of the Faction and got All Mother's journal back. Instead, he'd proposed to Magistrate Delenon. Our marriage hadn't come up at the regular council meeting either. All of a sudden, we weren't a priority again. Now that he was King, nothing had changed. I would always come second when it came to politics. Hadn't he given up on finding his Soul Mate? Dedicated himself to the Cause before hiring me to take him into the Deserts? Our working together had been a fluke. A way for the old Kronik to dispose of me the way he had my father. I was an afterthought even then.

"I'm sorry. Stay out of my way or it'll happen again."

He laughed as he held his forehead. Gelden glowered at me. He'd never seen me violent before. His Underground lens of the world had always painted me in broad strokes. I was CTF. I was a trained killer – I just preferred protective duty to soldiering. But I had no filter anymore.

"Load up your stuff. We're leaving in ten minutes." I walked to the vehicle and hopped into the enclosed cab to familiarise myself with the controls. Nothing digital. Good. Gelden slipped in on the other side.

"What was that all about?" he asked.

"Nothing. So, I'm assuming that once I've turned the key, the stored solar energy in the battery will operate the Caravan?" He nodded. "But is it one speed like the mini or what's this shifter for?"

"Yes, one speed but the shifter allows you to gear down for more torque in case you need to dune crawl or gear up if the ground is firm and flat so that you don't over-tax the motor. We kept it basic to see how it held up under the strain of the heat and sand."

"This is nice." I ran my finger along the thin, clear plastic stretched to form the bulk of the cab. "I like that you can see everywhere, including the cargo. Does it get hot in here? Is the screen UV treated?"

"You're avoiding talking, again."

"So, what if I am? Talking won't change anything. Talking won't bring Elix back or stop the terraforming—" my voice broke. I swallowed a sob and looked straight out the window. Neither of us needed this right now. I didn't want to burden him.

"Hey, now." He moved to rest an arm over my shoulders

but I shrugged it off. "You have nothing to worry about. My guides go there and back all the time. We follow Doire's maps, we take precautions, and we reinforce your training every few weeks. The creatures of the Deserts avoid us and we avoid them. You'll be there and back before you know it."

Yet, some small, dark part of my heart told me that wasn't true. Could I return somewhere if I wasn't the same person?

Gelden showed me the spare maps, backup verrin (the concentrated fake stuff), and satellite emergency beacon. He'd done well on his own. No wonder he hadn't been back to the Prime since they developed the guide headquarters.

"Hey, guys, all packed." The reporter popped his head into the cab by my elbow.

I jumped.

"Oh, hey, didn't mean to surprise you."

"Go around and get in," I growled and rolled my eyes at Gelden. He laughed as he slid from the cab to make room for the kid.

"Take good care of her." His hand drifted over the short nose that housed the battery, but his gaze fell somewhere back and to the left of the Caravan. I glanced over my shoulder but I couldn't see much behind me other than our supplies.

The reporter jumped onto the seat. "Are we expecting more cargo?"

"Excuse me – what?"

"It's just that a CTF transporter pulled up and the driver's wavin' at us."

I looked through the plastic back window and to the kid again. "What are you talking about?" I slipped down from the cab and walked the length of the magnetically hovering cargo bed covered in a darker anti-heat tent. The one we'd taken into the Deserts the first time hadn't been made that way. Another marked improvement on the original.

The sigh of a rig made me pick up my steps. In the open, my old pal Mac waved at me. I waved back and hopped onto the step of his rig by the driver's door.

"Hey, Mac. I didn't order any supplies. What are you doing here?"

"I've got an express package for you."

"You what? What is it?"

"Not what, who." He smiled and nodded behind me.

I swung away from the rig, holding onto the sidebar with one hand, and there stood Professor Gellik. The professor was fitted out in tan fatigues, oversized sunglasses, and a smaller pack than mine; he planted his hands on his hips and grinned.

"The CTF told him to find his own way, so he hitched a ride with me on my run out to Headquarters."

"Mac, I could kiss you."

He laughed as I jumped down and stutter-stepped up to the professor. "You came."

"I did. You were right. It's a chance of a lifetime. When I told the master keeper that the Kronik requested me personally, he gave me a leave of absence... and raised his eyebrows." He laughed and held his hands up. "Turns out, I wasn't lying after all. He really had."

"That's fantastic." When had Dez found the time to call

the CTF?

"It certainly is exciting."

"Come on, let's get your stuff stowed and head out."

When I started the Caravan, the motor hummed to life. Gelden and a couple of guides helping Mac unload their latest shipment waved as I shifted into gear.

"Hey, do either of you have an extra canteen? I think I left mine at the Station."

I glanced at the professor across the searching reporter and then looked up as if asking the gods for patience. "Professor Gellik, meet—" I looked at the kid.

"Kyler," he said and flashed a set of perfect white teeth.

"Meet Kyler. He's a reporter, also sent by the Kronik. Kyler, this is the professor. Do us a favour and try not to lose anything else while we're out here. I'd hate to bring you home without your Mini-View… or the head attached to it." Accidents happened, after all, and while I could certainly make sure I kept him alive, I'd make no such promises about his equipment.

With the professor aboard, my spirits lightened, at least until we reached the first checkpoint in the Barren Desert at the Ancient Memorial for the Dead. Crews had removed millennia of accumulated sand to reveal two large bisecting grave markers the size of a house. It's where Dez got his idea for the Memorial Gates. Gellik and Kyler admired the structure as we passed, commenting on it as a great historical find. It only reinforced death for me: the Ancients, the Dakturians, the assassination attempts on Dez… and me. I was tired of tempting fate.

Chapter 30
Many Happy Returns

Gelden

I held my breath as I stepped off the long-distance transport down to the docks of Nova Leau. The old replica ship of Darius's towered over the port with the rise of Beta, our second sun. As I waited to retrieve my travelling gear from the lidez's cargo hold, I exhaled and watched the bustle of the seaside town, so different from the ports at the Prime, where this ship had sailed from twenty-two years ago with my mother on board.

Swimmers in full scuba gear cycled in and out of small huts at the base of each pier. Those incoming hauled different coloured bags the size of their bodies. In the Prime, divers looked mainly for rare stones and gems along the cliffs. Some caught fish using the dual-thrust subs so that one person could drive and another hunt, but the bulk of Xannia's seafood came from Nova Leau.

The LRM's lidez pulled in and a small crowd gathered,

clogging the streets. Taya had said most of the survivors weren't willing to make the return voyage. I kept an eye out for a Nirian woman exiting the vehicle. Several men disembarked, followed by Thenticia, one of Uncle Gerry's sergeants. I thought she'd gone south with him. Guess she made the trip back for the memorial. She clung to a tall older gentleman's arm – her Grandfather? They certainly looked alike. My heart swelled for her good fortune, and it drove my hopes higher. Out came All Mother, and a cheer rose from the crowd. The Talian engineer followed right behind her.

Five more people stepped from the transport, the last one a girl with light-grey skin about my age. Her red coliths flared and made her appear on fire. No one matching my mother's description stepped off the lidez.

Maybe this is a mistake. If she's not here, why bother? I rubbed a hand over my face, then dropped onto the curb as the transport drove off. The Talian helped All Mother up onto a crate so the crowd could see her better. More people had arrived in the midst of the workday – some looked nervous, others excited. A group of nearly twenty stood to one side, as casual as could be. Something about the assuredness of their stance and the cut of their clothes made me wonder if this was the returning crew.

"I can't thank you all enough for volunteering to return to Darius's Island with us. We will spend the rest of today training you on the basics of sailing before launching at first light. We are tasked with an important mission by the Kronik and Magistrate Delenon. Your help will be invaluable."

She explained how to board and what to expect, but as the group moved single-file down the far pier to the massive sailing ship, I didn't budge. They didn't need me. I shook my head. If Taya was right, and my mother had been back in town for two weeks, why hadn't she tried to find me? Neither Aunt Kaynee nor Uncle Gerry had heard from her either. It made no sense.

"I shouldn't have come. Just chasing shadows," I muttered and shifted to stand. Before I did more than look up, I hesitated. The girl who'd stepped off the lidez last stood before me.

"Hi there. You okay?" she asked.

"Yeah, I'm all right."

She dropped onto the curb beside me. "Because you've got that look."

"What look?" I faced her, resting my arm over one raised knee.

"Like you hoped to find someone. I've seen it a lot since we visited Darzeth Prime. Who are you looking for?"

I sighed, closed my eyes and let my head flop back a moment. *What did it matter?* "My mother."

Something flickered in her eyes. Recognition? Sympathy?

"Gee, you must've been a baby during the Resistance."

"Yeah. I don't remember her. I've only ever seen old photos of her and my Dad. He never made it to the ship. I lost a lot of family that day. I was kinda hoping— ah, it doesn't matter." I grabbed my pack and stood up. She did too.

"Do you want to see the ship?"

"What? Really? Am I allowed?"

"Training won't start for another half hour. We need to give all the volunteers a tour, show them their beds, talk to them about the seas and the kind of work that'll be expected of them. I've bet my lunch rations on half the volunteers leaving within the first hour. Anyone who can handle Marxx's drills, and his attitude, for that matter, is likely in it for the long haul."

"Not everyone will sail with you?"

"If we lose too many, I doubt we'll be going anywhere. We need a full crew compliment for the day and another one for the night plus relief for both sides."

"But doesn't Taya, I mean the Kronik's rep, need something from the Island? Something to help stop the terraforming?"

Her eyes twinkled. "Well, don't you know an awful lot about something we've been told not to discuss?"

I blushed. "I— Well, I know—"

"Taya, is it? I gathered as much." She laughed. "Come on. Let me give you the tour. You can at least see the ship that your mother sailed. That might help." She held out her hand, and I took it without question.

"I'm Teena, Teena Myyup." My heart skipped as an invisible vice crushed my lungs, and I froze for an instant.

"Gelden," I choked out. *Gelden Myyup.* She didn't balk at my name or flutter her eyes; she just held my hand, turned and led me across the street to the boardwalk onto the pier. My feet couldn't help but follow her. I needed to know more. Was she my sister? No one said anything about my mother being pregnant and fighting in the war. Did she meet someone… *after*? But Teena had light-grey skin. Her mother would have been Glaaon, and her fiery coliths meant her father was Matin. How could she be a Myyup? *Is this why my mother never bothered to find me? She'd replaced me?*

I followed the girl up the wooden ladder built into the side of the ship. The wood under my hands smelled of the sea, and I had to watch that my fingers didn't get pinched between gaps in the treads where the old wood separated along the grainlines. On deck, I hovered at the back of the group of new recruits. Captain Marxx and Quartermaster Neldek Denton – Tony as he asked to be called – went over the basic structure of the ship on this deck.

"Excuse me a moment," Teena whispered in my ear. "I'll be right back."

A commotion over by the hull where a winch system sat drew Teena away. I skirted the edge of the crowd, half-listening, half-tracking the girl. I didn't normally indulge in eavesdropping, but when I got to within a few feet of Teena, All Mother, the Talian, and a town messenger, I paid more attention to them than to the captain.

"You're sure?" All Mother asked. She looked from the messenger to the Talian and back. "Teena, he says the new Kronik's Special Ops team has located the Faction's headquarters. They think the journal might be there."

"Will they raid it?" she asked.

"Not until both of the tagged Faction members return. It could be as early as tonight or as late as next week," the messenger said.

"What do you want to do, Satie?" the Talian asked.

"I don't know. I thought I'd already decided. The

voyagers need me."

"You don't have to stay. I can do the rites with them as we travel and take care of the Med-Bay. If this is your chance to find the journal, take it," Teena said.

The Talian placed his arm around All Mother, gave her a squeeze and a kiss on the forehead. I blinked out my surprise. I thought Sun Guardians abstained from relationships – but then again, they'd been on their own for over twenty years. If that was long enough for my mother to forget about me, it was certainly long enough for a Guardian to fall in love. Interesting that she paired with the only Talian on the ship. I watched her out of the corner of my eye. She wrung her hands and bit her lip in consideration.

"No matter what you decide, I'll stay with you," the Talian said as his arm dropped and he clasped her hand.

She shook her head. "No. It's just a book."

"Satie—"

"It's true, Drax. We carry our experiences here." She rested her hand over his heart.

Teena nodded. "For all we know, the Faction might have destroyed it already. Then where would I be? Stuck here when it's the ship's crew who really need me. Besides, we could always do a video documentary about our experiences. We don't necessarily need my journal. It's— I was just being sentimental. Never thought we'd be going back." She turned to the messenger. "Please inform the Kronik that I wish his team well, but my decision to return with my crew stands."

The messenger bowed and then hurried over to the side

of the ship.

"Are you sure, All Mother?"

"Yes, Teena. Now go on. You were escorting that young man somewhere, weren't you?"

My cheeks flushed hot. She'd noticed me. So much for casually eavesdropping. I tried to focus on what the Quartermaster was saying about the night shift, but his words were all a jumble. Teena appeared beside me and bumped my elbow with hers.

"Still want that private tour?"

I almost said no, then thought better of it. I might not get this kind of one-on-one time with her again.

"Lead the way." I went from being one of the dropouts to one of the committed volunteers – I had to know the truth. And if that meant stealing every moment I could on this voyage in order to figure it out, so be it.

"Tell me," I asked as she steered me toward a staircase leading down, "What's it like growing up on an island?"

Chapter 31
Battling Ghosts

Taya

I regretted telling Kyler to shut up. Now I had nothing to distract me from my thoughts. Just prior to the rise of Alpha, we'd entered the Powder Sands Desert, more or less on track with the way-markers the guides had planted every half-mile. We diverted around the Spike Beast nests without incident, but my nerves twitched from knowing what lay beneath the sands.

I tried to force my thoughts elsewhere, but they only landed on another sore spot – Dez. We'd argued instead of spent the night in each other's arms. Then, time disintegrated between us until only a whisper of thought caressed my damaged mind as I left the Compound. But even that went unanswered.

I just wanted to do my job as head of security. I didn't have to personally guard him – I knew that now. I also knew I wanted to be with him, not all the way across the world working on some project I wouldn't have agreed to if he hadn't put me on the spot. Here I was in the middle of the blasted Deserts. Again. Why must history repeat itself?

Twilight had settled several hours ago when we passed through the Valley of the Dunes. Kye had talked incessantly at that point, so I'd been able to bury my emotions. Now, the image of my father's mummified remains kept superimposing the image of the last picture taken of us. Mom and I never discussed Dad. I tried to once, but she got a faraway look in her eyes and then left me at the park without warning. I took that as a strong hint not to broach the subject again. After nearly two decades under house arrest, she didn't have much else to say, and I was tired of the blame game. I understood, now, why she and Dad gave me up. It wasn't their fault the Fyces took me in as a foster kid – that was just dumb bad luck.

"I see the next mile-marker," Professor Gellik said, lowering the binoculars and mounting them back into their dashboard holster. "The map says we should see the Ancient City soon."

I nodded, driving along the top of the sand dune. Maybe we'd finally be able to talk openly about the project. I'd formed a plan during the long quiet.

Sweat beaded on my forehead and upper lip. I took a sip of verrin and then let the canteen dangle from my neck. Kye might have been assigned to catalogue our efforts, but he didn't have clearance to hear about the details of the project. As far as everyone knew, the professor and I were experimenting with getting the tech operational – nothing more. Thanks to the Faction interrupting Dez's announcement at the Memorial Rally, the details of our mission were never revealed. Kye turned on the Mini-V clipped to his hat. He did that every once in a while, but with the city coming up, he wouldn't want to miss anything crucial.

I was surprised the network allowed another one of their reporters out into the Deserts after the last fiasco. *Had they actually let Zaith go? Or was that just another lie?* I tried to squash the hot flare of hatred, re-bottle it, so I could think clearly. But that didn't come easily anymore. Maybe it never had. I breathed deep and focused on Kye instead. He didn't strike me as being the same calibre as Zaith. Whatever she was, reporter, spy, assassin, best friend, she did it well. My skin crawled. Not just from battling ghosts, but because of what lay ahead.

"What are all those red flags?" Kye asked, leaning forward.

"It says here"—the professor turned a page in the map book—"a red flag denotes a danger zone. Those must have been red flags by the triple dune we passed early this morning, sun-bleached orange. But there were only a couple along the way." He glanced up at the hundreds of small red flags lining the edge of our dune. I gripped the wheel of the Caravan tighter but refused to turn my head. Refused to acknowledge the place where I'd almost died – the first time. I clenched my teeth. *Focus, focus, focus.*

"Do you know why they've flagged it, Taya?" the professor asked. Had it been Kye, I would have ignored him.

"The Pit of Chance."

"The what now?" Kye asked.

"The old amphitheatre is down there, covered by a ceiling of silk-sand. You go down there, you might get sucked under." Neither man asked more. Maybe something in the tone of my voice warned them off. Good. I concentrated instead on the pale pinkish-tan mound growing on the horizon.

Fifteen minutes later, both Kye and the professor leaned forward to get a look at the Ancient City: the home of our ancestors. It looked much the same as I remembered it, except for the small splashes of colour dotting the ruins and the temple itself sporting a communications tower. A mess of other tech also hugged its roofline.

I stopped at the gateway to the city before a new sandstone garage and checkpoint. One of two guards approached the Caravan and checked the number painted on the snub-nosed front housing.

"Hi there." He tilted his wide-brimmed hat up in salute. "Are you the council's delegation?"

"Yes," I said.

"Just leave the Caravan here and we'll make sure it's at the exit garage for you when you leave this evening. Guide Vitine will take you to the temple to register and then show you where you'll be staying." He pointed to a young woman who looked vaguely familiar. She wore a long, loose cotton shirt over equally loose pants, both dyed a rust-orange, complimenting her black skin and sunny yellow coliths.

We hopped out of the Caravan, grabbed our packs from the back, and met the girl by a bank of sliders – the modified ones from the Underground.

"Welcome to the Ancient City, travellers. Choose a slider and follow me."

As I walked past the garage, a faint hum followed. I selected one of the two-wheeled light-frame devices and balanced on the thin platform holding the handlebars with one hand. Even as we rode, the hum stuck with me. I forgot about it as I listened to Gellik and Kye talk about the sights. Workers affixed tarpaulin roofs and patched the adobe buildings that once crumbled. I waved at a crew chief when we slowed around a bend, recognising him from my time with Gelden in the Underground when we'd helped build those new homes...

I still didn't know how I felt about that. The time and energy and resources Gerrund and so many others had put into the Underground infrastructure were no longer needed, yet that was a good thing. No one was exiled. No one was trapped anymore. Kaynee and the Dias oversaw a community who called the Underground home. It shouldn't be surprising to see their developers out here or in the Alien City –*South* City. Dez hadn't wanted to call it Augitmein or the Great City the way the Dakturians had. It was our city now. I was so used to referring to it as the Alien City, my brain resisted the new name. It resisted a lot these days.

The closer we got to the temple, the more recognisable the building became – both from my scouting mission all those months ago in search of Dezmind and by the simple signage adopted from the Underground merchants. The ruins had truly become a hub, an epicentre for travel south. Clothing, merchandise, supply shops – you name it, they had it. People milled about the streets, though most stayed under the bright awnings that now made up the roofs along this corridor.

At the temple, a solar recharging rack for sliders modernised the ancient building. I plugged my vehicle in and followed our guide and the others.

I halted in the doorway.

Other than the fountain, which *worked*, people thronged everywhere, and nothing looked the same. The stone benches no longer faced the altar in multiple rows but ranged around the walls – one set with its backs to the wall, the other set facing it. Citizens lounged in the cool interior, reading, crafting, and chatting. The altar now acted as a service desk.

Voices came at me from every direction. Too many people shifted and moved for me to keep track of them with any level of accuracy. Gellik and Kye were halfway across the room and had passed several other stone desks where guides checked in and visitors checked out.

I forced myself to put one foot in front of the other, catching snatches of conversations about route updates, Henith herds, and news from both the north and the south.

I couldn't prioritise.

I couldn't focus.

My breathing quickened and my palms grew moist. My gaze flicked to each upper corner as my brain unearthed memories of creatures that used to make this place their home, layering even more information amongst everything else.

"Please take a moment to register your business and your stay. I'll wait for you by the door," our guide said and disappeared. My gaze tracked her as she sliced back through the room and out into the open air. The man behind the altar-desk looked up. A smile lit his face when he saw me. My heart jumped and my mind cleared. No cobwebs blocked this memory.

"So, the rumours are true," Laiviis said. "You've come back."

Gellik and Kye stepped aside and looked from the head guide to me and back.

"Laiviis, it's been too long. Please tell me you're keeping out of trouble," I said, forcing my voice not to waver or crack. I grabbed his extended hand and brought him into an awkward hug across the stone table. His eyes widened in surprise. I hadn't intended to hug him, but after everything, his friendly face did wonders for my soul.

"I try, but you know me."

We shared a laugh. Mine didn't quite mask my brush with hysteria.

"Let me introduce you to Professor Gellik and Reporter Kyler Zide with Network News Now. The guards at the gate mentioned you'd received word of our trip?"

"Yes. Gelden contacted us before taking a leave of absence. It's a marvel, really. We're still working on getting our array and com station fully operational, but it does allow us to receive a digital signal from the new satellite once a night. Usually around twilight." He slid a clipboard and pen over to me. "I just need you to sign in to register your party, and then we'll get you set up with a temporary residence."

I smiled down at the clipboard, the paper actually. Nearly everything in the north worked digitally these days, and the south utilised the Dakturian traditions of metal tablets and books. But, here in the Deserts, they embraced the ancient ways. All of my original notes on the Deserts had been written in paper notebooks, just as my father's had. I blinked back a wave of emotion as I filled in the details of our travel plans. The sudden quiet drew my attention back to the incessant hum. I slid the form over to Gellik to sign and wiggled my finger in my ear.

"It's the buzzing, isn't it?" Laiviis asked.

"You hear it, too?"

He looked at my travelling companions. "What about you guys?"

"I think so."

"Sort of."

"What is it?" I asked, looking around for the source. I wasn't surprised the sound was louder for me – my Talian genetics at work.

"The Frequency Emitter on the roof. It keeps the crawlies away."

"Does it, now? What is it? A digital signal? That would be hard to keep working with the sand and static storms that come through here."

"Yeah, but we also have smaller mechanical units spaced throughout the city and an entire crew dedicated to making sure they keep working. I've seen first-hand what those creatures can do to someone." He absently rubbed his chest. "The Painted Corridor has been incident free for over a month."

"Painted Corridor? Is that the line of colourful roofs bisecting the city?" Gellik asked, passing the clipboard over to Kye.

"That's right. If you decide to go exploring, you're safe inside the Corridor. If you plan on going outside the range of the stationary FEs, you'll need to sign out a personal emitter. It won't stop them from chasing you, but it will slow them down until you can get back to a safe zone."

"So, in other words, don't go wandering off," Kye said, handing Laiviis the clipboard as he looked around. He reminded me so much of Zaith. Not physically. They couldn't be more opposite. No, I could practically see his mind whirring with possibility.

"Before Vitine shows you where you'll be staying" —he waved a nearby guide over to us, away from her station— "you'll need to go over the rules. This is my second-in-command."

"Hello, everyone."

I recognised her, too. Another of the original crew of guides I'd trained months ago before sending Bazdin south to find his fiancé. "You're Robin, right?"

"Robin Leigh, yes. It's nice to see you again, Jutaya."

She never forgave me for using Laiviis as bait during our fake Deserts training down in the tunnels. He wouldn't have become half the guide he was without it, but I couldn't expect everyone to understand my tactics.

"She'll take care of you. We're in mid-transition. I'm expected back at Headquarters. Everyone cycles out after a week," Laiviis said.

"Everyone?" I asked.

"It's the buzzing from the EFs. The workers cycle south and the guides mostly cycle north unless they're on a run."

He smiled and then shifted over to speak to a small group of Citizens who waited behind us. I hadn't even noticed their arrival. Not good.

Robin Leigh escorted us to her desk and went over the basics: where to get water and verrin, where to get a complimentary meal or purchase delicacies from one of the local shopkeepers, how to dispose of garbage, what to do if we see a creature, how to use the com array (when it was working), and when to sign out, among other things.

"Everything is listed in a small laminated booklet in your suite. You might want to review it before you decide what to do next. Enjoy your stay." She waved over our personal guide. As we stood to meet Vitine and crossed the floor toward her, my body sagged and my energy drained faster than expected. Since I'd started training with Tek, these moments of extreme fatigue pulled at me – yet another sign that I wasn't the same person anymore. I was Dez's Plan B, but I was also the All Mother's Plan A. The fate of the world sat on my shoulders. I needed sleep, but when the suns set and we woke for the second stretch of our journey, I wouldn't be any closer to breaking free of the damage done to me. It was time for Plan C.

After Vitine showed us our huts and the main cafeteria, I grabbed my side satchel, slipped out the back window, picked up some food, and backtracked over to Gellik's place. I knocked on the door, hoping Kye was focused on getting settled and was not, in fact, spying on us.

The professor opened the door, and I held up two plastic containers.

"Care for some dinner before your nap?" I asked.

"That would be lovely. I was also hoping to go for a short walk with – Kye!"

I looked over my shoulder and tried to keep from giving him a death stare.

"Hey, Professor, Jutaya. Ready for that walk?"

"Taya and I are going to have dinner together. Why don't you swing by in twenty—"

"Forty minutes," I corrected. Professor Gellik gave me a quizzical look but nodded.

"A bite to eat sounds good. I'll see if I can get a few interviews while I'm at it."

"Good plan," I said and closed the door on him before he even had a chance to leave.

"Taya, what's going on? I get the feeling this is more than just dinner. Forty minutes?"

I set the meals on the small table and dug a number of papers, as well as my travel utensils, from my bag. Gellik grabbed his own from his pack and we sat down.

"I had hoped that we could go over the scope of the project before arriving." I popped the lid off my meal and breathed in its steamy goodness – so much better than travel rations. "I had no idea Kye was coming with us."

"And you knew I would?"

"No, that's not what I meant. I actually figured I'd be travelling alone after the way our conversation ended. I hoped you'd come, but when I hadn't heard anything before it was time to catch a transport out to the Expanse, I resigned myself to the inevitable. I packed these because I'd need them, regardless. They're the notes Professor Elix and I made over the last two weeks."

I scooped a mouthful of food and spread notes and images out on the table between us. I didn't want to rush, but the more I explained our theories and discoveries, the better I felt. In fact, Kye gave us over an hour before he returned. By then, the professor and I had even started bouncing ideas around about the modified battery core installation.

As the two men set out to explore the Ancient City, I collected all the notes and placed them back in the satchel. When they were well down the crooked path, I tucked the bag between Gellik's pack and the back of the bench before heading to my hut for a quick nap.

* * *

Taya

Six hours later, I snuck out again, only this time Alpha had set and Zerameteth chased Zita across the sky. I peered into Kye's, and then Gellik's, back window – both men slept in anticipation of tonight's travels. *Good.*

I skirted the back alleys behind the Painted Corridor, doing my best not to travel too far from the safe zone. Still, as I maneuvered over rubble and around unused buildings, the hum of the FEs wavered in and out. I spotted the large cocoons nestled into semi-sheltered overhangs and protected corners, harbouring the *critters*, as Laiviis called them. Nothing stirred. For once, the gods were on my side.

The watch at the main entrance lounged against the side of the garage. I crouched on the far side, listening for any noise from inside. Nothing. My heartbeat tripled as I slipped around the corner and into the shady interior. I let my eyes adjust and scanned the space, focused on my task. The two-seater Desert Vehicles were nestled in this bay. I slunk over to the one at the front and placed my pack on the back holder.

"Going somewhere?" Laiviis asked.

I jumped and whipped around. "What?"

He peeled himself from the shadows in the back corner. His grey guide garments materialised with the sound of his voice. *I shouldn't have missed that. Why did I miss that?* My gaze darted around even as I stood frozen. Caught. I'd been too focused on the D.V.s and not enough on the shadows. But why was Laiviis here? Why was he hiding?

"What are you doing, Taya?"

"Scouting ahead."

"No, you're not. You'd be at the south gate."

"I thought the only vehicles at the south gate would be the outgoing ones. I didn't want to take the Cara—"

"Stop."

"Stop what?"

"Lying."

Part of me wanted to jam my fists on my hips and rip him a new one. Another part of me just wanted to curl up and cry. I didn't do either. I hadn't anticipated this outcome. I hadn't planned for this variable. I was useless. My shoulders drooped and I hugged myself.

"I'm leaving. Vitine or one of your other guides can bring them the rest of the way. I'm going home." I turned away from him and straddled the Desert Vehicle. Laiviis moved in front and blocked me.

"Why? I don't understand. Gelden said the Kronik

assigned you this task. That you agreed to work on the south project. Why are you abandoning your mission?"

I felt the blood drain from my face, but I doubted he noticed in the dim interior. I swallowed past the constant grit in my mouth. "It doesn't matter. I just am."

I released the kickstand and pushed the D.V. forward. Laiviis straddled the massive front tire and gripped the handlebars. I scowled at him.

"Shall I let Gelden know about the change in plans? What about the Kronik? Will he be pleased to see you back so soon?"

I doubted it. But I wasn't really going home. Not right away. I was going to the Underground. Talk to Jak, train with Tek, work on becoming whole again. Not be thousands of miles away from the man who'd promised a future with me and had yet to keep that promise.

"Taya, this isn't you."

"Who says it isn't? A helluva lot has happened to me since our training. Everyone keeps telling me I'm still the same person. How would they know? I certainly don't feel the same."

"What are you talking about? I don't understand."

"No, you don't. You don't have all the facts and even those people who do, label me. I don't want to be here. I don't need to be here. Professor Gellik knows the scope of the project now. He and Gerrund can figure the rest out."

"So, you'd rather be a quitter than a fighter. It doesn't matter if you're not the same fighter you used to be. You don't abandon people for selfish reasons regardless if you're different or not."

I blinked as flashes of memory overwhelmed my brain: Dez, preaching about taking a Kahn-Lea into the Deserts and me firing a warning shot at the Rally; him, threatening to lead innocent Commoners into the Deserts with or without my help; me, challenging to leave him stranded but unable to; leaving the Kahn-Lea to run the generator so I could warn Dez; building the D.V. with Gelden; training the guides… dying for the Cause.

"I can't do it anymore," I whispered.

"Says who? How much work have you put into this project already? I know about the timeline, Taya. Do you honestly believe your professor is capable of getting that spaceship up and running in a month?" He pushed off from the handlebars, walked around, took my hands in his and, after I kicked the stand back into place, led me off the D.V. "Remember, you're not alone."

I wanted to fall into his arms bawling, but instead, I swallowed the fear. I swallowed the bitterness. I swallowed my selfishness and nodded.

Chapter 32

The Queen

Taya

That evening, everything went according to plan – just not my plan. Laiviis headed north after our encounter, and I admitted to myself he was right: I was being selfish. I had a job to do. So, south we went.

The next morning, as we stood gawking at the giant WELCOME sign high overhead on the outskirts of South City, Gellik and Kye fussed over its engineering and design. My eyes didn't focus on the patinaed welds and patchwork puzzle of riveted panels. Instead, I saw myself standing on the boulder at the head of the path, giving the speech Dez should have given and leaving the Kahn-Lea in the hands of a supposedly reformed assassin.

"Hello! Jutaya!" The familiar voice dragged me back to the present. A woman waved as she walked along the pebble path beneath the sparse canopy of trees. The dappled light of Zita's first rays traced shadows over her already dark features.

When did I start thinking of the suns by their Guardian names? I shook the thought from my head and squinted. It could have been Zaith's self-assured stride and wild hair approaching, but the nanosecond of ignorant joy soured. Zaith was dead. What did I care for a spy? A traitor? I pushed past the memory. Found Tek's reassuring presence in my mind and a smile.

"Lutrice! What are you doing all the way out here?" I asked.

She laughed. "Oh, lady, are you in for a surprise. *Out here* is not so far from civilization as it used to be." She walked right up and gave me a hug. Since when had I become a huggy person? Usually, people found me too prickly. Professor Gellik grinned at my shocked expression. I hugged her back.

"So"—she pulled away and opened her arms wide— "who have we here? The General said to expect you but didn't elaborate on details."

"Oh, right. Lutrice, this is Professor Gellik, head of sciences at the CTF. He's agreed to help with the spacecraft." Her gaze flickered a moment. "And this is Kyler. He's with Network News Now."

"Here to document our discovery, are you?"

"Yes, ma'am," Kye said, stepping forward and offering his hand.

"Please, call me Lu. Everyone does."

"It's a pleasure to meet you." Professor Gellik also shook her hand.

Voices filtered through the trees down the path. Lu

caught me glancing up the way.

"That'd be our Runners. They'll collect your things from the Caravan and return with them in a few hours." For a moment, the joy drained from her face. "Did you bring anything for us? Any verrin? I know there's a situation and all—"

I placed my hand on her arm to reassure her. "Yes. Half the D.V. is loaded with kegs. Gelden asked me to tell you that another full transport will be here in less than a week – with more migrators."

Lu motioned with her head toward the growing voices on the path. I shifted the weight of my pack and walked beside her as we headed toward Central Commons.

"More UGC?" she asked.

"Yes, as far as I know. I think he mentioned something about extended family members and a few guides to switch shifts. Why? Are you running out of room?"

"Goodness, no! I just hoped the Kronik had received my message, that's all." She smiled, but it didn't reach her eyes. Something was amiss here. I didn't push.

Eight youths and four all-terrain carts with cargo straps materialised ahead. Gellik, Kye, and I skirted around them but Lu allowed herself to be pulled into their midst.

"Hey, Mamma Lu!" the guys and girls shouted in casual greeting. Some high-fived her, others just touched hands briefly, but she connected with each one of them as they laughed and teased. The joy radiated from Lu as she rejoined our little band, her gait now matching that of the youths – easygoing and relaxed, as if this had always been their home.

"How many citizens live in the south now?" Gellik asked as he took in the greenery.

The air grew heavier the tighter the canopy became, almost as if the rainforest tested me. Knew I'd tried to run from it. I might have promised to return all those months ago when right and wrong had been so clear. In truth, this was the last place on Xannia I wanted to be. Even sailing out to Darius's Island sounded more appealing than coming back to where Dez had left me the first time and everything had fallen apart.

"Registration has us at nearly eight hundred permanent residents and about one hundred temporary ones – workers, guides, visitors and the like."

"I had no idea so many citizens had come south," Gellik said.

"Most used to live in the Underground. Approximately a tenth are families from the main cities – Topside, they call it."

"But not you. You're one of the Kahn-Lea, correct? You came here with the Kronik and Taya looking for the Chronicles."

"That's right. There were ten of us initially. Due to the virus and other duties, we lost a few. We were down to six for a while – nearly drove each other crazy. But when a young girl in our group was reunited with her fiancé, who helped us find a vaccine, people learned about our little colony. Luckily, they don't arrive in groups larger than ten at a time, but as soon as we get one group settled, another arrives."

"Have you thought about setting up an outpost at the

cliff?" I asked.

Lu's frame stiffened. "Yes, the General and I are working on that."

As the first signs of civilization grew, more and more people went about their routines.

"What does everyone do here?" Kye asked, touching his Mini-V recorder on its headband and taking in the dark, metallic alien dwellings. Guide Aelix had been right. Based on the schematics Gerrund photographed and sent via the new satellite com, the homes were made from the fleet of alien ships that had arrived thousands of years ago. And we were on our way to see the last surviving one.

"At first, we took turns getting food and making fabric for clothes and bedding. I work in the clinic and have a small team who help me with the herb and healing gardens. Others monitor the larger general gardens. We have a team who fish and a rotating group to collect the special seaweed we use in the vaccine and for other health experiments. Lately, though, we've set up schools and more libraries, teams of crew members who salvage what they can, and others who are able to build what we need." She sighed.

"The general spends a lot of time at the South Sea watching over the spaceship, the dive teams, and coordinating with the guides and the Kronik. With the com system up, we're monitoring and scheduling time for citizens to talk to those back home, and we're working on expanding a local signal. Come, let me show you the city. You can grab a bite to eat at the Central Commons Market, and then I can bring you to see the General before you settle in. I'm sure the extended trip from the Ancient City has tuckered you out."

Just as I thought I might have overreacted about returning, we walked through a bustling suburb and into the core of the city – the Commons. At first, the small wooden and metal booths surrounding the inner circle where the main fountain sat captivated my attention. They had everything from clothing to smoked and dried meats to artistic figurines made of glass and metal. The long tables we once used for food prep had been converted into fruit and vegetable stands. The people still used the old shops around the Commons as dwellings, but some made use of their large front windows to sell pastries and other sweet treats.

My gaze fell on the end unit to my left. It was exactly as I remembered it, but why?

"Taya, if you'd like to leave your pack here, we can—"

They'd kept it for me. All this time, the Kahn-Lea had expected me to return and saved this prime piece of real estate for me.

I didn't want it.

"What? No, Lutrice."

"Lu."

"Right, of course. Lu. I—" I didn't know what to say. "Uh, please assign it to a merchant. I need to be closer to the work site."

Confusion played over her angular features.

"Thank you, for saving it. For thinking of me. But I can't. I mean, I'd like someone else to have it." This was not my home, and the memories of Zaith and me bunking together, trying to pretend we were still friends after everything that had happened… it was too much.

I hadn't realised my body shook until the professor stood shoulder-to-shoulder with me, his presence the brick wall I needed in order to remain standing.

Lu nodded, then gestured toward the fruit and veggie stands. "We take turns collecting food each day. Everyone is entitled to their own share. If someone wants more, they need to leave a sampling of what they make on the table in the middle for anyone to choose in place of raw goods. We work on a barter system right now. We're considering developing our own currency, but so far, this is working."

"Mamma Lu!" someone across the Commons called.

Lu turned and waved.

"Keera, how are you?"

"Frustrated. Lekka's still at it."

"Really? I spoke with her a couple of days ago. The same white root?"

"Yes. It's not fair for the rest of us. I told her I'd take it to the General if she didn't stop."

"No need to be hasty, now. Let me talk to her again, and if I think it warranted, I'll go to the General. Okay?"

Keera nodded, then her gaze flickered over us as if she'd just realised Lu had been in the middle of something. Lu turned to us.

"Would you excuse me for a moment? Feel free to grab a snack or pick up a few items for lunch and dinner later. At the very least, you can trade the raws for something pre-cooked if you'd like. There's a tally sheet on the far booth. Just add your names and mark down what you take." She hurried away, Keera following.

We wandered over to check out the selection.

* * *

Taya

It took over an hour to walk to the beach site. Mamma Lu, as she seemed to be commonly called, took us on a meandering path, pointing out the cloth factory, libraries, clinics, and a whole host of other businesses that came with the necessity of supporting hundreds of people. I didn't see any temples, but that didn't mean they weren't there.

The last large building we passed before the homes went from spaced out to non-existent housed the vaccine lab, research centre and clinic.

"What are you researching?" Professor Gellik asked as we caught sight of a slice of cerulean blue on the horizon.

Lu paused as if contemplating just how much to reveal. This wasn't like her – at least, not like the woman she'd become in the last half year since the Kahn-Lea's arrival.

"A verrin supplement."

"Oh." Both Gellik and Kye perked up. I did, too, but not noticeably. This *was* news.

"Have you discovered anything?" Gellik asked.

"Nothing concrete. We've isolated the chemical make-up of verrin – nothing outstanding there, that's what the Kronik did in order to create the concentrated sludge we used on the quest for the Chronicles. We're looking at how it bonds to water particles and if, perhaps, there's something in that bonding agent key to finding a way to bio-replicate it rather than synthetically produce it."

"Wow. You have the capacity for that kind of research

down here?" Kye asked. The green light on his Mini-V blinked. Mamma Lu noticed it and gave a full, welcoming smile.

"The Dakturians were an advanced species. We're utilising their facilities. Since their buildings, and much of their equipment, are made of a resilient metallic structure, we just had to sanitize our workspace and supplement with items from the North. Many of the citizens now living down here have scientific backgrounds."

And I knew one of them: Tamaine's fiancé, Bazdin. *I wonder if they ever got married?*

"We've made interesting discoveries regarding the marrow-weed used in the Dakturian Vaccine," she said.

"Do you think you'll find a way to recreate verrin?"

"I don't know. But we'd be insane to ignore the verrin shortage. It's imperative we stop the alien terraforming, otherwise, we may not live long enough to reap the fruits of our labour regarding this research."

I smiled at her and she winked back. Lutrice had been a government population analyst before getting stranded in the south – she and Deltek, her husband, both were. She knew how to work the system. No other familiar faces were around. I supposed I shouldn't be surprised with over eight hundred people living and working there. Still, it seemed odd.

We passed some kind of invisible threshold around a bend in the trees, and, like magic, our quiet tour exploded with the bustle of business at the South Sea Cove. A din of voices and machinery echoed rush-hour traffic back in the Prime. I clapped my hands over my ears and waited for my senses to adjust as we walked along a boardwalk skirting the divide between grass and sand.

A stationary crane sat rooted to a dock across from the broken rock pedestal Elix and I had seen countless pictures of. Several rowboats bobbed on either side of a narrower dock nearby with two other empty docks. I gazed out to sea and spotted a couple of them working together to cast a net and catch fish the old-fashioned way.

A holler from up high pulled my attention back to land and toward a lookout tower as tall as the trees. In fact, it was made up of three of the taller trees on the beach line. The rest was a wooden structure that reminded me of scaffolding. The only walls were at the top, and those were giant cloth sheets pulled taut and tied in place. Large leaves covered the roof. On the platform immediately below the treehouse stood a large metal table, its base made up of drawers like a filing cabinet. Rocks littered its surface. I could only imagine their purpose. The large sheets on this level were tied back against the posts, as were the ones on the next level down, which held a number of chairs and small bistro-like tables. One long table held jugs and bins of prepared foods. Two people worked on filling the bins.

The real feat of engineering here wasn't the tower, but the lift system. The cage of thin trees enclosed a platform that could easily hold four people. Maybe six. It worked on a self-pulling winch system so that whoever rode had to help pull on the rope to raise and lower the elevator.

Behind the tower base a long, roofed structure acted as the hub of the beach. Mamma Lu led us toward it. We gawked at the multitude of men and women in dive gear or fishing outfits as they brought their haul into the open-fronted building for collection, separation, and, in the case of the fish, cleaning. As I glanced past the last processing stall, I gasped. Gellik and Kye whipped their heads around and followed my gaze.

There, nestled in the sand, just past the dock with the crane as the beach curved away from the main cove, sat a gleaming masterpiece of engineering.

"Dear gods, it's gorgeous," I whispered, slowing my steps to take it all in.

The spaceship was the size of a single-storey house and anything but boxy. Its curved body rivalled the best hover racers in the Prime and simply screamed *blast off.*

Chapter 33
The King

Taya

"This is as far as I go," Mamma Lu said, hands planted on her hips.

I blinked to try to clear my head, so full of the possibilities of that technological marvel, and turned to look at her. "What? Why?"

Out of nowhere, four soldiers with short metal staffs surrounded us. Instinct kicked in. I shoved Lu between Gellik and Kye, then disarmed two of the men.

"Taya! Stop! It's okay!"

I froze, the third staff held between me and a Matin guard as the Metek guard stepped back and shouted for reinforcements.

"Don't move." The lead soldier's eyes narrowed, pinching his gold coliths.

"Oh, for the love of Zola, Erik. It's just me. I told you I'd be by with the delegation."

"Apologies, Mamma Lu. Protocol. General's orders."

Lu placed a gentle hand on my shoulder. "It's okay, Taya. Stand down."

Confusion crept in... *Why soldiers? Why guards? What protocol?*

"You can let go of the staff," she said.

I did.

The guy stepped back to join his partner as Gerrund jogged over and six more guards converged on us. Gerrund signalled for two of them to remove the ones lying unconscious on the ground between us, then waved away the others. Without hesitation, they disappeared back into the working throng. This time, though, I caught snatches of the green and brown of their basic uniform. Nearby gawkers also melted away, but no one had come within ten feet of our party.

"Well, that was quite the entrance. I don't think you'll live that one down anytime soon." He smiled, but I didn't believe it. The old edge clung to his voice. I'd hoped it would disappear once he'd moved out here – so much for wishful thinking. My heart still hammered in my chest as I willed my brain to catch up with the moment.

"What the hell was that, Gerrund?" I asked, finally wrapping my head around the confrontation.

"A precautionary measure."

"For what?"

He looked from Mamma Lu to me. Lu shrugged and cocked her head as if waiting to hear his answer. The look on her face told me she already knew and didn't agree with it. I was starting to see a pattern here.

"An attempt was made to sabotage the spacecraft."

"Says you." Lu crossed her arms over her chest. "They told you they were curious about the ship, but you wouldn't let them see it. Just because someone is curious doesn't mean they're dangerous or trying to sabotage something."

"Just because we're living topside now doesn't mean the rules go out the window."

"If you would bother to explain to people why—"

"I shouldn't have to. I never had to before. We had a system. It isn't broken. They made the choice to ignore the rules. They pay the price. We placed the ship under our protection."

Lu heaved her arms up and waved Gerrund off. She turned to leave. "Let me know if you need anything. I'm staying beside Merik's Library back at the Commons." She disappeared into the crowd of workers.

Gellik and Kye glanced from me to Gerrund, looking as confused as I felt. I decided to start over.

"General Kipling, I'd like to introduce you to Professor Gellik and Reporter Kyler Zide."

Gellik held out his hand and Gerrund grasped it. "Call me General, everyone does." He shook Kye's hand, too. "A reporter? Dez— the Kronik mentioned something about that. We'll have to go over some ground rules."

So, even Gerrund slipped up and called him Dezmind from time-to-time. Probably said it to his face often enough that the formal moniker never stuck. I understood who he'd become, but for me, he would always be Dezmind, that pain-in-the-ass Talian with a death wish. Then Gerrund's words clicked in my head.

"What do you mean, *rules*?" I asked.

He inclined his head toward the spaceship, and together, we walked over to it. Kye and the professor followed.

"No society can function without rules. You know that. Many of them are unspoken: don't steal, don't kill, try not to be a jerk."

"Right, but something tells me this is more." I wanted to ask him what was going on between him and Lu but now wasn't the time.

"Unfortunately, that last rule has needed clarification more than once since I arrived with the first group of citizens. At first, everyone helped out and did what they could, but soon, curiosity overpowered common sense. People would disappear for hours or days at a time, exploring. Lu got worried and would send out search teams. Large animals live around here and poisonous plants grow everywhere. We couldn't allow people to wander off. Others would hoard food instead of sharing. Lu is big on the whole communal experience, not realising that everything had been taken from these people, and life in the Underground worked on barter and trade."

"Looks like you've successfully blended the two practices. At least based on what I saw in the Commons."

"Today must be a good day, then. The point is, not everyone felt inclined to help with all projects. Certain people were more willing than others to perform tasks involving greater risks and felt they ought to get compensated for it. Including Lu's people."

"I don't understand. What do you mean *greater risks*?"

"Not everyone can hunt the larger game. Those animals

get kinda mad when you don't kill them right away. Then there's the team who collect the marrow-weed used in the vaccine. Before we had dive suits, they risked sodium shock. When we found the spaceship, people started forgetting that Dezmind was the new Kronik. They reverted to their old suspicions, and people without access to the ship are trying to break in. You'll notice a fair amount of damage to one of the panels just inside the main door. Might be nothing, might be the interstellar life support system. What do I know? That's why you're here. Still, those unspoken rules no longer seem to apply to those people."

"So, you've had to lay down the law."

"And enforce it."

"Oh, what is wrong with people?" I sighed. "Have you reminded them who Dez is? How he's different from the old Kronik? Why we need to fix, not destroy, this spaceship?"

"Not everyone believes that Gamma is a fake sun."

"What?"

"Or that we're running out of verrin because of terraforming."

"You can't be serious? Then why are they here?"

"Ah, the Big Question."

"And?"

"To live topside as far away from anything to do with *any* Kronik as possible. Doesn't matter if he's a nice guy or if they've met him before. Anything he says or does is suspect, and people will remain suspicious of the position regardless of the man."

I decided to test the waters.

"But Lu doesn't see it?"

"Lu only sees the good in people. She thinks I'm being heavy-handed."

"And you think she's being too soft?"

He didn't answer me, but he didn't have to. They both wanted the best for this new society. They just had trouble seeing eye-to-eye.

The closer we got to the alien spaceship, the more imposing it became. Ten feet from its curved hull, I stopped. The others did, too. We stood shoulder-to-shoulder for a long time, staring at the last piece of truly alien tech left behind.

The large raised and lowered panels were etched similar to the metallic orb of the Chronicles. I shifted to touch it but stopped myself.

"Go ahead," Gerrund said. A gentle playfulness teased at the edge of his voice, something I hadn't heard since the day I woke up in the Underground hospital after calling him Spark Bug. Maybe a bit of the man who'd saved my life still rattled around inside the hard exterior he'd crafted into "The General".

I moved the few remaining steps forward. My fingers hovered over the metal sheathing, its skin. The heat radiated off the hull as my fingertips made first contact.

Chapter 34

Fool Proof

Jezetek

"Yes," I said over the coms for the fifth time, "I'm certain. We've got the right place. We're in position." A street lamp flickered in the distance.

"We can't afford any mistakes," Dezmind's voice rumbled through my ear-piece.

"I know. Trust me." I wanted to check the power cartridge on the laser gun one last time, but I didn't. It was just nerves. These weapons hadn't been in operational use since the Nine Seas Massacre, but Dezmind insisted we use them. No more mistakes. This ended here. Tonight.

"Going radio silent. Mark." I nodded to my team in the dim light of the lamp affixed to the side of the building. Two agents dashed left and two dashed right. The remaining three followed me up the steps and into the front door of the engineering building. No one had wanted to believe that a respected member of the Kronik's team had been a mole, but after Professor Elix's assassination, everything fell into place. However, that also meant that the Faction now needed a new base of operations and would be on the move.

Red Team unlocked the double doors and dispersed into the halls of the main floor. I led Blue Team downstairs, activating my night vision goggles. The forms and figures took on a pale green glow. Several doors lined the main hall, but it didn't make sense for a hidden base to be behind any of them. Still, SO Kellum and I cleared every room just in case. The location in question presented itself when we studied the blueprint layout of the building and discovered a crosshatched section in the original plans that didn't transfer over to the final ones.

A bunker. There but not there.

Kellum and I cleared the last two smaller labs at the end of the hall and met in the corridor between them. I motioned with hand signals to move forward with the plan. We each disappeared back into the two labs. I moved around the drafting tables and desks to the back concrete wall and changed the setting on my goggles to thermal.

And there it was: a perfect rectangular outline around a hidden door where the warmth bled through. *Now, to open it...*

The transmitter on my utility belt vibrated. I sent the same signal back. Kellum was ready. I marked the edge of the door in bio-luminescent marker, changed my goggles back to infrared, and pulled my oxygen mask up over my mouth and nose. The sound of my breath rasped in my ears as I placed the casing charges on the four corners.

My transmitter vibrated again. I returned the signal and activated the charges.

Four silent puffs of smoke oozed through the angular cracks, forcing the knock-out gas into the chamber beyond. I took three steps back and raised my gun, straining to hear anything. The beat of my heart ticked off the seconds and then the minutes.

Stay still. Hold your position.

I knew they were in there. Their trackers didn't lie.

The wall shifted out. Lens flare from the bright light forced my goggles to switch to standard mode. The nanosecond hesitation was enough to let three targets through before I could take aim. I fired.

One down.

Two down.

Underlings.

I whipped around and fired, blasting a fist-size hole in the concrete block beside his head. I didn't think the stun setting was supposed to do that...

I glanced at the Faction members, unmoving on the floor. I couldn't afford a split focus. *Stick to the plan!* I ran after my mark, joining Kellum in the hall.

"One!" he shouted.

"One plus one!" I amended.

We each chased our mark, our footsteps echoing in the stairwell. Red Team fell in with us on the main floor.

"This way!" Red Leader called. The marks separated into different offices and smashed out the windows.

"Green Team. Converge on targets," I said over the coms, then dove out the window into a tumble and back on my feet. Green Team took out one guy before he disappeared into the neighbouring housing complex. Kellum and I dogged the last man, deking in and around houses, riders, and fences. Two spotlights pierced the depth of night as Gamma set. The hum and buzz of a crowd filtered between the houses. Kellum slowed and fired a volley of blasts, narrowly missing our mark.

I sped past him, holstering my gun across my back as I followed the slippery bastard into the midst of a solstice celebration. I scrambled to keep up with him, pushing past citizens dressed in yellow and Guardians robed in white. As I passed the front of the temple by the two strobe spotlights, our man was gone and so was his tracking beacon.

No one I asked could tell me anything about the soldier I chased. No one wanted to.

Chapter 35
Work

Taya

The next morning, Gellik and I stood in the middle of the cavernous energy room after a complete tour of the spaceship, led by none other than the General. I planted my hands on my hips just as the professor crossed his arms. Kye hovered by the door to the antechamber.

"Get lost now, Kye," I said, not even looking at him.

"But I'm supposed to—"

"What are you going to do? Take pictures or record me and the professor staring at the walls? We need to work. Go explore the rest of the city. Check in with us at dinner."

"Oh, all right." He hurried off, his hiking boots echoing along the metal corridors.

Gellik chuckled and shook his head.

"What?" I asked, opening my arms and shrugging.

"You treat him like an unwanted pet. Watch out, he might grow on you."

"Not likely." I stared at the mostly smooth chamber and noticed a pattern of indentations on the ceiling, concave walls, and floor – the same ones Professor Elix and I had seen in the pictures Gerrund had taken. Whatever device the Dakturians had used to power this craft was long gone, but clearly, it connected to these ports.

"Shall we bring in the ion charger?" Gellik asked, his gaze following mine around the chamber.

"Yeah, let's grab it and see what we can rig together."

It didn't take long to get back to the main corridor that looped the ship. The Dakturians were a tall people, so it was actually quite spacious. Outside, a red glow from Zola highlighted the entrance/exit. Gellik and I walked down the ramp that also acted as the air-tight hatch to the ship. Mama Lu's Runners had brought all our supplies to the beach and set them up under a new tent canopy. I grabbed a couple of pry-bars from the supply Gerrund had left and handed one to Gellik.

The long crate held the oversized Whipstaff Elix and I had engineered into a giant ion battery. I jammed the end of my crowbar into the wooden box and heaved. The planks whined as the nails pulled away. I worked around one side and Gellik the other. It didn't take long for a light sweat to moisten my forehead. The humidity in the south made even the simplest task an effort.

With a final snap, the lid popped up, and we pushed it off a box large enough to hold a person. We shifted a layer of straw from the top and unwrapped the giant cylinder.

"Ready?"

Gellik nodded.

"On three. One, two, three, lift."

It went up and then his end went right back down. I lowered my end, too.

"Everything okay, Professor?"

Before he could respond, a diver in full bubble-fish gear walked over carrying his flippers. The diver pushed down his mask and let it hang. "Need a hand?"

His pale blue skin took on a darker hue next to the charcoal-hued diving suit, but I'd recognise those intense eyes anywhere. "Bazdin? You're a diver?"

He smiled and set his flippers and gloves down on a pile of smaller crates, then held out his hand. I took it without hesitation. He'd been a royal thorn in my side four months ago when I went topside with my first mission – almost cost me my reputation. But he was a good guy. Laiviis had made sure Bazdin arrived here safe and sound.

"How's Tamaine doing?" I asked.

"She's good. We're married now." He grinned like a fool.

I couldn't help but laugh. "Looks like you finally got your wish."

"We make our own fortune, right? I wasn't about to let her slip away."

My smile faltered. His words opened fresh wounds of my own.

"I don't mean to intrude, but I noticed…"

"Professor Gellik." Gellik held out his hand in greeting.

"Do you need some help?" Bazdin indicated the cylinder.

"That would be much appreciated, young man."

"Do you have time?" I asked.

"Yeah. My shift is up. I won't have another for a couple of days, and I'm not due at the lab until later. Come on, let's get this thing mobile."

Without even waiting for a count, he reached down and grabbed hold of Gellik's end. I followed suit, and we hefted the energy cylinder up out of the crate.

"Follow me inside." I walked backwards, marking where I was in relation to the craft for future reference. At least my basic sensory perception still worked. Tek would chide me and tell me everything still worked, just differently. Bazdin gave a strained smile and a curt nod, the weight pulling most of our concentration. A tiny part of me noticed the small crowd gathered to watch us, but the second we were on board I forgot about it.

Maneuvering through the ship was relatively straightforward, only the access portals were a bit tricky. With a bit of leverage, we managed to get through them just fine and set the ion cylinder down in the middle of the energy room. The professor shuffled in behind with a cloth bag full of wires and connectors.

"Thanks, Bazdin. We'll take it from here." I turned toward Gellik but Bazdin didn't leave. As I crouched down beside the professor, I looked up at Bazdin and raised my eyebrows as if questioning him.

"Are you sure you don't want me to stick around? Just in case?"

I smiled. "I think we'll be fine today. I'll track you down if we need your help again."

Gellik spread the connectors out between us on the floor. I took a cursory glance at the ends of each one before moving over to one of the inset ports around the room. Gellik followed. I tugged at the edge of the rectangular piece of metal no bigger than my hand. Nothing happened. Gellik pushed at it and it slid inside the wall. A three-pronged multi-phasic port stared back at me. Nothing we had would work. I didn't really expect it to be that easy, but you need to start by eliminating the simplest answer.

"Let me get the toolkit. We've gotta open this thing up." I rose and walked back out, admiring the beauty in the alien engineering, hoping I hadn't made a promise I couldn't keep.

* * *

Taya

My stomach growled, reminding me that choosing not to have breakfast meant skipping lunch wasn't on the menu today. I popped open the last port and disconnected the receiver from the wires behind. Nothing strange about their appearance. They didn't operate on stardust or blood. They'd take an electrical current, but I wasn't sure what kind: AC or DC.

"What do you think?" I asked Gellik, letting my eighth batch of wires hang down from the wall. I spun around on my ass to face him over the energy cylinder. He wiped his hands on his pant legs and turned on his knees.

"Well, we essentially have a giant battery sitting here. Let's run with DC and see what happens."

"Is there any way we can figure this out without risking an explosion?"

He laughed. "I think we're well beyond that. Nothing

else is strong enough. You said yourself that we'd be lucky to get a handful of systems operational on this run. It's not like we could do this on a smaller scale with your side-arm."

I sighed. "Yeah, that's what I figured, too. All right, let's do this." Gellik and I each grabbed eight cords, the ends already stripped back to reveal the wires. We systemically twisted together and then soldered the Dakturian wiring to the Xannian wiring. My gut groaned and gurgled.

"Do you want to take a break?" Gellik asked?

"No. I'll eat later."

I focused on the task at hand, careful not to melt away the connections, just reinforce their stability. I sucked in a heavy breath. Gerrund had warned it got hot in here mid-day. I wanted to get this done before—

"Hey, guys! I brought lunch," Kye called.

I nearly jumped out of my skin. "Kye! Get lost."

"I think what Taya means is thank you for thinking of us, but please wait outside."

"Oh, uh, right. Sorry about that. I'll just—"

"Now, Kye." I pointed my soldering gun at him, and he disappeared back the way he'd come.

"Go easy on him, Taya. He's just trying to make himself useful."

"I don't care what he's *trying* to do. He's throwing me off. There. That's the last one. How about you?"

"Another minute."

I put my tools away and collected all the rejected wire ends and stripped housing as Gellik finished up. I moved slowly and inhaled deep, heavy breaths. When Gellik joined me by the toolbox, a sheen of sweat glistened over his face and upper body. He'd ditched his sleeveless shirt an hour ago. I wore my bra. The groin area on both our shorts looked like we'd wet ourselves.

"Maybe we should wait?" He wiped a damp arm across his already wet forehead. "This humidity probably isn't good for the device."

"It should be fine. We tested it back home."

He stretched his neck and then raised his arms above his head with his hands clasped and straightened his back. Several vertebrae popped.

"Okay then, have at it," he said.

I wiped my hands on my shorts and moved over to the activation switch.

"Here goes nothing."

I gulped in a thick breath, licked my salty lips, and flicked the switch.

Nothing happened.

"Something's not right." Gellik looked from the cylinder to the wall ports nearest him. "Turn it off."

I did, but a heaviness that had nothing to do with the humidity hovered in the air. I allowed my hand to linger over the switch on the cylinder. Heat radiated. A low buzz that reminded me of the FEs in the Ancient City vibrated the base of my neck at the top of my spine. The heat under my hand spread, radiating along the length of the cylinder along with a faint *tick-tick-tick*.

My chest contracted. Everything became overly bright. *That sound.* I tried to analyse the situation. My brain faltered but my heart didn't. *Listen to your body,* Tek had said.

"Run!" I shouted, scrambling around the device to the

door on the far side. Gellik only frowned and took a step back. "Run! Run!"

The ticking increased. The buzz shifted frequency from low to high. I launched into the air, tackling Gellik. The world folded in on itself a nanosecond before the blast launched us out the door.

Heat flared along our bodies as we slammed into the far wall. I went limp, losing hold of the professor. Smoke filled the chamber. I coughed. The fierce jolt brought my senses back. I couldn't see. *Listen.*

Gellik coughed, too. I found his arm, grabbed his hand and forced myself to my knees, dragging him with me toward the hall. My chest tightened and my heart vibrated.

Rhythmic banging echoed throughout the ship, getting louder as the smoke followed us into the corridor.

"There they are!" a man yelled.

Strong hands wrapped around my ribs, lifting me to my feet. I felt the presence of a second person helping Gellik.

"One foot in front of the other," a hoarse but familiar voice said in my ear. I gripped his shoulder tighter, fighting off the urge to take care of Gellik myself. The right side of my body ached from the impact with the wall, and I couldn't stop coughing.

You don't have to do this alone. Jak's voice rang through my head. *Broken doesn't mean useless.*

I certainly felt useless. I tripped over my own feet, but the arm around me kept me upright as I stumbled through the corridors and out into the blinding mid-day light. I squinted, rolling my forehead onto my helper's shoulder.

"Over here, Jutaya," he said, and guided me toward the

lunch table under the fabric canopy where the supplies sat. That voice made my eyes pop open. I looked down at the arm supporting my body. Broad silver coliths wrapped a muscled, moss-green forearm. I only knew one Metek-Glaaon, and we hadn't exactly parted on good terms.

"Raylan?" I rasped, then coughed. He sat me down and passed me a canteen of water. When I looked up from a long pull, I watched my old second-in-command, Syvis, carry the professor out of the spaceship. Gellik didn't move. I grasped Raylan's wrist.

"Gods, what have I done?"

"Don't move." Raylan stood and helped Syvis lower the professor onto the sand. Syvis pulled his sleeveless shirt over his head as Raylan soaked it with water from another canteen. Authoritative shouts carried from somewhere nearby. Then I noticed the ring of shoes surrounding three sides of the tent canopy. I looked up as the crowd parted to let the General through.

"What in the world happened? Is everyone all right?" Gerrund dropped to one knee beside the men as Raylan moved the damp cloth over the professor's face and neck. I leaned forward, hovering on the edge of the seat where I'd been told to stay put. I listened because it was a direct order, because my brain shifted through surfacing logic that fewer bodies surrounding Gellik would help him recover faster.

We hit the wall so hard... My hands shook. I dropped the canteen and rushed to pick it up. My lungs ached as I breathed in the salty, moist air of the South Sea.

I looked at my favourite professor, willing the gods to make sure he was okay. Cursing myself for relying on a myth to save a man's life, I then berated myself for not telling him to wait in the antechamber.

He coughed. The professor sucked in a shuddering breath as the men helped roll him onto his side. Then the General raised his head and glared at me as wisps of smoke wafted from the spaceship.

I shouldn't have come.

Chapter 36
Invitation

Taya

Mamma Lu arrived at the beach a lifetime later, swooping in with her team of healers and scattering the onlookers. My gut twisted as I watched them lift Gellik onto a triage cot and carry him to the forest line. A cart attached to an original-model D.V. waited on the path. I stood to follow them, wavering slightly. Raylan shifted to support my elbow.

"Thank you," I whispered, then realised exactly who was helping me as the General turned and closed the gap. I tensed, not in the mood for a fight.

Raylan stepped between us.

"I'll be escorting Jutaya to the clinic at the research centre to get checked over. I'm sure Mamma Lu will arrange for you to speak with her after lunch. I'll be back shortly for my shift."

"I'll get the gear ready," Syvis called and moved toward

the dive hut. No one went anywhere near the spaceship.

Raylan guided me, by my elbow, away from the General. I didn't look back. I knew what I'd see.

"I'm okay, now," I said.

Raylan relaxed his grip and released my elbow but still kept close. We walked in silence until the canopy overhead afforded a hint of cooling shade. I didn't know what to make of this man. He'd been a thorn in my side the entire journey across the Deserts with the Kahn-Lea six months ago, and yet he'd put himself between me and the General. I gave him a side-glance. The look on Ray's face matched the way he used to look at me. Maybe it *was* meant for me.

"It's that cluster of small huts over there." He pointed down a path beside the research centre and then turned and walked back to the beach. Still a man of few words. The closer I got to the clinic, the more I realised the cluster of huts were interconnected with clear glass walkways. No other Dakturian building I'd been around was made like that, yet I doubted supplies from the north consisted of perfectly formed, curved glass walls. It had to be alien. The main door stated CLINIC in bold, Dakturian text. I ducked inside.

The domed interior felt anything but alien. I stood gawking at art on the walls, a minimalist yet plush sitting area, and a pretty Glaaon girl who worked behind a desk separated by filing cabinets. Then it clicked. White walls. Someone had painted the metal.

"You must be Jutaya." The girl's matching crisp uniform paled her already wash-out pink skin, but her golden coliths gave her a sunny aspect perfect for her position.

"Yes."

"Please, have a seat. Mamma Lu will bring you to see the professor shortly. She and the team are making sure he's stabilised."

"Right. Of course." I gave my head a squeeze with my hands, shook off as much of the panic as possible, and sat down with a long exhale. Pamphlets littered the low round table in the middle of the main grouping of chairs. I only spared them a glance, used to the Cause literature from the Underground. But the Cause didn't exist anymore…

I leaned over and pushed the small booklets around, reading the titles.

Living South.
Sodium Shock Facts.
Getting Vaccinated – Your Health, Your Life.
Dehydration – It Can Happen to You.

What did Gerrund do? Bring his printing press along? I squeezed my eyes shut a moment and leaned back in the chair. My stomach grumbled. *Shut up.* We were so close. *So close! What did I do wrong?* I'd checked every connection. Even if the ship took alternating current, the few seconds the cylinder operated shouldn't have caused a power surge that bad.

What am I missing? My brain fought to make the connections to the material filed away in my head, but with my thoughts spinning in a dozen different directions, nothing made any sense. My pulse raced. I shut my eyes to try to eliminate one source of irrelevant information, but every line of questioning I followed only led to another block.

I growled.

A throat cleared.

I jolted and opened my eyes.

Mamma Lu sat a chair away. "He'll be fine. Don't worry."

Heat rose to my cheeks. I hadn't even been thinking about Gellik. I'd been too focused on what went wrong. Guilt twisted my heart. "Thank the gods."

"You'd better come to his room. He's worried about you. I almost had to strap him down."

"Worried about me?"

"He didn't see you after the explosion."

I stood and she rose with me.

"This way."

She led me down a hall inside the waiting-room dome, past a couple of offices, and into one of the clear corridors. The trees, flowers and bushes in the area crowded around the glass. The warmer air here made it feel like outside was inside.

"I'll talk to the General after lunch. He should be calm by then. Well, calmer." She glanced over her shoulder at me and winked.

I tried to smile, but even such a simple act was hard with fractals of information replicating and then competing for attention in my head.

"I'll tell him you'll assess the damage in the morning. He'll demand tonight, then I'll relent and settle on dawn. So, be ready for dawn."

We passed into the next dome and took the right leg of the Y. She paused a few feet from the first doorway and turned to me. "I'm going to insist that Professor Gellik remain here until that time. He's fine, but we've had cases in the past where symptoms of something more major didn't show right away. This is just me being cautious. Take the afternoon off." She grabbed my shoulders, demanding my gaze not drift away from hers. "Don't think about what happened or what to try next."

"That's impossible."

She sighed. "Promise me you'll distract yourself, at least for the afternoon. Go visit Jan and Tami at the cloth factory. Then, come to my place for dinner. It's potluck, so give yourself time to make a dish. Doing routine tasks will help you focus more than beating the problem to death in your head. Okay? Promise me, now."

"Yeah, okay."

"Good. So, no talking about what happened. Let the man know you're all right and then off you go."

I stepped into the small room. The professor lay on a cot by the wall, staring at the ceiling. A long bruise blended the green of his coliths with a yellowish tinge of battered skin down the side of his swollen face and neck. He raised a cold-pack up and turned to lay his head on it. He caught sight of me and smiled.

Oh, gods. I did this to him.

I plastered a false smile on my lips and sat in the chair beside his cot, a plan forming in my mind. As promised, I stayed long enough to prove that I only had a few bruises. I reiterated his need to remain for observation because of his head injury. I told him I'd see him in the morning and gave him a brief kiss on the forehead. He closed his eyes and slept.

I didn't see Mamma Lu on my way out, but the receptionist/nurse waved goodbye. I planned to hold up my end of the deal with Lu, but I had to do something first.

After walking a mile back toward the Commons, still in the less developed area, I slipped into a copse of trees, sat on a log, and popped open my watch-com. The voice detection line blipped, then fell straight.

"Dezmind Lisle."

I had programmed in the south satellite code as soon as Lu mentioned it on our tour of the city. Luckily, I was close enough to the tower that it would still work.

The countdown of numbers fell in slow-motion from three to one. It clicked through to voicemail. *Of course. He's in council.* I sighed.

"Hey, it's me. I just needed to hear your voice. I'll try again tonight."

I hesitated to shut the com, wanting to talk to someone. My hand twitched. Tek was the only other person I might call, but he'd be just as busy as Dez. Snapping the com shut, I left the trees to get my bearings. Lu was right. I needed a distraction.

Before I could find the cloth factory, I had to figure out where I was. A slight breeze lifted, accompanied by a faint tinkling and hum. I hesitated, then turned a full circle looking in all directions. The memorial grounds. My pulse quickened.

You should go in.
No, I shouldn't.
You can't avoid this.

I'm not avoiding anything.

I pressed my fists to my closed eyes and pushed until the pain drove the madness from my head. When I looked up, I turned to the right and headed for the factory. Jantice and Tamaine would be more than enough of a distraction. I just hoped they'd be happy to see me. I'd allowed one to become a breeding ground for an eight-legged Deserts creature, and the other I'd ordered to keep away from her family and fiancé. I could only hope time had healed those wounds.

* * *

Taya

The Central Commons buzzed with activity that evening. While Zola hovered full and red above the horizon, families selected raw goods or sold pre-made meals and after-dinner sweets as last-minute bundles of produce and fresh kill were added to the tables.

I tried to take in the myriad of choices, but there were too many options and too many people grabbing what they needed – what *I* was considering choosing – and then leaving again. In the end, I kept it simple and selected what I recognised from my first travels out this way. Mamma Lu had said to make something for a potluck, so I only had to worry about one dish.

Using one of the outdoor cookhouses, I emptied my pack of supplies from the hut and got to work. I cracked open the spiky fruit and caught the juices in an earthenware bowl. Setting the rind and flesh aside on a plate, I pre-cut chunks of lizard meat and soaked them in the juice. After washing up at the central fountain, I worked on bringing my cookhouse to temperature, utilising all my old training. *Old.* It felt like five years, not five months. It felt like it had happened to someone else. It did, in a way. Before I could fall into the well-worn pattern of self-depreciation, a flurry of activity across the Commons caught my attention.

A small crowd, constantly changing and revolving around a core, bobbed from one seller to the next. As the group neared the tables of raw goods, several people broke away to grab an item or two, revealing a cream-clad figure holding an industry-standard View-X recorder.

Kye.

The huge smile on his face drew people in as he chatted. *Probably talking to them about their trip south and life down here.* He laughed with the crowd and continued his circuit. Had it been Zaith, she might have smiled, but she always strove for the big story – she would've been more at home sneaking shots of the spaceship.

And there it was. I'd managed to push the beast in the room to the back of my mind for all of half a day. Now, it was back, and with it came the certainty we were not meant to get the spacecraft working. I was not supposed to be back here – the unrest All Mother thought she'd picked up on wouldn't manifest. And if it did, Dez had the means to calm it. He had the gift. He just needed to talk to the Guardians and the Followers of Light and everything would be all right.

I turned back to the prep table and wrapped the dripping chunks of meat in large sweet leaves before setting them on the grill to cook. Watching the steam coil up from the wrappings lulled my brain into a place where time didn't matter, only the play of marinated meat and wood smoke. I followed the twirl and waver of the pale swirl rise until it got lost in the sky.

"Hi, Jutaya!" Kye and his View-X crashed into my quiet space. "What's it like being back where it all started?"

An invisible blade knifed me through the chest. I tried to smile through the grimace but gave up. I covered the lens with one hand and turned the recorder off with the other.

"Hey! What are you—"

"I'm sorry, Kye. I don't want to share that. You can record me from a distance all you like per your instructions from the Kronik, but you do not get exclusives on my feelings. Understood?" I turned and flipped the meat packets on the grill.

"Oh. Sure." He lowered the device. "So, are you back to work on the spacecraft in the morning? I'd like to get shots of Alpha rising in the background with the waves lapping onto shore before too many people start work for the day. What do you think? Then maybe I could follow you and the professor around for a bit? Now that you're familiar with the ship and all? Hey, how's he doing? Word is he'll be back to work tomorrow."

"Yes. Gellik will be fine and the sunrise shot sounds like a great opening. We'll figure the rest of the day out after that." I watched the grill instead of looking at the reporter. The pain from the invisible blade had lessened but not disappeared.

"So, one of the library collectors told me we'd be here for the Generator Cycle at the end of the month. I can't wait to get some footage of it and—"

"You'll need to run that past…" Who? The General? No. I'd left Zaith and the Kahn-Lea in charge. "Mamma Lu. There's a memorial garden in the same location. A sacred place. You can't just show up and start filming."

"Oh, I didn't realise." He went quiet and looked at his feet. "Is that where Reporter Beji is?"

"No." The idea of her being buried like a common pet rubbed me wrong.

"I didn't mean—"

"She probably has a memorial pipe. Just don't go snooping around in there without Mama Lu."

"Yeah, I'll find her. Thanks for the heads up." He turned his View-X back on and carried on the whirlwind tour of the Central Commons, unfazed any further by my comments. Like with Zaith, he didn't hear *no*; he heard *try again*. The invisible knife twisted deeper. I pulled in a shaky breath before refocusing on the task at hand.

I put the meat in its little leaf packets on the plate, cleaned the grill with a charred piece of wood, then stepped aside for the next person. After reorganising my pack, I hauled it over one shoulder, grabbed the plate and headed across the Commons to Merik's library. The door of the hut immediately behind it stood open, and a jumble of voices filtered out.

I paused mid-step. Lu lived with her husband, Deltek, but there were more than two people in that house. She'd said it was a potluck. I groaned. I wasn't in the mood for a party.

But you promised her you'd come for dinner – and I kept my promises. I glanced at the time. Too early to try calling Dez again. *Just think of it as another distraction.* Inhaling a deep breath, I forced myself to take another step and another until I stood outside the door. No one would hear a knock, which is probably why it stood open. I cleared my mind and shook off my reservations, then walked in.

A blast of brilliance wrapped the metal walls: yellow and orange and red – the colours of the suns. Just like the clinic, Lu's house became something more than the shell of an old alien ship compartment. The tapestries and pottery and paintings told the story of Lu and Deltek's life here in the south.

"Taya! You made it. Welcome." Lu rushed over from the large round table near the kitchen, wiping her hands on an apron before throwing her arms wide. I let my pack slip off my shoulder to the floor and returned her hug with one arm. Deltek separated himself from the small crowd in the open-concept living space and came over to shake my hand.

"Jutaya, it's great to see you again. I can't thank you enough for setting up the guide network. We couldn't have survived without it."

I blushed. "Well, it wasn't all me. Without Gerrund's nephew, I couldn't have made it happen."

A brief, dark flash crossed my host's eyes at the mention of the General. I made a note not to slip up again.

"If Gelden hadn't believed in me, in the project, I don't know what might have happened."

"Yes, Gelden is a sweetheart." Lu turned to Deltek. "He sent an extra half-shipment of verrin this month."

"That will help more than he likely realises."

"I'll be sure to tell him," I said. I glanced past their shoulders and leaned in toward them. "I didn't realise this potluck was a party."

Lu and Deltek smiled, and Lu said, "Not a party – a tradition." She and Deltek separated to reveal everyone else in the room. "The Kahn-Lea, those of us who are left that is, meet for dinner every night. Tonight, it's our turn to host."

Deltek relieved me of the plate of meat and Lu placed her arm around my waist. I had seen everyone at some point during the day, but being in their presence, now, brought a rush of mixed emotions I couldn't sort through. I blinked semi-transparent spots from my eyes.

Raylan, Syvis, and Bazdin stayed in the living area chatting to each other, but they looked my way as Jan and Tami rushed over to join us. Lu bowed out to take care of the dinner table with Deltek, leaving me with the girls. Technically, Bazdin wasn't one of the original Kahn-Lea, but it made sense that he be amalgamated into the group after crossing the Deserts to be with his true love. That and helping these dedicated people find the vaccine for the alien virus cemented him in their hearts.

"You came!" Tami squealed as Jan leaned in for her second hug of the day. Both girls radiated their youthful exuberance, as they had all those months ago when Dezmind first convinced these people to trust him and venture into the Deserts. At the factory, their subdued and professional manners were both impressive and a little off-putting. Now, beyond the office, they embodied that adventurous spirit again. And, clearly, I'd been forgiven.

Tami crushed me in a hug right after Jan released me and whispered in my ear, "Oh, Taya, I can't thank you enough for finding a way to bring Bazdin back to me."

She kissed my cheek and the heat of a blush crept up my neck again. I didn't know what to say, so I just squeezed her back. I hadn't wanted to help him – he'd blackmailed me – but she didn't need to know that. Bazdin met my gaze across the room, over his wife's shoulder, and nodded a salute. The grief that man had given me in order to get him here melted from my mind.

"Dinner!" Lu called.

The six of us joined Deltek and Lu around the table. Everyone grabbed a plate and served themselves. It was a good thing I'd decided to chunk the lizard meat. There was just enough to go around. After a complete circuit of the table, everyone sat down, and Lu passed a water jug. But no one started eating.

The jug made it back to Lu; she filled her cup and then set it on the counter dividing the kitchen from the living and dining area. Facing the group, she raised her arms, elbows bent, palms up, her fingers touching those of the person next to her. I followed along, lightly touching Jan's and Syvis's fingers. Everyone bowed their heads, like a Guardian's Prayer, for just a moment.

"Community," Lu said, voice strong.

"Community," the others chimed in. Eyes opened, heads raised, arms dropped, and people ate. I sat still, trying to take it all in.

Syvis leaned over and touched his bronze shoulder to mine. "We honour Zaith. She made sure we shared a community meal every morning and relayed news about the previous day as well as plans for that day," he explained, emotion choking the words. "She wanted to keep us strong and feeling connected, whole..."

I couldn't help but wonder what might have been between the two of them.

"Breakfast is difficult to coordinate with everyone starting jobs at different times of the day, but the City's rule is everyone breaks for dinner – *together.*"

Zaith had inspired this connectivity. I'd left her in charge when I returned north. Told her to watch over these people, and still... The woman who claimed she was my best friend and then tried to kill me had kept her promise on that score. It didn't make sense. I shook my head. I couldn't figure it out then, and I certainly wasn't going to now. Did it really matter anymore? Instead, I focused on the plate of food before me as general chatter about who brought which dish and what they did differently this time dominated the conversation between mouthfuls.

"Oh, who brought the lizard?" Tami bit into my grilled offering. "Holy Trinity, it tastes just like Zaith's!"

"Really?" Syvis and Deltek echoed and bit into their portions. They groaned in appreciation.

"Taya brought it. How do you know Zaith's recipe?" Lu asked.

Zaith's recipe? My mouth grew dry. Of course. That's how I knew what to make. She'd cooked the small jumping lizards just like that the night of her betrayal. My food stuck in my throat.

Lu quirked her head to the side and looked at me with

narrowed eyes. Her gaze cut through everything – straight into my heart. "Oh, no doubt Taya and Zaith figured this out together when they first arrived. Before Taya and Dezmind had to return north."

I gave her a weak smile and thanked the gods when she turned the conversation to the events of the day… until Raylan asked me how the professor was doing and a whole new cascade of emotions threatened to overwhelm me. Under the table, hands in my lap, I forced the tip of my thumbnail into the top of my finger.

I wanted to leave. To get out and run. But the weight of expectation, of duty, immobilized me.

Chapter 37
Promises

Taya

I smacked a tube-light, making it glow, then shut the hut door and fell onto my cot. I lay there and stared at the ceiling. The weight of my body pulled at me, urging me to forget everything else and just sleep. Crowds did that to me now. The effort of being *on* all the time. Of doing my damndest to keep the threads of conversation in my head and even contribute, all while pushing unwanted thoughts of the day from my mind. But I couldn't give in to the pull yet. I flipped up my watch com.

"Dezmind Lisle." The screen counted silent rings, my heart contracting as each one echoed his busy schedule and the utter unimportance of our relationship in the grand scheme of—

"Taya?" His face materialised on the screen. A firework ignited in my chest, and I released the breath I held.

"Hey, Dez. Can you talk?"

"Sorry I missed your call earlier – bad timing."

"Yeah, I figured."

"You okay?"

"Exhausted." I rubbed a hand over my face and pinched the bridge of my nose.

"Long day?"

"You could say that. Long and disastrous."

"Something tells me this isn't a personal call." His voice fell. I couldn't tell if he was upset that I had bad news or that I had called about work... or both. A loud purring came over the com. "Someone here misses you." The subtle catch in his voice told me it wasn't just my lynx. Jadis's tongue flashed across the screen, and then her nose and face came into view.

"Hiya, girl. Are you being good for Dez? You reminding him to take you for walks?"

Her purrs grew louder, and she half yawned, half meowed, and snapped her jaws shut. Her face disappeared and the purring subsided.

Gods let me go home.

"So, what happened down there?" Dez asked, his voice guarded.

"The energy coil exploded this morning."

"Meeka." He sucked in a huge breath between his teeth and closed his eyes.

"Maybe it's a sign. I don't know. Maybe we're going about this the wrong way. Maybe the Followers of Light can be reasoned with or the All Mother was wrong—"

"She wasn't."

"Huh? What do you mean? How do you know?" My

chest tightened. The all too familiar ache of being inadequate forced the air from my lungs.

"We have a mole." He scrunched his face up as if trying to decide how much to say.

"We knew that. Elix—"

"Not Elix."

"Tell me what's going on."

He sighed, long and deflated. "Tek and his team found the Faction's Headquarters."

"Isn't that a good thing?"

"It was a hidden room at the back of the labs under Professor Elix's offices. You were right. We shouldn't have trusted him."

"But we could trust him. I don't understand. Elix is dead. The Faction—"

"—basically executed him in front of us when they couldn't get to me. He wasn't a casualty of a botched assassination attempt. They meant to kill him."

"How do you know? As much as I hated the guy, we were really making progress together."

"We caught them."

"The Faction? Did you find All Mother's journal?" I remembered when the secret agents for the old Kronik had caught me. What they did to me in search of answers...

"Yes."

I struggled to refocus on the conversation. "Again, isn't that good news?" My brain hurt. I rested my free arm over my forehead and closed my eyes.

"One got away. A different someone on the inside is still feeding him intel. He's leaked it to the media that we plan to blow up Gamma. That this administration can't be trusted if we plan to destroy a god."

"No…"

"Taya, I need to tell them we have a plan. That we won't destroy the sun."

"You can't. We can't say that – can't promise that. Even if the cylinder had worked, we have no idea if the super lodestone is even compatible with the ship. My being here was always a long shot – Plan B!" My throat tightened, constraining my voice. My heart rate doubled, and I sat up struggling to breathe. I was supposed to be going home. I was supposed to be head of security. I was not supposed to be—

"Promise me you'll do everything you can to make this work."

"B– but–"

"Promise me, Taya. Please."

The signal cut off.

I cried out and collapsed in on myself shaking, the whisper of the word *promise* echoing in my head.

Chapter 38

Borrowed Clothes

Dezmind

Jadis lifted her head from my lap as I re-entered the com sequence for the south satellite and Taya. Their system was still fidgety. I didn't want to leave things like that. The lynx growled. A knock at the door stopped me mid-sequence. I set my vis-u-fax on the coffee table and slipped out from under the big cat's head and paws, giving the nape of her neck a quick scratch.

"Sorry girl, I gotta get that." I didn't want to, but a knock at twilight meant business. I passed into the main hall, checked the peephole and opened the door.

"Tek," I said.

"We need you in the Command Centre."

I nodded, slipped my shoes on, and locked the door. We walked side-by-side through the corridors leading to the main building, by-passing the Government Wing at the main security station, and waited for the elevator to the lower levels. Only a few security personnel wandered the halls this late at night. The dim lighting cast soft shadows into every nook.

The elevator dinged and then brought us down to the sub-basement – the next level down from the ops planning room, where I'd spent most of my time lately. Tek led the way down the dim corridor and into the quiet room. The moment the door shut, my ears ached for the normal chatter of sound.

"What is it, Tek?" I asked, not bothering to sit at the small conference table in the middle of the room. The space reminded me of the back room where Gerrund used to have the Cause meet in the Underground – not because of how it looked but because of the need for its existence in the first place.

"We're at an impasse."

"What does that mean?"

"It means, the standard questioning methods aren't working on the prisoners. We need to know how to proceed from here."

Neither of us spoke. I'd hoped it wouldn't come to this. I'd hoped the decision wouldn't be mine to make, and it wasn't. Not alone, anyway.

"Where's Kronik Delenon?" I raised an inquiring eyebrow.

"He hasn't been sworn in yet—"

"That's just a formality. I offered. He accepted. The council approved. Get him."

"Right away. And Daria?"

"Only if he insists. She waits outside."

"Yes, sir." Tek hurried out. The door swung shut behind him.

I leaned my back against one of the dense, carpeted walls and closed my eyes. Three Talian citizens, former special agents for the old Kronik, remained locked up in separate cells just down the hall. When Gerrund showed me the warehouse where Taya had been tortured all those months ago, I wanted to kill the Kronik and everyone who'd done his bidding. Levelling the building and destroying the tech felt insufficient at the time.

But now, the diplomatic approach wasn't working. I had three of the four major players involved with the Faction in my reach, yet my hands were tied. We had to find the fourth leader. We had to find the mole. Was this how the old Kronik justified his actions? Or did he simply not see Commoners as equals and they were, therefore, dispensable?

The airlock on the door whooshed. I opened my eyes, and the one man who truly represented the Commoners stepped into the room. Tek and Daria followed.

"Leave us," I said.

Tek bowed out. Daria locked eyes with Delenon, flashed her gaze my way, and then gave a nearly imperceptible nod. She closed the door behind her. Delenon sat down and rotated his chair my way.

"What's all this about, Dezmind? Surely it could have waited until morning?"

"Perhaps. It depends on what we decide to do with the Faction leaders in holding. Seems that being polite isn't working."

"That's... unfortunate." He leaned forward and rested

his forearms on his thighs. "You're concerned about the mole?"

"Yes. I can't deny the leak."

"We discussed damage control at the council meeting this morning."

"And then Taya blew up the energy cylinder. I can't in good conscience tell the people about Plan B and pass it off as Plan A if there isn't even a hope of getting that damn ship operational. I'm starting to sound like the old Kronik, placating the masses with general misinformation just to save face."

"It's not just to save face. You tell the truth and we have a religious revolution on our hands. Just because destroying Gamma will save the world, doesn't mean our people won't destroy it, and us, first. I had many conversations with the old Kronik about maintaining balance – about finding a way not to hide, but to bend, the truth. Unfortunately, his decisions made matters worse. Maybe it was bad advice."

"I don't want that to happen again. There has to be a measure of transparency here where we don't cause a war or mass panic. Right now, the only way I see this new government surviving is by plugging that leak." I pushed off from the wall, restless, and paced with my hands clenched behind my back.

"Why don't we bring it to the council in the morning? If everyone has a say—"

"Don't you see, Del? We can't trust them. At least, not the Talians. The only people who knew about Denali's findings and our two plans were present in the council room."

"What? You can't really think—"

"Why not? Look at it this way. A mole is leaking intel to the Faction. The Faction hates the new regime and everything we stand for. They're pro-Talian. Therefore, there's no way a Commoner would work with them to destroy the future of equality. The only Talians left in-the-know are those on the council."

"I thought you replaced all the old councillors with more open-minded reps?"

"I did. Obviously, I'm not as good a judge of character as I thought. Either that or the Faction turned someone. It wouldn't have been hard to do. The reps I chose followed blood-lines and traditions, but we've never had a council this young since we first migrated north. The young are… *impressionable.*"

He raised his eyebrows at me. They were my age or a little older. The comparison wasn't lost on me.

"I'd hoped to help mould them. Someone else thought the same thing – and obviously succeeded."

"Then how do you know it's only one?"

I thought back to the inside man Gerrund had thought we could trust. The Talian double-agent who said and did all the right things until Taya revealed exactly who he was and everything nearly fell apart. It had fallen apart. She'd died. I blinked the memory away.

"It only takes one. Maybe a year from now there might be more if the Faction were allowed to grow stronger – but not now. Not yet."

"Okay. So, we can't trust the Talian reps on the council, and we have three of the four Faction leaders locked up, not talking."

"Exactly." I flopped down into the swivel chair beside him. "So, who is more likely to crack? We've hit a wall with the prisoners. The way I see it, we have two choices. Take the questioning of the Faction leaders to the next level or begin question the Talian councillors."

Del balked and sat up straight. "Those can't be our only options. Either one will work to undermine and destroy everything you've built. Torture isn't the answer, but neither is sewing distrust among the new council."

"So, then, what do we do?"

Chapter 39
Keeping Promises

Taya

Near-dawn threatened the start of a new day. I stood with my supplies before the entrance of the spaceship, now sealed off from wind and animal by a taut tarp. The sharp, salt air needled at my nose as steady waves broke against the beach. Dez's words echoed over and over in my head. *I need to tell them we have a plan. That we're not going to destroy the sun. Promise me, Taya. Please.*

Even if he hadn't heard my answer, I'd still said it. Now, I had to keep my promise.

I walked up the ramp and yanked the tarp off one side, letting it dangle like a curtain, and went in. The acrid taste of electrical fire clung to the back of my throat. I pulled a light-tube from my satchel and hit it against my thigh. Forget the engine room; I went straight for the cockpit.

In the main area, I lit and dropped light-tubes like falling stars, over the main panel, on the floor, any surface. Then I dropped down, grabbed a small pry bar and slid under the bulkhead. Elix and I had spent enough time staring at pictures of the cold, stark panels to have a sense of the layout and operations. If our hunch was right, this area would give me access to onboard schematics, star charts, navigation, and any stored travel logs.

The panel cracked open. I dug my fingers into the narrow space and searched for a release catch.

There!

It gave way and smashed me on the forehead before clattering on the ground beside me.

"At least I'm in."

I yanked down a thick electrical cord and sliced it open with my knife, peeling back the protective sheathing.

"Right."

The bluey-green glow from the light-tubes made discerning colour difficult, so I concentrated on the gauge of the wire instead. Leaving everything hanging from the open compartment, I slid forward and rummaged through my satchel. I couldn't see anything and dumped it out. Tools, more light-tubes, scavenged wires, connectors, nodes, and a jagged piece of wood I'd stolen from a wide crate slat littered the floor.

I took a deep breath. I knew how to do this, but I not only had to wade through conversations with the two professors – one recent, the other several years ago – but also a ton of emotional baggage. Thoughts of Dez, All Mother, my foster parents, my real parents, and that last battle in the caves below the Capitol Building pulled me farther and farther away from my goal.

"Arugh!" I pushed the heel of my hands into my closed eyes. For this, I had no muscle memory to rely on. I had to remember; I had to find a way to help my brain locate those memories and discard the noise. Hot, frustrated anger welled up inside me, and I swallowed, forcing it down with deep breaths. Into my mind's eye popped a vision of what I needed.

I got to work.

I could have constructed the adapter outside in the early morning light, but the ship had drawn me in as if it knew I could fix it – even if I couldn't see how. I clung to my limited electrical engineering knowledge from my time studying at the CTF. Something Elix said about the energy source popped into my head. Then, the image of Tek hauling his limp body away from the carnage of the Memorial Rally flashed behind my eyes. I blinked over and over to get rid of it, shaking my head to knock it loose, but the signal, the memory, kept repeating. I growled and grabbed my Whipstaff from my thigh holster.

"Not so fast, J.J." Gerrund's voice ricocheted against the metallic interior. I rolled onto my back, weapon still drawn, and looked up. The General took a wide stance, his hand hovering over his own armament.

"What in Zita's name?" I slammed my hands down and pushed my torso up.

"I could ask you the same thing." He growled low.

"Oh, for Trinity's sake, Gerrund." I slumped back down and stared at the ceiling, arms crossing my chest – still holding my Whipstaff.

"Put the weapon down, J.J."

"It's Taya. How many times do I have to—"

"Stand down!"

I did a stomach crunch and threw the damn staff at him. The memory of him holding me up by my throat back in the Underground flashed through my mind. I said now what I'd wanted to say then but couldn't. "What's the matter with you? I'm trying to do my job. Go jump in the sea and get off my back already."

He snatched my weapon up from where it landed. "Where've you been, Taya? You were supposed to check in with me last night, and then Lu tells me to bugger off, you'll see me in the morning. I walk over here, see the ship's been broken into, and there you are reaching for your weapon. What in the Trinity is going on here? What happened yesterday? What are you doing now? Where's Gellik?"

I held up a hand. He shut up. I reach forward, and after only a moment's hesitation, he holstered his weapon and helped me up.

"We overloaded the energy cylinder yesterday. I don't know how, but I'm figuring the DC current from the battery didn't like the AC feedback and sent a power surge to the cylinder. It blew up."

"Why couldn't you say as much yesterday?" He rubbed his hand over his face and through his hair. The dark grey of his skin took on a greenish hue from the scattered lighting, making the hollows of his eyes appear even darker than usual. A haze of the disappointment from our time underground hung between us – him believing again that I did something for personal gain. Maybe this time it was justified.

"I couldn't face you. I blew it. Literally. Blew up our only chance of getting this alien bucket of bolts operational and..." I sighed.

"And?"

"And I was relieved. Sick that Gellik got hurt, but relieved this crazy mission failed and I could finally go home where I belong."

"I don't get it. Then why are you still here? It looks like you're trying to rig something else up. I thought you were aiming to blow the whole thing up. Regardless if we get the ship airborne or not, we still need to salvage the tech."

I side-stepped my mess on the floor and dropped into one of two command chairs on the bridge. "I talked to Dez last night."

"Told him you were on your way home?"

"That was the plan. Until he mentioned that Plan A would destroy us even if it succeeded."

"What? You're talking in riddles. What's going on?" The old edge to his voice was back.

I stared at him, numb from crying, from punching metal walls half the night, and from trying to deny my destiny.

"A mole in the council told the last free Faction member that we were going to blow up Gamma. The FOL and the Guardians are in an uproar now, believing the new Kronik is trying to kill the Child god."

"A religious revolution? Is that what you're telling me?"

"If we send Plan A rocketing up to Zerameteth, yes."

His gaze darted around the bridge, taking in the wires dangling from the control panel, the mess on the floor, my device, me, and finally, my Whipstaff in his hand.

"You're trying again."

"I'm trying again."

I held my hand out. After a moment's hesitation, he gave me the weapon. I pried off the end with a screwdriver and pulled loose the wiring.

"What's that going to do though? It's so small. The cylinder…"

"The cylinder should have powered most of the ship minus whatever propulsion we actually needed to get it off the ground." I dropped to the floor, rolled onto my back, and shimmied under the control panel, connecting my Whipstaff to the current adaptor I'd built from scratch. "Now, I'll be lucky if I can access one system at a time."

It was only ever a theory, the framework for creating the energy cylinder in the first place. But Elix had run the numbers, demonstrating everything should work. But it hadn't. Now, I was left with a hack job and no room for error. At least Gerrund shut up. I focused on the wires, my training, my breathing, and kept my mind clear of thoughts of the end of the world – or at least tried to.

I slid out from under the panel ten minutes later and sat up.

"Well, you stayed. Are you ready?" I asked.

"What do mean am I ready? That's it?" He pointed at the mess of wires and mixed tech on the floor and narrowed his eyes. "Where did you get your supplies from? I don't remember any of that coming out of the boxes you brought."

"Paid a visit to your satellite receiving station this morning."

"You what!"

"Here goes." I couldn't think about it. Couldn't let the

fear wake up my nerves. I turned on the Whipstaff and flicked the switched on the converter…

I held my breath.

Gerrund squinted and took a step back.

A quiet hum grew louder and louder.

We locked gazes.

The control panel flickered to life!

"Thank the gods, it worked." My knees wobbled as I bent to check all of my connections again. I looked up at Gerrund from the floor and nodded. "It's all good."

He let out a slow breath, ending on a chuckle. I dropped down onto my ass and leaned my back against the bulkhead. A giddy giggle bubbled out of me. I clapped a hand over my mouth. Gerrund laughed harder. I let my hand drop to my lap and joined him.

We hadn't blown up.

"What's going on?" Professor Gellik popped his head around the door frame from the adjoining corridor before walking into the room, escorted by Raylan who hovered at a distance.

"Professor! You're all right." I jumped up, spurred on by the giddy lightness inside me, and hugged him. He gave me a squeeze and then pulled away as he caught sight of the lit panel behind me.

"You got it going? A converter, of course. Naturally." He glanced back at me. "But what now?"

"Now, we get to work." I turned and held my hand out to Gerrund and pointed with my gaze to the only other Whipstaff in South City. He pursed his lips, shrugged and handed me the weapon.

Chapter 40
Birthright

Teena

"This is it," Mardel said, slapping Gelden on the back. Gel gripped the rail as our ship picked up speed, heading straight for the magnetised stone barrier surrounding Darius's Island. I leaned my forearms on the rail beside Mardel, close enough to feel the heat radiating off his body. Mom would frown at me, but Mom wasn't here.

The activity, both in the rigging above and on deck, stilled as if every person on board held their breath.

"I honestly never thought I'd come back." My stomach alternately jumped and clenched. I forced myself to take deep breaths and clasped my hands to lessen the shake.

"Nostalgic for home?" Gelden asked, that familiar bitter edge lacing his words. I couldn't figure the guy out.

"Mom never called this island home."

His lips twisted at my comment. I quirked my head to

the side. He looked like he had something to say then changed his mind.

"What exactly is supposed to happen again?" he asked as the wind vaulted us over crashing waves. The salt spray bit into our cheeks and forehead. He flinched even though I'd told him numerous times that small amounts of salt water wouldn't hurt. It was as if he didn't trust me. I mean, I'd done this before.

"You'll see," I said, my heart racing as the slap of the waves crashed faster and harder with each beat.

"It's the reason Captain Darius turned around, right? Why he risked returning home with only a skeleton crew?" Mardel asked of no one in particular.

Mom never spoke of the past. I'd heard snippets of stories from Tony and the others, but Mom had said none of that mattered – only the here and now. And tomorrow. No one spoke of the Rebellion, not during the day, anyway. Occasionally, I'd overhear the odd whisper around a twilight campfire. I knew we hadn't chosen this life, and Mom's warnings on the voyage about the Kronik and his contractors seemed impossible. Nightmares that made no sense.

"Hold tight, now." I wove my arm around Mardel's and snuck my hand into his. He blushed and rested his cheek on the top of my head for just a moment. Mom told Tony, Drax and Satie to keep an eye on me, so Mardel got Gelden to scout for us. He'd seemed so nice that first day, but he'd grown sullen and distant on the voyage. He never talked about his mom, like the other volunteers who'd lost family members.

The hull shuddered under my grip. I couldn't tear my gaze away from the rapidly looming rocks. A gap appeared and my heart jumped. I knew it wasn't a wall, but my eyes had refused to believe it until now.

Faster and faster we shot toward the narrow opening until…

The sky sucked the ship out of the water and my stomach dropped to my knees. Mardel pulled me closer in a half-hug. Gelden gaped, leaning nearly in half over the side, looking down at the sea rushing away from the hull as we hovered several feet above the surface. I swallowed and my ears popped. The ship shuddered and then the free-fall shoved my stomach up into my throat. Gel's knees wavered. Mardel's free hand grabbed the back of Gel's shirt and held him steady. We crashed down. Water sprayed up as the ship bobbed and rolled on the calm, clear blue waters. I licked my lips.

"Fresh water," Gelden said, pushing himself up enough to turn and look at me and Mardel.

"Home." I stared into the distance, fighting off a lifetime of memories I was instructed to forget.

"All hands!" Marxx shouted as Tony corralled everyone not actively working to pitch in and load the rowboats.

Tony and Drax ferried the boats to and from the shore multiple times as the bulk of the day crew weighed anchor, collapsed the sails, and readied the rigging. But not everyone made the trip to land. The hard look on the faces of the men was mirrored on the women's faces. They were here to do a job and nothing more.

I helped Tony tie the rowboat to the small fishing dock.

Gelden, Mardel and I hauled the last of the equipment to shore where sparse grasses met the onyx sand.

"We're starting in an hour, right?" I asked Tony. I grabbed both Mardel and Gel's hand, pulling them along behind me.

"Yes, 'n I expected ya back here in half that time, young lady."

I could only imagine what might be going through his mind. I'd grown up the only child on this island. Now, I had two guys practically my age to hang with. I glanced over my shoulder at them and smiled as giddy excitement bubbled inside. For once, Gelden smiled back. Then a dark shadow passed over his expression.

Out of sight of the shore, I dropped Gelden's hand but raced on with Mardel in tow. It didn't take long before the familiar shapes appeared on the horizon in the clearing just past some sparse trees. My heart walloped my chest. I was certain the guys could hear it. A small village of stone and wood houses ranged around a central well with a bucket winch. I let go of Mardel's hand and stepped to the well alone. I opened my arms, slowly turning a full circle. My face tilted to the sky, thanking the gods.

"Welcome to Trinity's Haven." I walked with measured steps to the closest house and let my hand hover over the wooden door knob. A roil of emotions battled in my heart and my head. My hand twitched.

"Are you going in?" Mardel's soft breath wisped against the back of my neck. I jolted with his nearness, sighed, and shook my head.

"No." I let my arm collapse against my side, and I stared

through the door, recovering the memories. "I might never leave." I shook off my thoughts and looked up at Mardel. "I promised Mom I wouldn't get caught up in the memories. There's nothing here for me now. I— I just wanted to show you the town. To prove that we weren't running away from squalor the way some of those reporters claimed. To show you we had a life – a good life. In fact, we'd still be here if the well hadn't run dry. Come on. Let me show you around." I pulled Mardel away from the only home I'd ever known and then glanced over my shoulder. "You, too, Gelden."

I got another one of those confused half-looks between hope and something else. Still, he followed. We toured the village for half an hour and then I led the guys back to the main port. I had to shake my head at that – *port*. Now, the finger docks at Nova Leau and Darzeth Prime, those were ports.

"Time to suit up!" Drax waved the diving volunteers over. I surged forward. Mardel walked a few steps and released my hand. I looked at him over my shoulder as I walked.

"Come on. I used to do this without a suit. We don't have enough people as it is. Please…" I looked from Mardel to Gelden and back. Gelden, his face a mask of stone, pushed past both of us and collected a suit from Drax.

* * *

Gelden

I shivered, but not from cold, as the water lapped against my shins, then my knees and my thighs. I wanted to stop, but Teena dove in just ahead of me with Mardel close behind. Drax, Marxx, Tony, and a bunch of former and current UGC – Underground Citizens – and volunteers with shovels also plunged in. I kept walking, the weights on my ankles heavy enough to keep me from immediately floating to the surface.

The mask sucked to my face as I carefully breathed the air stored in the tank on my back. The clear turquoise water crystallised everything: the multi-hued sand, the red seaweed, silverfish, and smooth, dark rock-teeth. The dig team followed close on Drax's flippers. I gingerly leaned and swished the large foot extensions behind me. I shot forward. My heart leapt into my throat. I shoved my arms out to the side and waved them around, slowing myself down.

Teena swam spirals around Mardel. Bubbles of laughter escaped his facemask. She'd opted only to wear the mask and flippers. Technically, the fresh water on this side of the rocks wouldn't send us into sodium shock, but what would happen when we removed a piece of the puzzle that made up this geomagnetic wall?

Drax gave the signal-wave and the dig team swarmed the sacrificial super lodestone. As the group of six worked on the base of the rock, Drax supervised above the diggers as Tony and Marxx floated just below the surface, nudging the rock from side to side. The tip of the oval stone didn't quite breach the surface. It was a lot smaller than the ring visible above the waterline but still nearly twice as tall as Tony – and he was a big guy.

During our tour through the village, Teena had talked

about how loosening a small geo-mag could take the better part of a day. Only so many LRM were willing to brave any kind of water over their heads and fewer still had the stamina for the cold. Resurfacing for air every minute or two slowed progress, too. With such a large team helping, Teena's *better part of a day* wound up only being a couple of hours.

As Teena, Mardel and I relieved half the group during our sixth dig swap, the stone tooth *shifted* and then swayed. Teena signalled for everyone to back away.

Oh, meeka. I looked up to the bright surface of the water, the weights on my ankles becoming cement blocks. The surge of my blood pumping past my eardrums and the pressure on my eyeballs from the facemask only added to the rise in my blood pressure. I sucked in a fast breath. It burned down my throat. I gulped another and another, too fast. The giant boulder fell. Everyone swam to the mark – everyone except me.

I scrambled to peel the weighted cuffs from my ankles but couldn't get a grip. Spots flashed before my eyes. I tried to catch my breath, but I couldn't. Squeezing my lids shut, I tried to remember Teena's instructions for staying calm, but I couldn't think. I couldn't breathe. I couldn't get to the surface. My heart beat faster and faster and faster—

Small, firm hands gripped my shoulders.

I opened my eyes.

Teena.

She knocked on my face mask and pointed two fingers at my eyes and then hers. I nodded and fixed my gaze. She gripped my arm just below my shoulder and squeezed once.

310

I took a breath, short as it was, and held it. I remembered that.

She squeezed again.

I let the breath out.

Again she squeezed, and I obeyed, over and over.

When my breathing evened out and the spots disappeared, I nodded. She pointed up. I shook my head no. She pointed up again. Again, I shook my head no. I wanted to surface, but I didn't want to give up. They needed my help. I held her arms, mine crossing over hers, at the bottom of a strange freshwater sea halfway across the world from the rocky caverns I'd called home all my life. I'd come seeking answers. I didn't get the ones I'd wanted, but maybe I'd found the ones I needed.

This girl had welcomed me onto her ship, into her home. She trusted that by bringing a piece of her habitat back to a government in a land she knew little about, she helped do her part in saving our world. She'd never once pried into my reasons for coming. Never asked who my mother was or what had happened to the rest of my family. All she saw was someone in need of a friend as I tried to come to terms with my own baggage.

I pointed to the group struggling to lift the super lodestone with two fewer workers than anticipated. Then I pointed to her and me and back at the group. She stared a long time into my eyes before finally nodding. She pulled away, keeping hold of one of my hands, and bent her knees. I copied her. She gave my hand a squeeze, and we pushed off from the sand on the bottom of the sea and swam over to take our place under the geo-mag to walk it slowly back to shore.

Chapter 41

Breaking Tension

Taya

"Knock, knock," Bazdin called as he walked from the main corridor of the spaceship into the cockpit. "You missed lunch again."

A giggle escaped me as the weapons array lit up on the panel. "It worked!" We'd combined the power from both Whipstaffs. The wiring was suspect, but it held.

"You didn't?" Bazdin asked, handing me half a sandwich over a small bowl of fruit salad and passing the other half of each to the professor.

"We did. I can't eat now. We just got the system up—"

"Taya – sit, eat, and talk me through it." Bazdin accepted the notebook and pencil from Gellik, who chuckled and then winked at me.

"He's right, you know. You work too hard." The professor sat down on one of the two command chairs and swivelled to face us as he took a big bite of his sandwich.

The crunch made my stomach growl. I rolled my eyes as he laughed again, and Bazdin quirked an eyebrow while trying to keep a straight face.

"Okay, okay. Can you start by sketching a diagram of the interface and labelling the controls?" I bit into my half of the sandwich and a soft groan escaped. "Oh, gods, how do you do it? I never find good stuff at the Commons to make for lunch."

"You just need some training up. Thank Mamma Lu's herb and spice garden." He turned his back to us and dove into the sketch as I flopped into the other command chair to devour my food.

Bazdin had been stopping by on his lunch break for the past week and a bit. At first, I thought he was spying for Gerrund, but he was honestly interested in how we were doing. We didn't get many visitors otherwise – well, none, actually. Gerrund made sure of it. But, somehow, when Bazdin finished his dive duties for the morning, he managed to slip on board past the General's guards. He often brought not just our lunch but also his inquisitive mind. Besides, he sketched better than either Gellik or me, so we let him help. Mamma Lu wanted a new metal book for Merik's library.

"Gerrund! Gerrund, get down here, you good for nothing, pompous ass, swindling..." Mamma Lu's voice echoed through the metallic interior as she passed the opening to the ship.

I slipped off my chair and pressed two buttons on the adjacent panel, also lit by the double Whipstaff battery. The whole front windshield of the ship dissolved from metallic grey to transparent, and with all the vents now open,

Mamma Lu's voice carried loud and clear when she poked Gerrund in the chest with her finger.

And he let her.

He stood in the sand just to the left of the screen, arms crossed, in a green t-shirt and cargo pants with boots cinched tight over his ankles and a brown cap shadowing his eyes. Lu appeared in all her Mamma glory: long black braids woven with colourful lengths of fabric and a flowing sundress to match. The deep scowl she reserved for Gerrund set her features livid.

"What did he do this time?" I whispered, even though I knew the pair facing off on the beach couldn't hear me.

"He's wondering the same thing," Gellik said.

"You never know with those two," Bazdin chimed in.

We stood still, trying not to betray the fact that we looked on.

"What is it now, Lu?"

"Don't 'what is it now' me, Gerrund. Those soldiers of yours need to be put in their place. They don't run this city, no matter what you tell them."

"You're making no sense. Come back and talk to me once you've calmed down." His voice remained calm, but that edge I knew only too well crept into his tone.

"I will not. You need to get your ass over to the Commons and see for yourself. They are intimidating the merchants and making demands for the best of everything. This city is equal opportunity, and you of all people should be working to keep it that way."

"Now, hold on here. What exactly is going on? It's not like we can just walk into town – that'd take too long. What do think you saw?"

"Ooo..." I breathed.

Bazdin sucked in air between his teeth and leaned forward slightly to get a better look. The beach was deserted, but not really. Everyone knew to make scarce when Mamma Lu and the General went head-to-head.

"They didn't *do* anything. That cultured air of superiority and the way they stand, like you are now, scare everyone. They may not demand the best of everything, but the merchants know to save it for them so they'll back off and leave them alone. You need to set this straight. They won't listen to me."

"Of course not. You're not their commanding officer. You're the freakin' sector keeper in their eyes. They need to look intimidating. How else will they deter people from acting out and breaking *your* laws? No one is forcing those merchants to do anything. This is something they've gotten into their heads. You said yourself, my guards don't say anything. Don't make demands. Don't tell folk off. They're not doing anything wrong."

"They're not doing anything right, either."

Gerrund leaned over so he stood face to face with Lu. Bazdin and I leaned forward, too. A siren wailed over the intercom. Bazdin, Gellik, and I jumped back. A blast of blue-white light fired from the nose of the ship. Gerrund and Lu dropped flat to the sand as it streaked past them and blew up a small stand of trees several yards away.

"Oh, meeka." I bolted for the door, Bazdin and Gellik close on my heels.

Outside, wood-smoke choked the air. Bazdin dropped to

his knees next to Lu just as I did next to Gerrund.

"Are you all right?" I asked.

Bazdin muttered something similar. Neither one of them moved.

"Gerrund, can you hear me?" I clasped his hands. His eyes blinked rapidly and he gasped in air. I pulled him up almost the same time Bazdin raised Lu. I knew she was in good hands, so I focused on Gerrund. He scrunched up his face, opened his mouth, and slipped a hand from my grasp to stick a finger in his ear and wiggle it. I swallowed a chuckle. Now was not the time.

I tilted my head and raised my eyebrows before straightening again. "Can you hear me now?"

He frowned. "You sound far away." He looked over his shoulder at the blast zone. "What in Zola's name just happened?" More surprise than anger seeped into his voice. I took this as a good sign.

"We just got the weapons system operational. We— someone, bumped the control panel and initiated a pre-set command."

Workers ebbed from between the huts and out of the shadows with curious murmurs.

"Hey! Go see if that blast did any damage!" I yelled. That's not what I was thinking, but I couldn't bring myself to say it.

Most of them headed for the tree line and the smouldering brush. The rest formed a wide circle around Lu and Gerrund. I helped him stand, sliding his arm over my shoulders when he stumbled. The problem with his hearing made him unsteady. He looked surprised to see so many people around.

I turned my head and said in a loud whisper, "They hide when mom and dad fight."

He made a face, unimpressed. I caught Gellik's gaze and motioned with my head in the direction of Gerrund's watchtower. He nodded and pointed in the direction of the clinic in the distance where Bazdin led Lu.

A gaggle of UGC soldiers jogged up and met us at the base of the tower.

"Everyone's accounted for and only a small group of trees suffered damage. A lot of damage. There are only stumps, really," one soldier reported. Gerrund waved him off.

"Secure the area and then get back to your duties," I said.

He looked from me to Gerrund, who, focused on staggering to the elevator, completely ignored the soldier.

"Do it," I said.

He nodded, motioned for the others to follow, and left.

As we rode up the elevator to his office, Gerrund sighed and said, "I suppose I shouldn't bother asking for a status report?"

I grinned. I think he was just happy we were making any kind of progress.

Chapter 42

The Sins of the Father

Dezmind

I nodded to Ynell, standing guard by my office door. "I don't want to be disturbed. By anyone. Do you understand?"

"Yes, sir."

"That includes SO Jezetek and Kronik Delenon."

She glanced at me before resuming her static post. "Yes, sir. What should I say if it's an emergency, sir?"

"Get them to text me on my watch com. I'll decide how much of an emergency it is."

"Yes, sir."

Once inside my office, I locked the door and faced the room with my arms crossed. Yet another council meeting where I said little and agreed to nothing. I had to find the mole or everything we'd worked so hard for would crumble. Tek searched for the last Faction leader. He also sent out squads to help keep the peace as Commoners gathered with the Guardians to protest the "imminent destruction" of Gamma outside sector buildings throughout the city and at the front gate. At least Taya was finally getting somewhere with the spaceship. Still, there was no guarantee.

I walked over to the gilt pedestal holding the Book of Law beside my desk. A thin gold chain lashed it in place. My father had me studying pocketbooks of the Acts all through my childhood – bored me to the heavens and back. I ran my fingers over the embossed leather cover and then grabbed the top of the podium and twisted it, harder than last time.

The corner section of shelving that wrapped around the walls shifted forward and swung to face the left bookshelves. I grabbed a light-tube from the back of my bottom desk drawer, snapped it on, and walked down the stairs of the dark mouth. I held the light before me. The tight tunnel walls nearly brushed my shoulders. Too many late nights I'd ventured down here, wondering where each tunnel led. Too many nights I'd slipped into bed when Taya was fast asleep.

A couple months ago, when the trouble with the Faction first escalated, I'd kicked the pedestal, frustrated that they were undermining everything, scaring the Commoners and now injuring them on Talian soil.

The pillar had moved.

And so had the bookcase.

Likely, each Kronik passed on the secrets of his station to the next in line, but I had never gained that courtesy. The old Kronik refused to speak to me – to anyone. His signature on Taya's Infinity contract had been coerced. I don't know why I never told Taya about the secret exit. She was my head of security. My Soul Mate…

I shook off the sentiment. Now wasn't the time. I had to keep a clear head. I had to find out how all this would end.

The concrete block of the tunnel gave way to formed stone and rough rock underfoot. The crevice widened every few yards until it hooked into the Talian Underground caverns. None of the natural tunnels I'd explored in the past two months ever reached the colossal expanse of Kaynee's Underground City or the opulence of the unexcavated caverns. Likely these were just old tributaries the underground verrin used to travel through before the Dakturian's terraformed our world.

My gut clenched. So did my jaw. I opened my mouth and tried to loosen my muscles. I still didn't know what to make of the Dakturians. They'd arrived when we were evolving and died when we were advancing. The last survivors of the super virus, bacteriophage, Bazdin had called it, had found a way to alter Talian DNA to procreate and live on. I would not be who I was today if Ketic and the others had never lived. I might not have ever been born. *Yet, it's their fault the verrin is disappearing. Their fault the Deserts exist. Their fault we believe in three gods instead of two. And my fault I trusted so blindly.* Taya had warned me not to keep the Talians on the council, but change had to happen gradually – a new twelve instead of no twelve.

My thoughts cycled and circled as I followed the etchings the ancient Dakturians taught me to make at junction points leading from one tunnel to the next. Taya would be impressed. No, she'd be mad I kept this from her.

I sighed and climbed the narrow, rough-hewn rock stairs toward a metal door set in a stone wall. I unlocked the latch, pushed the heavy door open, and walked through a mass of ivy and shrub out the side of a hill and into a backyard.

She sat some distance away, closer to the house than the berm, whittling while cross-legged on a short circle of grass. The silver-white of her skin and blank eyes contrasted against the depths of her long black hair.

Parting the knee-length grasses, I walked toward her. She neither smiled nor frowned, instead concentrating on shaping the wood in her hands with the small, fine blade. I paused at the edge of the short velvety grass. Thirteen years ago I'd walked out of this very circle angry and confused. So much had happened between now and then, and yet here I stood, bearing those same emotions, only seasoned this time.

"Well, are you going to sit or what?" she asked. Her clear voice startled me.

I sat, leaving the requisite three feet between us.

"I expected to see you sooner." She laughed at her own bad joke.

"How did you know it was me? That I'd come back at all?" I closed my eyes and gave myself a mental slap. She was the Seer after all. Of course she'd know.

"Only one person ever comes from that direction. I may be blind, but I know who's in power. And I know how you got there. Question is, why are you here?"

In that moment, my certainty about everything crumbled. Suddenly, her prophesy to an ignorant twelve-year-old no longer seemed wrong. *You will strike your own path in this world and help make Xannia a better place to live. However, your Soul Mate is the unborn child of an ill-fated union.* She had said so much more that day, but that was what stuck with me – had changed me.

If Taya was my true Soul Mate, then why weren't we married yet? Why were we always apart? It wasn't until I stopped looking for her that I was able to see how I could help Gerrund and the Cause – to *make Xannia a better place to live.* When I set aside trying to find someone who didn't exist, Lady Lynnia's child with her Soul Mate who died, my true destiny became clear.

But I love Taya.

That doesn't mean she's your Soul Mate. Lynnia loved Doir and he wasn't her Soul Mate…

But without Taya, I wouldn't be King.

She was always part of the Prophesy, just not in the way I thought. Falling in love with her wasn't Destiny, it was chance.

The Seer hadn't made a mistake after all… I did.

"I need direction. Advice—"

"You're afraid you're making the same mistakes as the man who came before you."

"Yes. Can you help me?"

"Maybe."

"What do you mean 'maybe'? Can you see beyond this? What do I do?"

"The man who came before you had the same questions. I will give you the same answer. How you interpret it will depend entirely on the man who sits before me."

Chapter 43
A Convergence of Fate

Daria

I followed Kronik Delenon off the long-distance hover transport back to the finger docks of Nova Leau. *Kronik Delenon.* I still couldn't believe it. This is what the Resistance – what *I* – had fought for, and lost, twenty-two years ago. I held his elbow before he crossed the street to the crowd gathered around our ship at the port. He paused and looked at me, an inner joy and excitement radiating. My heart dropped farther into my stomach.

"Del, are you sure this is the right move? Please, reconsider. We've only just achieved everything we've worked for."

"What do you think will happen, Daria? The ship won't sink. She's just gone all the way to the Island and back in a month. She'll make it to South City."

"Yes, but—"

"That's where our people are." He'd said the same thing

all week. "I must go to them. We need to be their voice. Dezmind said your brother's concerned about integrating non-UGC into the colony. Dez has enough on his plate here. I'm needed down there. Are you coming with me or not?"

"Of course, I'm coming. I'm not letting you out of my sight."

He gave me that look.

I knew what he was thinking. "I'm not avoiding my family and I'm not talking about it. Don't start anything."

He shrugged his shoulders and headed across the street. Most of those present were the same townsfolk who'd seen us arrive a month ago. A few new faces hovered near the front of the crowd, waiting for someone to welcome them on board for the trip south.

The group parted, allowing Delenon to pass. I doubted Marxx would come down and talk to everyone. Likely Satie would, but Drax never left her side, and his presence might cause another stir. It was bad enough the media and local temples took shots at them when they weren't here to defend themselves.

I scanned the new faces at the front. *Is Gelden here? Did he sail to the Island? Is he still at the edge of the expanse, managing the trade route south?* I don't know what I was expecting to see. He'd been a baby when I... left. I had no idea what he looked like. He had no idea what I looked like. *Thank the gods.* I wasn't ready for this.

I gasped as my gaze took in my mother's face – or at least the face I remembered from my childhood, not the hardened, stern one I last saw before the attack on the

Compound gates.

Kaynee.

My younger sister stood chatting with a small group, at ease and yet still quiet. I'd avoided her during our stay in the Underground. It wasn't hard. We were both busy, and Delenon often didn't leave the Compound until late. I glanced away but kept her in my peripheral vision. She was only four years old when… Did she remember me? Would she recognise me? *Do I even look the same anymore?*

She'd had twenty-two years to forget what I looked like. I only remembered snatches of Gerry's face, so like our older brother, Hez… like Gran Da. An ache welled in my chest and crept out with a chill. I gasped in a short breath and held it, wishing I were anywhere but here.

I'd never expected to see any of them again.

I'd never expected to be home.

Satie shimmied over the rail and down the ladder at the belly of the ship – the same one we'd been forced up at Darzeth's lone dock at the Massacre. It was our ship, by blood and by right, but it was also our prison and our death barge. I love it and I hated it and I was going back on it again. Satie pulled a crate from the dive hut, up-ended it and stood on the base. She opened her arms wide, smiling.

"Welcome, Citizens. Thank you for restocking our supplies before we head south to complete our mission. New crew and designated travellers, please take a moment to say your farewells. We set sail in twenty minutes. When you're ready, join me at the belly of the ship for a quick tour." She hopped back down and replaced the crate. Nothing said about the gods favouring our travels or what the cargo down in the hold might be. I knew, of course, as did Delenon and Kaynee, no doubt.

Keeper Gedrix and Delenon spoke briefly and answered a few questions for the ever-present media. Delenon's rumbling voice held both a serious note and a hopeful one, echoing Satie's tone.

We were on a mission, and for the Kronik of all people. The Kronik – a Talian *and* a Commoner now. I shook my head, reeling from it all. I shifted my backpack, filled with the few items I'd collected, and tapped Delenon on the shoulder. Most of the others stood with Satie. It was time to board.

He shook hands with Gedrix one more time, then walked with me onto the boardwalk over to the far pier. Satie nodded to us and motioned for the group to follow her up the wooden ladder set into the side of the ship. I kept half-an-eye on Kaynee and the other half on those travelling with us, trying to get a sense for who they were. After all, Delenon wasn't just *our* leader, he was the world's now.

I grabbed onto the sea-dampened wooden rungs, the last person to board. With every step and every reach, my body grew heavier and heavier. I forced myself to take even breaths, but it still took every ounce of willpower to haul myself onboard.

Satie divided the twenty new travellers into two groups – one to remain with her and one to stay with Tony. I knew Drax hovered nearby, but I couldn't see him.

"Kay!" a man shouted and swung down from the rigging. His button-up shirt had come undone, exposing his pale blue chest and gold coliths. The line of his jaw and sturdy build hit me like a hurricane. I hid behind Delenon and leaned against a barrel as my knees quaked.

Bridden?

But not. The man's coliths were gold, not purple. Gold, like Grand Mum's – skipping a generation.

"My baby," I whispered.

"Mum? You okay?" Teena gripped my arm and kept me from falling.

"Where–?" Where had she come from? And who was the tanned stranger shadowing her? A flash of blue drew my gaze back to the man now enveloping Kaynee in a hug, their voices muffled by the crowd. I was frozen and yet my insides flopped around like jelly. I kept gulping air into an unresponsive body.

"Mum. What's going on? Mardel, take her other arm and help me get her to the Med Bay."

"N– no. I need to stay with Kronik Delenon."

"What?"

"Who?"

Of course, they hadn't heard. I shook my head to clear it as they led me below deck. "Magistrate Delenon is now co-Kronik with Dezmind Lisle." Too many thoughts invaded my mind at once. I blinked and shook my head to try to get rid of them.

"Lay down. Mardel and I will keep an eye on Delenon. I'll get All Mother."

"Satie. Yes. Need to talk to Satie." I pulled my pack from my back and curled up on the cot hugging it to me as my daughter and her boyfriend left. I lay, muttering to myself,

327

reliving Bridden being shot to death right in front of me; of me whispering a broken promise to four-year-old Kaynee; watching Delenon's swearing-in ceremony; the new Kronik's face giving way to that contractor-bodyguard; and my chubby baby boy's face flashing back and forth between my last memory of him and the man outside who'd hugged my sister.

"Daria? Daria, what's wrong? What's going on?" Satie's cool hand touched my forehead. "You're not feverish. Come on, sit up now. Teena's worried. Look at me." She took hold of my jaw and turned my head toward her. My gaze met hers and my eyes finally stilled.

"Satie."

"Yes, it's me. What's going on?"

I gripped my pack, then released it and zipped open the top, never once taking my eyes from the one constant that had brought me back from the brink and never gave up on me. My fingers wrapped around the worn leather binding, and I pulled the book free.

"They found it," I said.

"My journal!" She gingerly lifted it from my grasp, turned it around and all over and then flipped through the pages. "In... tact! How? What? I thought for sure they'd destroy it." She hugged it to her chest and closed her eyes briefly.

I nodded. "They were going to – but publicly. To make a statement. SO Jezetek found it at the Faction's main hideout."

"Did they get them all?"

I hesitated before answering, "Not quite. There's still

one out there." I dropped the pack to the floor and rubbed my face with my hands. This, at least, was something I could focus on. "Between the Talian Citizens helping hide him, and the mole in the council, the new Kronik is doing everything possible to fix this."

"There's a mole in the council? How do they know?"

"They know."

"Okay. You can tell me about that later. What about now? What happened up there? Here? Talk to me."

I squeezed my eyes shut tight and struggled to push that one word past my lips for the second time in over twenty years.

"Gelden."

Chapter 44

Legacy

Taya

I turned and stared at the Mini-V's lens attached to the band on Kye's forehead. The usual fleeting traces of memory from the super quake at the Solar Plex flashed through my mind.

"Are you ready? We're only going to do this once," I said.

"Ready when you are, boss." He adjusted everything to the lighting levels, prepping for the official tour.

I glanced to the ceiling of the spaceship and knelt beside Gellik to hook up the double Whipstaff battery to the first section of the main panel. Gellik radiated heat. I glanced at him as he made the final connections. A volley of sweat slid down his face from his forehead. It was hot, sure, but still morning – nowhere near what it got to mid-day.

"You all right?" I nudged his shoulder.

He blinked and wiped his damp skin with the back of

his arm. "What? Yes. Just a little warm."

"Are you nervous about the ship arriving later?"

"Somewhat."

"Me too."

I never would've admitted that even three months ago, but both the world and I were very different these days. I turned back to Kye and stood up. The red recording light winked at me. My mouth went dry. He waved at me to start talking. I was not meant to be in front of a camera. Zaith knew that. He wasn't Zaith.

"In anticipation of the arrival of the LRM's ship, we're conducting a full-system review of the spacecraft. For the past month, Professor Gellik of the CTF, and I, as head of Kronik security—"

"And professor of languages," Kye interrupted.

I wanted to scowl at him, but I also didn't want to have to do a second or third take either, so I didn't.

"—have been tasked with learning all there is to know about the spaceship. Let me show you around." I turned back to the control panel and brought up the main display on the darkened windshield.

"You'll notice figures in the upper corners. These dictate direction in four dimensions: latitude, longitude, altitude, and relative speed. Everything is, as expected, in Dakturian, and only someone familiar with their language and culture could even consider taking it for a test drive." My heart jumped at the thought. It did every time Gellik and I talked about the possibility. I'd been teaching him the Dakturian language almost since our arrival in the south.

I triggered another button and the main screen

dissolved to reveal the beach, water, and distant hole in the trees from our accidental weapons test two weeks ago.

"You don't need to see where you're going in order to fly in outer space, but it does help with travelling in the planet's atmosphere – and it would be pretty cool to see the suns. But outer space is mostly black with distant blots of pale starlight, and interstellar travellers would rely mostly on the calculations you see in the upper corners to navigate."

Gellik took over. "We call it a theory even though we've read the Dakturian manual because we haven't actually done it yet. We have no way of knowing if the package the LRM and UGC volunteers are bringing will succeed in powering up the entire craft."

He motioned to an intricate set of slightly raised controls attached to the arms of the chairs. "These are used only once we pass from inner to outer space. They are the gamma controls. This ship requires two sets of thrust power – one set to get us beyond the ozone layer and the other to harness the abundant gamma rays leaking out into the solar system. The Dakturians would have us believe this ship can harness the power within those rays to affect pitch and yaw via their absorption and repulsion of the ship's alloy shell."

He sat down in one of the chairs, but it almost looked as if he fell into it, panting. I took over for him earlier than planned.

"As you can see on this panel here"—I pointed to the area in front of my vacant chair—"the controls for takeoff and thrust are similar to the heilos used around northern Xannia, though this craft is maybe twenty times the size of one."

I took Kye and the world through every inch of that ship. Gellik and I never once mentioned *how* to do all of these amazing things, just that they could be done. Beyond the dynamics of the dual-propulsion system, which no one was likely to believe anyway, Dezmind wanted us to give the appearance of complete accessibility without actually granting it. It was a fine line, but a necessary one. The last thing we needed was another group like the Faction spawning and using the alien tech against us. Besides, half the time Gellik and I still didn't know the how – just that it worked.

It took us the better part of an hour to complete the documentary. It would've been half that time if Kye hadn't insisted on motioning me to keep talking, but even that didn't bother me. We'd gone through and re-tested every operational system, panel by panel, with our mini-battery, and they all worked!

"That's a wrap," Kye said back in the cockpit as he clicked off his Mini-V. I turned to Gellik and hugged him. He nearly fell over.

"I'm so sorry, Professor." I laughed at my own over-exuberance.

He coughed out a chuckle, too. It lasted a little longer than either of us expected. I rubbed his back, but he manoeuvred beyond my reach, leaning forward on his knees to catch his breath. I caught sight of flaking skin on the back of his neck. Maybe he'd been spending too much time in the south's sun.

"Come on. Let's grab a drink and sit in the shade. We've

earned it."

I wanted to race off into the trees on my own to call Dez and give him the good news, but that could wait. As we found a shaded bench by the tree line, a cool breeze whisked in off the sea. Kye handed each of us a cup of water. Gellik eased himself down and nudged me with his knee.

"Go already."

"What?"

"Make your call. I'm not going anywhere."

"Are you sure?"

Kye laughed at us.

I blushed. "Okay. I'll be right back." I slipped away into the dappled light under the leafy trees and checked the time. Council had finished during our recording of the documentary. I dropped to a fallen log and flipped up my watch-com.

"Dezmind Lyle." The grey screen blipped in confirmation of my voice and made the call. I watched the numbers flash from three to one.

He didn't answer. I cut off the recording and tried to swallow the lump forming in my throat. I called again.

Three.

Two.

On—

"Taya?" His voice shot adrenaline through my veins.

I laughed.

"Who else would it be?" I said, and his face came into view on the small screen.

He sighed. "Tell me you have good news. Has the LRM

ship arrived?"

"No, not yet. But I do have good news."

His eyes brightened perceptibly. I hadn't noticed the deeper lines and darker shadows until that moment.

"Is everything okay?" I asked.

"You first."

"All systems are go! We just finished the documentary for the network. Everything worked as anticipated, and Gellik and I know that ship forwards and backwards now. We couldn't be any better situated." Except that I still had no idea how we were going to integrate the geomagnetic rock into the propulsion system – but he didn't need to know that right now.

"Thank the Trinity."

"What's happening over there?"

He hesitated as if debating what to say or how much to tell me. I hated when he did that. Thankfully, it didn't happen often. But it did remind me how impossible it was to be in two places at once. He needed me and I was here, thousands of miles away.

"I've disbanded the council."

"You've what? Why?"

"The mole is one of them. One of the Talians, I'm sure. But I can't point fingers and I can't play favourites."

"What did Magis— Kronik Delenon say?"

There was that pause again.

"I did it after he left."

"Where would he go? Wait. He's coming here? Why?"

"Mainly it's something he feels he needs to do. Most of the relatives of the LRM are down there along with over half of the UGC. That and something Gerrund said about not thinking it wise to send down any non-UGC other than family members. He wants to get to the bottom of it in person."

"And now it's just you and Tek looking for the mole and the last Faction Leader? Do you have any leads? What's the plan?"

Again, he fell silent.

"I—"

A cry went up at the beach. Shouts of joy and excited whoops. "Dez, I think the LRM just arrived. I gotta go. We'll talk tonight. I'll let you know how it goes." I kissed the air. He mimicked me and the screen went grey. I leapt up and crashed through the trees back to the beach.

I stumbled over the slight drop from earth to sand as I broke free of the canopy. Kye stood on the bench beside Gellik, who was hunched over with his elbows on his thighs, watching the crowds of people stream toward the small dock by the shore. Just rounding the straight sailed the largest sea vessel I'd ever seen. It looked exactly like the one shown in the documentaries on the Wire.

Three sets of sails billowed in the changing winds as it turned into the cove.

"Come on, Professor. I hear Kronik Delenon is on board. Let me introduce you." I turned to Gellik and smiled, holding my hand out to help him up. He grasped it and staggered to his feet. I frowned but shook the negative thought away.

"Could you really do that? Oh, I have been wanting to meet him." He laughed and then coughed, slowing down and falling behind. I paused and turned to wait for him.

"Gellik!" I shrieked. He lay on his side in the sand, coughing and hacking. I dropped beside him, not sure how to help or what was happening. I tried to help him sit. A blast of heat quaked off his body.

"Help! Somebody, help me!"

Two UGC soldiers noticed us and broke from the crowds. The one closest spoke into his com.

"Please, you have to help me get him to the Clinic. Something's wrong."

"Go," the lead soldier said, and his partner ran off toward Gerrund's tower. Moments later the soldier returned with a stretcher and the General.

"What's going on, J.J.?" He crouched beside me as his men worked to roll the professor onto the stretcher.

"He collapsed. He's feverish and can't stop coughing. I don't know what's wrong. We have to help him." I rose beside Gellik as the guards lifted him. A heavy sensation of dread clawed up my spine, needling things from another life. Gerrund supported the opposite side of the stretcher, and we kept the professor from falling off as we rushed against the thinning crowd, away from the impromptu celebration breaking out on the beach.

We didn't say anything. We just ran in the opposite direction.

When the clinic finally came into sight, I wanted to break away and bust the door down. But Gellik still coughed even though he moved little. A large burst of anything and he might roll off the stretcher. I gripped the pole, squeezing a scream into the innocent wood.

The front-man kicked at the door until the nurse from the front desk yanked it open. A shout for Mamma Lu echoed down the long corridor.

Even when Lu swung around the door of her office and came running, the inky dread wrapped tendrils of ache around my guts. She shouted for reinforcements. Two more nurses appeared as if from nowhere. I hadn't seen them coming, only Gellik growing more still.

Lu and her staff took over the stretcher and rushed the professor into an open room. In less than a nanosecond, they had him on a bed and Lu stood filling the door frame.

"You can't come in, Taya."

"Will he be all right?"

Lu pursed her lips.

"Give it to her straight, Lutrice," Gerrund growled.

I waved him off.

"I'll see you outside, J.J." The General left with his guards, the weight of expectation still clinging to the air.

"I don't know. I won't know until we can stabilise him. Come back in an hour. We should have an answer for you then."

"Promise?"

"No."

She shut the door on me. I reached for the handle, but a hard *click* snapped in the empty hall.

I wanted to collapse. To run. To scream and cry. To dive into the sea and just keep swimming.

In the end, I ran.

Chapter 45
Reunion

Taya

Branches whipped my face, arms and legs as I crashed through underbrush, overgrowth and shrubbery under the shifting shadows of the canopy. Fleeting shouts and yells of excitement wavered in and out, mingling with the snapping of twigs as I ran.

I ran and ran and ran.

Until the trees disappeared and I tripped over my own two feet. I fell to my knees, eyes unseeing as my sight turned inward and replayed Gellik's collapse and the clinic door slamming in my face. I squeezed my eyelids shut and screamed at the top of my lungs. Birds took off squawking and flapping from limbs high above. My skin prickled along the nape of my neck as haunting wisps of song wove through the clearing in their wake.

My heart leapt into my throat. I snapped my eyes open and looked around.

The memorial garden.

A bright metallic post at the base of the canopy goddess, the enormous tree across from the generator's aperture, held a single new windpipe. I didn't need to be told who it belonged to.

I crawled forward on the carpet of moss, each limb shaking; the heat of anger and months of frustrations radiating off me. I grabbed the staked pole and caught a flash of Dakturian writing spelling out an all-too-familiar name: Zaith Beji. Slamming my forehead against the shaft, I closed my eyes, opened my soul, and let everything go in one long wail.

The uncertainty – had she only been using me? I'd never had a truer friend.

The anger – her betrayal at the cliff. Her struggle to kill herself rather than me.

The confusion – her unwillingness to give up on a fractured friendship.

The pain – her sacrifice for Dezmind, for the Kahn-Lea, for me.

The love...

Tears coursed over my cheeks as my heart threatened to burst with the ache of it all. Zaith was dead. Dezmind was pulling away. Gellik was sick. And the fate of the world sat squarely on my shoulders. If I didn't get that gods forsaken alien spaceship operational, the people of Xannia would tear this world apart. A super virus had destroyed the Dakturians, but ignorance would be our undoing. Even if Dez launched the missile to blow up Gamma and save the verrin supply, the religious civil war that followed would devour us as surely as any deadly virus.

The hollow whisper of voices long past cradled my broken heart and empty soul, reminding me that I was here for a reason.

I was the first naturally born half-Talian.

I'd survived the streets.

I'd worked the mines.

I'd put myself through school.

I became the youngest contractor ever.

I'd been sucked into the Pit of Chance, had scaled the underground verrin cliff, crossed the Deserts, saved the future Kronik, stopped the super quakes, discovered an alien civilization, and sacrificed myself to ensure the Cause won the coup. Zaith once said to me, "You've done everything you needed to in order to survive." That wasn't about to stop now.

Gripping the pole tightly, I hauled my sorry ass off the ground and wiped the tears from my face with the back of my hands. I turned and walked back to the beach.

I had a job to do.

* * *

Daria

As the rowboat glided toward shore, Satie grabbed my hand and squeezed. I squeezed back but for different reasons. A bitter ache consumed my chest. I'd tried several times to approach Kaynee and Gelden. I'd even gotten so far as to reach out and touch a shoulder or arm but pulled back and turned away before either noticed. Before I knew it, two days had passed, and the cove came in sight. I'd run out of time.

I glanced back at the vessel that had brought us halfway around the world and back. I'd spent all my time trying to get off that ship, and now I wanted nothing more than to be on it again. Stroke after stroke, the rowers brought us closer to what the Island had given us false promises of – hope. But all it brought me were random shudders and spikes of fear-laced adrenaline.

I watched Teena and Mardel walk so close along the beachfront they might as well have been holding hands. I had to watch him. I had to watch all of them because Teena wouldn't. Gelden stood with Kaynee, talking to one of the UGC soldiers, judging by the tan fatigues and muscle shirt. Hundreds of people milled about on the sand. A wooden tower and marketplace edged a line of tall trees.

Satie and I helped moor the boat, then she and Drax walked with Delenon down the short dock toward the waiting crowd. I followed, scanning the people milling about. Most of the LRM disappeared into the smiling and laughing crowd. No one yet realised who walked toward them. My pulse ratcheted higher. I took a long, shaky breath and shook out my hands.

A tall Danieth couple detached from the closest pocket of LRM and walked toward us, the others trailing behind, immersed in their conversations. Though the couple walked side-by-side, the commanding stature and presence of the woman told me who she was. I searched the crowd for a Nirian man. The deeper shade of grey popped out but I couldn't get a good look at any of them. We stepped from the wooden planks onto the soft sand, the breeze bringing a fresh scent from the woods after too much saltwater.

"Welcome to South City! I'm Lutrice, and this is my husband Deltek. We are two of the Caretakers here." She spread her arms wide as if to offer a hug, and maybe she was, I don't know. And that's when I saw it. The flash of recognition sharpening every feature. But it wasn't Drax who caused it—

"Magistrate Delenon?" Her arms froze at their apex, her fingers jolting open.

"Actually, it's Kronik Delenon these days," he said, stepping forward and giving her a hug. Her husband stared at the two, as did the rest of us. I coughed.

"Sir?"

He pulled back with a chuckle. "Don't worry, Daria. Lu and I go way back. She worked as a Junior Staffer back in the day. We had—"

"Did you say Daria?" a deep voice rumbled. My heart careened around in my chest as a familiar face on a much older body parted the three Danieths before me. "Gods, it is you."

I froze. My breath. My heart. My brain.

He burst forward, grabbed me in a giant hug and swung me around, laughing. The ice inside me melted and I folded into him.

"Gerrund," I sobbed, taking a shuddering breath. "You didn't do anything stupid like get yourself killed."

He laughed and hugged me tighter. "I almost did. But I'm sure you've heard about that by now. I, too, have a Talien friend, only mine's the other half of the team leading this gods forsaken planet." He pulled back, still holding me tight but giving himself room to look at me. It was the same look I'd seen over and over again as the LRM reunited with their families after our return: joy, shock, disbelief. But in that moment of glances, my gaze slipped past him to my little sister, jumping and tugging on a young man's arm. I saw her mouth form words I couldn't hear but saw echoed on my daughter's face as she looked from me to the boy and back.

I gripped Gerrund's arms tighter, my breath catching in my throat. He turned and looked over his shoulder.

"What? Gods, Daria, don't tell me you sailed all this way and never introduced yourself."

"I didn't know what to say," I whispered, holding fast as he supported me with an arm around my waist, and we all moved as if in slow motion toward each other. Everyone except Teena. A piece of me fractured at that moment. The little boy I never thought I'd see again stood before me as a man.

"Daria!" Kaynee shrieked. "You kept your promise!" She crashed into me. My baby sister had never forgotten I'd told her *I'd be back, I just didn't know when.* "Why didn't you say something on the ship?"

Gerrund kept us from falling over as we staggered in one giant hug. Good-natured chuckles came from my LRM family and the South City Ambassadors, but I still couldn't breathe properly as my daughter stared at my son staring at me.

My siblings must have sensed something amiss. They pulled open the hug, me still standing sandwiched between the two, and followed my line of sight. My baby still hadn't moved. His expression was unreadable, just like Brid's during a planning session or when he chopped raw veggies and got lost in thought.

He looked from me to Teena.

He knows. Oh, Sweet Zerameteth, he knows what I did.

"Gelden!" Gerry called. "Get your ass over here. It's about time you met your mother."

He didn't move.

A lifetime passed inside a nanosecond.

He wouldn't move.

I had to.

Did I have the strength? I had to try. I gave each of my siblings a squeeze, let go and took a step forward. The gaping cavity in my chest ached for the little boy I'd left behind twenty-two years ago; for the husband who'd died in my arms and now stood re-born in our child before me. Did he know he looked like his father? Did Gerry have any pictures? No. We had nothing when we were forced Underground – nothing but each other.

I commanded one foot to step in front of the other, focusing on my son yet keeping my daughter in my peripheral vision. The disbelief etched onto her face screamed my incompetence as a mother. Her unspoken words echoed inside my head: *Why didn't you ever tell me?*

Why didn't I? My gaze locked with Gelden's as I stood just over an arm's length away. No words could ever convey how sorry I was for making the wrong choice – or maybe it was the right one, but I hadn't been strong enough to survive it.

Tears slipped over my cheeks as I held my hand out to

him. No one spoke but the buzz of excitement swelled around us.

My arm shook. My lips trembled. A hand reached out and grasped mine, tight. I smiled, then looked at Teena and held my other hand out to her. She frowned and cocked her head to the side as if asking, *Then what?* I raised my eyebrows to say, *Why not find out?*

And she walked forward and held my other hand.

Chapter 46
Cursed

Taya

From the back of the crowd, I watched Gelden reach out and claim his mother's hand along with the youth Teena's. Gerrund and Kaynee joined them, and the family that had once been torn apart by the old Kronik went off to rediscover themselves. Daria glanced over her shoulder at Kronik Delenon but Drax waved her off and stepped forward to act in her stead.

Another ache in the long list of aches that plagued me this morning was the sight of a lone Talian amidst a flock of Commoners. But this was not *my* Talian. He stood with Delenon and All Mother, speaking to Deltek and… Lutrice. I frowned. Lu was supposed to be taking care of Professor Gellik. I dragged my black mood through the happy reunions along the beach and tapped Lu on the shoulder mid-sentence. She turned, confusion shadowing her gaze.

"Taya? I thought you'd be waiting at the clinic."

"I thought you'd be diagnosing at the clinic."

She turned back to the small, important group. "Excuse me, I'll be right back." She grabbed my elbow, much as Zaith might have done, and walked me away from the crowds to the edge of the water.

"What are you doing, Taya?"

"What do you mean? I should ask that of you. You said it would take an hour to diagnose the professor, and yet not twenty minutes later, I find you schmoozing with the big-wigs."

"I'm not the only one capable of taking care of Gellik. My staff are all highly trained. And, I'm more than just a nurse. I'm the head of this community. I had to be here for this."

"So did Gellik and me. We need that super lodestone. We need to get that damn spaceship up and running to save the bloody planet. So, I ask you, how is chatting it up at an impromptu soiree more important than getting a handle on Gellik's health? We're down to the wire here. Save the celebrations for when we have something to be thankful for."

She slapped me – full across my cheek. My eyes bulged before the burn set in.

"Listen to yourself! Gods, Taya. It's under control."

My hand itched to hit her back. I wasn't the one who needed the sense knocked into her. She grabbed my arm and yanked me around the edge of the crowd back to the tree line. I shook free of her once we hit the path back to the clinic.

"Gellik probably has some form of heat exhaustion, or

he got bit by one of the many bugs out here and we just need to figure out which one. He'll likely be back on his feet by tomorrow when we can focus on transferring the lodestone to the spaceship, and then the two of you can tinker to your heart's content."

"Dezmind was supposed to order the rocket launch two days ago. It's all on us. We can't wait another month. We can't wait another week. Gellik and I need to be working on this now. We can't be complacent. The FOL is threatening a religious revolution if we blow up Gamma. What don't you get? We're out of time and I need the professor."

She paused and turned to me. "You sound just like the General."

I jammed my hands on my hips and stared at her.

"But you're right. I had no idea it was this bad. He doesn't tell me everything. Doesn't respect me enough to keep me in the loop, and I don't have a direct line to Dezmind the way he does. The way you do. Instead, I'm left dealing with the everyday problems without fully grasping why everyone is on-edge all the time." She waved the air in front of her as if to push all this aside. "Come on. Let's check in on Gellik and my team." She turned and jogged the remaining distance to the clinic. I followed a half-step behind.

Why has Gerrund been keeping Lu in the dark? It didn't make sense. No wonder they were constantly at each other's throats.

The mild breeze cooled my stinging cheek as well as my temper. She didn't think Gellik was all that bad off. A bite. A day out of commission. Serious but treatable. I'd overreacted – again. Still, I knew very well I couldn't do this alone, and seeing Gellik collapse like that brought everything I'd been keeping at bay crashing down at once.

I took several steadying breaths as we walked through the main entrance of the clinic. Lu left me by the door as she spoke with the nurse at the desk. The two of them disappeared down the hall. I eyed the chairs set around the bright, white room but couldn't bring myself to sit. I didn't pace either. Now I was back and questions were being answered, my body refused to listen to me. Wait. Just wait.

So I did.

I stared at the opening between Reception and the hall that led to the treatment rooms. The last time we were here, Gellik had been dehydrated. We'd been good this past month, balancing our verrin intake with water – it had become a science around here with everyone. I hadn't taken the time to do my research on South City. It was an entirely different eco-zone. Lu and the remaining Kahn-Lea had lived here for over half a year and knew this place inside and out. A bug bite. I had no idea which bugs were poisonous and which weren't. I'd been so focused on getting the job done that I'd ignored my CTF training.

Footsteps softly whisked down the hall. Lu's cadence. When she materialised, her frown deepened. Something wasn't right. She should be smiling, at least a little.

"Why don't you sit, Taya?" She held my arm and tried to steer me toward the chairs. I shrugged her off.

"What's wrong? What bit him?"

She inhaled a deep breath.

I held mine.

"It's not a bite. He's got the alien virus."

Flashes of false memories flickered through my mind as I imagined Ketic, the Dakturian whose journal I'd translated on our journey through the Deserts, leaving this city and searching for a chance to live. Only nine had survived...

"But— but that's not possible, is it? The vaccine— We all took it. Dezmind mandated that everyone back in the prime get vaccinated. Even the LRM were given shots their first week back."

"Just because something is mandated, doesn't mean everyone listens."

"What?"

"In Professor Gellik's case, he admitted to always being too busy to make his doctor's appointment and then just forgot to reschedule. That was months ago. It didn't even cross his mind that he still needed to get it before travelling south. He's not immune. The bacteriophage has progressed into stage two. We have successfully treated most stage two infections. He should recover."

I sucked in air and let it out slowly. "Most stage two infections? So, there's still a chance he might die?" I couldn't think straight. If I hadn't convinced him to come down here, this never would've happened.

"We've only ever lost one stage two case. And that was because she walked into a sealed-off lab looking for the cure and stopped taking proper care of herself."

"Zaith?" I whispered. No one had ever explained it to me, just that she'd caught the virus – bacteriophage.

Lu nodded. Then the timeline set off alarm bells in my head.

"Wait. How long does it take to recover?"

"The only other serious case of stage two infection took several weeks. But he was fit and stubborn. It might be another month before Gellik is well enough to get around unaided."

But I didn't have months.

I didn't even have days.

"Meeka."

I'd lost my partner – again.

I looked up at the heavens and screamed inside my head, *I can't do this alone! Why do you keep insisting that I do?* I refused to let fate dictate my actions. I turned and left.

This was war.

Chapter 47

A Conversation with the Gods

Dezmind

I paced my office, glancing at the time far too frequently. After Taya's call about Professor Gellik's condition and needing to find yet another co-pilot for the mission, I finally understood what to do with the Oracle's advice. I ran my plan by Delenon. He agreed, but he was also thousands of miles away in South City. I needed back-up in case something happened.

A firm knock altered my circuit around the room. I opened the door.

"Tek, thank you for coming."

I stepped aside. He stood a few inches taller than me, filling the space with his mass as well as his height. Taya had been right to suggest we hire him, but he still made me nervous. They had a history. He'd saved her life after the coup. She'd turned to him when I wasn't available – no, when I'd refused to see how much help she needed after the coma. I knew this man still loved her. I could only hope he'd do right by her and help me, now.

"You called for me, sir?" He stood at ease in the middle of the room, feet shoulder width apart, hands clasped behind his back. A good soldier. A dedicated officer.

I closed the door behind him and sat on the corner of my desk facing him. "You're the only one, other than Kronik Delenon, I can trust with this. I need to take you into my confidence because, quite frankly, I don't want to die today."

"Sir?"

I clasped my hands loosely on my one raised knee and studied my Special Operatives' commander and wondered if the old Kronik ever did this with his head secret agent. The Oracle was right: we really weren't that different. That was about to change.

"I'll be leaving the Capitol Building today, unescorted, to a clandestine meeting. A call for a truce with the Guardian overseers of the Followers of the Light from across Xannia."

"But, sir, where will you meet with them? If you leave the building unescorted, you'll be open to attack by the remaining Faction Leader."

"As I've said, no one else knows about this – not the council, not even Taya. I have a way out of the building and from the Compound using the Underground tunnel system. What I need from you is twofold: one, contact Dias Betauni – she's acting in Kaynee Kipling's stead. Arrange for her to have these tunnels clear at these times."

I picked up a sketch I'd drawn of the area and passed it

to him.

"Two, have a covert extraction team at the ready outside the address on the back of that sheet. That's where we'll hold the meeting. I wish I could say I have faith that the Guardians won't break their promise and try something, but I don't. If this job has taught me anything, it's to over prepare. Can I trust you to be discrete? No one can know of my absence or why they're watching that building. I'll keep a digital flare"—I picked up the small signalling device between my fingernails from a black dish on my desk—"under the flip-screen of my watch-com. The tracking code is below the address."

He glanced to the page to verify and nodded.

"May I ask why you're hiding this meeting? Wouldn't it look good if the citizens saw you reaching out to the Guardians? Especially now?"

"Yes, I'm sure the Commoners would see it as such, but I need to keep everyone in mind right now especially those who would see this as a move by me to secure secular backing in an impending war."

"You don't want to give the FOL the wrong idea."

"Exactly. I can't let this become another red flag in their eyes – me trying to show I'm better than they are. Between announcing that Gamma's a fake sun, the leaked info about the rocket plan, and no Guardian Rep on council, my actions could easily be misconstrued. We're on fragile ground, and this mole has escalated a complicated situation from bad to worse. We've stopped the flow of intel to the remaining Faction Leader. Now, it's time to cauterise the wound. I'm leaving in one hour."

"Yes, sir. You can count on me."
Gods, I hope so.

* * *

Dezmind

My footsteps echoed down the eerily silent Underground tunnel. The Dias had cleared out this bustling sector in less than an hour. I only hoped she hadn't given Tek too much of a headache about it. I walked into the Underground temple where, Taya had told me, All Mother had made a stir on her first day back in town.

Chairs and crates stood to either side of the door that had once been a transpoint for the Resistance. The knob had been removed from this side, so I knocked.

No answer.

I checked my com – five minutes early.

"Really?" I breathed low. They were sending a message. So, I waited.

At exactly noon I knocked again.

The door groaned open. A single Guardian stood before me. She stepped aside and moulded her body to the wall. *Must be a trusted Devout.* We'd agreed not to speak of this meeting to any of our followers. However, just as I had looped in Tek, so she would've patched in her security, too.

I nodded to her.

She closed the door and motioned for me to follow her farther along the lower corridor. I had no idea they'd have rooms below ground. I hoped a signal could get out should I need it to. My pulse raced even through my slow, steady breathing. This was unprecedented.

The Sun Guardian opened the door for me, and I stepped into a dim space. As my eyes adjusted, twelve Guardian overseers, one from each sector, stood in a circle before me. A single crate rested slightly apart from the open ring. I glanced around the room. Storage containers and supplies climbed the walls, and stacks of crates dominated the lower spaces.

An impromptu meeting space.

I stepped forward but didn't speak. This wasn't my turf.

When no one else spoke, I bit my tongue. This was a test.

Again, I waited. Instead of counting the beat of my own heart, I studied the faces of the men and women standing with me – representations of all the races of Xannia save one. I had to admit I didn't have a clue what the Talian Guardians thought of all this. The ones making the most noise lay on this side of the wall.

A Guardian stepped forward and spoke a prayer:

May the Trinity's light illuminate
Our souls and their worth.
Bring guidance to the lost,
Strength to the weak, love to those forsaken.
May the warmth of Your rays brighten the dark
Within and without,
Uniting each soul with grace and wisdom.

"Zozizer," they all responded.

"Welcome, Kronik," she said, but I didn't feel welcome.

"Thank you for agreeing to meet," I said.

"An odd request during this volatile time, to be sure. However, you have done as you've said and come alone. We recognise this as grounds for open and honest communication." In other words, no media influence and no way for me to twist their words against them in the eyes of the public. I understood that.

I nodded to her and to each side of the circle. They sat down. I did, too. I don't know if I was supposed to or not, but for me to remain standing would have been a power play. We were all equals here. I only hoped they saw it that way.

"I would like to share my concerns with you one-on-one. No more second-hand information and unanswered questions. You have serious apprehensions, as you should, about the state of the planet. I have notes and journals and images I'd like to share with you. Some you may have seen before on the Wire but some not." I pulled my shoulder satchel around in front and removed several Dakturian books, including Ketic's journal, and my vis-u-fax.

A young male Guardian held his hand out for the device. I passed it to him and he opened the screen.

"The password is UNITED."

He keyed it in. His fingers breezed over the board, no doubt searching the device for anything untoward. There was only one file on it and nothing more. He passed it back to me. I called up the images of the Chronicles and the Aperture.

"This is why we believe Zerameteth is an even younger god than we first thought." That got their attention. I'd been working on that line for hours. I had to show them I respected their beliefs, and that I took this meeting seriously.

"You'll notice, in these books, images sketched by the

Dakturians. Here they're transcribed into Xannian. I am willing to instruct anyone who is interested in how to translate their language so you can see for yourselves that we're not making anything up. This is simply what we discovered when we went south.

"As you're all well aware, the scientific community has long debated whether Zerameteth is a sun or a moon. Most experts agreed that because Zerameteth gives off light and heat, even as little as he does, that he is, indeed, a sun. The Dakturian's verify this as well, here and here." I pointed and gave them time to digest the information.

"They claim, here, that they helped birth Zerameteth to make the planet more habitable for them – what we refer to as terraforming."

"Gods cannot be created by mortals," an older, male Guardian grumbled. The others murmured in agreement.

"I didn't say they created him. I said—"

"I heard you. Just because you say 'birthed' doesn't mean you believe it."

"What I believe doesn't matter. This is about what you believe. You believe Zerameteth is a sun. We agree on that. You've long upheld that he's the youngest of the gods. We also agree on that. What I'm trying to do is show you why I believe he was born – to help the Dakturians. The problem is, his light and heat, little though they may be, are having an adverse effect on our planet. He was born to change the world, and that's what he's been doing for thousands of years. The problem is, if he doesn't stop soon, what's left of our verrin will disappear and us with it."

"So, your solution is to blow him up," the female

Guardian who welcomed me spat.

"Maybe. No. Not necessarily." I sighed. I didn't think it would escalate this fast. "There may be another way, but it's a longshot. Something the media isn't aware of."

Several of the Guardians present leaned forward, their faces open instead of a mask of hostility. *Taya's gonna kill me for this.*

"And if it's going to work – if we're going to even have a chance of saving Zerameteth – we'll need your help."

"What is it? What can we do?"

"Pray."

Chapter 48
Destiny's Wager

Taya

I stood at the tree line on the path, watching the laughter and smiles, hugs and handshakes, as the UGCs welcomed the LRMs. A rustling came from behind me up the path. Mamma Lu stood beside me.

"What are you going to do?" she asked.

"What needs to be done."

"Can't you give them at least an hour of joy before—"

"Before what, Lu?" I confronted her. "We're already behind schedule. At the very least we need to learn if that lodestone will even work. If it doesn't, it's out of my hands, and Dezmind can launch that missile."

I turned back toward the crowd and caught sight of Delenon, All Mother, and Drax speaking to a group of youths. Gerrund and Daria were huddled with their family on the edge of the crowd near the marketplace booths. Piercing the throng, I wove a path toward Delenon's group.

Lu followed.

From behind the young men and women formerly of the UGC, I made eye contact with All Mother. She cocked her head to one side and excused herself from the conversation. Drax asked a question of her with his eyes, and she inclined her head toward me. I met her by the shore just off to the side of the group. Lu followed.

"Taya, it's good to see you. Is something the matter?"

"Do you remember our conversation in the Underground?" I asked.

"Yes, of course."

"You were right. It's happening, or it will if we don't succeed."

"What do you need me to do?"

"Find a way to get your cargo to shore while I prepare the engineering room on the spaceship. The sooner I can report back to Kronik Dezmind, the sooner we can move forward with one plan or the other."

At that moment, part of me hoped the geo-mag didn't work so I wouldn't have to face piloting the craft alone; another part of me hoped it did work so we at least stood half-a-chance of avoiding another rebellion.

"Will do. I'll get my team on it and send word when we're ready."

All Mother led Lu over to Delenon and tugged Drax aside. The second his face morphed from jovial to serious, I knew I'd chosen the right person to help me. Lu had also been right. These people needed some time to be happy. Drax and All Mother had a team and a plan. They'd pull away only those individuals necessary to help get the job done.

I followed the line of damp sand around the curve of the cove, past the milling crowd, and over to the spaceship. Inside the main area at the top of the ramp, as the tarp fell back to cover the opening, I stared at the mass of metal before me. My mind peeled away the layers of shrouding, conduit, and electrical wiring as I envisioned what Elix and I believed might be the skeletal structure of this craft. Some of the library diagrams of the larger ships echoed our theories; some didn't. We had so much still to learn about this technology.

Are we in over our heads here? I knew I was. I shoved all my misgivings aside, cracked a light-tube on, and headed for Engineering.

* * *

Taya

The com on my belt pack squawked, "Ready when you are."

I checked the double-Whipstaff battery connections for the fifth time. I held my breath and punched in the cargo-bay opening sequence from the small control room just outside the cargo area. We'd managed to manoeuvre the ion cylinder in and out using the side hatch, but we'd known from day one that these super lodestones were huge.

The rear portion of the ship peeled away, gears groaning. I ran into the cargo-bay and followed the worst of the noise to its source, tracking exactly what and where we'd need to add lubrication. A blast of cool sea breeze forced away the stifling hot air that always rose with the mid-day heat.

Gerrund, Gelden, and Daria worked with a crew to lay a ramp from the water over to a reinforced flatbed hauler. Even the General had been busy with his part of this task. Drax, Tony, Mardel and Captain Marxx grabbed onto netting surrounding an enormous oblong boulder floating on a giant raft. A team held the raft steady as the men heaved and dragged the monolith up the ramp and onto the hauler.

Muscles strained, tendons tightened, and teeth ground together as Marxx call "heave" and the others echoed "ho" with every haul forward. UGC guards kept onlookers a safe distance. Wisps of my hair, loosened from the day's events, fluttered up around my face. I pushed the larger strands behind my ears as Gerrund, Daria, Gelden and Teena pulled the hauler across the short distance of sand to the tail opening where I stood.

"What now?" the General asked.

"Can we reverse the water ramp and slide this thing in the rest of the way?"

He nodded and everyone moved to shift the ramp around. I walked the length of the lodestone. On the hauler, it went from my knees up past the tip of my fingers as I raised my arm to touch it. The dark exterior reminded me of petrified wood, but it was cool to the touch. A soft hum tickled the back of my ears.

Does anyone else hear it or feel the pressure change? Maybe. Maybe not. Twenty-five paces along, the end rounded to a gentle, elongated egg shape. Drax's team jumped up onto the back of the hauler bed as Gerrund's team gripped the netting to either side.

Marxx called out and his group pushed while the other pulled. Foot by foot, the exotic stone shifted closer and closer into the Engineering cargo-bay.

And then it was in.

The hauler and ramp disappeared as did most of the helpers. Only Gerrund, Drax, Daria, Delenon and All Mother remained.

"Come into the Engineering Control Room. I have no idea what will happen," I said.

"No idea at all?" Delenon asked.

"Well, almost no idea. See those small rectangular hatches scattered all over the sides, ceiling and floor? They contain connectors. I'll initiate the sequence for them to release and then figure out how to harness the magnetism from the super lodestone from there." I slid my make-shift battery over to allow for more room in the small space, closed the rear of the ship and the Engineering-bay door. They crowded around the large, convex window. I peered through a portal above the control panel.

"Here goes nothing," I said, heart beating into my throat. I pushed the initialisation button.

The rectangular hatches slid open and dozens of connector arms dropped out. I sighed in relief and swallowed past the lump in my throat. I moved to wipe both the sweat and loose hairs from my eyes but froze. The flat circles on the end of each hose-like protrusion rotated open. Arm-length strands of clear tentacle-like fibres shot out and danced maybe a handbreadth away from the geo-mag.

Various gasps escaped the onlookers, but no sound

made it out of my mouth. The giant lodestone lying on the floor of the bay shifted and hovered in the air as more access ports opened beneath it.

"Heavens above! It's floating." All Mother gasped.

"Taya, this is incredible. Did you know this would happen?" Gerrund asked.

Of course, I didn't know this would happen. I would've told them. Gods! But it was happening. I shook my head.

The soft buzzing that accompanied the geo-mag intensified and grew, vibrating my eardrums. I covered my ears with my hands, but it barely helped. Everything hummed as the control panel flickered and lit up. Even the recessed lights turned on! I let my arms fall to my sides and stared, open-mouthed, as the ship came alive.

"How…?" I muttered, trying to figure out how this could be possible. I mean, no rigging or alterations or piecemeal engineering required.

Gerrund caught my gaze and held it. "It's the Dakturian's again, isn't it?" He looked at the LRM, who lived on the Island surrounded by these super lodestones. "They didn't just put a sun in the sky to erase the inner verrin seas, but to grow these space rocks."

"Maybe." I shrugged my shoulders. But that didn't sound right. Professor Gellik – but the professor couldn't solve this mystery for us. Not now, anyway. I mashed my eyelids shut and focused on trying to find the right information locked away in my brain. "I don't think so. Maybe that's why the Dakturians chose Xannia to settle on in the first place? Maybe they were looking for them. But, even that doesn't sound right. Why would they destroy all of their generation ships and turn them into housing if they planned on using the geo-mags as generators? There would be some kind of record. But we haven't found anything, have we?"

"No," Gerrund said. "No one has ever mentioned it. There's nothing in the journals and schematics we've found. But neither was anything specified for what did run these things."

All Mother looked to the heavens and whispered a prayer.

Maybe she was right. Maybe it was Divine intervention.

I closed my eyes, a palpable weight settling over every inch of my body. Now I had to figure out how to fly this thing... *alone.*

Chapter 49

Double-Down

Taya

I flopped onto my chair and stared at the readings on the display screen for the fiftieth time that hour. I rerouted every major system over to my workstation, but I still couldn't do more than power up the thrusters and whip sand everywhere. Not a soul remained on the beach, not even the divers. Everyone had been given the afternoon off to celebrate the arrival of the LRM.

Everyone except me.

My hands hovered over the control panel. In my mind, I reviewed the sequencing, step-by-step, but I lost it all when I had to juggle three sets of calculations. I kicked the base of the control station and whipped around in a circle on my chair, face in hands. I grappled with anger and frustration, tried dousing them with calming breaths and repetitive actions, and I failed every time.

"I can't do this!" I shouted at the Heavens. Fate had a

sick sense of humour.

I shut it all down. The core pulsed in time to a green light on the main panel, but all systems were off. My hands shook. I waved them by my sides and leaned back in the chair, eyes closed. So far, the system showed the spaceship as fully operational, but I had no idea if this super lodestone was a one-time-use thing, self-regenerative, or something entirely new that we couldn't even define. We really had no idea what we were dealing with here. It was one thing to get a handle on the operational systems, another entirely to think we understood how any of it worked, and another thing to *actually* control it.

I rubbed my hands over my face and opened my eyes. If the powers that be insisted we get this thing in the air, then I needed help doing it. I needed a replacement for Professor Gellik, fast. I wasn't the only one who could read Dakturian script fluently. I sprang up and jogged off the ship.

* * *

Taya

Finding Mamma Lu wasn't as easy as I expected. She wasn't at the clinic, and by the time I got back to the Commons, the celebration superseded everything. Music blasted from two different locations as people danced and laughed around the central fountain and in the nearby side-streets.

I glimpsed Bazdin and Tamaine, twirling around with Jantice, another young man, Teena, and Mardel. Daria shadowed Delenon while Gelden, Kaynee, and Gerrund chatted in a group, occasionally including her in a shouted comment. I followed my nose to the outdoor cooking ovens and fire-pits.

Deltek, Syvis, Raylan and several other South citizens roasted meats for the dinner to come. I skirted around their helpers and caught Deltek's gaze as I neared. He smiled and inclined his head in greeting while he continued to turn the spit. I got close enough so I didn't have to yell to talk to him.

"Have you seen Lu?"

"Not recently. She's in charge of salads. Check over at our place. She'll probably want her own kitchen to organise everything from."

"Thanks. Smells great." I clapped him on the shoulder, nodded to the other two Kahn-Lea, and then wove my way around the edge of the packed Commons, past the Library, to Lu's house. The door stood open, but I knocked before walking in.

"Lu? Are you here?" I asked.

All her furniture stood pushed to the far reaches of the living room, and three tables joined her dining table in the cleared space. At least two dozen helpers of all ages lined the tables and made a variety of different salads. But no Mamma Lu. I frowned and stepped to the closest table.

"Does anyone know where Mamma Lu is?"

Several hands pointed toward the open back door.

"Thanks!" I slipped out back.

Mamma Lu and two helpers carrying baskets picked herbs from her garden. It looked exactly as I imagined it would when we talked about it all those months ago before I left to follow Dez back across the Deserts to warn him about the old Kronik's plans.

"Taya!" She straightened when she saw me. I gave a small wave and nod. "Have you come to help?"

"I can, but I need to talk to you first."

"That sounds ominous. What can I do for you?"

"Before dinner tonight, I need you to make an appeal to everyone gathered."

"Me? Why don't I just introduce you?"

I shook my head. "No. They all look up to you. They'll take you seriously. I'm just the crazy North girl who works for the new Kronik. This is important."

"I see. What's it all about?"

"I need a volunteer."

* * *

Taya

While Zola broke free of the night's embrace and pierced the sky with her deep red resonance, I sat on a crate outside the entrance to the spaceship and waited.

And waited.

I watched divers come and go on their shifts all morning, saw the beach collection booths grow with the day's finds, tracked the comings and goings of soldiers, and followed the slow rise of the suns. Not one person approached to even ask a question about the volunteer position, let alone offer their assistance.

Lu had been quite clear last night: if I didn't find a co-pilot, we couldn't launch; if we couldn't launch, Xannia would face another war. The only stipulation was the volunteer had to be able to read Dakturian and be older than sixteen.

371

I didn't eat lunch.

I didn't want someone to come looking for me and not find me.

I didn't need food; I needed help.

By mid-afternoon, my mind held fast, but my stomach revolted. It gurgled and ached and I was dehydrated from sitting so long in the suns. Still, I didn't move. It was a matter of pride now. Yet, the longer I sat there, the emptier my body became. I didn't hunger for food, but I wanted someone – anyone – to throw me a bone.

By dusk, I sat cross-legged on the sand, meditating. The last of the beach crew readied to return to the Commons. I closed my eyes, steadying my resolve for a long, chilly night.

Soft steps padded through the sand and stopped before me. I opened my eyes and looked up as Bazdin crouched before me. My heart jumped. He must have seen the desperation in my eyes for he shook his head in warning as he sat down across from me.

"I'm not here to volunteer."

"Then leave. I don't want someone to think the position's been taken."

"No one has come?"

I narrowed my eyes at him. "No."

He sighed and rubbed his hands over his knees. My stomach growled. He cocked his head to the side and raised an eyebrow at me. "Have you eaten today?"

I pursed my lips and crossed my arms.

"Starving yourself won't prove anything. Come to dinner." He reached forward as if to pull us both up to standing together. I leaned out of his reach.

"This is ridiculous, Taya."

"No, it's not. I need a co-pilot. I should have dozens of people eager to learn how to fly this thing – help save the gods damned world!" The last word echoed against the tree line, taunting me.

"Do you know why no one has come? Have you even allowed yourself to think about it?"

"Nothing should stop any of them."

"Oh, come on. You don't believe that. Why do you think I haven't offered to help you? Hmm?"

I glared at him.

"You can read Dakturian script?"

"Yes. Fluently."

A flash of hot anger blazed over the surface of my skin. I ground my teeth.

"Think about it. Why am I in South City to begin with?"

My food-deprived brain chugged to resurrect the memory of his threat to hire a contractor to take him across the Deserts if I wouldn't... so he could be with Tamaine, his fiancée. My brow softened and my arms dropped, hands in lap.

"Now, think of why I know how to read Dakturian script and why other people might have learned."

I wasn't in the mood for a lesson. But he had a point. Why would someone living in the south bother to learn a dead language? Bazdin helped figure out the vaccine. He was taught for a purpose. Anyone else who knew how to read it likely used that knowledge in a key way, helping the colony thrive from day to day.

"I'm not asking them to do this forever. We're going up,

seeing what we can do from outer space, and then coming back. That's the mission."

"Are you coming back? Can you guarantee that?"

"I—" He was right. I couldn't promise that. I couldn't even promise we'd make it into the outer atmosphere without crashing or blowing up. It was all theory.

"You're not just asking for a volunteer to act as your co-pilot, Taya. You're asking them to risk their lives for a government they left behind on purpose. Yes, Kronik Dezmind is different, but it's hard for anyone down here to trust him – except maybe the Kahn-Lea. But they are the backbone of the colony."

"Gods, Bazdin. I need to get this ship airborne! If we can stop Dez from launching a missile to destroy Zerameteth we can stop a—"

"A war. I know. But remember, ninety-eight percent of the people who live here now have survived a war. And those problems are in the north. Not here."

We sat staring at each other as Zita cursed my fate. At least I'd tried…

"I tried… I can't do it alone." My voice wavered with the truth, my curse.

He reached out for my hand again, but I shook my head. He rose without me and looked as if he might say more, but really, he'd said enough. Bazdin turned and walked away. I watched him slowly disappear along with the last of the guards.

I should have joined him. But I couldn't. Couldn't move. My brain reeled with the fact that no one here was willing to take that risk – to believe in something bigger than themselves. But then, maybe that's why it'd been me all along. I loved Dez, and that meant I'd lay my life on the line for him. He asked me to make this work, so I came. I was willing to sacrifice never seeing him again if it meant he survived to lead our world toward unity... even if I couldn't be there to see it.

Tek would have done it.

Even Ynell or anyone on my security team. I'd picked them because they were dedicated. Hell, even my mother would've done it if she knew how to read Dakturian.

I lost track of time sitting there, in the sand, listening to the waves break on the nearby rocks. The silhouette of the LRM's ship played over the choppy water as the rustle of leaves mingled with the rush of the water pulling me into and outside of myself as I searched for a way to make that call; say those words...

I failed.

As I tried to rehearse what to tell Dezmind, finding and rejecting words and phrases until I'd twisted my thoughts into knots, a lone shadow separated itself from the tree line. I watched it without realising what it signified. Until...

"Hello, Jutaya." He sat down before me, where Bazdin had sat, I don't know how many hours ago. I blinked, trying to force my eyes to focus properly.

"Raylan?" My skin prickled just being near him. My brain recalled his condescending sneer seven months ago when I demanded he empty his pockets and let me check him over before the Kahn-Lea left the Expanse. Him, directly disobeying my order to stay put in the desert cave as he dug furiously at the wall of sand keeping us safe from the storm while trapping us at the same time. And then a false memory based on the explanation of how Zaith died – by having this man ignore her warnings and break into a sealed Dakturian dwelling just to save his own ass from a storm.

The limits of my self-control dissolved with the setting of the suns. I glowered at him. I know he saw me – the starlight bathed the beach.

"I'd like to volunteer," he said.

"No. I'll do it myself."

But somehow, his gaze called my bluff.

Chapter 50
A Twist of Fate

Taya

Time was up. I don't know why I even bothered to walk back to the beach. No one else stepped forward to volunteer, and anyone I asked for help repeated what Bazdin had said. Even Gelden. Especially Gelden. I shouldn't have asked him. He'd only just met his mom after believing she'd died in the Nine Seas Massacre. I'd even tried Jantice, someone loyal to Dez who didn't have family or a spouse to worry about abandoning – but she was afraid to die. Afraid that the ship might blow up or not be able to re-enter the atmosphere or crash... I knew those possibilities existed, but they didn't stop me from doing my job.

I had to wonder why.

I had Jadis. I had Dez...

A rhythmic scuffle and faint regular thumping told me I wasn't alone. But it was morning; I wasn't the only person going to "work" at the beach. I ignored it. A disturbance at the base of Gerrund's tower carried across the beach, distracting me instead.

Mamma Lu and the General were at it again. Workers gave the pair a wide berth as they went about their business, as did I. A third, softer voice added into the mix. As I got closer to the spaceship, I recognised the cadence in the tone.

All Mother.

I paused on the ramp and leaned my shoulder against the ship's bulkhead. It's not like I could do any work now that I'd arrived. In fact, I'd avoided calling Dezmind since I woke up. Fragments of opening lines battered around in my head. I couldn't focus on what the others said, but I could watch. All Mother kept them calm. She stood between them, arms relaxed, voice low. Lu and Gerrund actually took turns speaking without yelling for a change. If All Mother could work miracles, maybe I ought to ask her for one. Last night was a bad joke.

I slipped inside the ship and headed for the cockpit. I activated the front screen, put my feet up on the control panel and watched the trio talk. My finger traced the outline of my watch-com as my brain prattled on.

Dez, I tried everything…

We need to talk. Things have taken a turn…

Dez, it looks like Plan B just moved back to Plan A…

Ready the launch…

"If this is what you do every day, flying this thing should be easy," Raylan said.

I dropped my feet and spun my chair around.

"Don't even bother. There's no way we can work

378

together. I'd have a better shot trying to fly this thing solo." I stood and placed my hands on my hips. "I don't know why you even bothered to make the offer." A cruel joke, perhaps? One last chance to rub in his aversion to—

"Do you know why things didn't go so well the first time, with the Kahn-Lea?"

Was this a trick question? "You have issues with strong female authority figures."

"What?"

"I didn't have a lot of time to dig into everyone's background before we left Vitexid's Lakes on Dezmind's quest, but learned enough." Werks excluded since he led a double life.

Raylan crossed his arms and frowned. "Oh? And how do you figure I have issues with women?"

"Not all women. An old boss of yours had a restraining order against you. Your scholastic grades were noticeably lower with female instructors. Your ex-girlfriend had a lot to say when I messaged her, and your mom—"

"Okay! I get it. But you're generalising. My ex?" He waved it away. "You're right, though, they each had something in common with you – and about a dozen men I've known over the years."

I tilted my head slightly, waiting for this huge reveal.

"You were all self-absorbed, self-righteous, know-it-alls. And, in your case, you flaunted it. Because you were CTF, you assumed you were better than any of us. *That* is what I take exception to, Jutaya. Why should I trust someone who thinks so little of me? Who hasn't given me any reason to trust them?"

"Then why are you here?" My voice wavered. I didn't deny it. I didn't deny any of it. I was entitled to respect but never got what I deserved – and that made me bitchy. I wasn't proud of that, but I didn't deserve to be reduced to my age or my gender or someone else's preconceived notions about who I was and what I ought to do. Not that any of it mattered anymore.

"Because you're different now." His baritone voice oozed through me as his words struck me down at the knees.

"I am." It wasn't a question or an admission though it could very well have been both. It was a statement of fact, pure and simple.

"Since you returned, you haven't once acted superior. You've been patient and kind to everyone – even me. You smiled at me. You've never done that before. You accepted my help with the professor and even thanked me. You don't avoid me, and you haven't once talked down to me until this morning. Though, I'm certain I've stirred up old feelings with this conversation that you haven't dwelled on in quite some time."

"I— I don't understand." I massaged my forehead with my thumb and forefinger, closing my eyes.

"You've changed. For the better. You've still got all these mad-skills and crazy abilities, but there's a humble, quiet nature about you now that makes you more approachable. That inspires me to want to help. Now, my knowledge of the Dakturian language is rough, but Merik taught me the basics before he returned north. I believe in the new world Dezmind is trying to build, and if getting this alien contraption flying is crucial to making that happen, then I'm here. Just as I was with him as a member of the Kahn-Lea."

The silence stretched between us. I couldn't get a handle on how being broken made me a better person. I had greater limitations now. I was no longer first among my peers at the CTF – in fact, I was no longer even CTF with the Infinity contract in play – yet, they still treated me as one of their own. Professor Gellik had practically welcomed me home.

"So, are we doing this, or what?" he asked, uncrossing his arms.

I looked up and met his gaze. "On one condition."

He raised his eyebrows, and I said to him what I'd said to Dezmind before we shook hands across his desk in the back office of the Chalklin Pond Restaurant before all this insanity began. "We're partners in this. You don't tell me what to do. I don't tell you what to do. We take sound suggestions and work together. Can you do that, Ray? I'm willing to trust you if you're willing to trust me."

Without hesitation, he held out his hand and we sealed the deal. I had my co-pilot. Now, I had to teach him everything he needed know in a day.

"We launch tomorrow."

* * *

Taya

Contrary to the high hopes and heartfelt promises shared over that handshake, Ray was no easier to work with than I was. Two stubborn and willful people do not make the best partners, but we managed to keep our cool and an open mind, and really, that's all I could ask for at this stage. I'd forced fate's hand and had to take what I could get.

Three hours before twilight I called it a night. We agreed to meet back at dawn with six hours sleep under our belts and the fate of the world at our feet.

I collapsed into my chair and stared out the main screen at Zerameteth, Gamma, the Child Sun, and for the first time since I was a child, I prayed to a god I knew didn't exist. Between Dezmind, the Followers of the Light, and All Mother, I knew something in the universe had brought me to this moment – something more than just a scared girl making the only choices she had to stay alive. Still, there was one more thing I had to do in case I did blow up tomorrow. I flipped up the face of my watch-com.

"Dezmind Lyle."

He answered on the first ring, still awake after all. "Taya?"

"Hi." Even that one simple word caught in my throat.

He sighed. "This is it, then? War?"

I shook my head. "We launch in the morning. It's only war if I fail. If I—" I couldn't say it. We both knew what I meant, anyway.

"At least we can say we tried, right? At least I can uphold my side of the deal with the Guardian overseers."

"You made a deal? When?"

"Yesterday."

"What— what did they say? How did you convince them to talk to you?"

"I went to see the Oracle. She gave me some sound

advice. I had to figure out how to find peace without suffocating the innocent. I came so close to repeating so many mistakes..." He took a deep breath and let it out slowly. "I told them everything – in terms they'd understand. I promised they could have a voice, but not a vote, on the council. No more second-hand knowledge."

"That's huge, Dez. First Delenon as co-Kronik and now religious representation in parliament?"

"If we're going to be the voice for all of Xannia, then I'd better be willing to listen. Tek is questioning *all* councillors. No one has admitted to being the mole, yet, but it's only a matter of time. We're digging into everyone's comings and goings of the past few months, not just the Talian councillors' movements. I think I was being narrow-minded, ready to blame my own people without solid proof. The truth is, it could be any of them."

"Yeah, I guess I never thought a Commoner might not want equality. There's always one person who wants to punish the powerful. If closing off the Compound brought the Commoners their own new government, separate from Talians, everything might change. I'm glad you found a way to salvage your goal for peace and equality."

"Ah, it's a long road yet."

"Isn't it always?" My words echoed more than just truth about politics. They resonated on a deeper level between us. It almost looked as if Dez flinched.

"Listen, Taya, I don't want to put off getting married any longer. When you get back—"

"No, Dez. It won't work."

Fear flickered across his face and the determined hope

disappeared.

"I love you. It took a while for me to realise that two people could be in love but not meant to be together. Everything that's happened since we met has pulled us in two different directions. The more we try to cling to each other, physically, the farther apart we become."

"Nonsense. We'll find a way. There's always a way."

I gave him a sad smile, my heart breaking a little more with every word. "It started small. You believed in the Chronicles and I didn't. I believed in the government. Your quest brought us together and showed me I still didn't understand much and I could take nothing as absolute anymore. But the moment I sealed my love for you, circumstances forced me to remain Underground while you stayed topside.

"Then, I sacrificed everything at the battle for the Compound in order to change the world so we could be together, and I died."

He cringed.

"You brought me back. I know you did. I heard your voice when I was in a coma. No one else's voice came clear but yours. When you made me the head of security, I hacked into the hospital video records and saw you visit me. I still have the note you left me.

"But then my brain damage shoved a wall between us. You saw me as the same even though I tried to tell you I was different. I tried to be the person you fell in love with – but I couldn't. This new mission to learn about Dakturian space technology goes from being a recovery operation to the best hope for keeping us all alive. And I'm here and you're there. As much as I've learned about this spaceship, there's a real chance this is the last time we'll ever see each other." My voice caught, and I pushed the tears I hadn't realised were falling off my cheeks. "I can't even hug you. Can't wrap my arms around you and let you convince me that the gods have some kind of Divine plan for us to be together. Because they don't. I wouldn't be here and you wouldn't be there if that were true."

"Taya, you will come back to me. The gods be damned. If your mother could find happiness with Matheson, even for just a little while, then we can, too. Don't give up on us."

"I'm not. Or, at least I'm not giving up on love. I do love you. I will always love you. But even if I somehow survive this insanity, you will need me here – not there. You've got Tek and Ynell to watch out for you now. You don't need me."

I closed my com and gave in to the tears.

Chapter 51
A Breath Held

Taya

I didn't sleep. I couldn't. I had to get ready for the launch. That meant getting travel bags together: one for food and one for personal hygiene. I lay down for three hours before dawn and tried to meditate. Problem was, I couldn't get Dez's face out of my mind. I shouldn't have left things the way I did. I needed him, now, more than ever.

The walk to the beach revived my spirit some; a spike of adrenaline took care of the rest.

I chose not to tell Mamma Lu or the General or All Mother. They'd find out soon enough if we managed to break through the atmosphere to the vacuum of space or just break our necks. I didn't need a crowd of innocent people gathered if the latter happened.

As I stepped onto the beach from the main path, I glimpsed Ray, leaning against the hull of the ship. I dropped my packs at his feet next to two of his own.

"Seems we had the same idea," I said.

"No sense in causing a scene."

I nodded and activated the sequence to lower the hatch. We walked in and I shut it behind us. The ship's interior sensed our presence and lit the corridors. I tucked my bags into a bunk on the opposite side of the spaceship and then went straight to its heart – the super lodestone.

Staring at it, I cleared my mind while the node arms hovered more than a foot from its surface, the whole thing levitating in the engine room. I took a breath and held it, held it a long time.

Ray tapped me on the shoulder. I jumped, my heart fluttering.

"It's time. We wait any longer and the morning divers will be here along with the change in guard."

I nodded and followed him back to the cockpit. We sat at our respective control panels. His hands shook as he held them over the board. Mine didn't, but only just. Besides, this wasn't a pissing match. He'd learned a lot in one day. If we had a week, he might even remember it all. But we were out of time.

"I'm activating the external shields and locking down the interior for take-off," he said, fingers flying over the keys and buttons the way we'd practiced two or more dozen times.

"I'm calling up the pre-set coordinates for Gamma's orbit and bringing the thrusters online."

The ship vibrated with a hum. I could only imagine the noise it made outside. By now, everyone knew what we were doing. We just had to take off before they arrived. A tightness invaded my chest, but I ignored it and woke up the forward screen. Zola peeked over the treed horizon, staining the sky red.

My fingers followed the sequence we'd rehearsed hour after hour. The muscle memory allowed my mind to focus on one task at a time as my body, my fingers, repeated a dance meant only for them.

The thrusters whined. Ray and I hit the green button on the arm of our chairs, and a five-point harness rose from hidden compartments, locking us in.

The ship shook and rattled.

I double checked every last setting entered into the panel as it flashed across the screen.

"Ready?" I asked.

"Punch it."

I did, just as Gerrund's silhouette materialised across the beach at the base of his tower.

The ship shifted.

The stats displayed that we now hovered. The Dakturian numerical system counted down.

I raised my hand and gave a wave.

I think he waved back, but the sheer force rocketing us up knocked out my vision.

"I can't see," Ray's voice wavered.

"Me neither," I whispered as the breath left my body. *Please don't blow up*, I thought and blacked out.

* * *

Taya

An incessant beeping pulled me from the haze of unconsciousness. As my vision wavered in and out of focus,

I forced my gaze on the red numbers in the lower left of the screen.

"How long were we out?" Ray growled.

"Five minutes."

"We en route?"

I checked the navigation readings. "No." I sighed, tapped the green button to release the harness, and grabbed the front of the panel to pull myself closer. "What do the Readings show?"

"Steady gamma rays from a distant pulsar and faint but steady readings from Alpha and Beta now we're clear of the ozone."

"Initiate the ray drive."

He entered the sequence – the irony not lost on me.

We jolted right and nose-dived toward the planet. My heart leapt into my throat, so I couldn't properly appreciate the turquoise pearl we threatened to crash back down to.

"What the Hell!" I yelled, my stomach floating somewhere behind my eyes. I nearly hurled but managed to hit the symbol for gamma on my chair. Two joysticks popped up from the raised portion of the front arms.

"I guess there's no such thing as automatic pilot," I said. Ray just stared at me with "do something" plastered across his face. I swore he crossed his legs to keep from pissing his pants.

"Now or never."

I grabbed the sticks and moved them. We jolted in the opposite direction – my stomach following several nanoseconds later.

"Moderate that!" he yelled.

"Moderate what?" I snapped. I had no idea what I'd done. I tried to reverse the move with a little less force. We levelled out some.

"It's the pitch and yaw!" I shouted. They weren't just buttons you pressed but actual devices to control. "You manage the external vents, and I'll take care of the pull from the gamma rays." The relative quiet and lack of hum finally registered in my brain. The engines turned off once we breached outer space. The geo-mag no longer acted as our propulsion source but as a battery core for ships' systems. If we wanted to make it into orbit around Zerameteth, I'd have to get us there.

A twitch of fear needled my brain as I worked on matching the wildly fluctuating coordinates in red with the green orbit set. I couldn't think about everything else that needed doing. I had to leave it to Ray. If I could just get us there… I bit my bottom lip and put all my focus into steering the ray drive. Just the slightest touch took us several degrees in one direction or the other.

Facing the small sun once again, I noticed the main screen tint to shield us from the brilliance. I couldn't feel the ship speed up and slow down with Ray's tweaking, but the numbers relayed the information as I handled the directional maneuvering and learned how to manipulate the hull in response to the gamma rays.

I stared at the navigation alignment as it went from red to yellow, shifting in smaller increments now. When the numbers flashed green, Ray initiated the synchronisation sequence, and I let go of the joysticks.

"Well, we didn't blow up." He let out a shaky laugh,

staring at the contrast of deep black space next to the pale-yellow brilliance of our smallest sun.

"Not yet, anyway."

I sat back to take a moment – let my heart rate slow and rid my ears of the pounding. A tremble shifted from my left foot and travelled up my body. I clenched my teeth to keep them from chattering and shut my eyes. Ray's comment repeated over and over in my head. *We didn't blow up. We didn't blow up...* We could have blown up.

I don't think I honestly let myself believe those words until now. I opened my eyes and stared at the navigational calculations flickering in all four corners of the main screen as the stars winked in the distance. No Xannian had ever been close enough to touch one before.

I caught Ray staring at me. "You okay?" he asked.

"Huh," I forced out on a shaky breath and gulped more air. How could he be so calm? *Why can't I? What's wrong with me?*

Ray pulled himself forward and out of the chair. His legs wobbled and gave out. He crawled the rest of the way over. I glanced at the gravity ratings on-screen. Everything worked as it should. Everything but us, anyway.

Ray sat with his back to the console, looking up at me from his place on the floor. I still shook, but a laugh, verging on hysterical, bubbled out. He laughed, too. Something blinked on the panel and the navigation field went purple. All the numbers were correct, so I ignored it as we continued to orbit the sun. I wasn't ready to push buttons again. Wasn't ready for what came next.

The gamma rays feeding the drive system propelled us

on our path far faster than a natural geo-synch orbit would. I was all for a one-hour tour as opposed to sixteen days. Most of that hour Ray and I dozed, not fully asleep, but in desperate need of a biological recharge nonetheless. I don't know how much sleep he'd had last night, but it probably wasn't much more than me.

When the shakes finally stopped, I just sat and breathed... until my stomach gurgled. Ray cracked a grin.

"I missed breakfast, too." He stood.

I sat up straight. "I could do with a bite."

"I'll grab something from my stash. Be right back."

Six months ago, I would've spouted some asinine line about being able to serve myself. I could see this, now. It was amazing anyone had bothered to get close to me back then. Maybe Zaith didn't want to at first, just like Ray. Maybe she only did because it was her job. Maybe Dez only did because he figured out who my parents were and thought I was the missing piece of his destiny. But what about Tek and Gelden and even Niless – if I let myself go there? Professor Gellik... I looked up to him as a father. He and Niless were my pseudo parents at the CTF for four years. Where had that gotten them? I'd given Niless the cold shoulder and Gellik lay bedridden with an alien virus.

Gods, I'm a walking disaster.

Flying disaster, now.

I gripped the control panel and hauled my ass from the chair, using the console to help with balance as I gained my bearings, then walked around. Ray returned and tossed me an eppal. I caught it. Everything seemed to work again. Leaning back against the panel, I bit into the fresh fruit and looked out into space. Ray joined me, leaning against his own console. I never thought I'd see the day when we'd work together. Maybe I wasn't the only one who'd changed.

He'd become a respected leader in South City. I saw the way he worked with his Dive Team and Hunting Troop. They looked up to him, respected his knowledge and advice. He'd made a name for himself, built friendships, and a home. Still, he was the only one willing to sacrifice it all.

Ray held out a spiky-fruit leaf sewn into a bag. I put my core in before he pulled a pair of drawstrings tight and disappeared back down the hall. Sitting down, I wove my fingers together and cracked my knuckles. I flicked the stiffness from my hands and got to work.

I did a scan of the sun, initiating every sequence I'd discovered when Gellik and I had nosed around, and even a few new ones that popped up now we were in space. Ray sat down, placing our canteens between us against the base of his console. *At least a rider came with cup holders.* I smirked at the stupid thought.

"What have we got?" he asked, looking over the readings on the screen.

"Nothing. It's exactly the same information the old Kronik got with their satellites." I hit the edge of the console with my palm. "I thought for sure we'd get different readings with the ship – that it would know what to look for. An energy signal or hotspot or a way to detect where the core of this thing is… wait."

"What?"

"Call up the weapons system. Lock onto the sun."

"Okay. Why exactly?"

"Maybe it's not in the diagnostic systems. Maybe the

trigger will reveal itself when the weapons are engaged."

"But we're not engaging them."

"No. Of course not. But we need to lock on and see what happens."

Ray did his thing and a moment later a large crosshair inside a target came up on the screen. He input the coordinates for Gamma and the image zoomed in on the small sun. Still no red flags or new information. It just locked onto the centre of the mass.

"Okay, stand down. That didn't work." I rubbed my hands over my face and through my bangs. "What are we missing? What are we missing…?"

The purple figures flashed on the screen again. Nothing had changed except their colour. Wait. One button on my panel glowed purple, too.

"Ray, look at this."

"Yeah, purple. Like before."

"No. This!" I pointed to my console. He slipped out of his chair and came over.

"What's it do?"

"The database manual said something about being part of the scanning program. I pressed it earlier but got no new information."

"But now it's purple, not green. It might do something different."

"Sweet Zerameteth, what do we do?" I knew what I had to do, but an icy coil of fear wrapped around my spine. Was this it? Would this identify the core?

"Press it."

I did.

Chapter 52
Locked On

Taya

The craft jolted. I gripped the edge of the console as something pulled us from orbit.

"We're on a collision course with the Sun!" I jumped to my feet and pressed every button that might reverse what I had done.

"You already tried that. What about this?" Ray hip-checked me out of the way.

For once, my natural instinct to dig in and fight didn't rear its useless mass. I saw nothing but the sun as it filled the forward screen. The navigational numbers flipped and flickered – then froze. Our fixed course brought us toward the back of Gamma, away from the planet, on a declining arc. Ray slammed the controls and raised his hands in the air before attacking the mass of thick hair on his head.

We stared, side by side, at the stupidity of fate. Every muscle in my body tensed, anticipating impact within twenty minutes. Until…

"What's that?" Ray pointed to the corona.

"It's dark."

And we watched as a strange shadow gradually ate away at the fullness of the Sun, like approaching the dark side of a moon. Flashes of lectures and arguments bombarded my brain – fragments of old and new memories jumbled together and overlapped. I squeezed my eyes shut and held my head just as tight. I knew something but couldn't say what; the fractured memories were pieces to a puzzle my brain used to process in nanoseconds.

I slumped to the floor, staring at the enlarging Gamma and yet not seeing it… seeing the repeated flashes in my mind's eye.

"Taya—"

I absently waved Ray off and he let go of my shoulders. I was so close! I almost had it.

As the density of the growing darkness took on actual mass and dimensionality everything finally fell into place.

"Dear gods," I whispered, and crawled forward on my knees, staring at the screen, but seeing the reality unfold.

"What?" Ray crouched beside me.

"It's fixed. I'd forgotten the early readings that gave viability to the argument that Gamma was a moon. I ignored the possibility because moons don't give off light and heat, but it's not a natural phenomenon. The Dakturian's put it here. It doesn't rotate. It's a static mass – unlike Alpha and Beta. It has a fixed orbit around Xannia, hence the Deserts, but it also has a fixed rotation. We never see the back of the sun."

"But we saw it an hour ago when we did our first orbit."

"Before we pressed the purple button. Now…" The edges of a network of mechanics and structures slid into place. "Now the illusion is gone." In its place, a space city grew larger and closer with every passing minute.

"No way…" Ray collapsed all the way to the floor, and we sat there as some kind of homing beacon drew our ship into a pre-programmed docking sequence. The ship guided itself toward the concave metal city built by an advanced alien race thousands of years ago.

The ship jolted again and all the navigation information went green. I looked at Ray and he looked at me.

"We're here," I said.

He blinked out of his trance and scrambled over to his workstation. "The readings are showing a solid airlock between the ship and the— the space city." He fumbled over what to call it.

"Spaceport?" I offered.

"Yeah. That. Systems say everything is stable on the other side of the hatch. But…"

"How do we know for sure? It fell into disrepair when the Dakturian's died off. Who's to say there isn't some kind of breach on the other side?" I finished his thought.

"So, what do we do? How do we know we aren't being fed false readings?" he asked.

"We don't." I pushed myself off the floor and straightened my clothes. Ray narrowed his eyes. I didn't look right at him, but I knew. I turned and walked to the corridor.

"Where are you going?"

"To face my destiny."

He raced to catch up to me and grabbed my elbow. "Don't open that hatch. We need to find a way to test the accuracy of the readings."

I shook him off and kept walking.

"Who knows how long that could take? We have no idea how this thing operates. Any information we do collect would still be suspect. Lock yourself into the engineering control room. That way, if something happens to me, you can initiate Plan A and fire at will. But we're here to see if Plan B has a hope of showing us how to do this without blowing up a god, so I'm going to see if they really do exist."

He stopped and stared holes into my back until I rounded the bend toward the main hatch. I stopped in front of the door I'd freely walked in and out of for just over a month now, never once having to worry about what might happen when I crossed the threshold.

The smooth metal filled my vision as I tried to picture what the airlock on the other side might look like. I swallowed past the lump in my throat, but no matter how many deep breaths I took, my heart just raced faster. Clenching and unclenching my fists didn't help. I bounced on the balls of my feet, puffing air from large, rounded cheeks. I had to stop though. It made me dizzy.

The control panel to the right of the door flashed green. One button glowed all the way around. One button stated HATCH. One false move and I'd fail.

My arm shook as I reached forward. I snatched it back, shook it out, and then slammed the heel of my palm over the button.

The hatch slid left instead hinging forward. *That's a first.*

A blast of stale air made me cough – but it was air. I clicked my com on.

"Not dead yet."

Static crackled over the line and then, "Try to keep it that way."

I gave a wry smile, clipped the device onto my belt and stepped from the ship into the short passageway. I initiated the lock sequence behind me, just in case. It closed, sealing me into the curved portal that suctioned to the side of the spaceship. A level walkway led to a wall and a control panel off to the right.

I certainly hope I don't need to know any kind of secret passcodes to get in here. I stepped closer to check it out. A bright blue fan beam scanned me from head to foot and back up again. My chest tightened. *Are Xannians even allowed here? Is it going to vaporise me on the spot?*

Stats flashed in Dakturian across the screen attached to the panel:

Hybrid.
Native 85%
Dakturian 15%

And then another hatch slid to the side. I staggered back holding my breath – not that it would help in any of the crazy scenarios that zipped through my head. Part of me was amazed that much alien DNA survived while another part tried to work out how it was possible after two-thousand years. *But it makes sense. The Talian's built a wall and restricted procreation with other races for a reason – a reason other than simply being elitist. That's what they'd become but not where they'd started. The existence of Chief Elder Nerroi and his daughter Anna from the alien journal proved as much. I just never let myself wonder how so much could be forgotten.* An image of Dez flashed in my mind as my oxygen deprived and damaged brain tried to piece everything together.

My chest burned.

Would the door have opened for Ray?

I gasped, forced to inhale. Cool, filtered, but slightly stale air caressed my aching lungs. I gulped greedily and forced myself past the last barrier and onto the spaceport. Dim lighting illuminated a large, squared corridor with three options: left, right, straight ahead. I grabbed my com.

"Still breathing. I've sealed the ship from the port so you can come out of engineering. I'll explore a little to make sure nothing untoward is lingering around a nearby corner."

"Don't get eaten by some strange space creature."

Dear gods! He said it in jest but what if there is such a thing? Those giant arachnids in the Deserts' cave crawled around my imagination. *What if some space entity has evolved to consume electricity or metal and—*

Stop it, Taya.

I pulled my reconstituted Whipstaff from the upper portion of my right boot and switched it on. Just in case. But, after walking a couple hundred cautious yards in either direction, I got nowhere, so I returned to the ship.

Ray stood on the other side of the main hatch when it opened. He looked me over.

"Still you, then?"

"Huh? What?"

"Not a clone or husk being worn by some creepy alien entity?"

"No. You're stuck with me. You've been watching too many shows on the Wire."

"Not in the last six months." We walked back to the cockpit.

"Well, then, let's put that over-active imagination to work. Can you do a scan of the port and get a working layout? We need to figure out how this fake sun works before we can even attempt to turn it off."

"If it even has an off switch," he muttered, heading over to his station. But he just stood there, staring at the control board. I walked over.

"What's up?"

He sighed and whispered, "I don't remember the sequence for using the scanner." Ray scowled. Not at me, and probably not at the electronics, either.

"Hey, don't be so hard on yourself. You learned in a day what Professor Gellik and I studied for weeks. Here." I punched in the sequence, cleared it, and let him do it. The anger that once might have bubbled over and left us wrestling on the floor, dissolved.

He was right. A lot of the tension between us in the past had been me being a jerk. Would the old Taya have cleared the sequence to let him try? No, probably not. She would have shoved him aside and did it herself all while complaining of the lack of comprehension of some people and grumbling about not having someone trained here to do the job.

Gods, I used to be so full of myself.

The main screen brought up three levels of corridors with intersecting hubs. The top two squiggled maze-like but the lower level showed us what we'd been looking for.

The power source.

"Okay. Now, we're getting somewhere. Let's see how this thing works."

Chapter 53
Priorities

Dezmind

My hand hovered over the lower viewing room doorknob. Three times in as many days I'd walked in certain we'd found the mole. *Why is today any different?* I pushed the thought aside and entered. I never used to second-guess my instincts but now… nothing was certain.

Tek stood staring at the large multi-screened monitor, his profile to me. He didn't turn to greet me. The frown drawing his eyebrows together said it all – deep in thought.

"What do we have?" I stood beside him and looked at the image on the wall.

"We found him."

My heart jumped and I squashed it back into place. "How can you be so sure?"

The others had all been Talian. I stared at the Metek man sitting shackled to the metal desk in the small room down the hall. His mussed hair and rumpled suit meant he'd been in holding since yesterday. The usually mossy-green of his skin greyed and his gold coliths no longer shimmered. He looked ill.

"We've picked through every single councillor's history now. He's the only one who's got holes and shady connections."

"Connections to what? Why would a Commoner want to hurt his own people?"

"A means to an end, sir."

"Why him?" I nodded at the screen.

"Sir Hetrick was a sector keeper during Kronik Delenon's time as magistrate. He's a staunch Resistance supporter."

"I don't understand. We're talking about the Faction here – Talian super soldiers trying to keep Commoners out."

"Flip that notion and you've got it."

Commoners trying to keep Talian soldiers in... of course! I groaned. "It's my fault, then. I knew he was sceptical about what I'd discovered in the south when I brought the sector keepers together to learn if they'd support the coup. I thought he was against my findings in general, not because he wanted only Commoners in power."

I stared at the man on the other end of the camera feed. He'd sacrificed so many innocent lives for his own agenda. If Taya knew, she'd destroy him. I let myself smile a little at the thought. She'd almost done the same to me when we'd first met, and I hadn't put anyone's life at risk, yet. The old familiar ache resonated in my chest, but this time, I let it stay. I didn't want to forget about what mattered to me anymore. *I'm not just a leader, I'm a person, too.*

"Has he confessed? I can't afford to be wrong again."

"It's him. He met with the last Faction leader yesterday. Hetrick takes walks after council Sessions. There haven't been any meetings, but no one else knows that. Each day, without fail, he stops at four spots on his tour of the park grounds. Yesterday, he spoke to someone. We tailed the go-between back to the Faction leader."

"Why didn't you pick him up?"

"We tried. I sent someone into the café, but he was gone. Either the owner hid him, which wouldn't surprise me, or there's a Talian transpoint under that café into the tunnels below the Compound. We're watching the café now. It's only a matter of time before he resurfaces."

"Why not flush out the tunnels?"

"Not enough manpower and we don't know where all the exits are." He gave me a knowing look. I nodded. I took a risk every time I used the one leading from my office. "Besides, we don't need Hetrick to talk."

"Oh?" I turned to look at my Special Ops commander, intrigued by his certainty.

"We've got a guard undercover posing as the councillor right now. Between our man on the inside and a clear image for facial rec to go from, that Faction leader is as good as ours when he makes his next move."

"Excellent. Keep me in the loop." I clapped Tek on the shoulder, spared one last glance at Hetrick, and went looking for the councillors. They were required to enter and exit the building every day as though nothing were amiss even if we weren't officially meeting.

In the corridors above, the plan formulating in my mind since my last conversation with Taya solidified. I knew what I had to do, I just needed to find the right person to help me with it.

Most of the councillors who weren't in their offices lounged in the Atrium Library. The individual I sought had never set foot in their office even though we'd had it refurbished since Taya's *visit* over seven weeks ago.

I passed through the Atrium, noting that the Talian councillors still didn't willingly mingle with the others. At least they were civil during sessions now. Everything took time. The Hetrick plant argued with councillors Enay and Saritt. I slowed down and listened to the gruff cadence of his voice and followed his mannerisms.... Whoever Tek found to portray the man was a master. I couldn't tell the difference. *I wonder if his wife can?* I filed that away to ask Tek later.

Only one other place made sense to search, so I headed to the public courtyard through the cafeteria. A few groups of guards and aids and assistants sat at the lounge tables eating, but one man lay on a bench with his eyes closed soaking in the mid-morning rays. I stood at the end of the bench where his feet crossed at the ankles.

"Guide Aelix."

He jolted to sitting. "Kronik Dezmind! I— uh— To what do I owe the pleasure?"

I waved off the formalities and sat down, turning with one knee up on the bench between us. "When are you scheduled to return south?"

"Tonight, sir. I'll head back to headquarters at the

Expanse right after session lets out – or would normally let out, all things considered."

"Do you have an itinerary, yet?"

"No. Assignments are coordinated on arrival."

"What if came with you?"

"What? I mean, excuse me, sir?"

"I need to travel south. Plan B launched early this morning, and I'd like to be there when they return."

A shadow of worry flitted across his eyes.

"I know. But regardless of the outcome, I need to be there. I have to be there. Can you take me?"

"Just the two of us?"

"No, I don't think Tek would let me get away with that. I'll ask him to assign Ynell. She's become my personal bodyguard in Jutaya's absence."

"With three people, we'd need to take either a Caravan or Cargo D.V. with supplies. That will slow us down. Not a lot, but since we don't know when Plan B will conclude, time is probably a factor."

"Hmm… yes. Faster is better. I think I know what I can do. I can make it work for just two people. Are you able to attach a small cart to the back of the D.V.?"

"Maybe."

"Can I leave you in charge of gathering the supplies we'll need and informing the station manager? Without mentioning who your passenger is?"

He paled and swallowed. Clearly, I was asking him to break rules. "I'll send you with a sealed letter explaining the need for discretion and sign it personally."

Aelix nodded. "I can do that."

"Good. When do we leave?"

"Second Sundown."

"If I'm not at Headquarters within fifteen minutes of departure, you have my permission to arrange for another passenger. Understood?"

"Yes, sir."

"Good." I gripped his shoulder and smiled before I stood to leave. I had a number of things to see to before taking a working-vacation south. Foremost was finding someone to run the place in my absence.

* * *

Dezmind

It took the better part of the day to settle the majority of my loose ends and find my stand-in. I glanced at my watch-com They were due to arrive any minute. Instead of pacing around my office to burn off the excess energy, I figured I'd watched for their arrival from the main door. I pulled it open and there she stood poised to knock.

"You summoned me?" Lynnia brushed past me. Shifting loose strands from her long braid behind her ear, she took command of my office. In the middle of the room, she turned to face me with her arms outstretched in question. I shut and locked the door. She cocked her head to one side and raised her eyebrows.

"I need your help."

"Clearly. What's going on?" Though she and Taya hadn't spent more than a few dozen hours together since their reunion, there was no mistaking their likeness – in their mannerisms, that is.

"Taya launched the spaceship this morning."

"She did what now? I thought it was going to be live on the Wire?"

"You know Taya. Plans changed. She didn't tell anyone. Raylan's missing so they think he's with her. They'd been training together – though not long. She knew we were behind schedule on this already. This is, of course, need-to-know information. Only a handful of my top people are in the loop."

"Okay." She crossed her arms and narrowed her eyes at me. That look stabbed knives into my chest from the first time I saw it when she sat trapped in a garden prison confined to a wheelchair.

"So now what?"

"I'm going south to welcome her home, but I need someone to oversee things while I'm gone."

"Hmm… That Special Ops commander of yours, what's his name? Tek? He'd do a good job."

"Agreed. But I don't want to give everyone the impression that only military personnel can handle this job. That could have dire consequences."

"True. So, what about letting the council do it? Have them each take a turn running sessions until you get back."

"That would be ideal, except that one of them is a mole."

"What!"

"We know who and we're handling it, but I'm not ready to tell the others who it is yet. I need everything to appear as normal so we can root out the Faction leader still out there."

"I see. Well, no, I don't see. How can you be leaving if all this is happening?"

I dropped into my chair and leaned back, closing my eyes for a moment. "That is the exact excuse I've been using since I took this office seven months ago. And I needed to be here. But everything else not directly related to running this planet has dissolved. I don't meet with friends anymore, I don't leave this complex to go out or take Jadis for a walk. And I've ignored Taya – made her promises and not kept them. It's time to fix that."

"That's the price of being Kronik, or hadn't you thought that far ahead?"

"It doesn't have to be. I can still have a life. If I don't, I'll end up just like the old Kronik and every one before him. I have an excellent team here that I trust implicitly. Tek is handling the mole and Faction leader issue. What I need is someone who knows all the people – Commoners and Talians. I need someone both sides respect and yet don't see as a threat. I also need someone capable who understands what we're faced with and how to neutralise problems before they explode. I need you, Lynnia. Will you do it?"

"You want me? You didn't bring me here to get my advice on who should do it, you've already settled on... me?"

I leaned forward and rested my arms on the desk, hands clasped together. "Yes. I do value your advice but today I called you here for something bigger. Delenon is already down south, and if I leave, too, I need to make sure whoever is in charge knows what they're doing and what's at stake – it has to be someone I trust. I know you've been touring the museums, libraries, and art centres across the north inside and outside the Compound. And we both know why you're doing it. It's a powerful message. But I need you here, for maybe a week or so. None of us know what's going on up there." I pointed to the ceiling, but she knew I meant outer space. "I'll be back to make the hard call if I need to, but right now I have to go south, for Taya."

Jutaya's mother stared at me long and hard. The two of them had become friends, but I knew they were both so set in their ways that neither of them had really been able to connect on that mother/daughter level. It kicked in now. Heat rose under my collar and up my cheeks. She knew it was my decisions that kept putting her daughter in harm's way, but would this be enough to convince her of my intentions?

"I accept. When do you leave—"

A knock cut her off and Tek let himself in. "Oh, sorry. Please excuse us, Ms. Doire."

"That's okay, Tek. She knows about both situations. You can talk freely."

He frowned, confused. I hadn't told him I was leaving, yet. He glanced from me to Lynnia and back. His eyes twitched as his brain likely calculated all the reasons I would have for letting a civilian in on council matters.

"Hetrick's talking."

"What did he say?" I asked. Lynnia's eyes widened as she connected the dots.

"Told us the schedule for the meets. It's not just the park and there's one coming up soon."

"How soon?"

"Tonight."

Warning signs flashed in my brain. If we could catch the last Faction leader tonight… "How do you know he's not lying? Why is he even talking to us? What's changed?"

"He said he's not in control anymore. Hasn't been for a long time. He's worried about his family if he doesn't make this meet. So, he struck a deal."

This was real.

We could end this tonight…

I looked at Lynnia and she stared a challenge right back at me, echoing my own thoughts: *What's more important? My job or my heart?*

Chapter 54
The Gods Speak

Taya

I was afraid to sleep. Hour after hour, I lay on my bunk shivering even though the temperature controls said it was warm. Since we'd breached outer space, a chill had settled over me. I stared at the bottom of the bunk above me, trying to make sense of everything. The spaceport's schematics etched lines in my mind and I followed every corridor, envisioning each hub as Ray and I had scoured it hours before.

So many hours.

So much information.

My com-timer beeped as the hatch to my room slid open. Ray stuck his head around the corner. Wise – smaller target. Lucky for him I was awake.

"You ready?"

"No." I swung my legs out of bed, sat up, and rubbed my face with my hands.

"Did you get any sleep?"

I sighed and let my hands drop to my lap. "No. Stop asking me questions you already know the answer to. I feel like meeka. Probably look like it, too."

His arm materialised and he tossed me a piece of fruit. I caught it. At least my hand/eye coordination still worked. I dug around in my food satchel and tossed him a packet of dried meat.

"Thanks. See you at the hatch in ten."

It was kinda funny: I'd packed more protein and Ray had packed more fruits and veggies. Neither of us had packed any grains.

I set breakfast aside, grabbed my brush and focused on re-braiding my hair. Even though I'd caught the fruit, my stiff fingers refused to twist and weave with their usual deftness. Two days without sleep affected even my fine motor control.

Ten minutes later I walked up to the main hatch with my gear, stocked belt pack and weapons in place. Ray nodded and then activated the door. It slipped to the side, and I gained us access to the spaceport with my DNA. We bypassed everything on the upper two floors and retraced our steps to the reactor portal.

I pulled a small pry bar from a loop on my belt pack and attacked the security panel at head height. Nothing we'd tried yesterday had worked. Time for brute strength. I maneuvered my way around two sides, creating a rim, then passed it off to Ray. He completed the task.

No alarms. Yet.

I grabbed a small light-tube and squished my face

against the wall to try to see under the lip we'd created. It latched in two places on all four sides. I jammed the bar in the centre of one side and motioned for Ray to join me. Two sets of hands devoured the shaft of the tool.

"Ready?" I asked.

"Yep."

"Now!"

We yanked together. The panel groaned and popped off, flying through the air. It clattered on the ground nearby. I gave Ray the pry bar, wiped my hands on my pants, and examined the wiring. The jumble of colours and sizes made my heart race and my brain shut down. I closed my eyes and took a couple of deep breaths, visualising my mechanical engineering classes at the CTF. I hadn't specialised in that field, but I knew the basics. My Talian genetics hadn't just given me better eyesight and hearing but also had given me a pictographic memory. I just had to access the right files in my brain, picture my textbooks and virtual presentations, and I'd have what I needed. I breathed out and opened my eyes.

I found the identification centre and fed a continuous loop back to it so the system didn't think I was breaking in – which I was. Then I followed each of the other wires back to its source.

I only had to cut one. The feed to the door lock.

"So be it," I whispered and pulled my snips from my pack.

"Are you sure? This whole place could go into lockdown if you miss."

Do it, the old Taya said.

What if I'm wrong? The new Taya whispered.

There's nothing wrong with your memory. Do it already!

I shrugged and cut the wire.

Ray cringed.

We didn't blow up. How many times could we claim that before we got back home? *Too many.*

The hatch slid to the side. I collected all my tools and walked through with Ray to an enormous viewing room.

"Wow…" It took my breath away. A protective force field or special type of glass swooped up from the floor and arced all the way to the second story above to reveal the inner workings of the sun. A single control pedestal bloomed in the middle of the floor, but Ray and I went straight for the window.

I stood there a long time just trying to soak in what I was looking at. Ray and I took turns remarking on what we saw as if hearing it out loud made it that much more real. *Huh – so that's what it was: a small nuclear reactor.* The photon beam from South City on Xannia reinvigorated the particles here in the core, which fed the light and heat back out again. I didn't have a half-dozen or more competing memories or theories or opinions rattling around in my head. I saw quite clearly.

"I know what we must do." I stepped back from the glass but still looked at the amazing feat of engineering before us.

"What?"

I pointed. "That's the core. Without it, the sun won't work."

"Doesn't that mean the entire spaceport won't work?

And orbit will decay again?"

I opened my mouth and then shut it. He had a point.

"Let's take a look at this thing. The energy reserves kept it somewhat stable for nearly two thousand years. The Dakturians had a yearly Regeneration Celebration and we've been activating the photon beam every week for six months now." I walked to the control console and studied the alien script. I pressed a few buttons, and a flood of information came up on the three-storey concave glass window before us.

"I bet there's a storage cell somewhere that operates the port. Yes. Here it is." I called up the schematics. "It's relatively accessible from both inside and outside the port. If we block off the incoming flow of energy from the reactor, it could power this place for some time. We might even be able to use two of the large super lodestones from the Island to power it instead. Keep it from losing altitude again."

"Then what? It's not like we can walk in there"—he waved at the reactor—"and just disconnect the core."

"No." My fingers called up information on the holding mechanism. "But we can jettison it. Look. The emergency code is right here."

"So, we shoot a nuclear device into outer space and just pray to the gods it doesn't fall to the planet?"

I sucked in a breath and held it, counting to sixty before letting it out again. Ray was being Ray – pointing out things we needed to consider, not being a smart-ass just for the fun of it. He had a point. How could we be sure it would jettison away from Xannia and not into it?

"The spaceship."

"What about the spaceship?" He turned to look at me. I met his gaze.

"Remember the tractor beam that pulled us into dock here? It came from the spaceship, not the port. What if I can reverse it to push instead of pull? You eject the core. I push it into space. We go home heroes."

"You make it sound so simple. How will you fly that thing by yourself? If you could have, you wouldn't have needed me or Professor Gellik. Your plan is flawed."

He was right, but I had to try. Time to listen to the gods and face my destiny.

"I have to believe it's that simple. We're out of time."

* * *

Taya

I nodded to Ray as the main hatch on the spaceship slid shut, sealing us off from each other. His deep scowl reminded me how crazy this idea was. Sometimes, you need to have faith. Zaith tried to teach me that, as did All Mother in her way, but just as I couldn't believe in the Chronicles all those months ago until I saw them, I had to be in this moment to understand.

The walk to the cockpit skipped time – or so it seemed. I dropped into my chair and rerouted all the major controls for space flight to my console. I needed Ray for re-entry into Xannia's atmosphere and landing, but if I organised my portion of the console more intuitively, I might be able to pull this off.

You know you can't. The old Taya could but she's long gone, now.

Shut up.

Raylan remained on the spaceport in the reactor room as I finalised everything on the ship.

I took a deep breath and then disengaged the docking sequence before calling the ray drive online and disengaging from the docking bay.

Within twenty minutes, I reached orbit.

At thirty minutes, a black spot formed on the dish portion of the sun. All the light drained away from Zerameteth and into the molten core now shooting away from the dead sun. It was twice as big as the ship and moving twice as fast.

I input the coordinates and grabbed onto the navigational joysticks with a set velocity to get me just close enough to lock on and then push the pulsing heart of our alien-made sun out into the vacuum of space. Just like we'd practiced.

The ship obeyed my commands. When I got into range, I set navigation to hold course and then focused on the tractor beam. I input the rerouting sequence into the ship's systems to reverse the polarity of the beam.

An alarm blasted.

I cringed and backed off the command.

Not good.

It stopped.

My fingers flew over the control panel, working to find a back door. Everything had gone as planned when we were docked. The modified beam pushed us out and pulled us in without issue.

The alarm screeched again.

I abandoned that approach.

I tried twice more to get in from another system to reverse the beam but the ship wouldn't let me. If I forced the issue, I'd blow up.

"Damnit!" I hit the panel with both palms and kicked it. Pain lanced up from my toes all the way to my knee. "Good gods!" A guttural scream launched from my throat. The beam wouldn't initiate outside the set proximity zone for the spaceport. Another warning light flashed in the upper right of the main screen.

"Oh, meeka." The core broke orbit and headed straight for the planet.

Blow it up!

No! The fallout from the radiation will kill everyone. Think! Think! Come on, Taya and use that damned broken brain of yours!

But I couldn't think. Too many voices vied for dominance: Old Taya, New, Gerrund, Dez, Tek, Ray, even All Mother. Then, a voice I hadn't heard since my early childhood ghosted through my head, silencing everything else.

My Mother.

Not Lynnia Doire, No. Mamma - Lilly Fyce from back before Blain was born, when she still loved me.

"Now, Jutaya, what are you trying to do?"

"Climb the fence, Mamma."

"Why?"

"To see what's on the other side."

"You know what's on the other side."

"Yes, but I want to see it."

"See what?"

"The over there."

"What over there?"

"The not here over there."

She sighed at my four-year-old logic. "Why do you have to go over the fence?"

"Because I'm not allowed to leave the yard."

But I did leave the yard, just as I'd left orbit to chase after that damn core. And if I couldn't lock on to push it, maybe I had to try something else entirely. Maybe I didn't need to scale the fence, I just had to use the gate. *What's my gate? What's the path of least resistance?*

"No." My real voice pulled me hard into the moment. "Could it work?"

I maneuvered ahead of the giant glowing bomb and reached a shaky hand to engage the tractor beam. If it wouldn't let me reverse its thrust, I'd just have to bypass the operating protocol and have it activate in standard mode as if to bring me back to the port. I had to trick it.

A jolt vibrated the spaceship.

I increased speed.

Different alarms sounded and red letters flashed across the screen. I slammed my ass back into the chair and absorbed every available gamma ray and altered course. "System Warning" flashed and blared as the ship shook with the effort of pulling the core onto a new path. Disengaging and letting it rocket off into space wasn't an option anymore. I'd never be able to pull it that far off course. But Zita sat on a relative trajectory.

I could slingshot the core on a crash course with a real star.

In theory.

Reversing the tractor beam away from port had been a theory, too.
Stop it. Focus. One step at a time.
First, pull the core on course.

I fought with it for nearly an hour – the ship shaking, alarms blaring, warnings flashing, and always the knowledge that one false move meant the end of existence. Not just for me and Ray but for everyone.

Zita's bright orange rays blurred the words on the screen until only a single phrase flashed in giant letters: WARNING! PROXIMITY ALERT!

I checked my velocity – not only had the ray drive doubled our speed, but the push of the core had added that much more to our momentum.

I'm too close.

I disengaged the tractor beam and pulled back on the steering. Once out of the core's path, I slowed down. But hitting the breaks in a spaceship was a lot different from slamming them down in a rider! The metal groaned under the strain. I had to let up, but if I did, I'd follow the core right into the sun.

I tried again.

The vibrations chattered my teeth.

I'm doing something wrong. But what? I couldn't treat the ship like a vehicle constrained to gravity. It's not an engine. It manipulates gamma rays for gods' sake! *So, what does that mean?*

An orange brilliance flared and then the screen went black.

"That's it!"

But was I too late?

Chapter 55
Xannia

Dezmind

Passing through the open black metal gates beyond the apex of the waterfall, I entered the outskirts of South City and shivered with remembrance. My first time through, I rode a cart, trying to prove I didn't need help. The second time, I left everyone, including the woman I loved, behind to fulfill my destiny. Now, a desert guide led me back to her.

So much had changed since that fateful day at the Spoken Truth Rally. Taya would still take a shot at me if she had the chance, but for different reasons now. She'd said it herself: once I'd found her, I stopped looking for her — stopped seeing her with my heart. I checked *Soul Mate* off the list and moved on to the next goal. But I'd been wrong — about so many things. I'd needed to believe she was something she wasn't in order to move forward with my destiny. Falling in love shouldn't have been the end; it should've marked a beginning. I meant to set things right.

A burble of voices rose in the distance, filtering through the trees. Lynnia made sure Gerrund, Delenon, and Lutrice knew I was coming. She wouldn't let me leave otherwise. Neither would Tek – something about not knowing if a Sand Eater had gotten me or if I'd decided to pick up Doire's mantle and wander the Deserts while the world crumbled around me. It wasn't a half-bad idea, actually.

As we hit the crest in the road, a horde of citizens waited on the other side of a huge, metallic WELCOME sign for the city. Three individuals stepped forward: Gerrund, whom I expected; Lutrice; and All Mother. Delenon and Daria remained at the front of the crowd, a group of guards immediately behind.

"Welcome back, Kronik Dezmind." Lutrice threw her arms wide but faltered when Jadis padded out from behind me and took a protective stance.

"It's okay, girl. They're friends."

The lynx sat down and I moved around her, smiling at Lutrice. She engulfed me in a hug.

I laughed. "It's been too long."

"Yes, it has." She stepped back, and I shook first Gerrund's and then All Mother's hand. Lutrice remained squarely between the other two, a buffer of sorts. I'd have to chat with her about it later. I turned to Gerrund. Jadis moved over beside me and tucked her muzzle into my hand. I scratched behind her ears.

"When did they leave? I only got hazy word."

"Yesterday morning."

"When do you expect them back?"

Gerrund just stared at me. Surprisingly, All Mother

Spoke. "Any time now, Kronik – if the mission remained straightforward. Taya confessed to me that the short timelines meant a lot of short-cuts, too. And any of their assumptions might be wrong."

"She was worried, then."

"Cautious. Calculating – and yes, a bit worried. I'd be concerned if she weren't. It's not every day we blast off into the heavens to talk to a god." She winked. She understood the stakes far better than her northern counterparts.

"When is D-Day?" *Detonation Day*, should Taya and Raylan fail.

Gerrund cleared his throat. "Tomorrow. She said if it took longer than three days, we should assume the mission failed and launch Plan A." He didn't ask if we were ready with the rocket; his tone and guarded stare did that for him.

"We're ready. Now, why don't you take me on a quick tour and end down at the beach Gerrund teases me about constantly? More beautiful than any in the north, I hear," I said.

Lutrice looped her arm through mine, sparing a glance for Jadis, who stood but remained by my other side and took the lead. Each of them had their roles, and clearly, Lu took pride in hers.

* * *

Dezmind

By mid-morning exhaustion set in, and I settled down for a nap to elude the hottest part of the day. That evening, Jadis and I snuck out of my apartment and walked over to the memorial grounds. They weren't on the tour, but I remembered where they were. As we passed through the trees and into the sacred space, the air cooled and the mists clung to the top of the grasses, short as they were. Pale purple moss draped from tree limbs, accenting the memorial pipes hanging there, too.

Jadis lay in the grasses, snapping at the bugs as I walked over to the aperture and clasped my hands low behind my back, staring at the very device we now had to make obsolete. The hours Taya and I had put into understanding this alien tech pulled shadow-memories from the depths of my mind. She'd tried to reach out to me then. The weight of her presence and her hand on my arm had made it that much harder to leave. I should've known she'd follow me. Should've known there was more behind the reason for her and Zaith's plan to keep me here than I could ever guess. I might have spared her the nightmares if I'd been thinking of more than just myself.

A rustle of leaves pulled me from my musings. Jadis didn't make a sound where she lay nor even turn her head. I looked around at the main entrance, overgrown as it was, and waited for my shadow-guard to appear. I knew Gerrund would be like Taya – always watching.

"I don't recall the memorial grounds being on your tour earlier," All Mother said, emerging into the clearing. She walked past Jadis and scratched the ruff on the back of her neck.

"I may not know all the little hamlets and new businesses that have sprung up since I last visited, but I know how to get to the one place that helped quell the super quakes. It's not something one easily forgets."

"I suppose not. What brings you here this evening?"

"Just saying goodbye."

"To whom? The past? The technology? Or to Taya?"

"Never Taya. I came down here to welcome her home."

She nodded. "The dinner market is starting. Mamma Lu thought you might be hungry."

"Yeah, I could eat." I chuckled.

She smiled back. "I'm glad you came."

I blinked at her unexpected comment. "Me too."

A rush of voices and the pounding of people running by made me jump. Jadis rose and growled, her haunches rising. All Mother and I looked to one another and then up through the clearing in the canopy to Gamma, sitting just by the edge of the leaves. The pale-yellow light wavered and drew to a fiery point, arcing like a comet across the sky.

"It's happening," I said.

"She's doing it."

All Mother grabbed my arm and pulled me out to the path. Jadis followed close behind. We ran with the others down to the beach for an unobstructed view. Where the boardwalk met the path and the trees, the reporter I'd sent along with Taya stood atop a picnic table on the sand, recording the event. All Mother and I scrambled up next to him, Jadis lay below, and the three of us stood in awe of that streak of light creeping across the sky.

"Network News Now is live from South City, bringing you the action as it happens. All Mother"—he trained the Mini-View on her—"can you tell us what's going on?"

"History in the making." She didn't hesitate. Her self-assurance was exactly what the people needed right now.

"As you know, a team from the government has been working tirelessly to learn more about the Dakturian technology discovered in the South Cove seven weeks ago. Yesterday morning, that team launched an alien spaceship into the heavens in order to talk to the gods. What we're seeing is Zerameteth's answer to our plea."

"And what plea is that, All Mother?"

"To ask the Child to return home, of course. Look." She pointed and he traced her trajectory into the evening sky. "His Sister is calling him."

It did look as though the God Comet headed for a setting Beta – or Zita, as any FOL would refer to our second sun. "He doesn't want to harm us. He has spoken to the sky-travellers and he has listened. We are saved."

An hour later the God Comet disappeared into Zita's orange glow, and a cheer rose up among the packed crowds all along on the beach. Impromptu instruments drummed out a celebration caught on record by a young reporter and commented on by the only Guardian in South City.

When Zita set, a faint orange glow reflected a perfect crescent down to us from the cooling surface of Gamma. I remained on that picnic table during the party and long after the revelry travelled back to the Central Commons, wondering about science and religion and how we would move forward as a world with one less sun – and one less Son. What we might call the new moon in our skies. Most of all, I thought about Taya.

At first, she punctuated my musings with her wry smile and full laugh, rare as it was. When only the stars shone, and the night chilled me, I called on the feel of her body next to mine as if drawing warmth from the memory.

I sat there, hour after hour, hoping she was okay, Jadis never once leaving me.

I watched Zola peak over the horizon for the start of a new day and prayed harder than I did as a youth for a Soul Mate denied – I prayed for the gods to bring Taya back to me.

Chapter 56
Bells Toll

Dezmind

A buzzing in my arm, or maybe in my head, woke me. I rolled onto my back. The thin slats between the hard wooden planks pinched tender skin. My mouth tasted like stale bread, and I had no spit to swallow. I sat up on the table and shook out my arm. The buzzing in my head persisted. Jadis jumped up beside me and rubbed her head into my shoulder. I massaged my jaw and pried open my eyes to search for that cup of water someone kept refilling for me. My foot collided with it and sent it flying into the sand. I scrambled from the picnic table and searched through the piles of blankets, pillows, baskets of food, and other offerings for Gerrund's canteen – he'd left it here that first night.

A blood-red glow inked the top of the dark sea waters, giving me just enough light to see by. Jadis yawned, closing her maw with a snap. I stuck a finger in my ear and shook it, but the buzzing didn't go away.

"Aha," I croaked, lifting the canteen. I twisted off the cap, closed my eyes, and took a long gulp of the warm verrin. I opened my eyes with my head tilted back, gulping what I couldn't bring myself to drink these past three days – and saw it.

A metallic wink high up.

I dropped the canteen, liquid sloshing over fabric and food. I stumbled over the mess, my bare feet scattering soft sand. Large paws thudded beside me. The speck grew larger and closer and louder… *louder! The buzzing in my ears.* I stood, jaw gaping, heart hammering, pulse racing as a craft the size of a house hovered over a patch of scorched sand before touching down. In the distance, bells clanged and rang out, alerting the city.

I froze to the spot as a large hatch slowly lowered toward the ground.

And there she stood, looking out at the beach.

At me.

A crazy surge of power burst through my veins and I ran. And she ran. Somehow, we ended up in each other's arms, on our knees in the sand, with the sun creeping higher and the waves lapping against the shore. Jadis bounded over, crashing into us and knocking us down before climbing over Taya and nuzzling into the nape of her neck.

I pulled Taya back to me and held her tight.

"I'm never letting you go again," I said into the hair by her ear.

She gave a half-laugh, half-sob. "You know, you can't keep that promise."

I pulled back, sitting us up and holding her shoulders. "Marry me."

"What?"

"Marry me. Now. Here. Today. I don't care if work separates us for a month or two at a time. I'll take regular trips south. You'll travel north. We'll make it work."

She held my face in her hands and tears coursed over her cheeks – but she smiled.

"Yes."

"You will?"

"Yes, I will marry you. Today. Right here. But not right now. You kinda stink."

I laughed.

Raylan's footsteps echoed against the metal ramp down to the sand. "What? No welcoming party? We did just save the world, you know. Well, a couple of days ago, but close enough."

Taya and I laughed as the citizens of South City spilled onto the beach and lifted him onto their shoulders. A circle formed around us, but Taya ignored them, and so did I, as Jadis guarded her people.

I kissed Taya, full on the mouth. I didn't care who saw or if that reporter streamed us live on the Wire. We were finally together.

* * *

Taya

Late afternoon, as Zola sank half into the waves and Zita hovered just above her, their radiance gave Zerameteth's shadow almost a full luminance. The deep-orange reflection

432

off the spaceport's planet-side exterior proved anything was possible. If we could turn an alien sun into the shadow-moon of a god, maybe Dezmind and I had a chance after all.

All Mother nodded, and Dez took my hands in his before a packed beach crowd, Jadis, and Kye's ever-vigilant Mini-V. The fragrance of the circlet of woven fresh flowers resting on my head mingled with the salty breeze from the sea. My borrowed dress fit a little snug, but Tamaine had assured me it created a perfect silhouette.

"Today marks a new beginning for us all." All Mother smiled as if we were the only people there and then raised her arms to the heavens. "May the gods bear witness, not only to a new age but also to a historical union between this man, Dezmind Lisle, and this woman, Jutaya Doire. Dezmind…"

He nodded to her and looked me in the eyes. "From the moment we met, you have kept me on my toes."

The crowd chuckled, likely remembering headlines about a near-assassination attempt at a Spoken Truth Rally many months ago.

"Every day you challenge me to be a better man, and your unfailing protective nature for the sanctity of *all* life, not just mine, has taught me to look beyond today into our many tomorrows. You have brought to my life, to my heart, an imperfect perfection, and I love you for it."

"Jutaya…" All Mother inclined her head toward me.

I took a deep breath, but a shiver of nerves quaked through me. Dez squeezed my hands, knowing such a public display went contrary to my wishes. But I'd agreed because even though it was a political move on his part, it was part of what made him special – wanting to change the world for everyone.

"I'm not one for purple prose or flowery language. You know me: I tell it like is. Dez, you are a pain in the ass, but you will forever be my pain in the ass."

The congregation laughed.

"I love you for seeing past my failings and for helping break down walls inside me I wasn't aware existed. Your unwavering belief in destiny and your interpretation of how fate and the gods work through our choices not only opened my mind to new possibilities but also opened my heart. Life together won't be easy, but it sure as heck won't be boring."

All Mother raised her arms high and clasped her hands over her head, a brilliant smile lighting her face. Dez released my hands, pulled me close, and kissed me as if there were no more tomorrows, only an endless today.

If you enjoyed reading *Forgotten Fallacy*, please consider leaving a review at your favourite online resource.

About the Author

Growing up in Ontario, Canada, M.J. was the only child of a single mom. M.J.'s passion for the arts ignited at a young age as she wrote adventure stories and read them aloud to close family and friends. The dramatic arts became a focus in high school as an aid to understanding character motivation in her writing. Majoring in Theatre Production at York University, with a minor in English, she went on to teach in both the elementary and high school divisions.

M.J. currently lives with her husband and young son. She keeps busy these days with her emerging authors' website Infinite Pathways, attending book fairs, and conferences as well as holding writing workshops and helping run the WCYR – Writers' Community of York Region.

Connect with M.J. online:

Author Website – www.mjmoores.com
Facebook – www.facebook.com/AuthorMJMoores
Twitter – www.twitter.com/AuthorMJMoores

www.ingramcontent.com/pod-product-compliance
Lightning Source LLC
Chambersburg PA
CBHW050021030726
47506CB00001B/53